HEROES IN

GRAPHIC NOVEL

TRAINING

No. 1

ZEUS AND THE THUNDERBOLT OF DOOM

created by
**JOAN HOLUB &
SUZANNE WILLIAMS**
adapted by **David Campiti**
illustrated by **Dave Santana**
at Class House Graphics

AUG -- 2022

Aladdin
New York London Toronto Sydney New Delhi

ALADDIN
An imprint of Simon & Schuster Children's Publishing Division
1230 Avenue of the Americas, New York, New York 10020
First Aladdin edition February 2022
Text copyright © 2022 by Joan Holub and Suzanne Williams
Illustrations copyright © 2022 by Glass House Graphics
Art by Dave Santana. Inks by Flávio Soares with João Zod and Juan Araujo. Colors by Felipe Felix and João Zod. Lettering by Marcos Inoue. Art services by Glass House Graphics.
All rights reserved, including the right of
reproduction in whole or in part in any form.
ALADDIN and related logo are registered
trademarks of Simon & Schuster, Inc.
For information about special discounts for bulk purchases, please contact Simon & Schuster Special Sales
at 1-866-506-1949 or business@simonandschuster.com.
The Simon & Schuster Speakers Bureau can bring authors to your live event. For more information or to book an event contact the Simon & Schuster Speakers Bureau at 1-866-248-3049 or visit our website at www.simonspeakers.com.
Designed by Nicholas Sciacca
The text of this book was set in CCMonologus.
Manufactured in China 1121 SCP
10 9 8 7 6 5 4 3 2 1
Library of Congress Cataloging-in-Publication Data
Names: Holub, Joan, author. • Williams, Suzanne, 1953– author. • Campiti, David, author. • Glass House Graphics, illustrator. • Title: Zeus and the thunderbolt of doom / created by Joan Holub and Suzanne Williams ; adapted by David Campiti ; illustrated by Glass House Graphics. • Description: First Aladdin hardcover edition. • New York : Aladdin, 2022. • Series: Heroes in training graphic novel ; book 1 • Audience: Ages 8 to 12 • Summary: Ten-year-old Zeus is kidnapped by the terrible Titans, merciless giants who enjoy snacking on humans, and when in self-defense he pulls a magical thunderbolt from a stone, he begins an adventure to rescue his fellow Olympians from the evil Cronus. • Identifiers: LCCN 2021015454 (print) • LCCN 2021015455 (ebook) • ISBN 9781534481152 (hardcover) • ISBN 9781534481145 (paperback) • ISBN 9781534481169 (ebook) • Subjects: LCSH: Graphic novels. • CYAC: Graphic novels. • Zeus (Greek deity)—Fiction. • Gods, Greek—Fiction. • Mythology, Greek—Fiction. • Adventure and adventurers—Fiction. • Classification: LCC PZ7.7.H656 Ze 2022 (print) • LCC PZ7.7.H656 (ebook)
DDC 741.5/973—dc23
LC record available at https://lccn.loc.gov/2021015454
LC ebook record available at https://lccn.loc.gov/2021015455

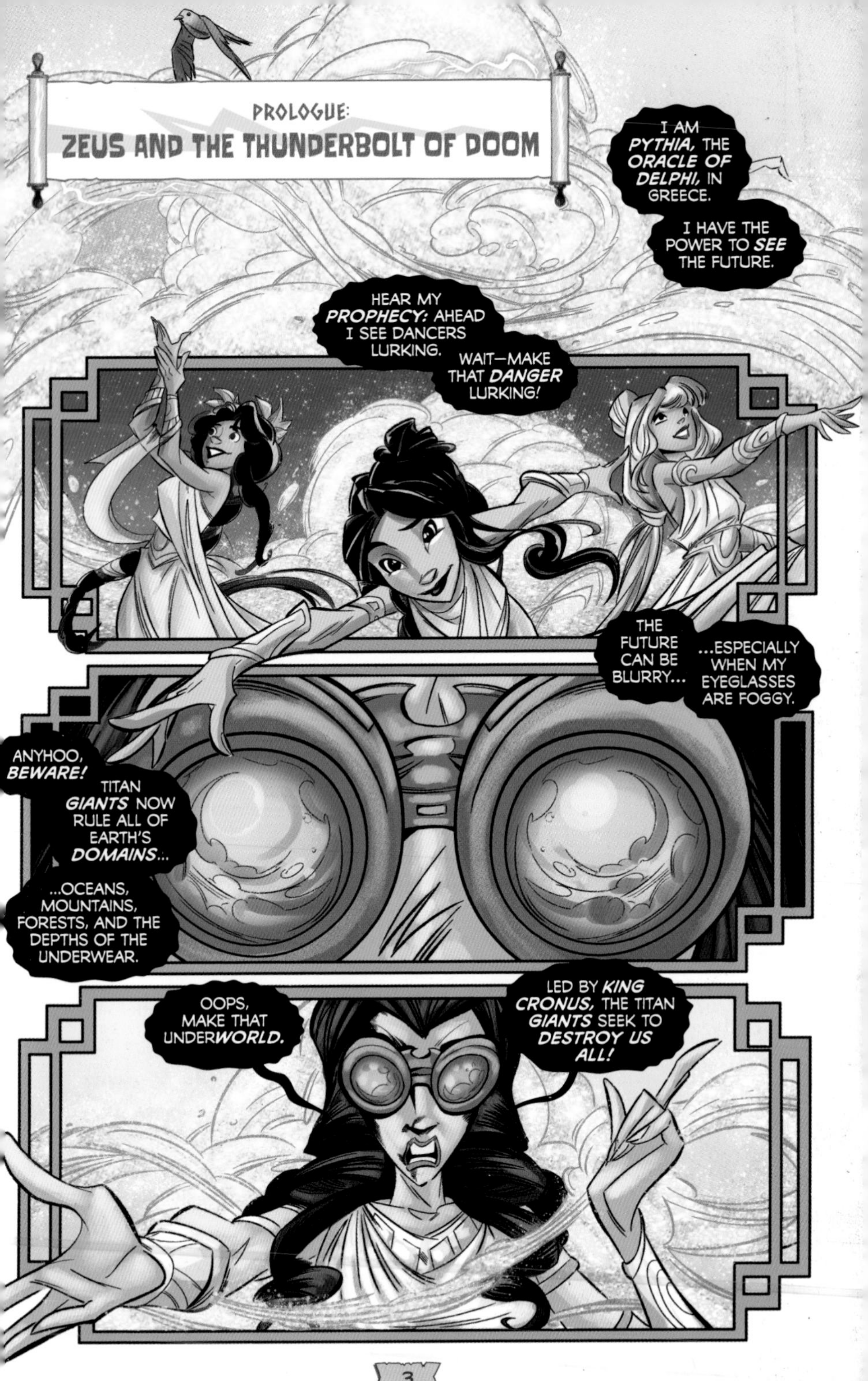
PROLOGUE:
ZEUS AND THE THUNDERBOLT OF DOOM
I AM PYTHIA, THE ORACLE OF DELPHI, IN GREECE.
I HAVE THE POWER TO SEE THE FUTURE.
HEAR MY PROPHECY: AHEAD I SEE DANCERS LURKING.
WAIT—MAKE THAT DANGER LURKING!
THE FUTURE CAN BE BLURRY...
...ESPECIALLY WHEN MY EYEGLASSES ARE FOGGY.
ANYHOO, BEWARE!
TITAN GIANTS NOW RULE ALL OF EARTH'S DOMAINS...
...OCEANS, MOUNTAINS, FORESTS, AND THE DEPTHS OF THE UNDERWEAR.
OOPS, MAKE THAT UNDERWORLD.
LED BY KING CRONUS, THE TITAN GIANTS SEEK TO DESTROY US ALL!

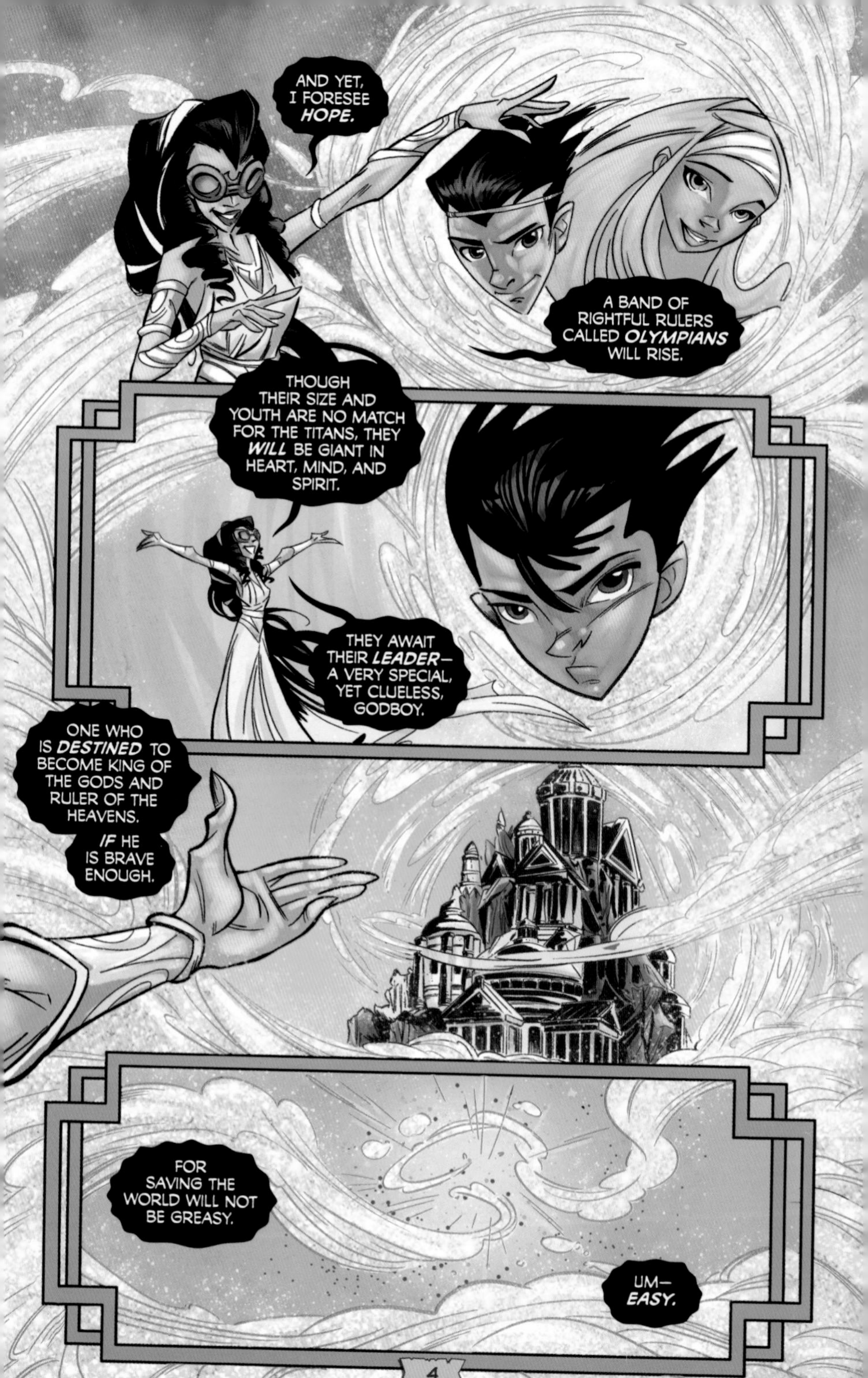
AND YET, I FORESEE HOPE.
A BAND OF RIGHTFUL RULERS CALLED OLYMPIANS WILL RISE.
THOUGH THEIR SIZE AND YOUTH ARE NO MATCH FOR THE TITANS, THEY WILL BE GIANT IN HEART, MIND, AND SPIRIT.
THEY AWAIT THEIR LEADER— A VERY SPECIAL, YET CLUELESS, GODBOY.
ONE WHO IS DESTINED TO BECOME KING OF THE GODS AND RULER OF THE HEAVENS.
IF HE IS BRAVE ENOUGH.
FOR SAVING THE WORLD WILL NOT BE GREASY.
UM— EASY.

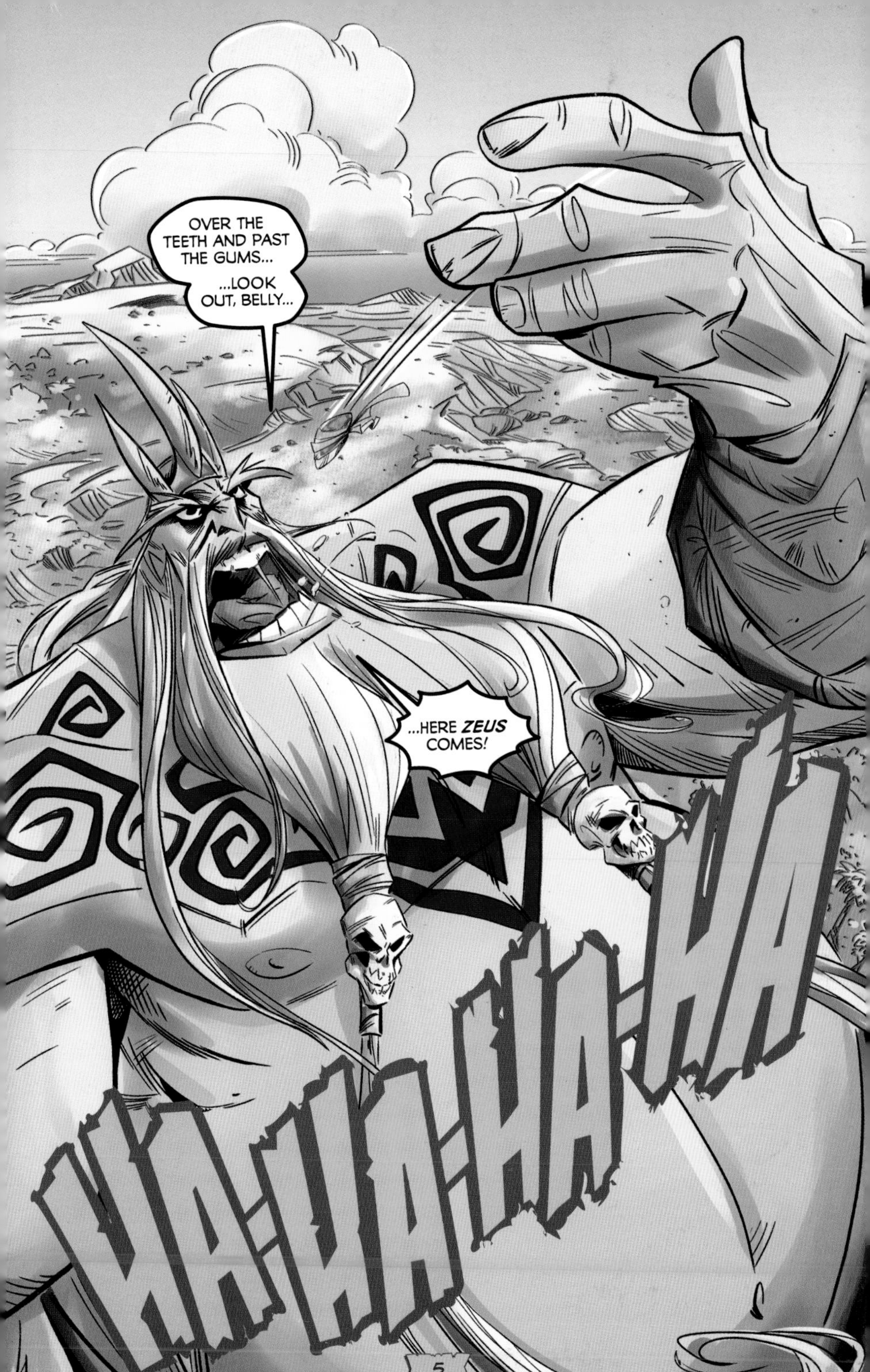
OVER THE TEETH AND PAST THE GUMS...
...LOOK OUT, BELLY...
...HERE *ZEUS* COMES!
HA-HA-HA-HA-HA

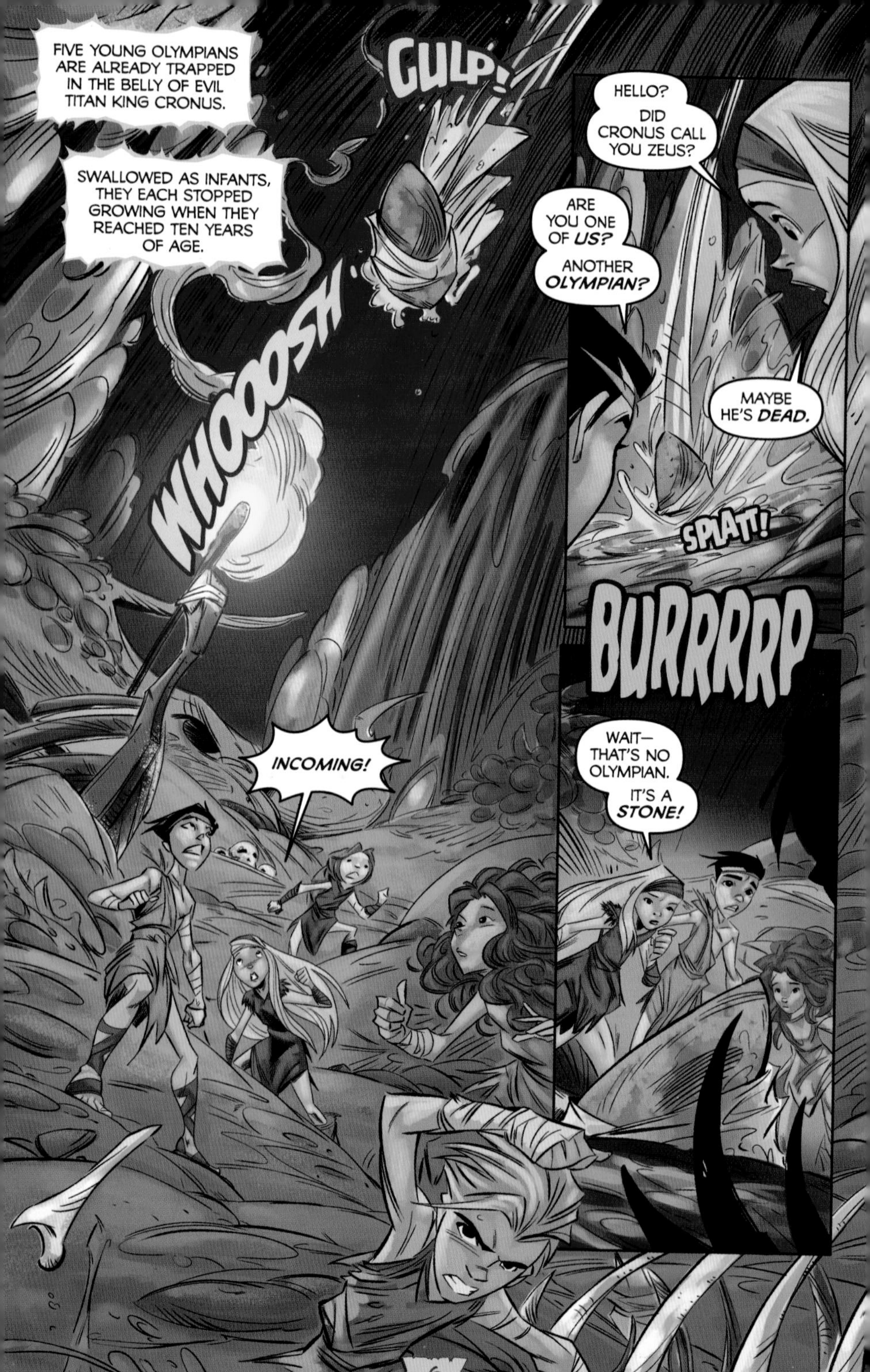
FIVE YOUNG OLYMPIANS ARE ALREADY TRAPPED IN THE BELLY OF EVIL TITAN KING CRONUS.
SWALLOWED AS INFANTS, THEY EACH STOPPED GROWING WHEN THEY REACHED TEN YEARS OF AGE.
GULP!
WHOOOSH
INCOMING!
HELLO?
DID CRONUS CALL YOU ZEUS?
ARE YOU ONE OF US?
ANOTHER OLYMPIAN?
MAYBE HE'S DEAD.
SPLATT!
BURRRRP
WAIT— THAT'S NO OLYMPIAN.
IT'S A STONE!

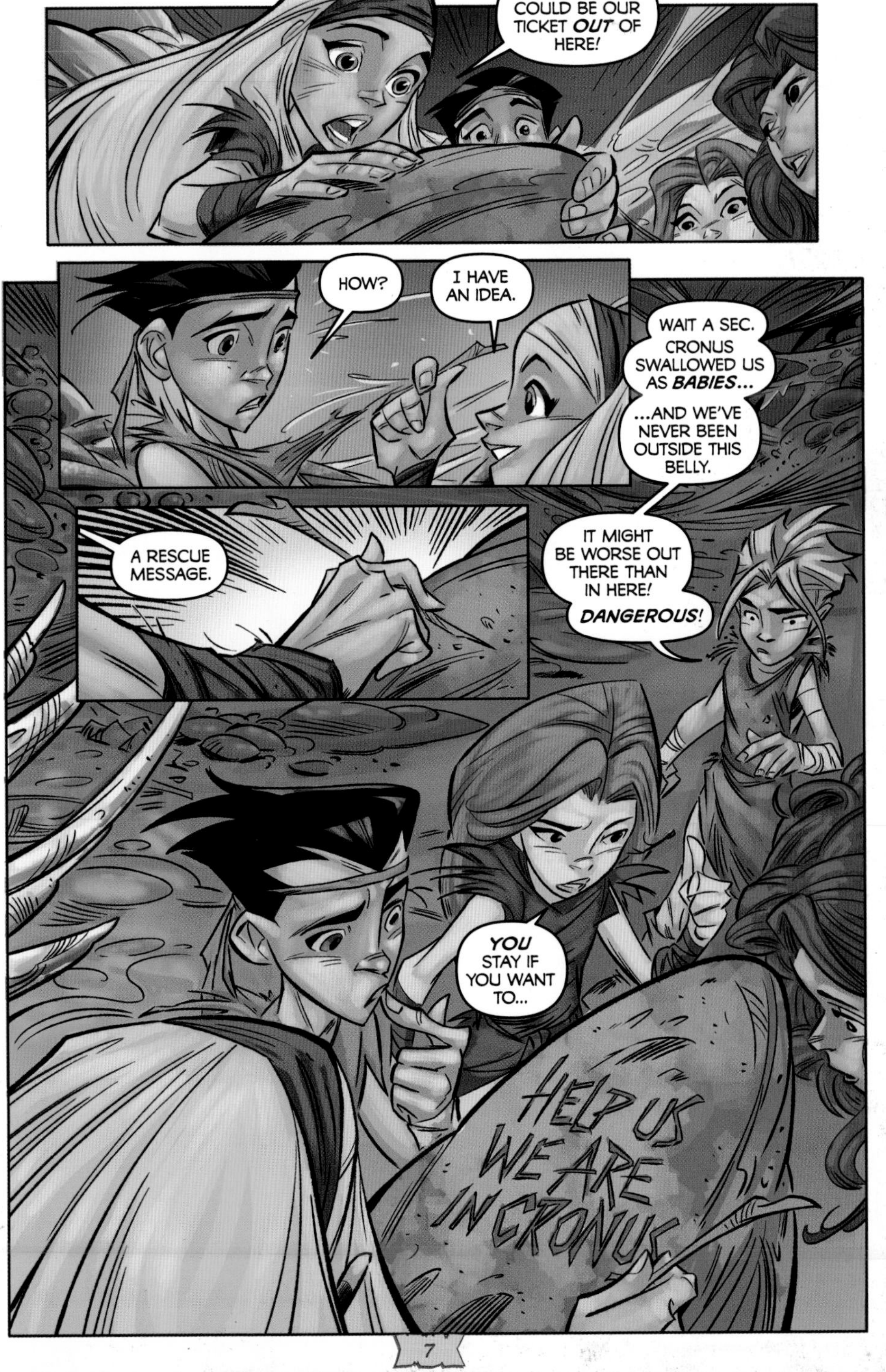
THIS THING COULD BE OUR TICKET *OUT* OF HERE!
HOW?
I HAVE AN IDEA.
WAIT A SEC. CRONUS SWALLOWED US AS *BABIES*...
...AND WE'VE NEVER BEEN OUTSIDE THIS BELLY.
A RESCUE MESSAGE.
IT MIGHT BE WORSE OUT THERE THAN IN HERE! *DANGEROUS*!
YOU STAY IF YOU WANT TO...
HELP US WE ARE IN CRONUS

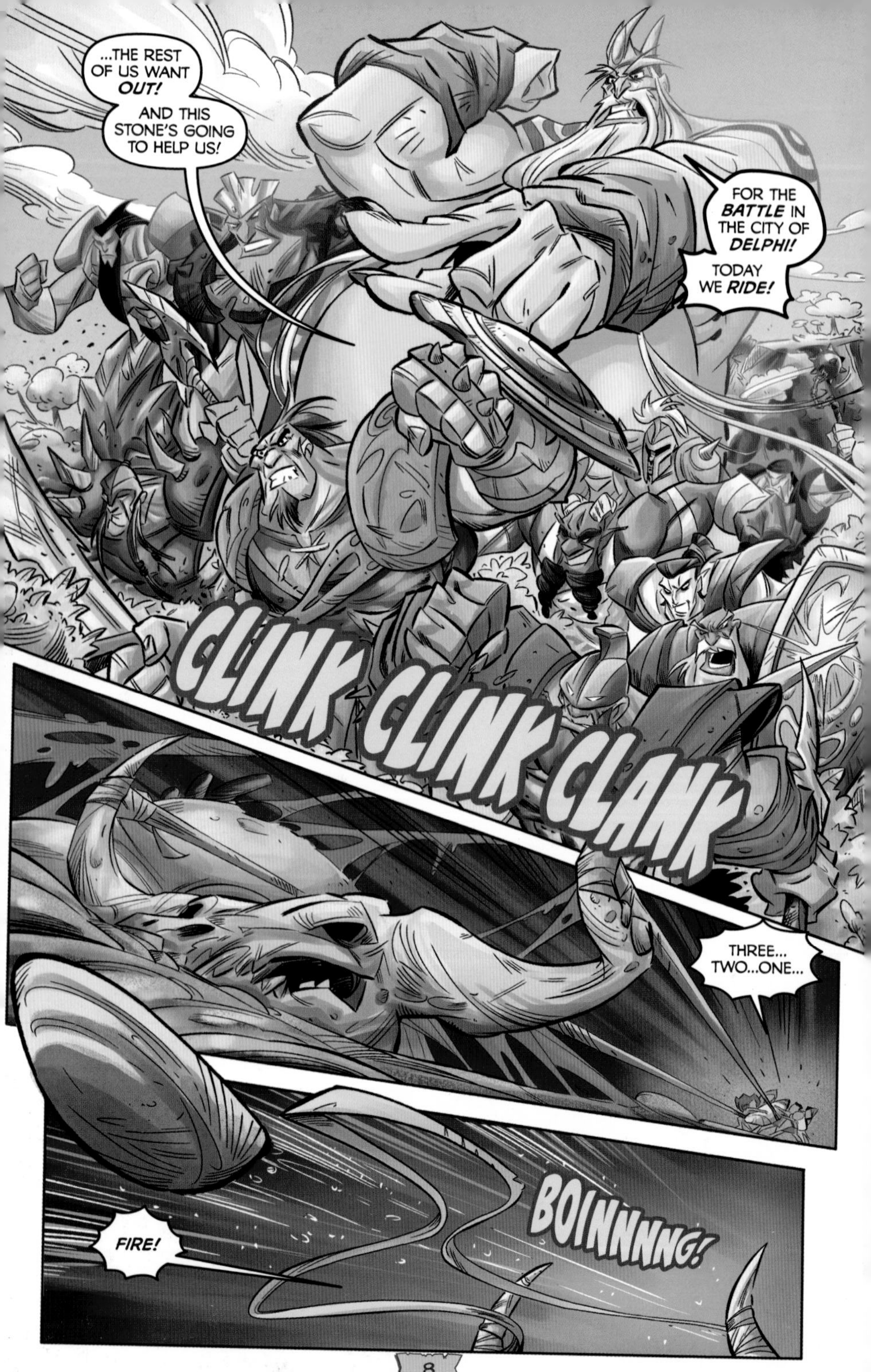
...THE REST OF US WANT OUT!
AND THIS STONE'S GOING TO HELP US!
FOR THE BATTLE IN THE CITY OF DELPHI!
TODAY WE RIDE!
CLINK CLINK CLANK
THREE... TWO...ONE...
FIRE!
BOINNNNG!

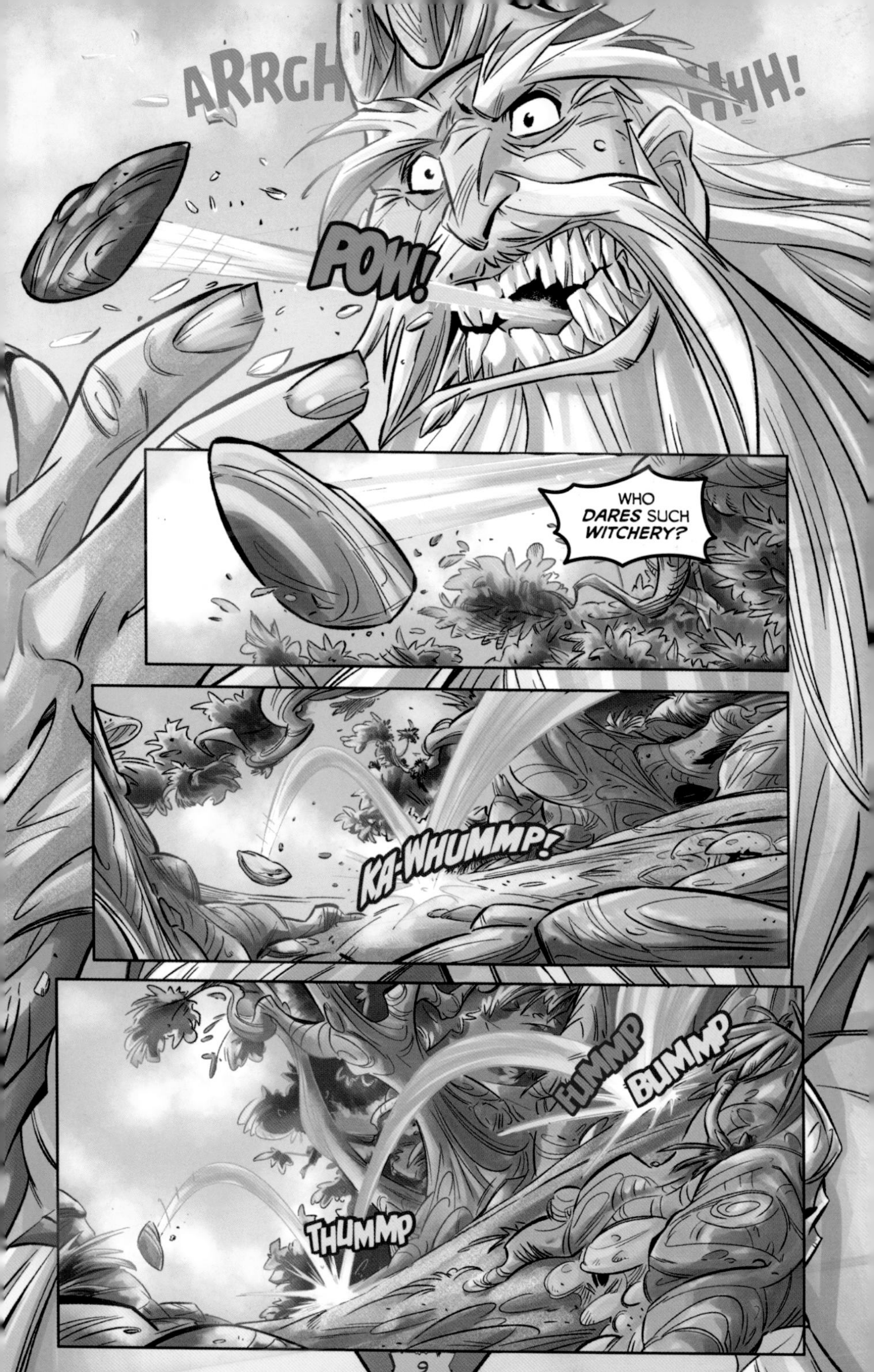
ARRGH
HHH!
POW!
WHO DARES SUCH WITCHERY?
KA-WHUMMP!
HUMMP
BUMMP
THUMMP

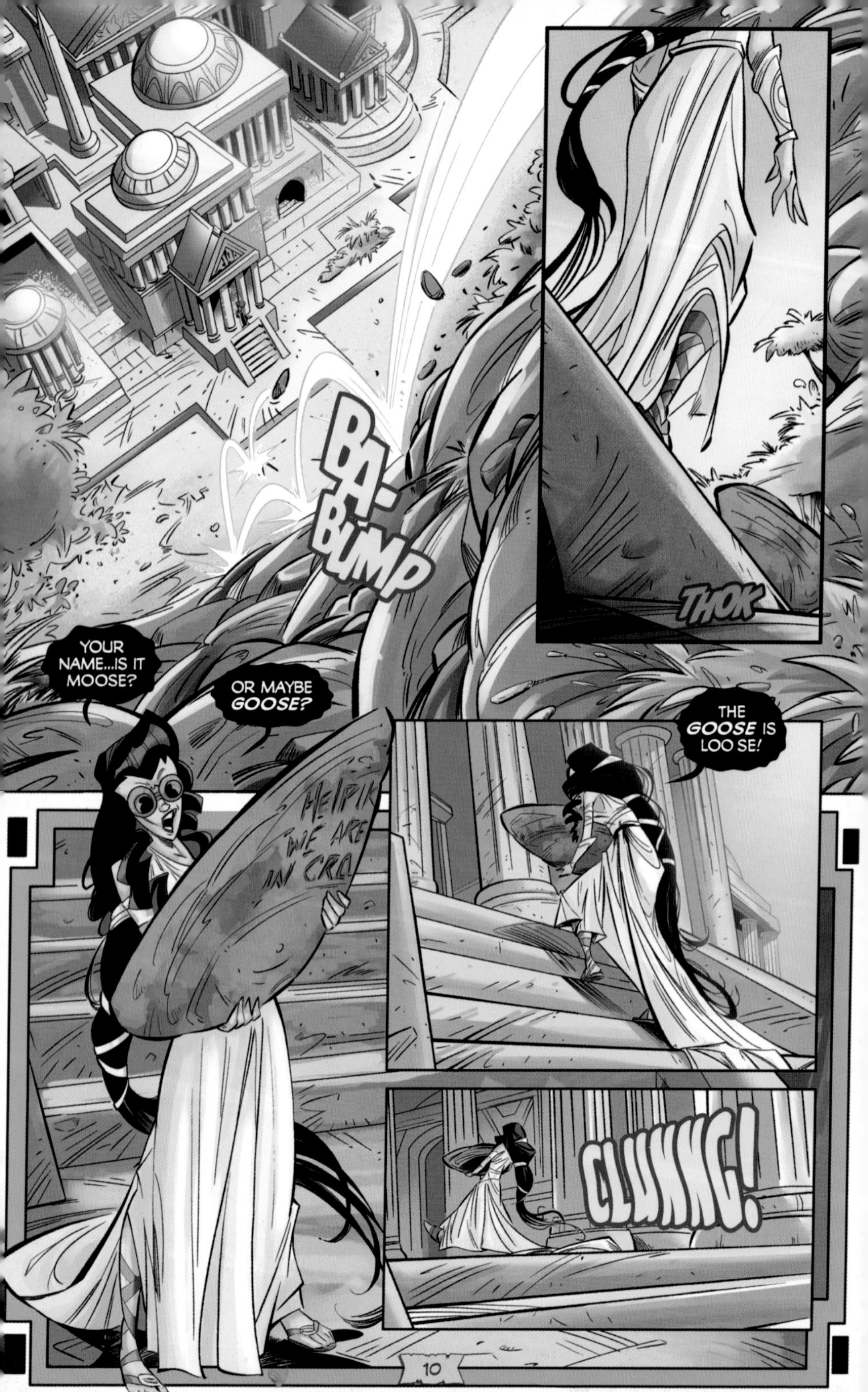
BA-BUMP
THOK
YOUR NAME...IS IT MOOSE?
OR MAYBE *GOOSE?*
THE *GOOSE* IS LOO SE!
CLUNNNG!

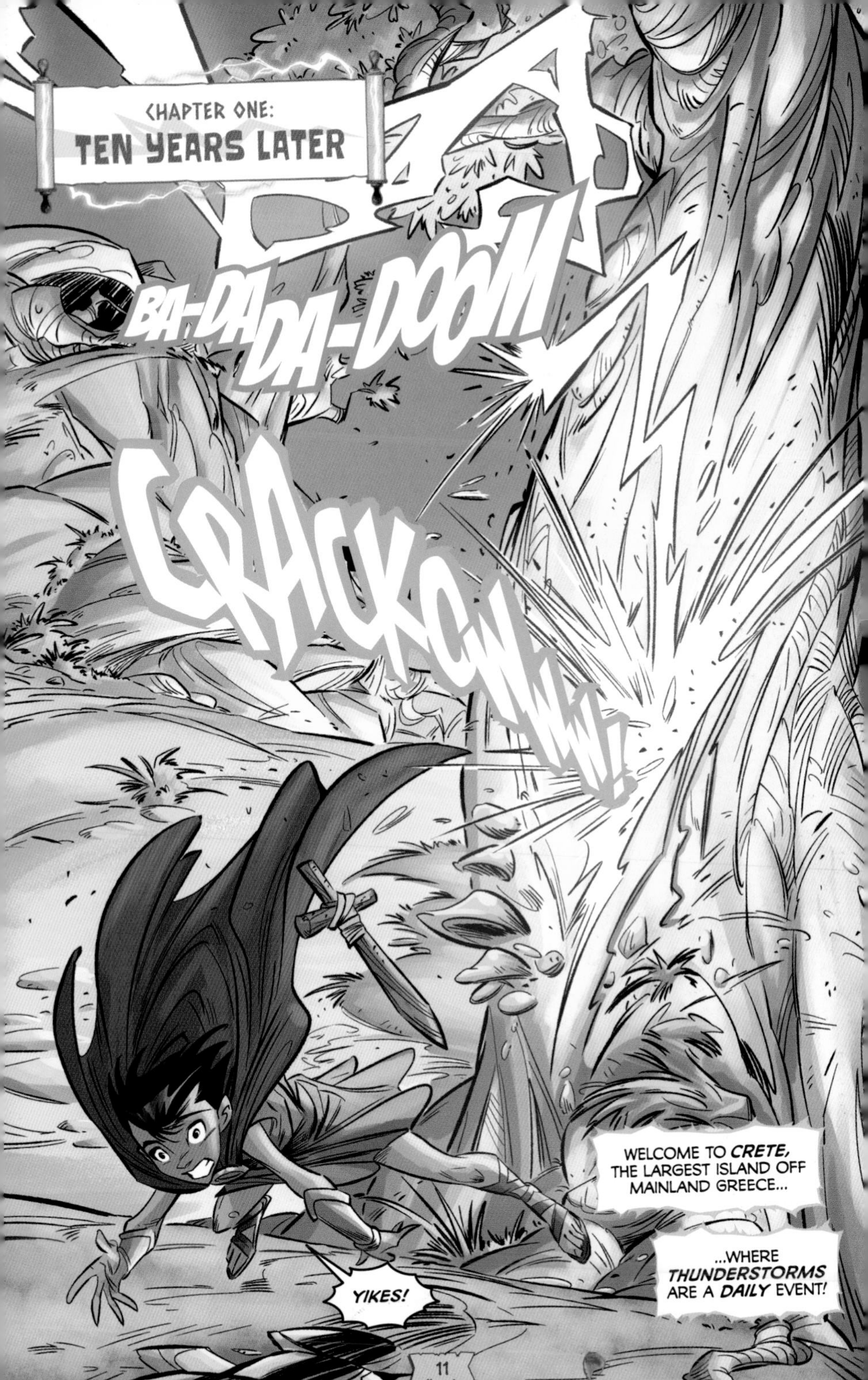
CHAPTER ONE:
TEN YEARS LATER
BA-DA DA-DOOM
CRACKOOM!
WELCOME TO CRETE, THE LARGEST ISLAND OFF MAINLAND GREECE...
...WHERE THUNDERSTORMS ARE A DAILY EVENT!
YIKES!

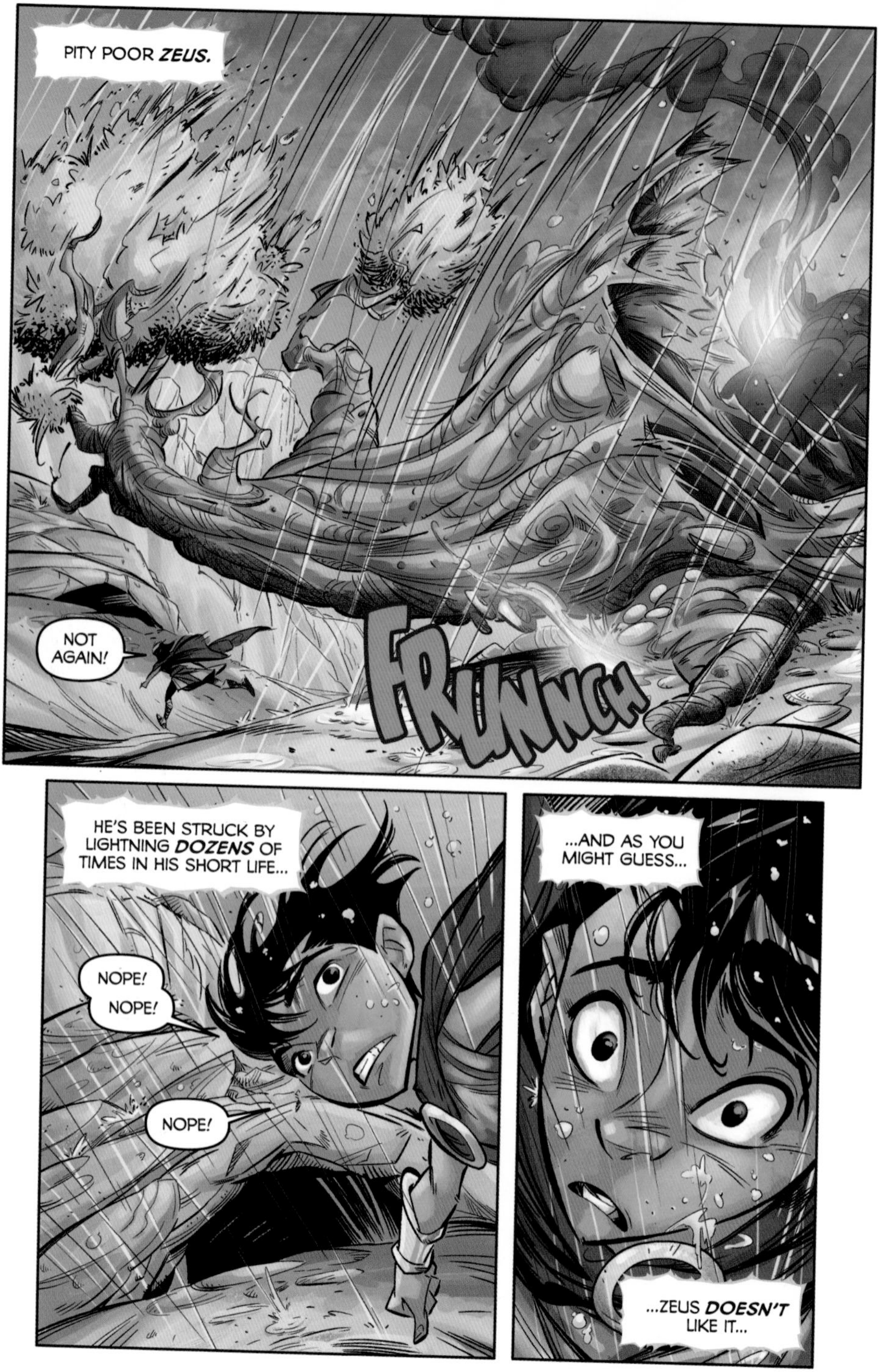
PITY POOR **ZEUS.**
NOT AGAIN!
FRUNNCH
HE'S BEEN STRUCK BY LIGHTNING **DOZENS** OF TIMES IN HIS SHORT LIFE...
NOPE!
NOPE!
NOPE!
...AND AS YOU MIGHT GUESS...
...ZEUS **DOESN'T** LIKE IT...

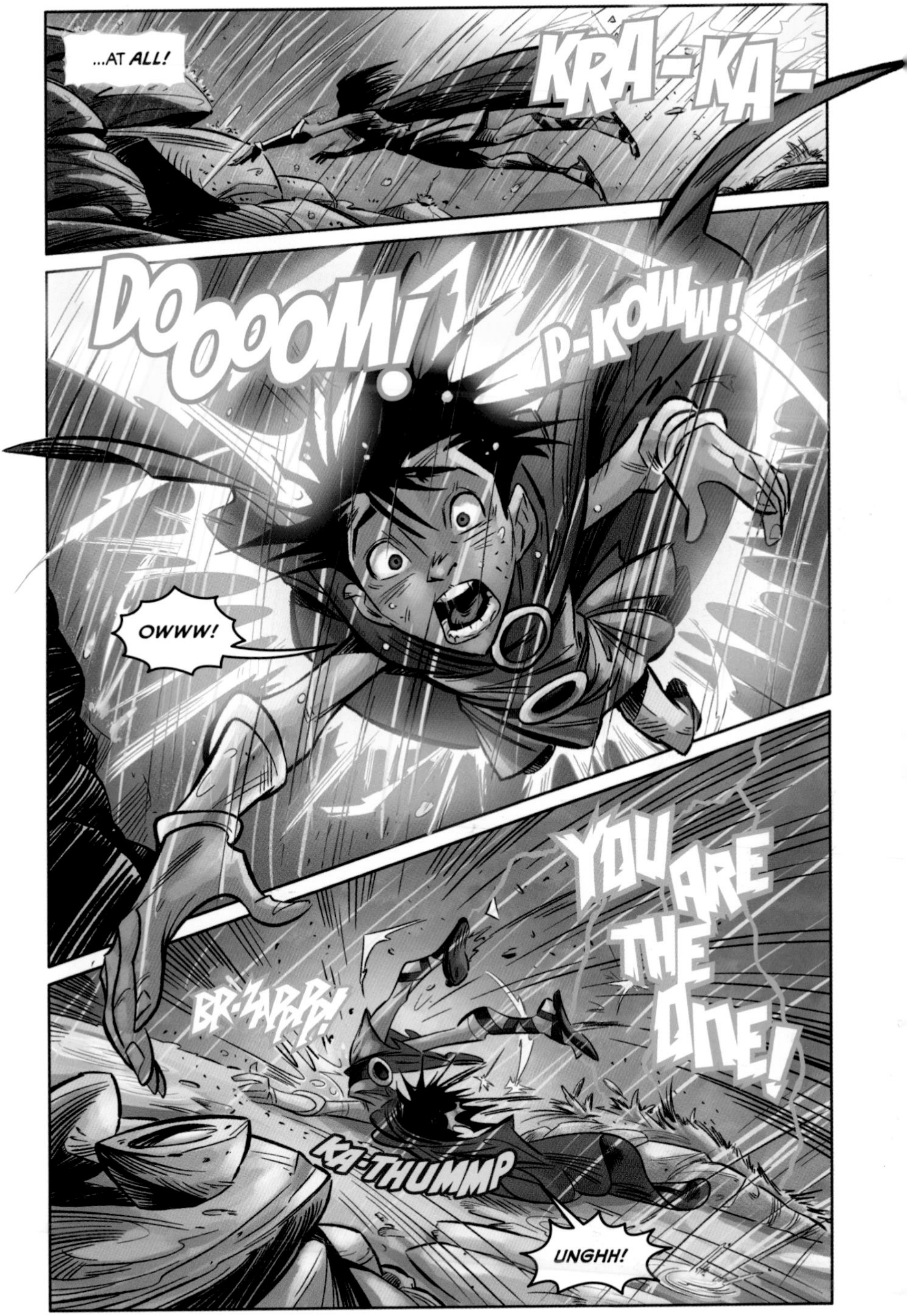
...AT ALL!
KRA-KA-
DOOOOOM!
P-KOWW!
OWWW!
YOU ARE THE ONE!
BR-ZARRP!
KA-THUMMP
UNGHH!

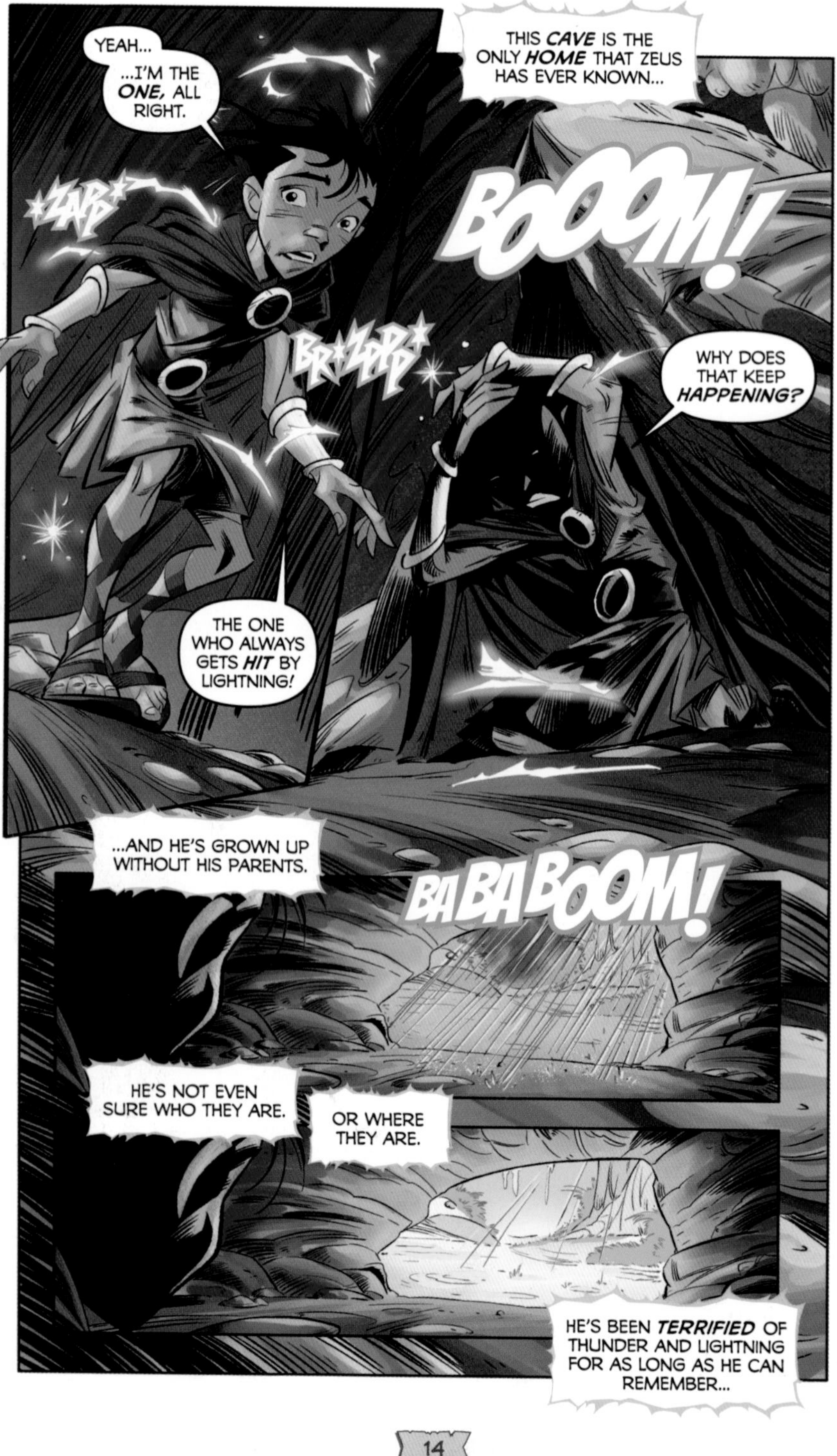
YEAH...
...I'M THE ONE, ALL RIGHT.
THIS CAVE IS THE ONLY HOME THAT ZEUS HAS EVER KNOWN...
ZARP
BOOOM!
BR*ZPP*
WHY DOES THAT KEEP HAPPENING?
THE ONE WHO ALWAYS GETS HIT BY LIGHTNING!
...AND HE'S GROWN UP WITHOUT HIS PARENTS.
BABABOOM!
HE'S NOT EVEN SURE WHO THEY ARE.
OR WHERE THEY ARE.
HE'S BEEN TERRIFIED OF THUNDER AND LIGHTNING FOR AS LONG AS HE CAN REMEMBER...

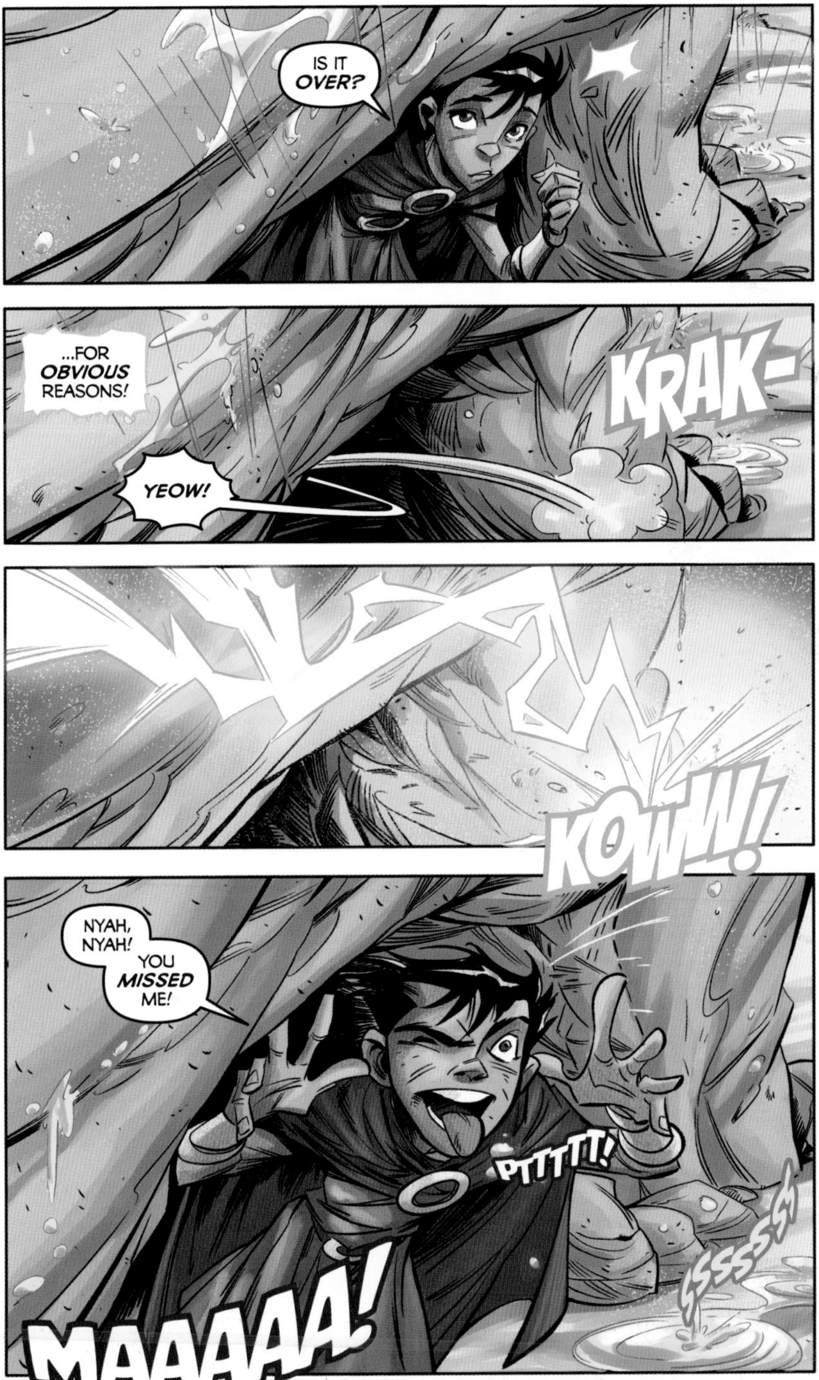
IS IT OVER?
...FOR OBVIOUS REASONS!
KRAK-
YEOW!
KOWW!
NYAH, NYAH! YOU MISSED ME!
PTTTTT!
SSSSSSS
MAAAAA!

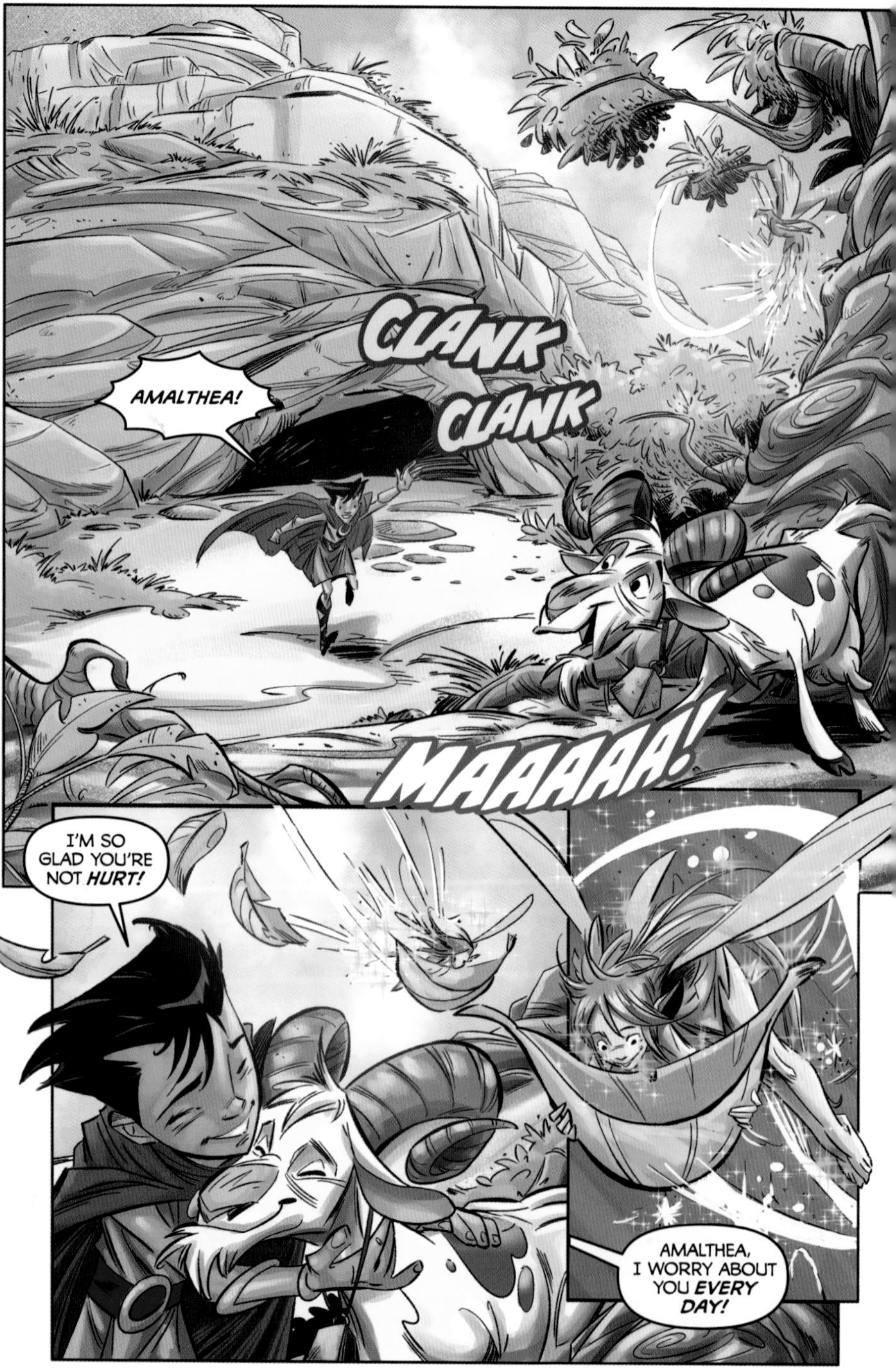
AMALTHEA!
CLANK
CLANK
MAAAAAA!
I'M SO GLAD YOU'RE NOT *HURT!*
AMALTHEA, I WORRY ABOUT YOU *EVERY DAY!*

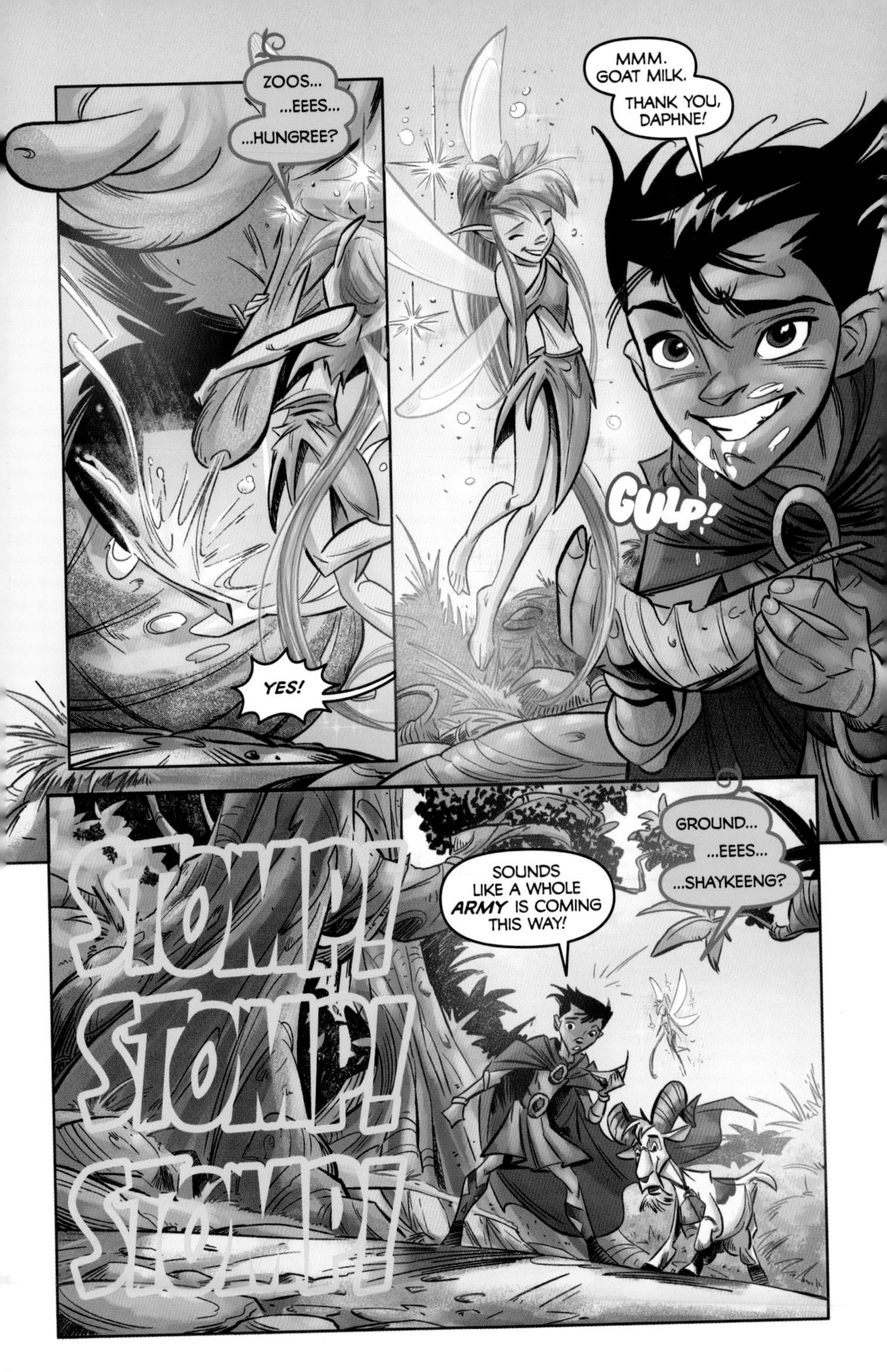
ZOOS...
...EEES...
...HUNGREE?
MMM. GOAT MILK.
THANK YOU, DAPHNE!
GULP!
YES!
STOMP! STOMP! STOMP!
GROUND...
...EEES...
...SHAYKEENG?
SOUNDS LIKE A WHOLE *ARMY* IS COMING THIS WAY!

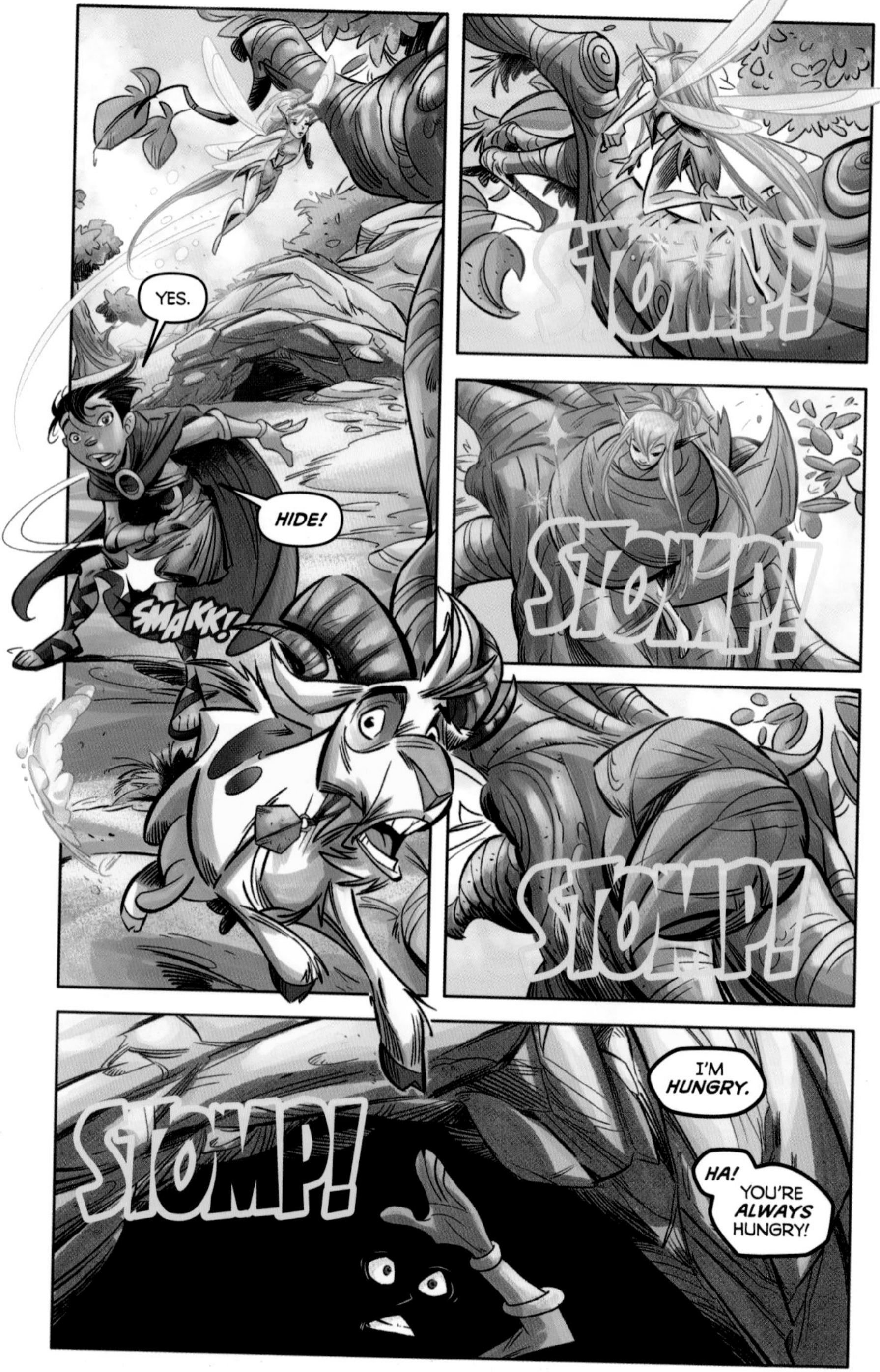
YES.
HIDE!
SMAKK!
STOMP!
STOMP!
STOMP!
STOMP!
I'M *HUNGRY.*
HA! YOU'RE *ALWAYS* HUNGRY!

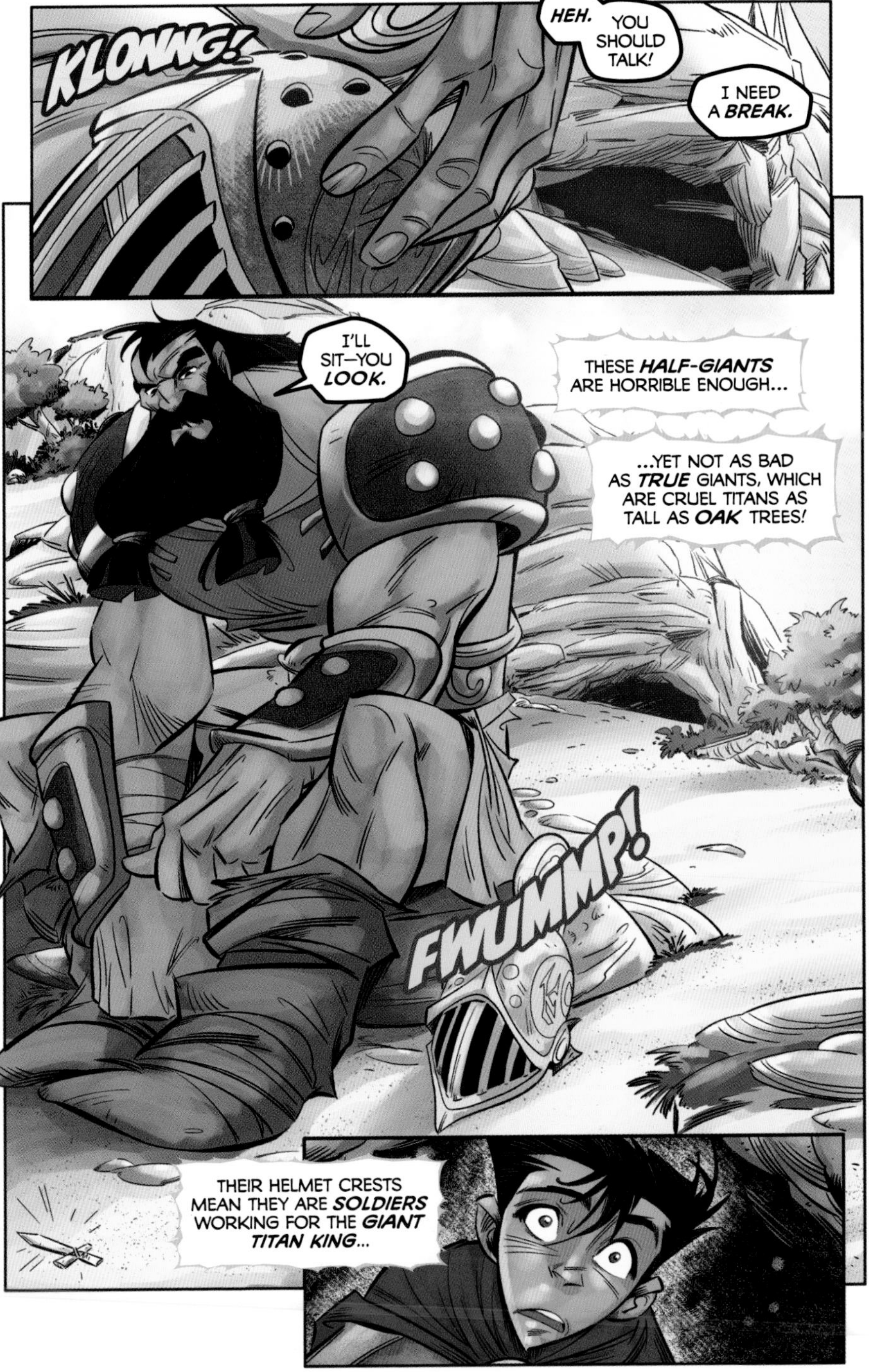

KLONNG!
HEH. YOU SHOULD TALK!
I NEED A BREAK.
I'LL SIT—YOU LOOK.
THESE HALF-GIANTS ARE HORRIBLE ENOUGH...
...YET NOT AS BAD AS TRUE GIANTS, WHICH ARE CRUEL TITANS AS TALL AS OAK TREES!
FWUMMP!
THEIR HELMET CRESTS MEAN THEY ARE SOLDIERS WORKING FOR THE GIANT TITAN KING...

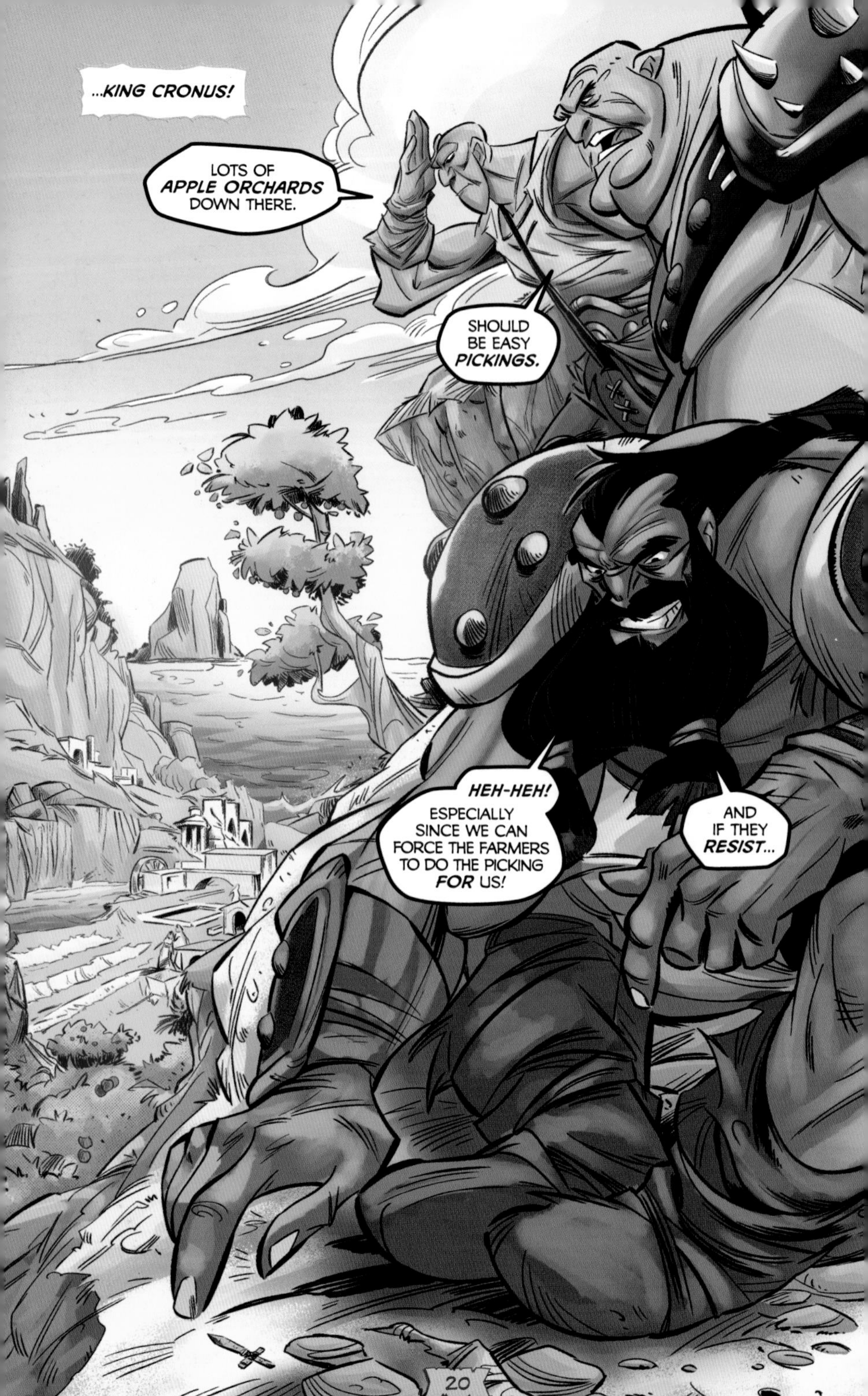
...KING CRONUS!
LOTS OF APPLE ORCHARDS DOWN THERE.
SHOULD BE EASY PICKINGS.
HEH-HEH! ESPECIALLY SINCE WE CAN FORCE THE FARMERS TO DO THE PICKING FOR US!
AND IF THEY RESIST...

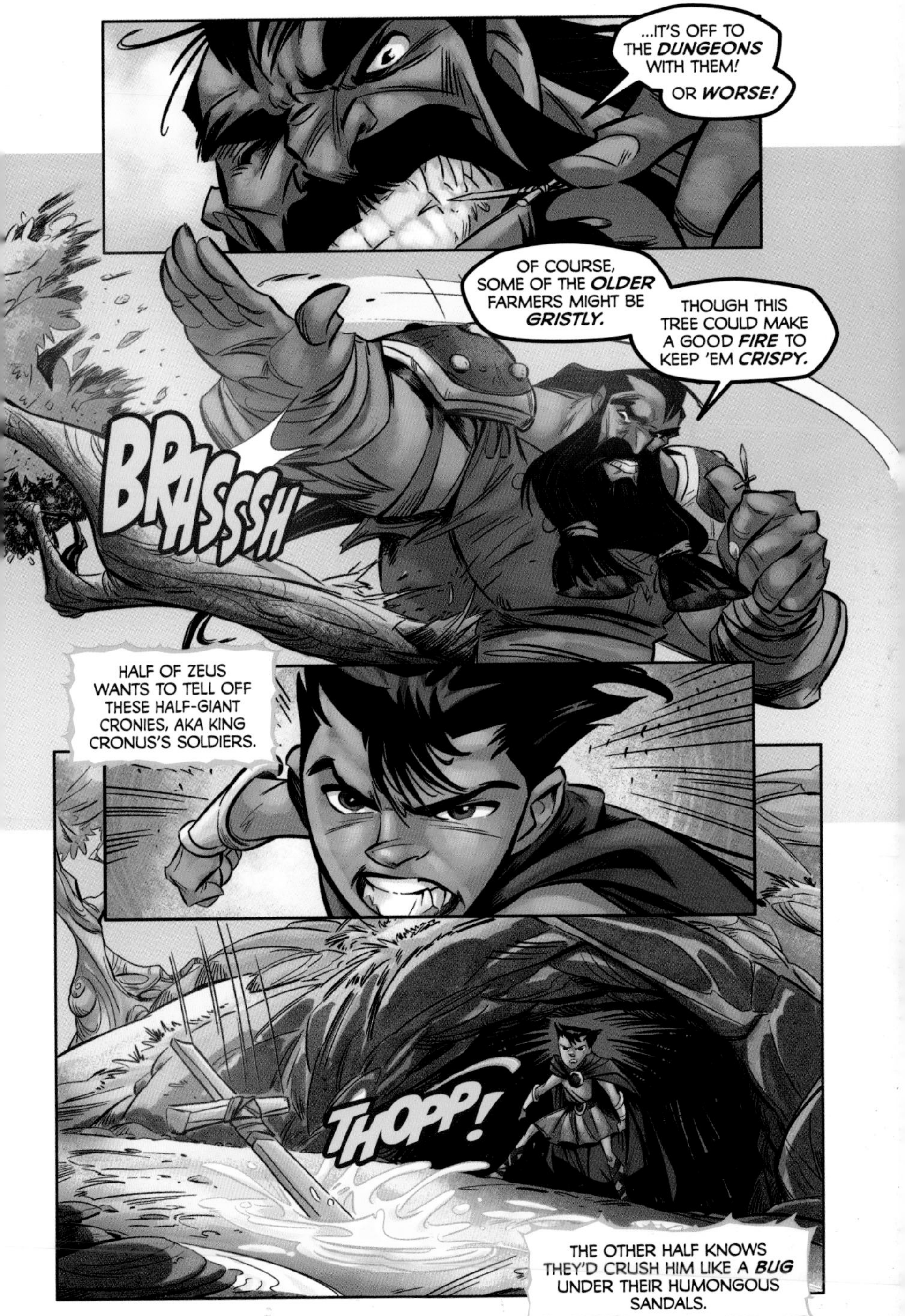

...IT'S OFF TO THE **DUNGEONS** WITH THEM!
OR **WORSE!**
OF COURSE, SOME OF THE **OLDER** FARMERS MIGHT BE **GRISTLY.**
THOUGH THIS TREE COULD MAKE A GOOD **FIRE** TO KEEP 'EM **CRISPY.**
BRASSSH
HALF OF ZEUS WANTS TO TELL OFF THESE HALF-GIANT CRONIES, AKA KING CRONUS'S SOLDIERS.
THOPP!
THE OTHER HALF KNOWS THEY'D CRUSH HIM LIKE A **BUG** UNDER THEIR HUMONGOUS SANDALS.

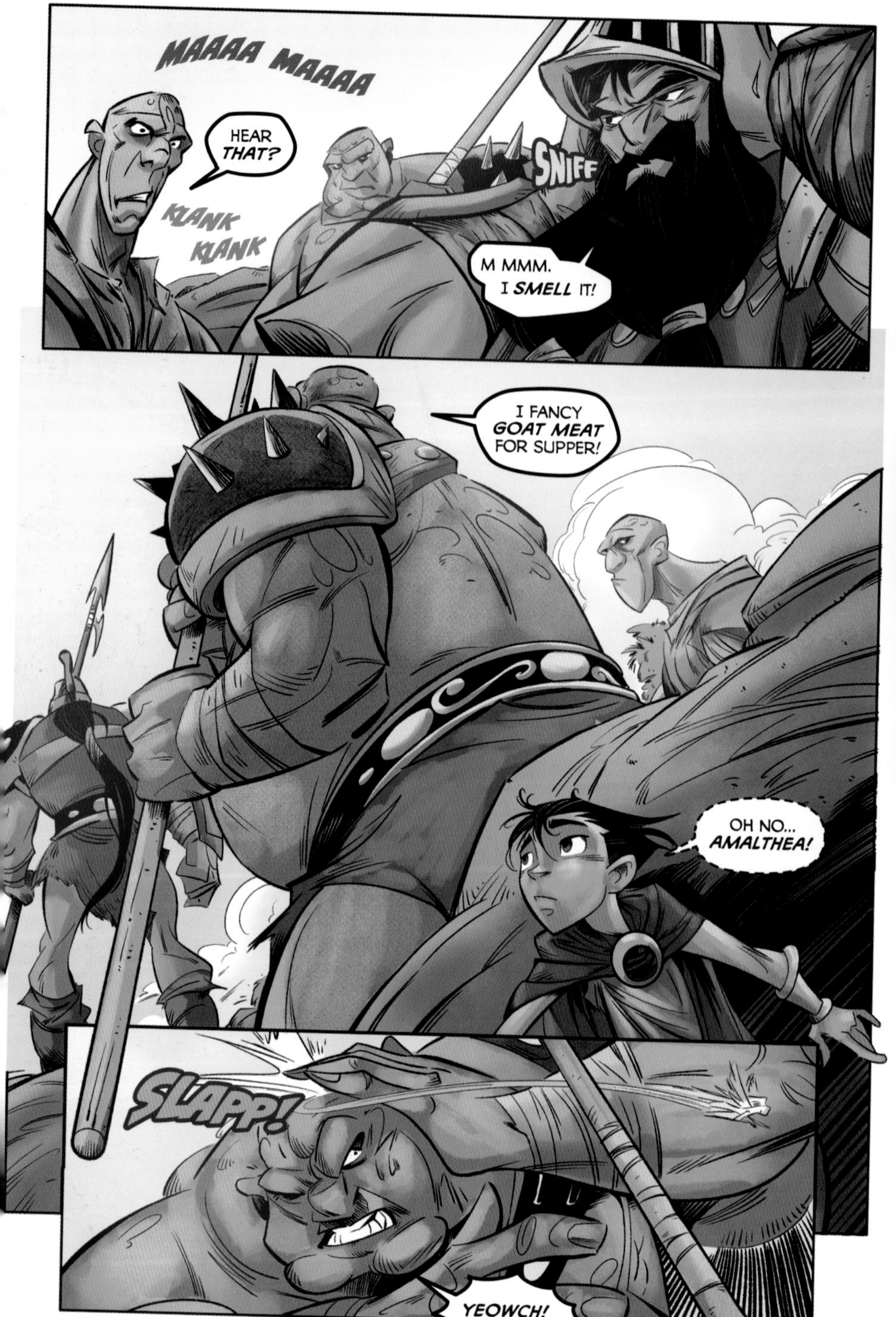
MAAAA MAAAA
HEAR THAT?
KLANK KLANK
SNIFF
M MMM. I SMELL IT!
I FANCY GOAT MEAT FOR SUPPER!
OH NO... AMALTHEA!
SLAPP!
YEOWCH!

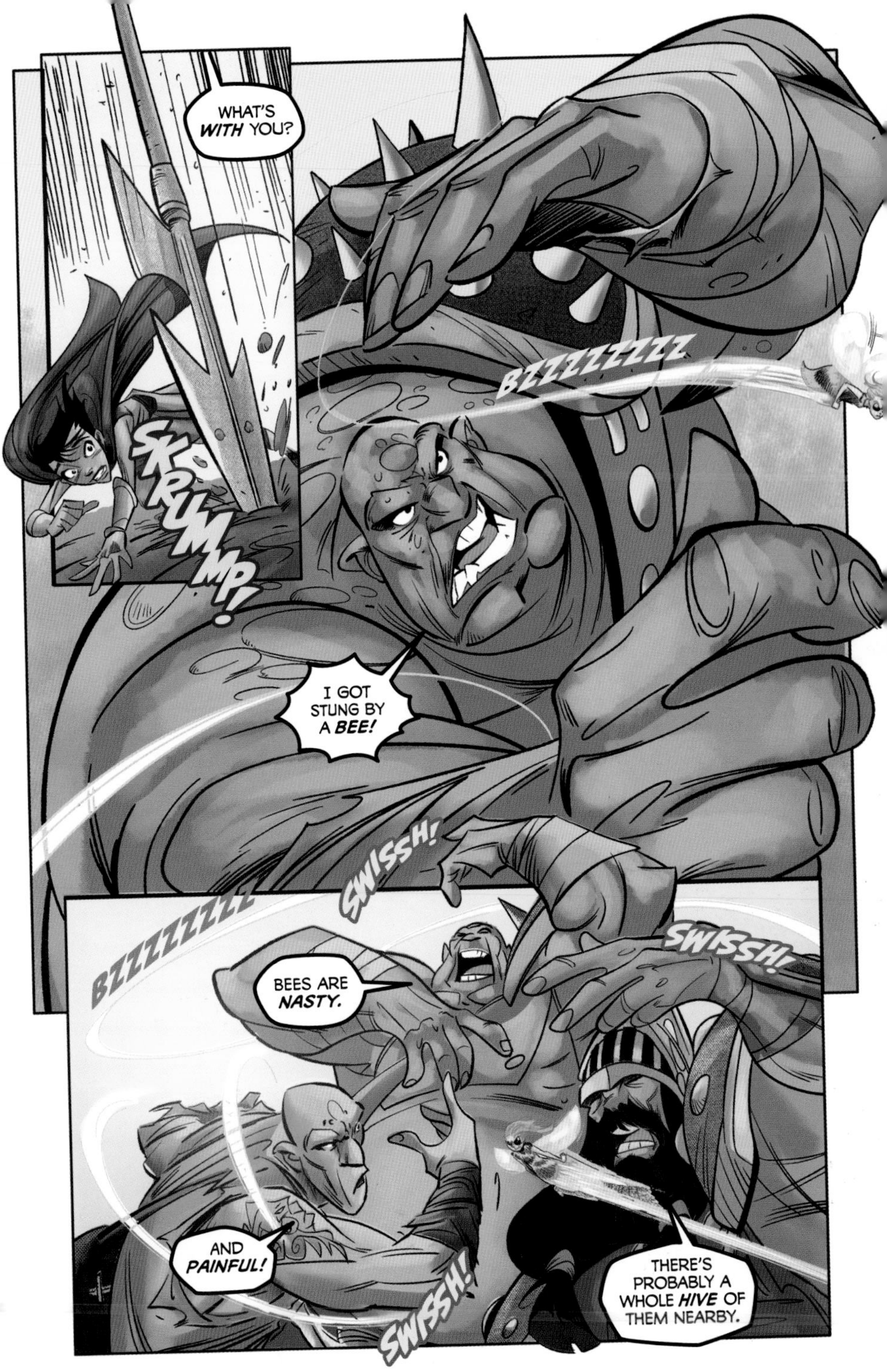
WHAT'S WITH YOU?
SKRUMMP!
BZZZZZZZZ
I GOT STUNG BY A BEE!
SWISSH!
BZZZZZZZZ
SWISSH!
BEES ARE NASTY.
AND PAINFUL!
SWISSH!
THERE'S PROBABLY A WHOLE HIVE OF THEM NEARBY.

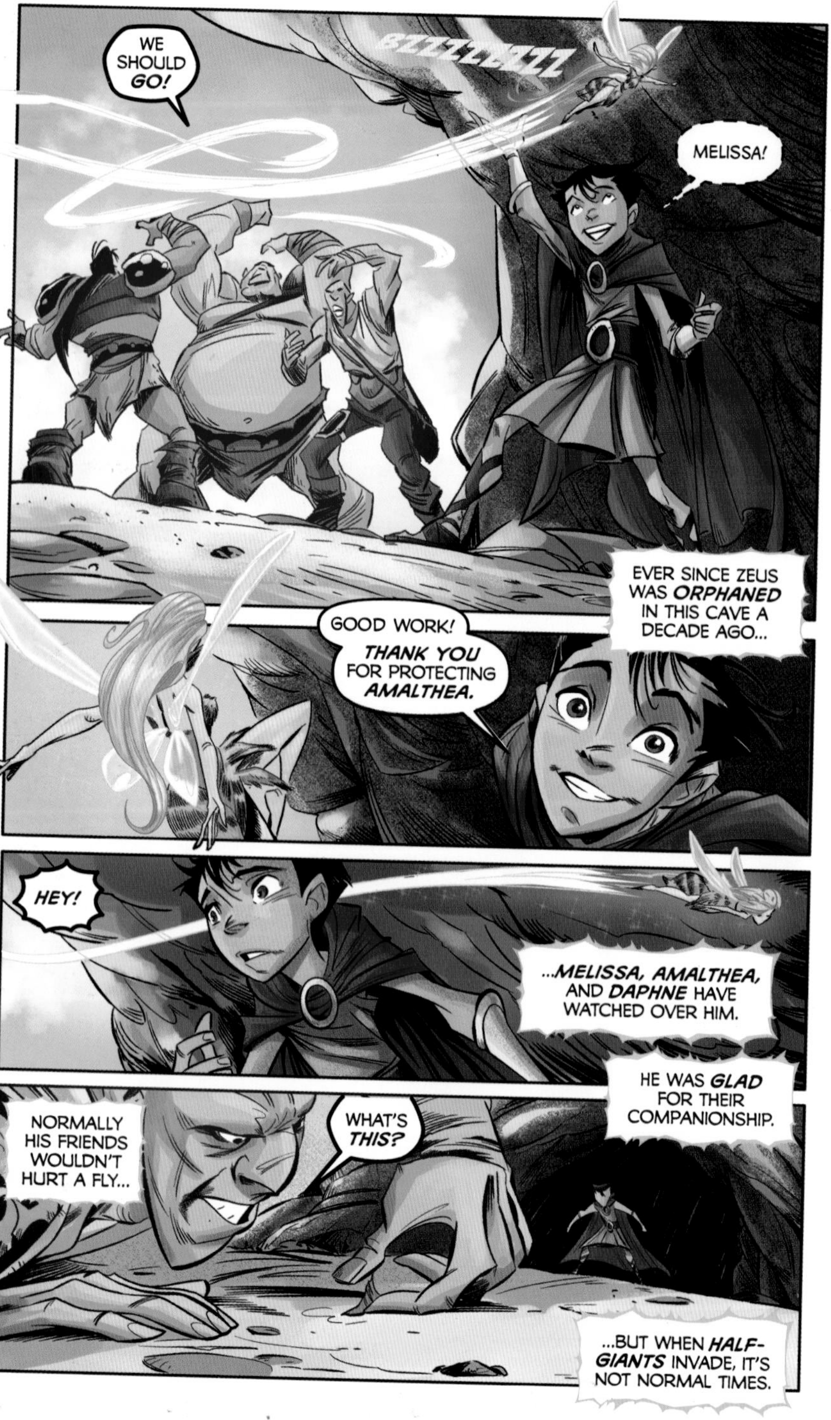
WE SHOULD *GO!*
MELISSA!
EVER SINCE ZEUS WAS *ORPHANED* IN THIS CAVE A DECADE AGO...
GOOD WORK! *THANK YOU* FOR PROTECTING *AMALTHEA.*
HEY!
...*MELISSA, AMALTHEA,* AND *DAPHNE* HAVE WATCHED OVER HIM.
HE WAS *GLAD* FOR THEIR COMPANIONSHIP.
NORMALLY HIS FRIENDS WOULDN'T HURT A FLY...
WHAT'S *THIS?*
...BUT WHEN *HALF-GIANTS* INVADE, IT'S NOT NORMAL TIMES.

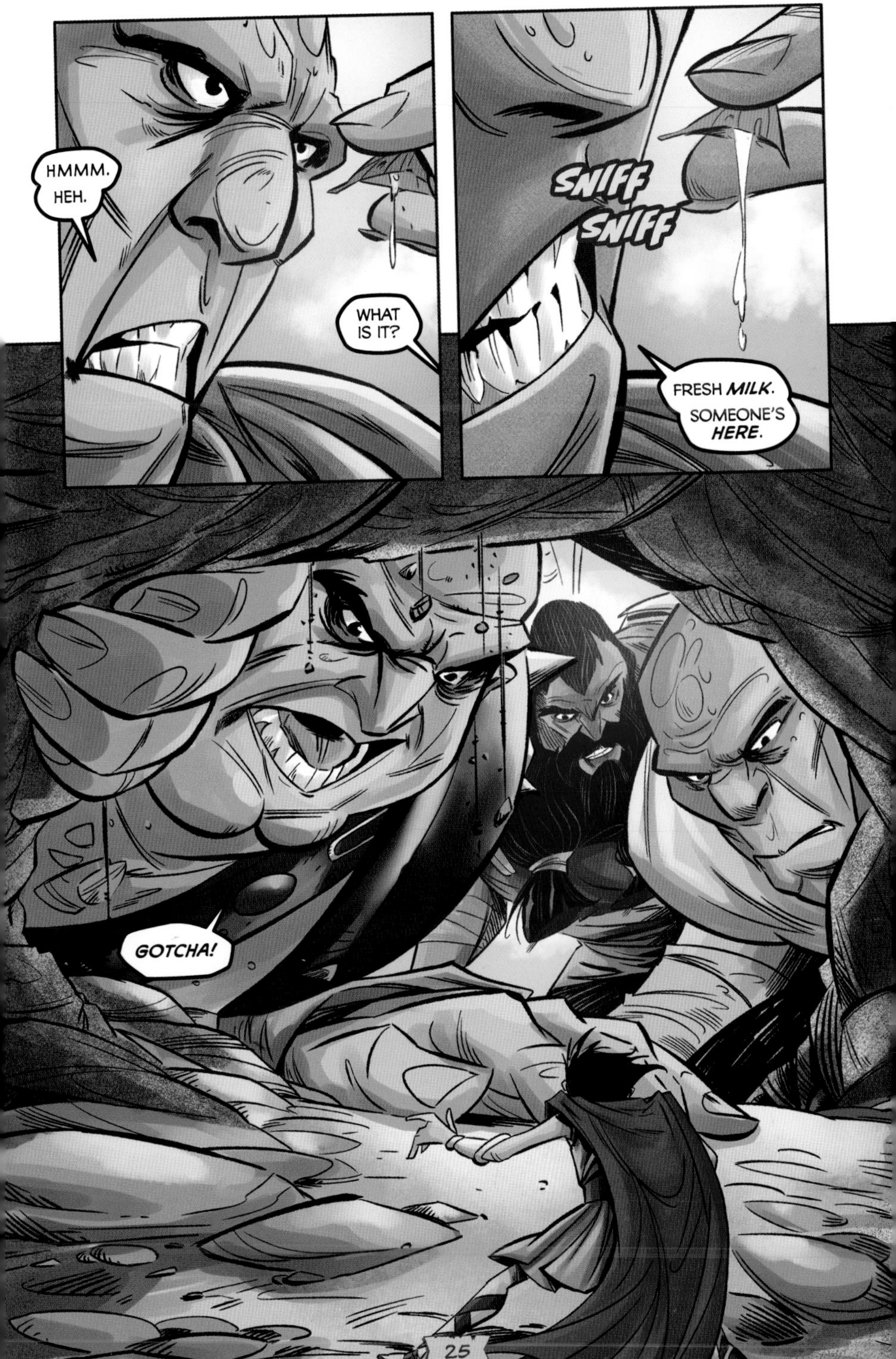
HMMM.
HEH.
WHAT IS IT?
SNIFF
SNIFF
FRESH MILK.
SOMEONE'S HERE.
GOTCHA!

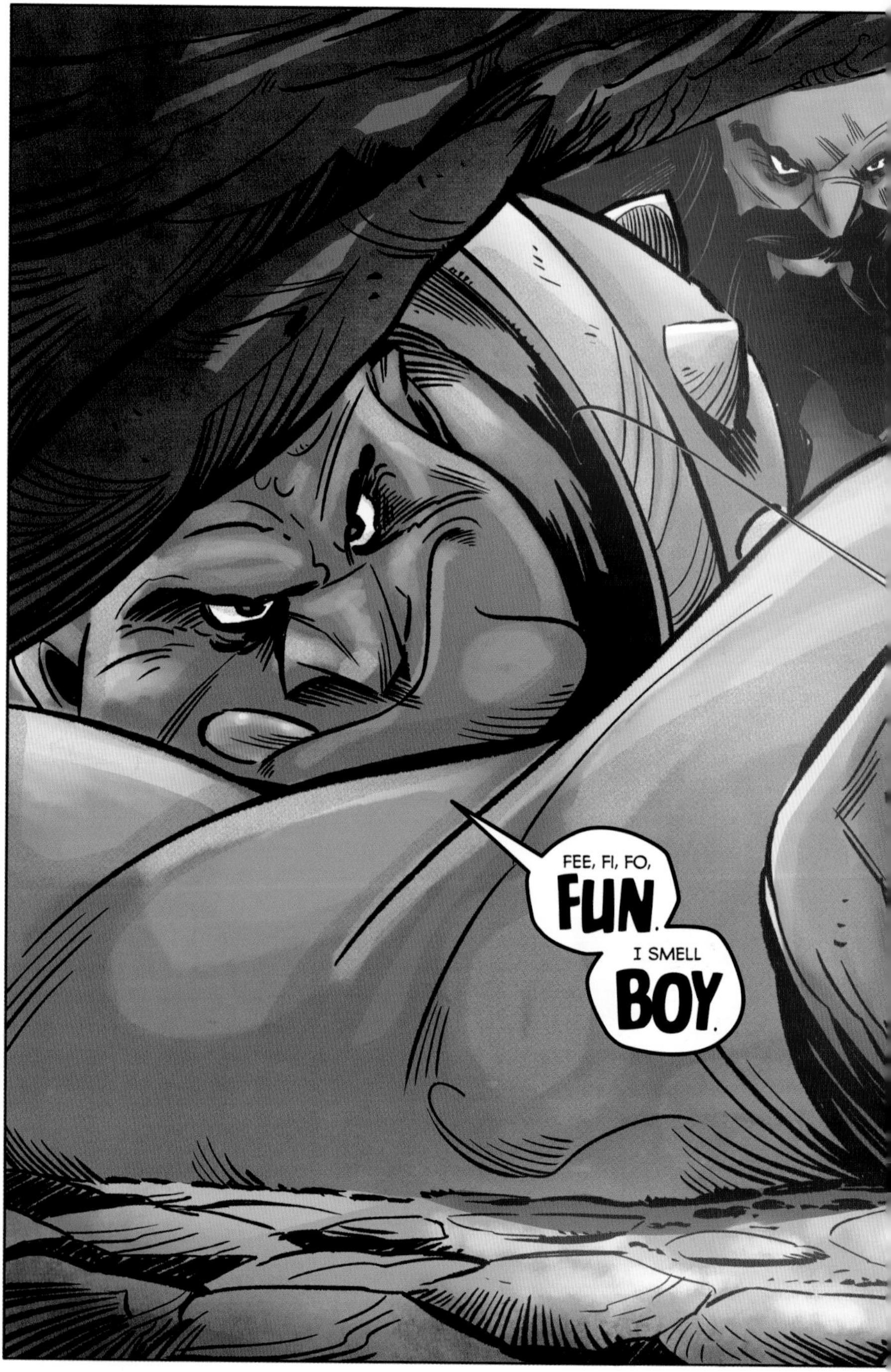
FEE, FI, FO,
FUN.
I SMELL
BOY.

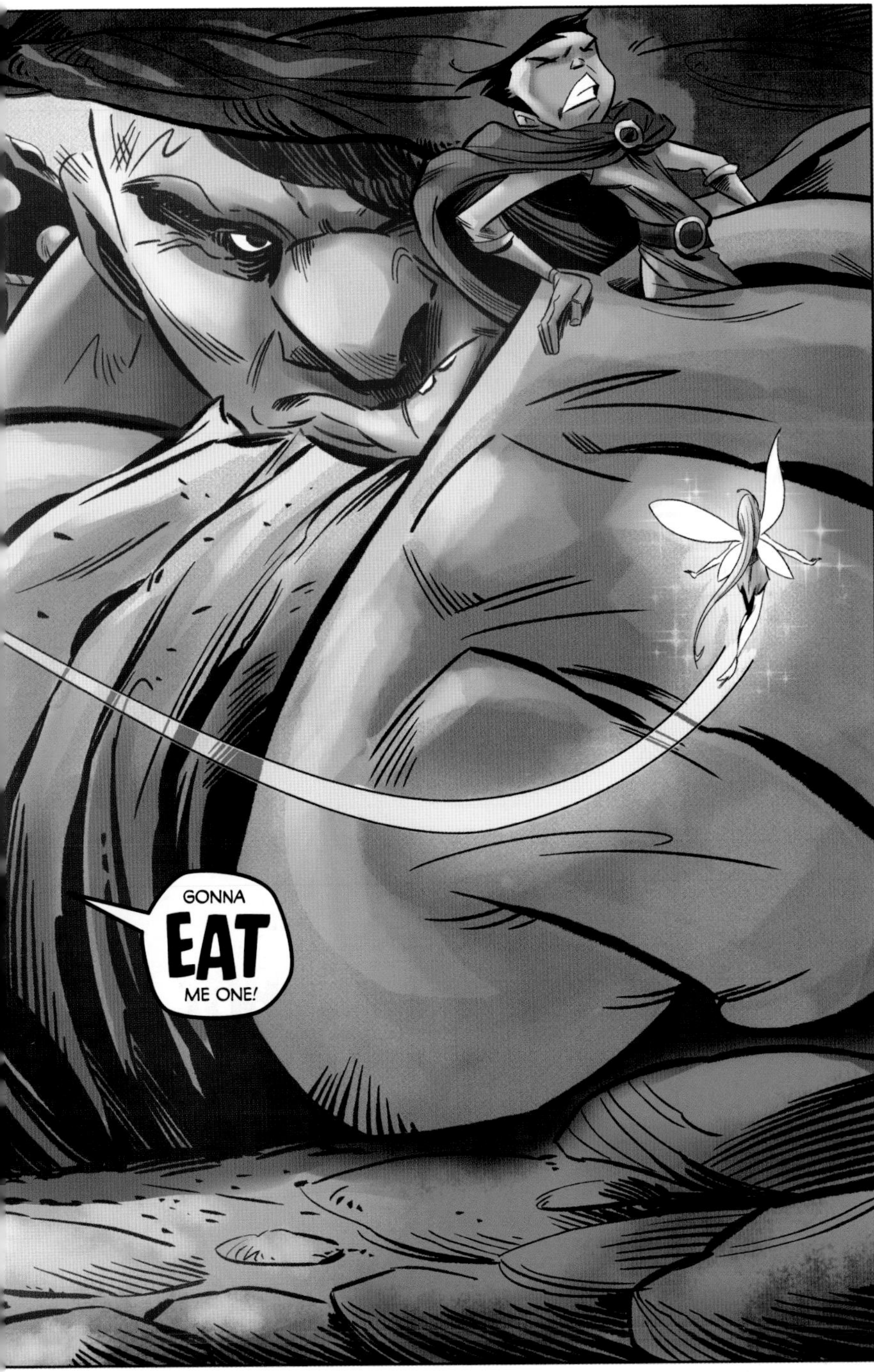
GONNA EAT ME ONE!

CHAPTER TWO:
GOODBYE, CRETE!

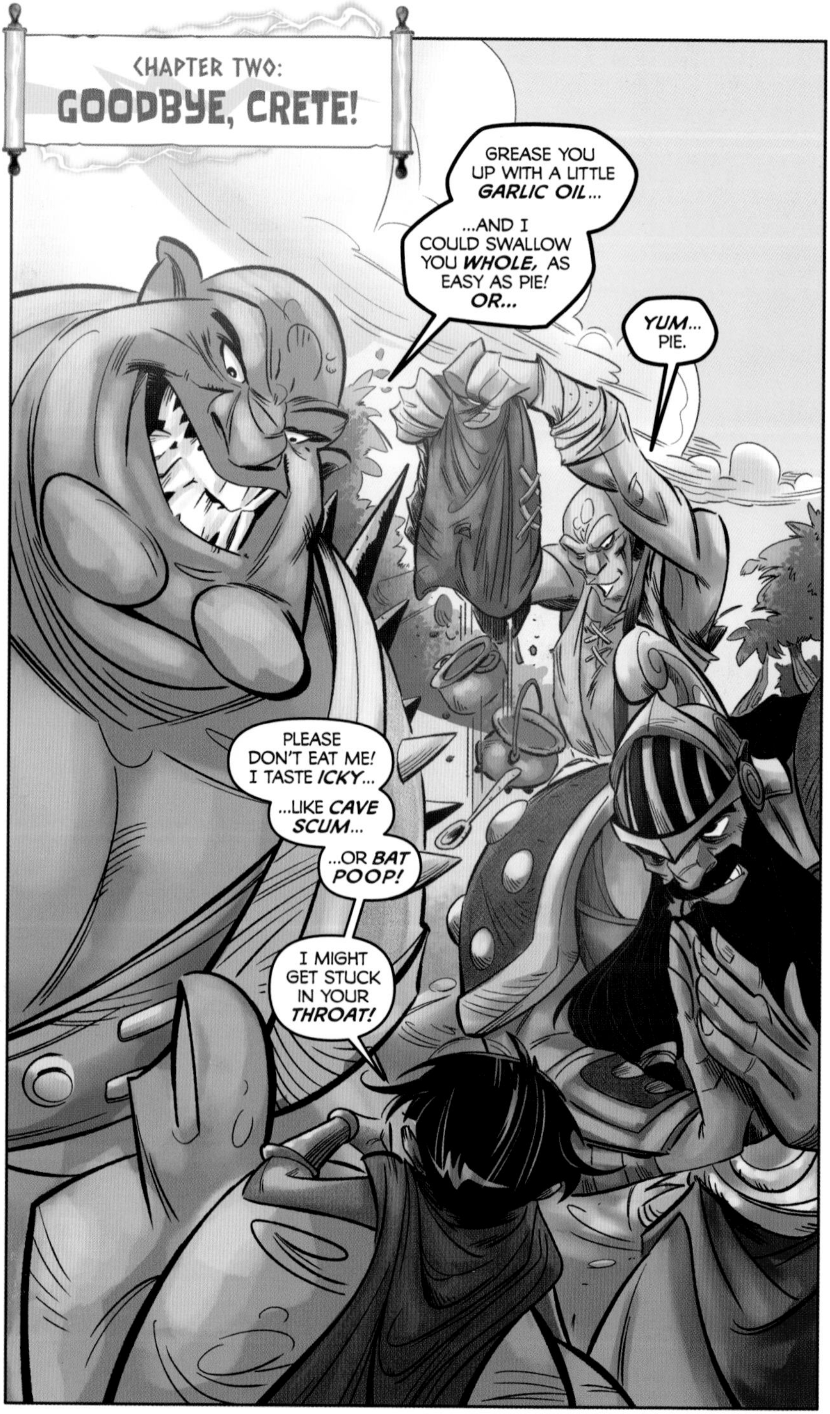

GREASE YOU UP WITH A LITTLE GARLIC OIL...
...AND I COULD SWALLOW YOU WHOLE, AS EASY AS PIE! OR...
YUM... PIE.
PLEASE DON'T EAT ME! I TASTE ICKY...
...LIKE CAVE SCUM...
...OR BAT POOP!
I MIGHT GET STUCK IN YOUR THROAT!

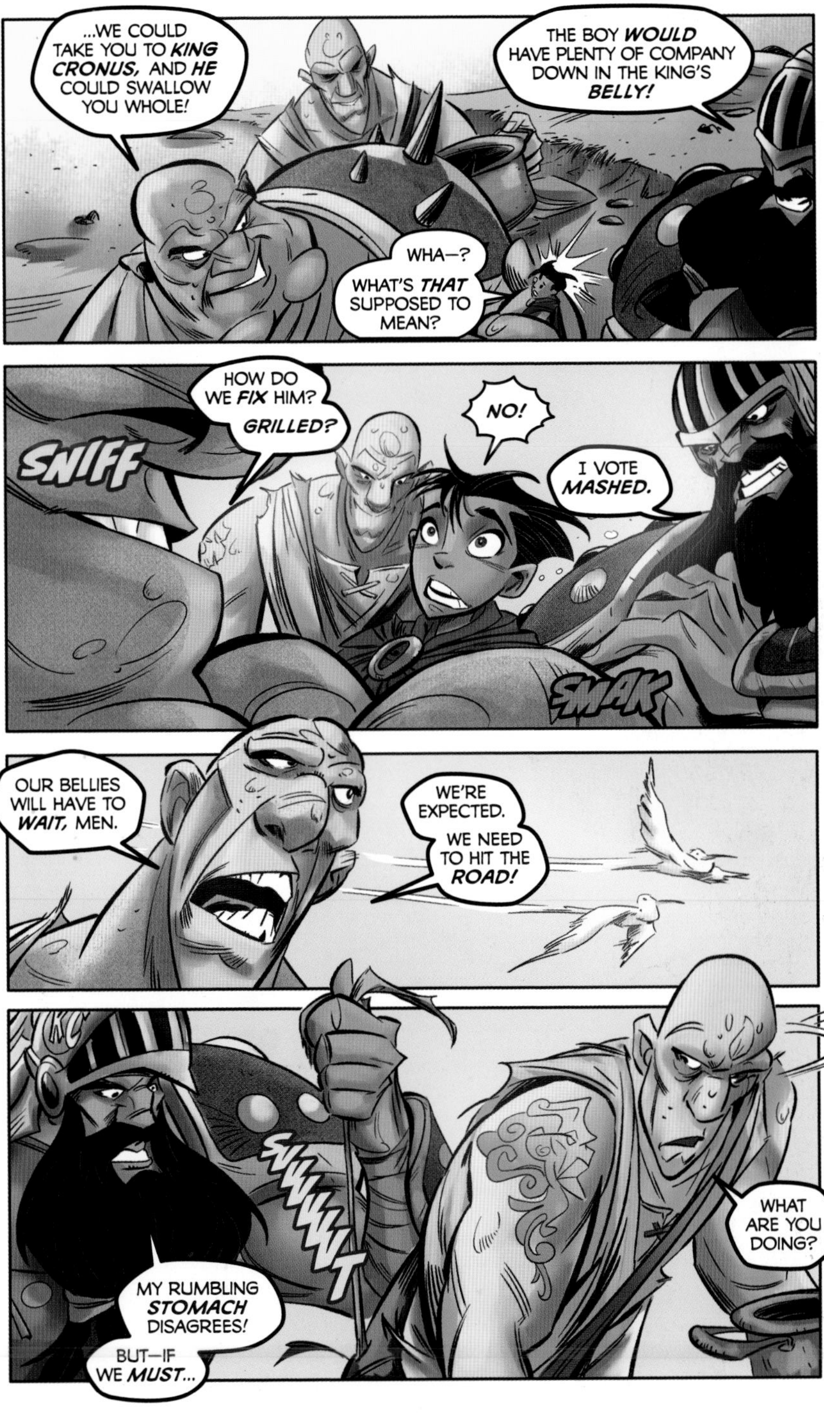
...WE COULD TAKE YOU TO KING CRONUS, AND HE COULD SWALLOW YOU WHOLE!
THE BOY WOULD HAVE PLENTY OF COMPANY DOWN IN THE KING'S BELLY!
WHA—?
WHAT'S THAT SUPPOSED TO MEAN?
HOW DO WE FIX HIM? GRILLED?
SNIFF
NO!
I VOTE MASHED.
SMAK
OUR BELLIES WILL HAVE TO WAIT, MEN.
WE'RE EXPECTED.
WE NEED TO HIT THE ROAD!
SWWWT
WHAT ARE YOU DOING?
MY RUMBLING STOMACH DISAGREES!
BUT—IF WE MUST...

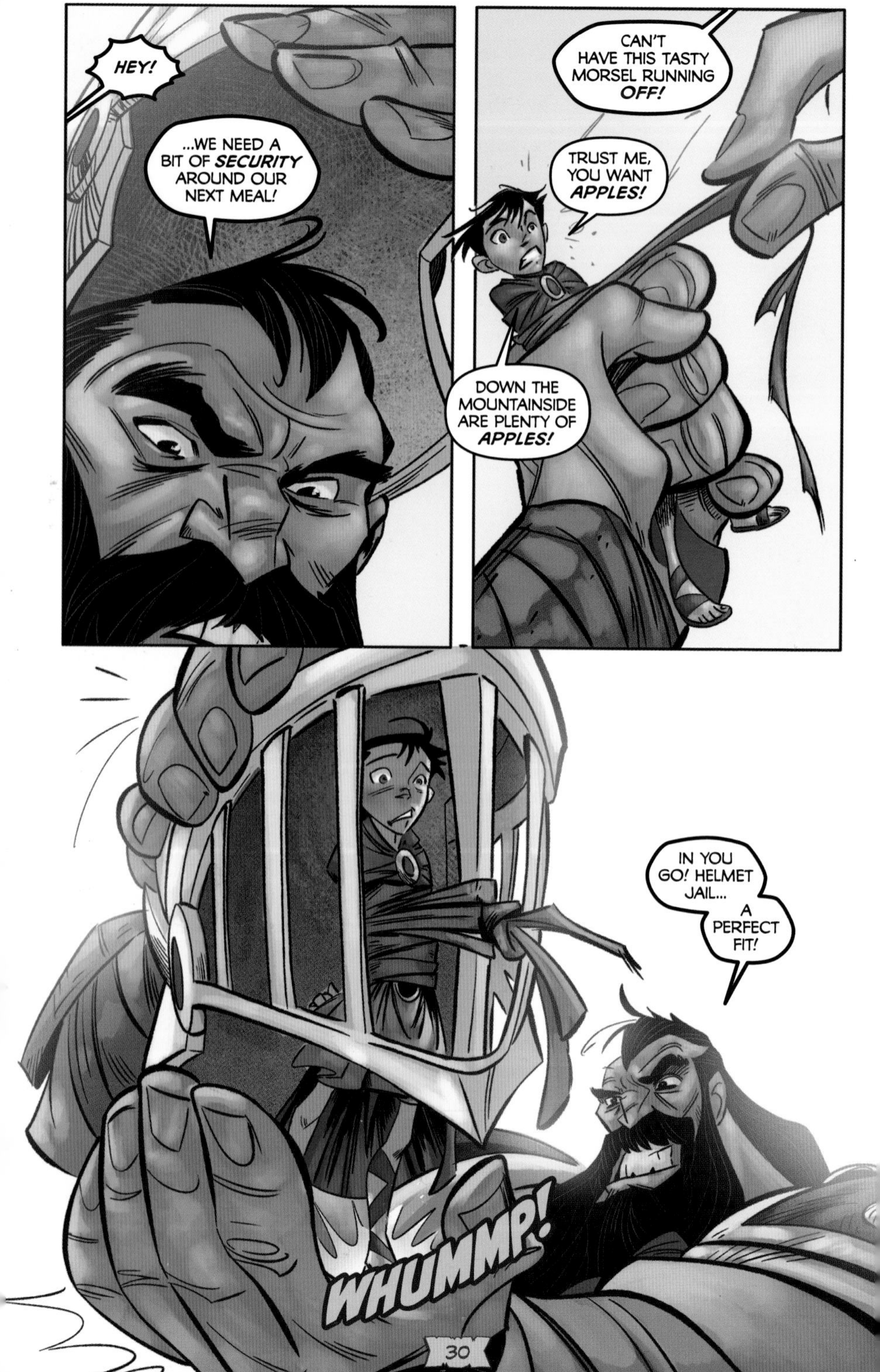
HEY!
...WE NEED A BIT OF SECURITY AROUND OUR NEXT MEAL!
CAN'T HAVE THIS TASTY MORSEL RUNNING OFF!
TRUST ME, YOU WANT APPLES!
DOWN THE MOUNTAINSIDE ARE PLENTY OF APPLES!
IN YOU GO! HELMET JAIL...
A PERFECT FIT!
WHUMMP!

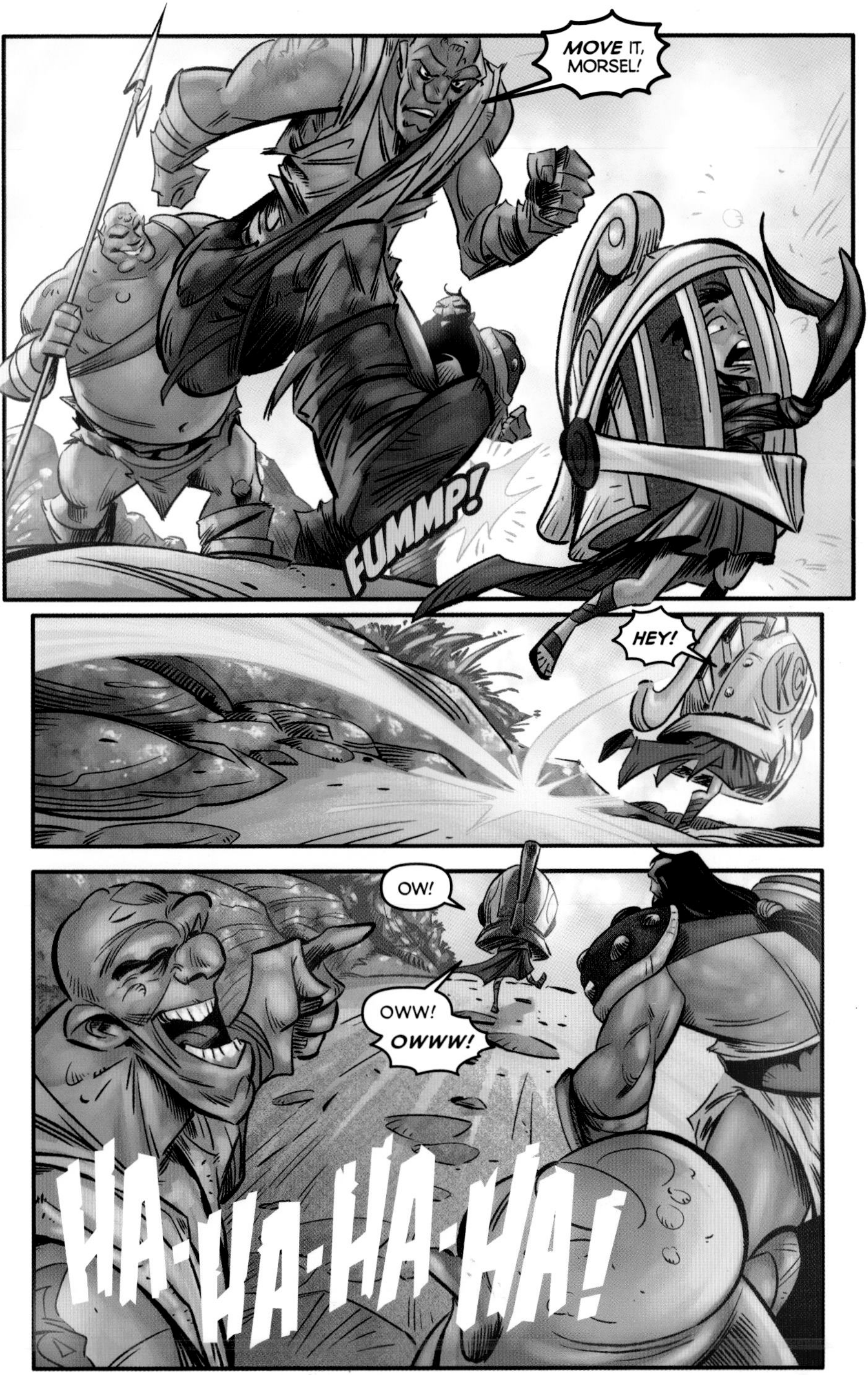
MOVE IT, MORSEL!
FUMMP!
HEY!
OW!
OWW! OWWW!
HA-HA-HA-HA-HA!

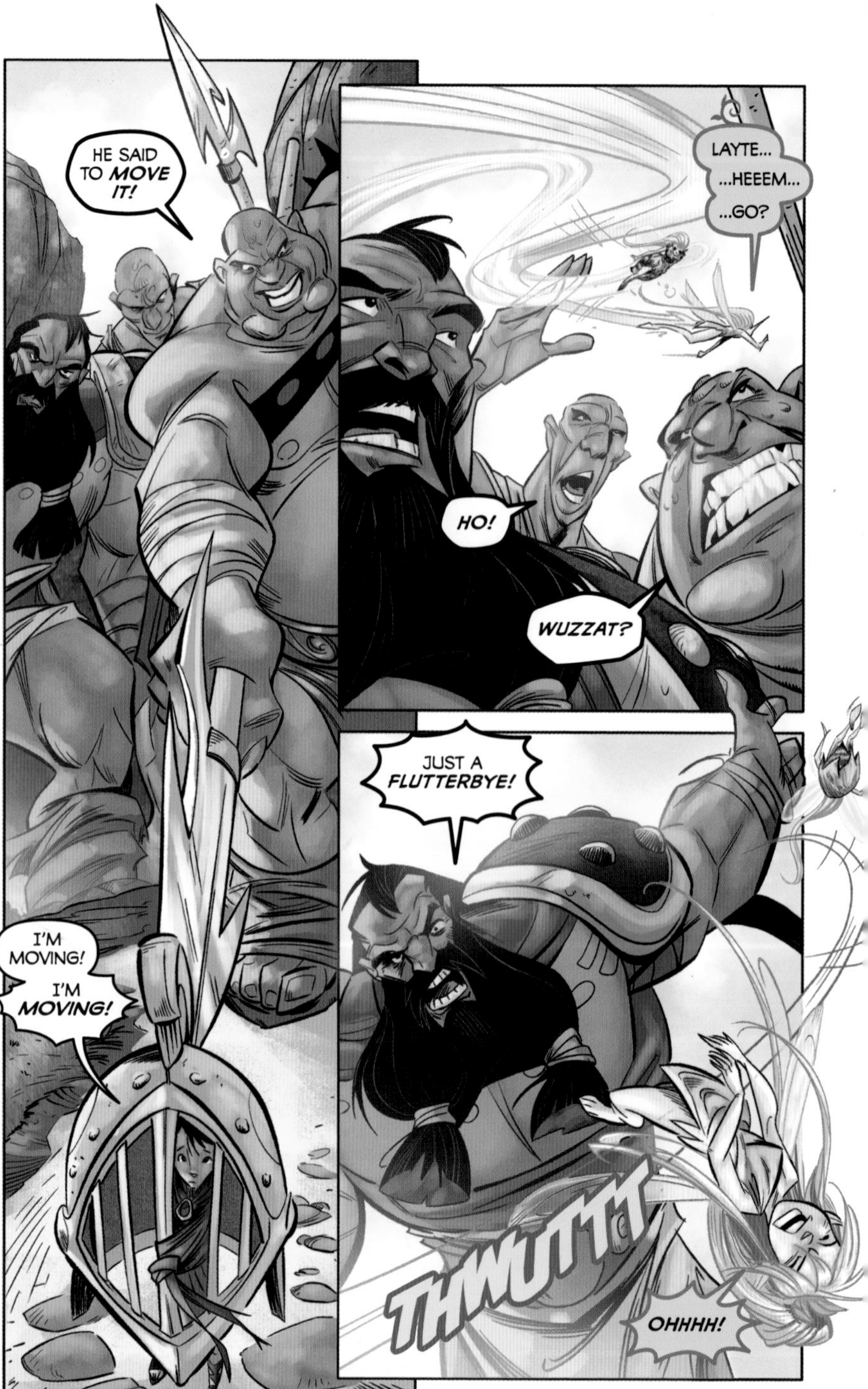
HE SAID TO MOVE IT!
I'M MOVING! I'M MOVING!
LAYTE... ...HEEEM... ...GO?
HO!
WUZZAT?
JUST A FLUTTERBYE!
THWUTTTT
OHHHH!

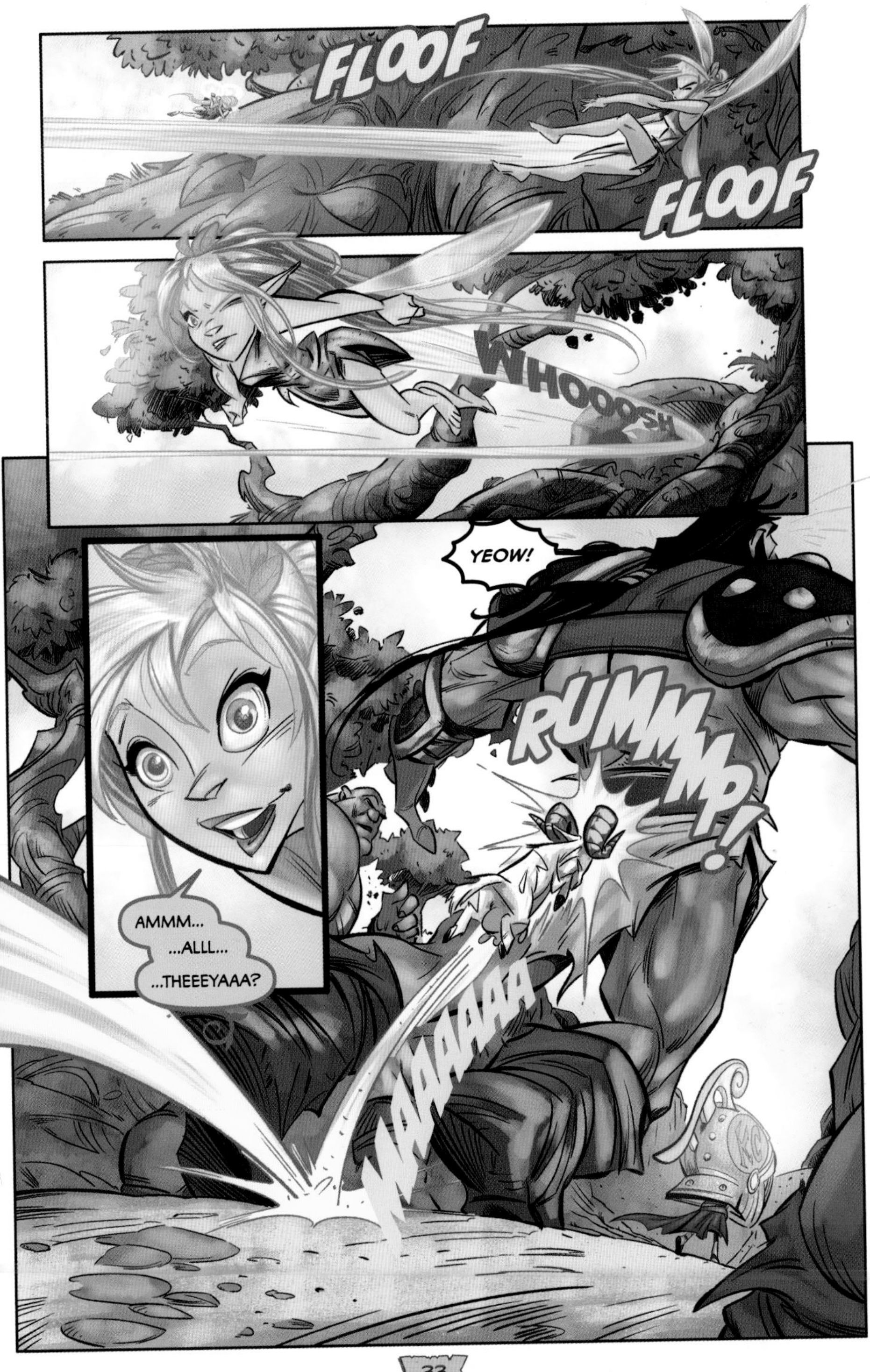
FLOOF
FLOOF
WHOOOOSH
YEOW!
RUMMMP!
AMMM...
...ALLL...
...THEEEYAAA?
WAAAAAA

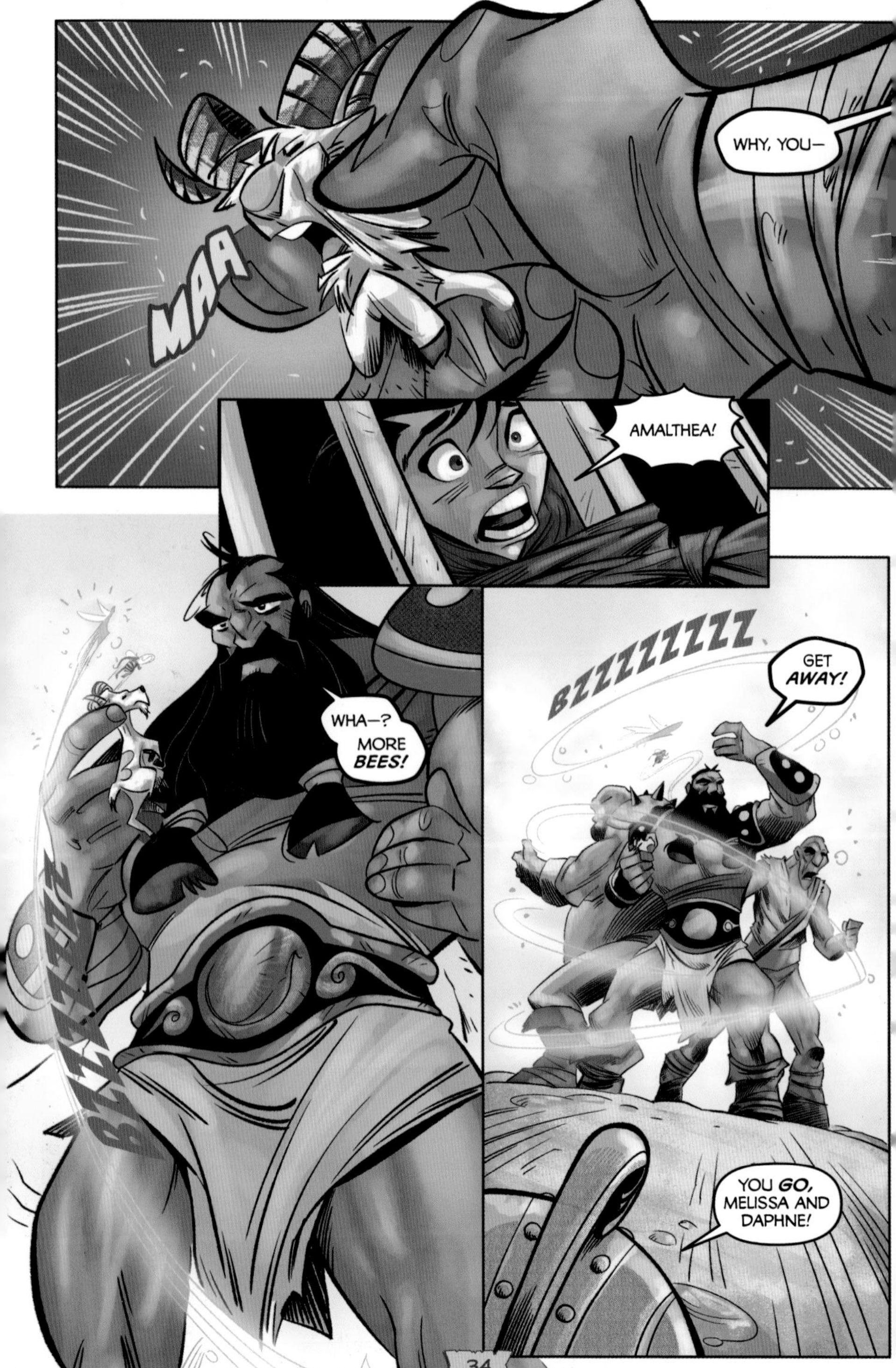
MAA
WHY, YOU—
AMALTHEA!
WHA—? MORE BEES!
BZZZZZZZZ
GET AWAY!
YOU GO, MELISSA AND DAPHNE!

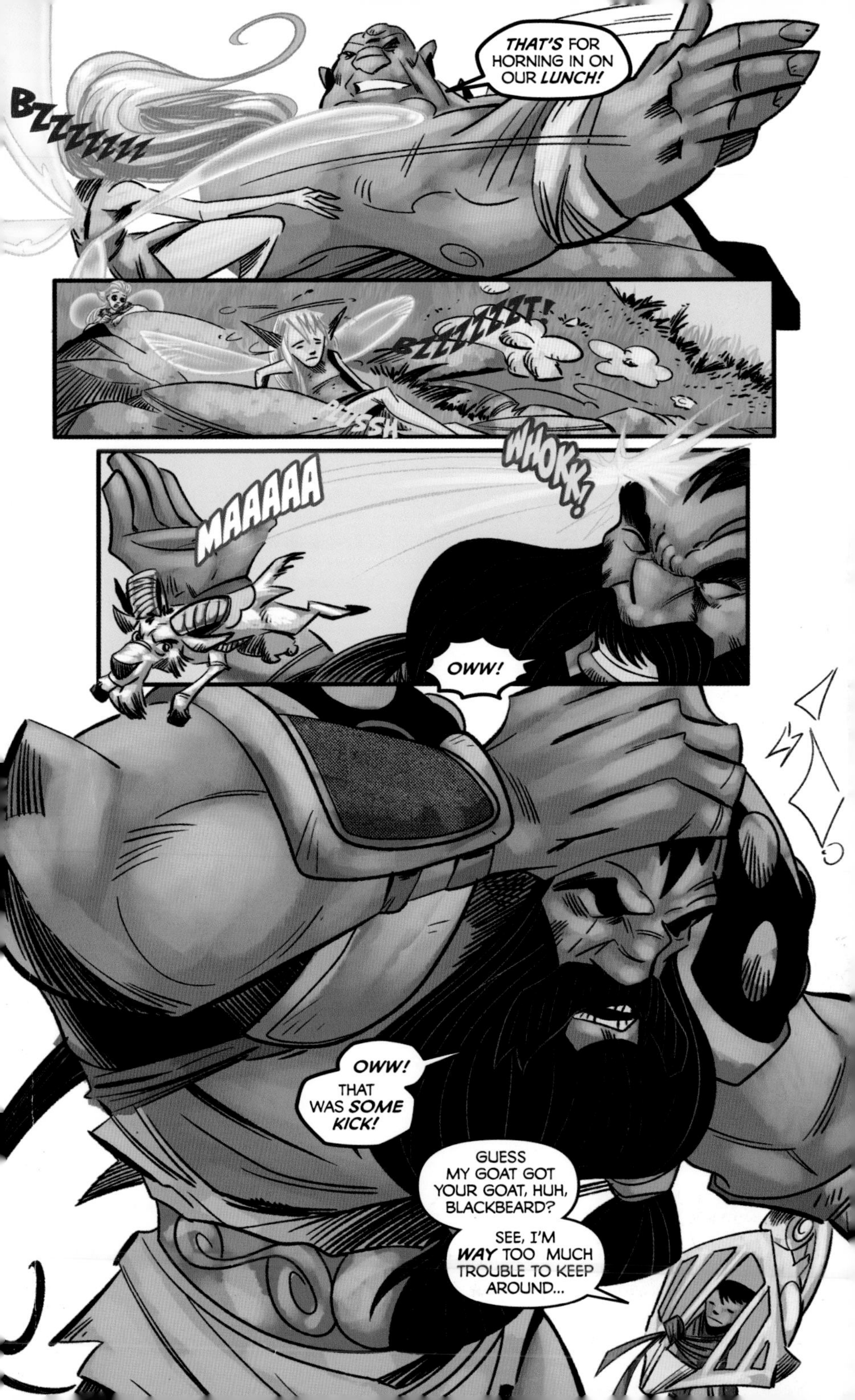
THAT'S FOR HORNING IN ON OUR LUNCH!
BZZZZZZZZ
BZZZZZZZT!
PLUSSH
MAAAAA
WHOKK!
OWW!
OWW! THAT WAS SOME KICK!
GUESS MY GOAT GOT YOUR GOAT, HUH, BLACKBEARD?
SEE, I'M WAY TOO MUCH TROUBLE TO KEEP AROUND...

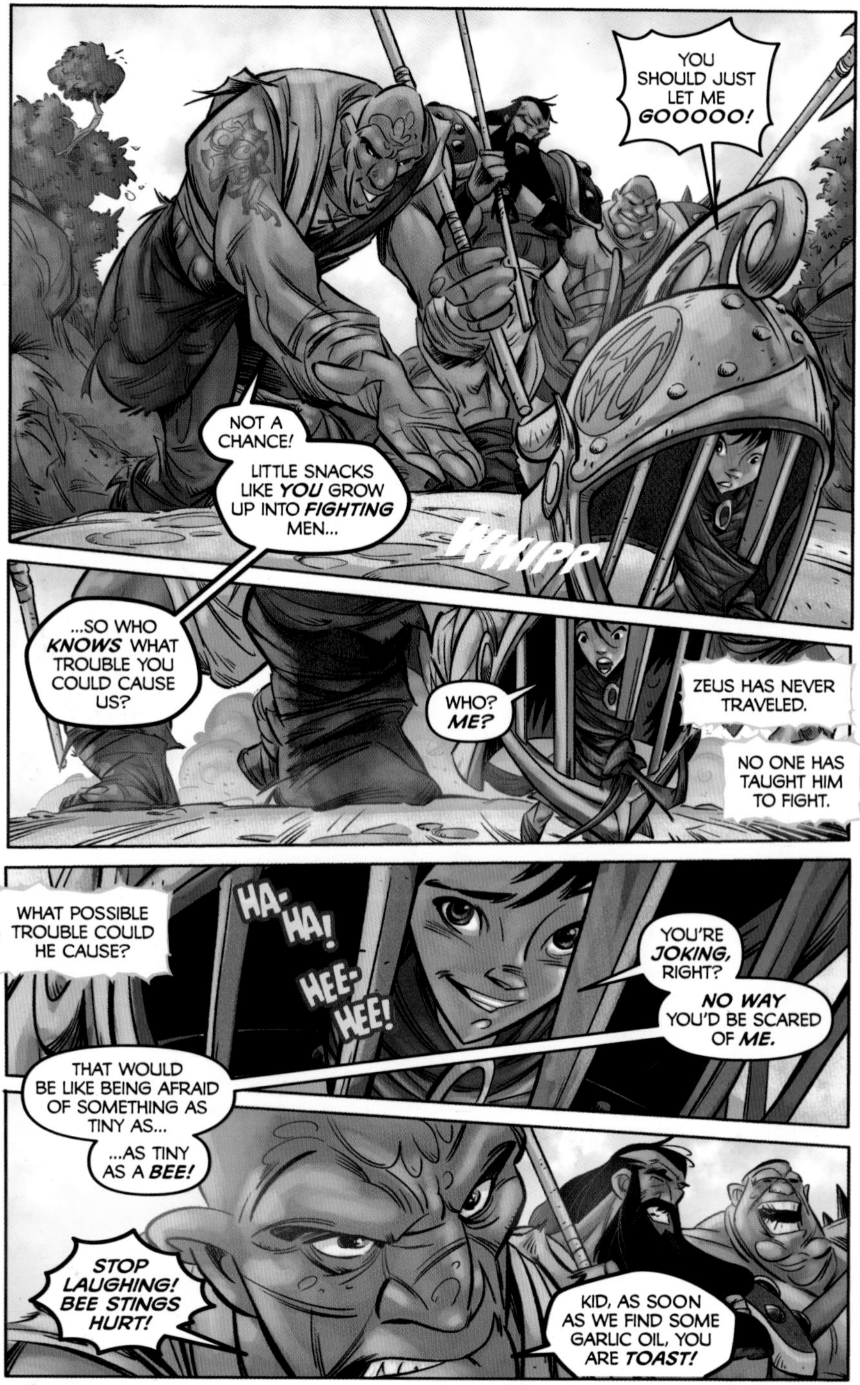

YOU SHOULD JUST LET ME GOOOOO!
NOT A CHANCE!
LITTLE SNACKS LIKE YOU GROW UP INTO FIGHTING MEN...
WHIPP
...SO WHO KNOWS WHAT TROUBLE YOU COULD CAUSE US?
WHO? ME?
ZEUS HAS NEVER TRAVELED.
NO ONE HAS TAUGHT HIM TO FIGHT.
WHAT POSSIBLE TROUBLE COULD HE CAUSE?
HA-HA!
HEE-HEE!
YOU'RE JOKING, RIGHT?
NO WAY YOU'D BE SCARED OF ME.
THAT WOULD BE LIKE BEING AFRAID OF SOMETHING AS TINY AS...
...AS TINY AS A BEE!
STOP LAUGHING! BEE STINGS HURT!
KID, AS SOON AS WE FIND SOME GARLIC OIL, YOU ARE TOAST!

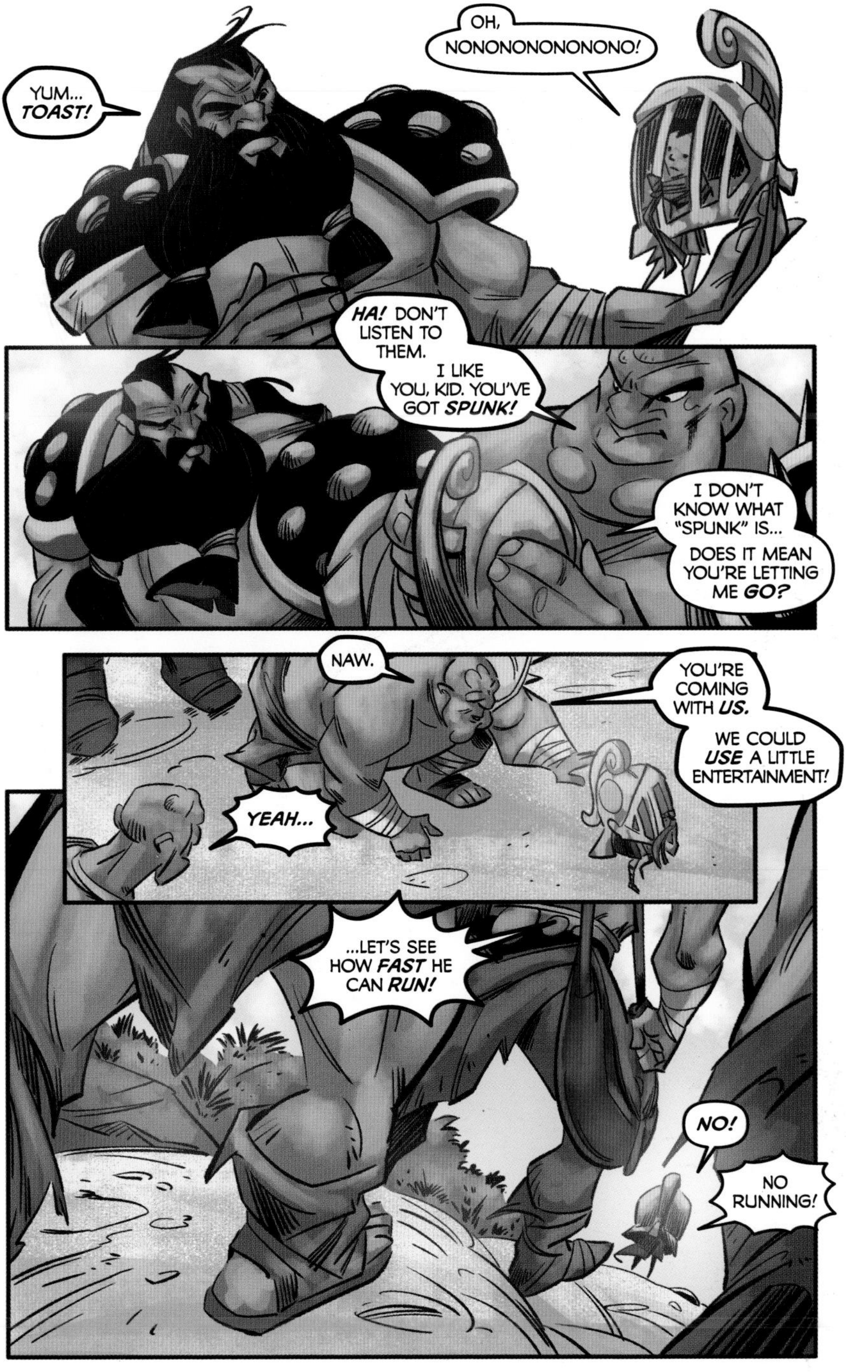
YUM... TOAST!
OH, NONONONONONONO!
HA! DON'T LISTEN TO THEM.
I LIKE YOU, KID. YOU'VE GOT SPUNK!
I DON'T KNOW WHAT "SPUNK" IS...
DOES IT MEAN YOU'RE LETTING ME GO?
NAW.
YOU'RE COMING WITH US.
WE COULD USE A LITTLE ENTERTAINMENT!
YEAH...
...LET'S SEE HOW FAST HE CAN RUN!
NO!
NO RUNNING!

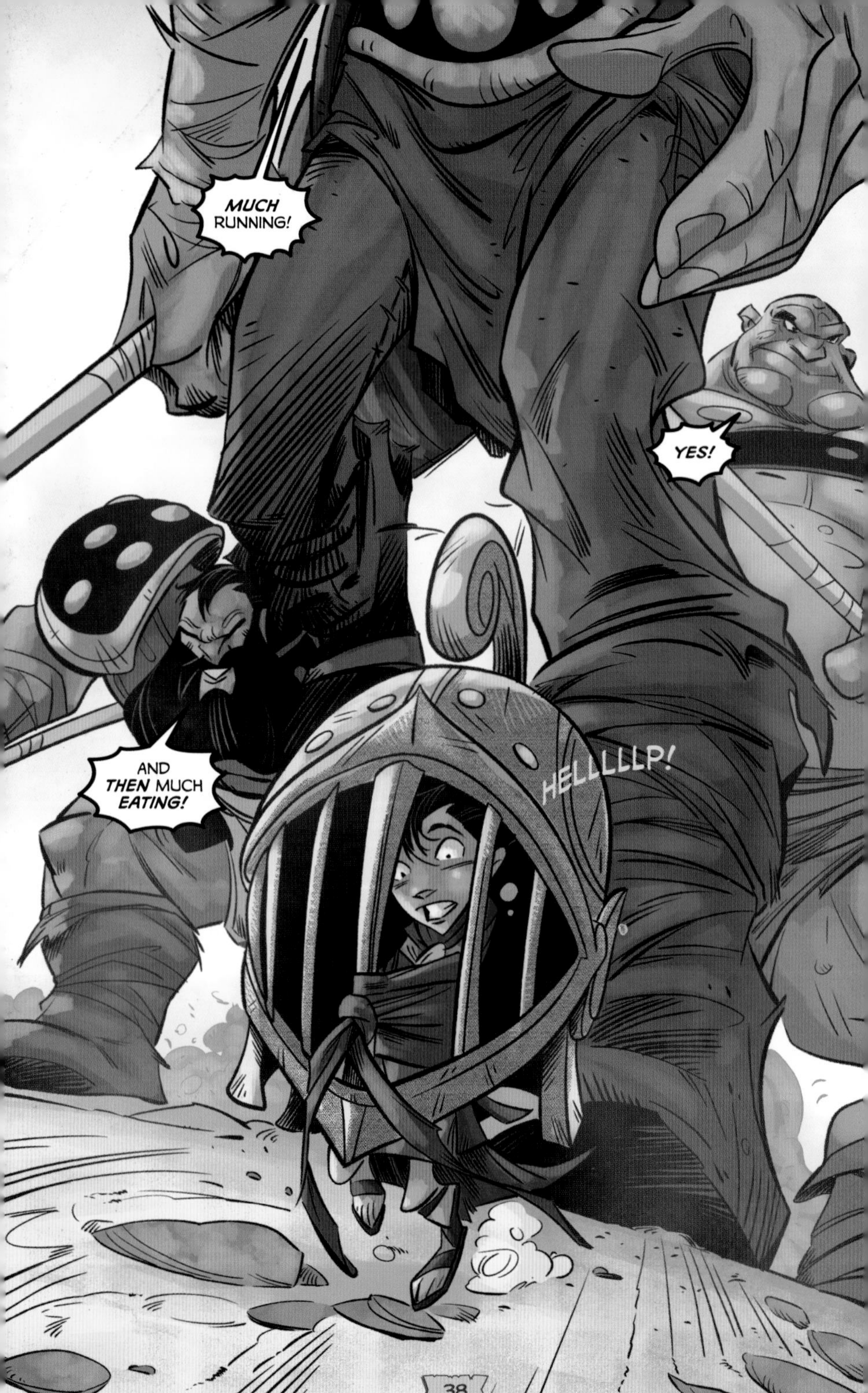
MUCH RUNNING!
YES!
AND THEN MUCH EATING!
HELLLLLP!

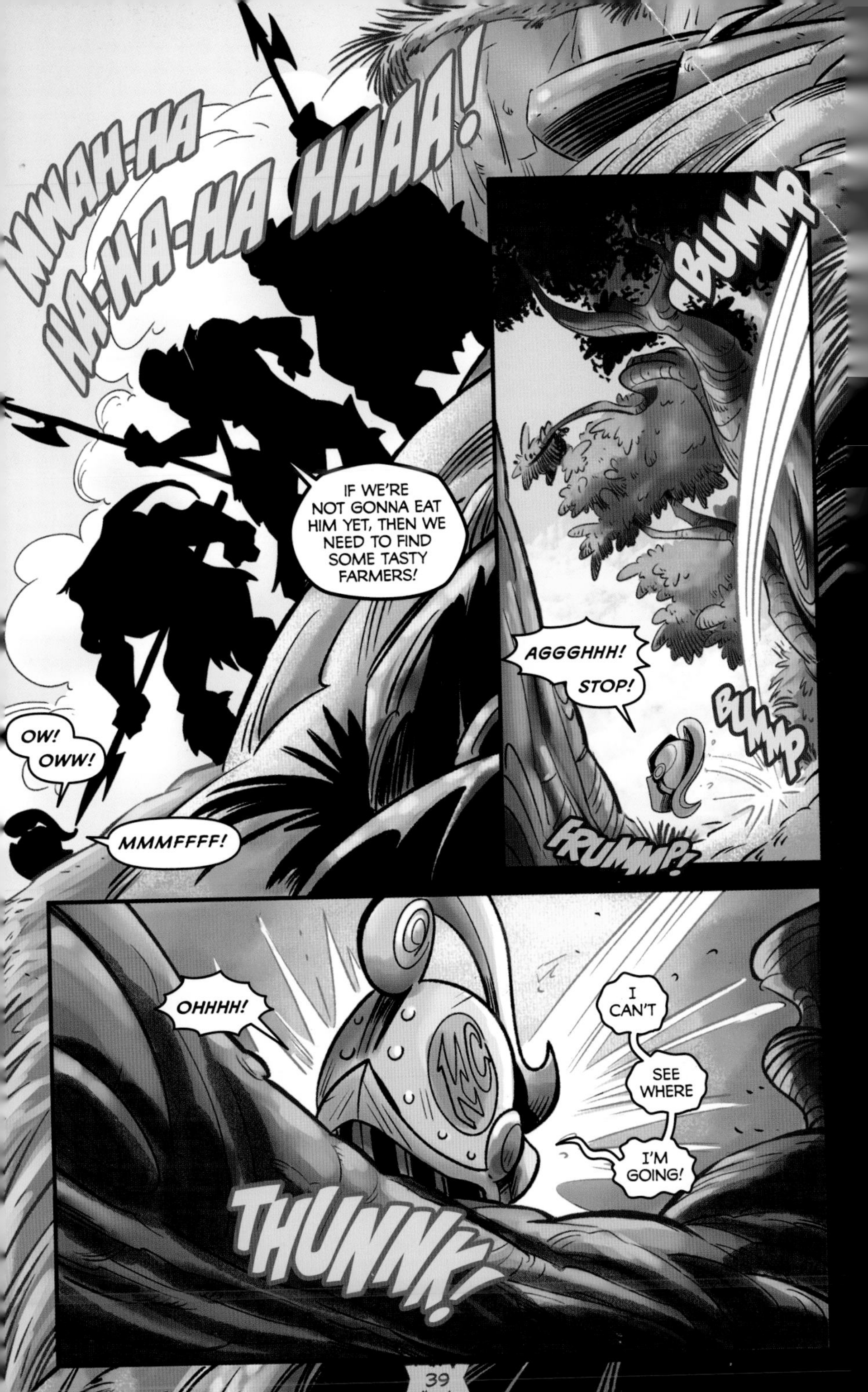

MWAH-HA
HA-HA-HA HAAA!
IF WE'RE NOT GONNA EAT HIM YET, THEN WE NEED TO FIND SOME TASTY FARMERS!
OW! OWW!
MMMFFFF!
BUMMP
AGGGHHH!
STOP!
BUMMP
FRUMMP!
OHHHH!
I CAN'T
SEE WHERE
I'M GOING!
THUNNK!

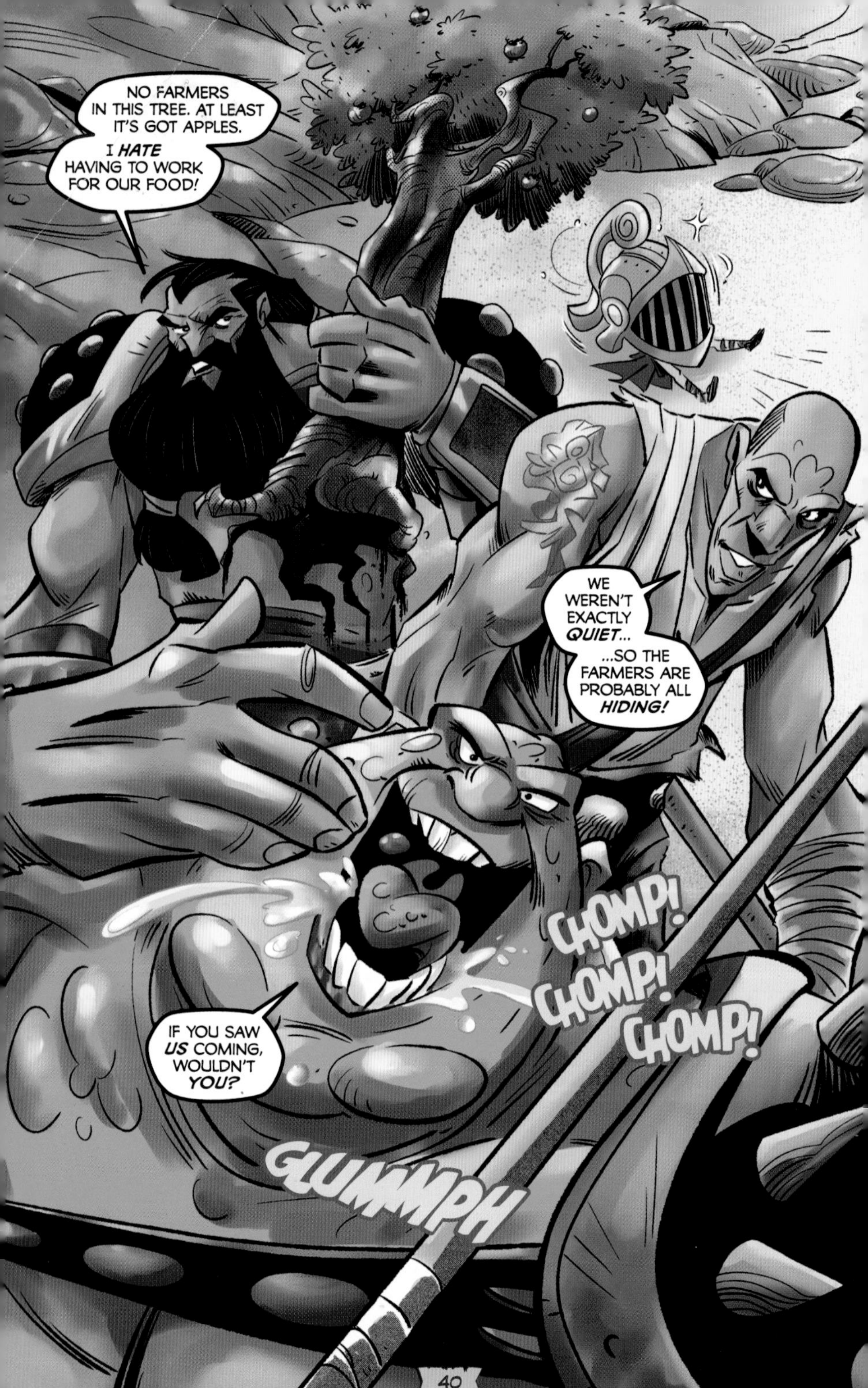
NO FARMERS IN THIS TREE. AT LEAST IT'S GOT APPLES.
I HATE HAVING TO WORK FOR OUR FOOD!
WE WEREN'T EXACTLY QUIET...
...SO THE FARMERS ARE PROBABLY ALL HIDING!
CHOMP! CHOMP! CHOMP!
IF YOU SAW US COMING, WOULDN'T YOU?
GLUMMPH

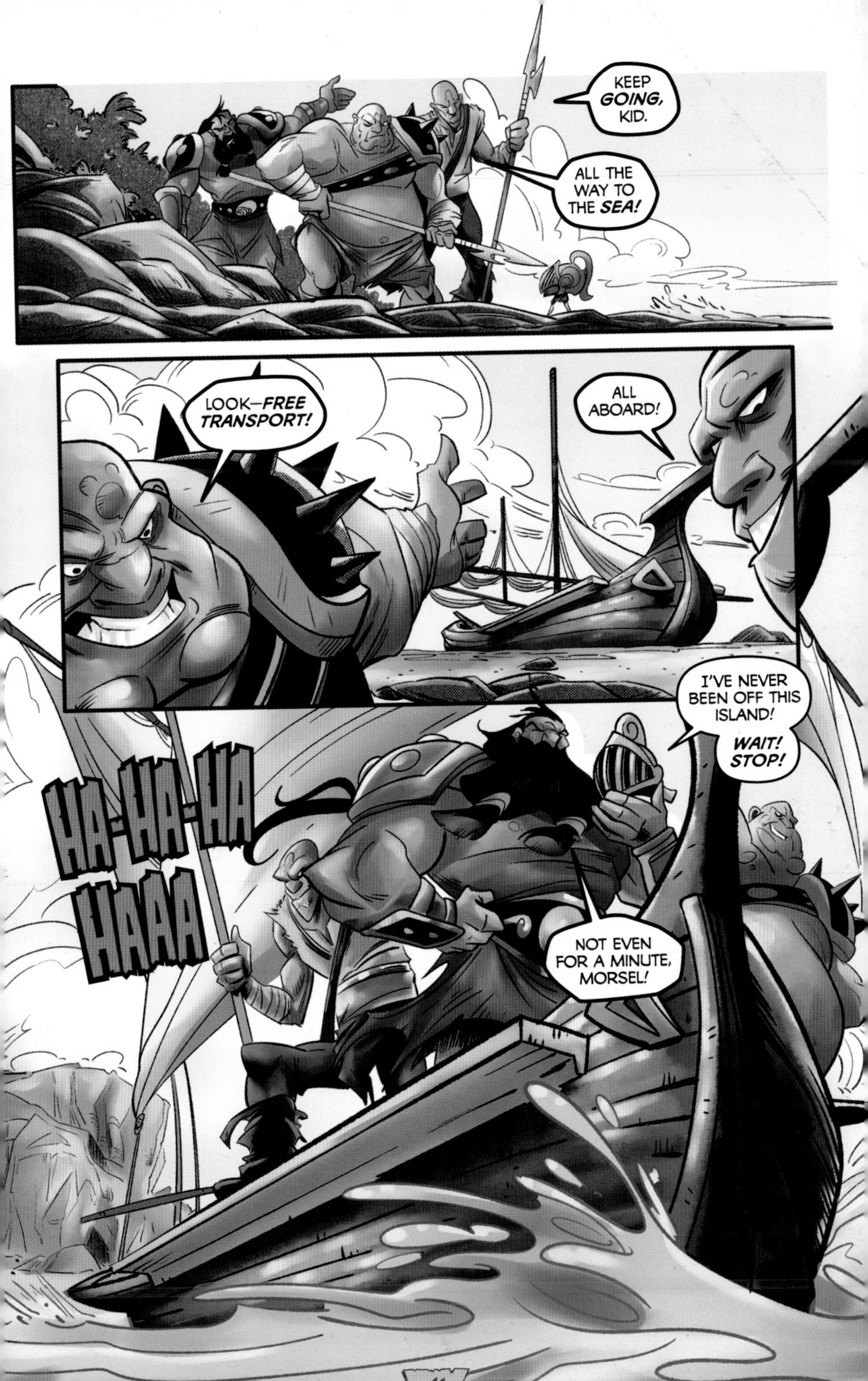

KEEP *GOING,* KID.
ALL THE WAY TO THE *SEA!*
LOOK—*FREE TRANSPORT!*
ALL ABOARD!
HA-HA-HA HAAA
I'VE NEVER BEEN OFF THIS ISLAND!
WAIT! STOP!
NOT EVEN FOR A MINUTE, MORSEL!

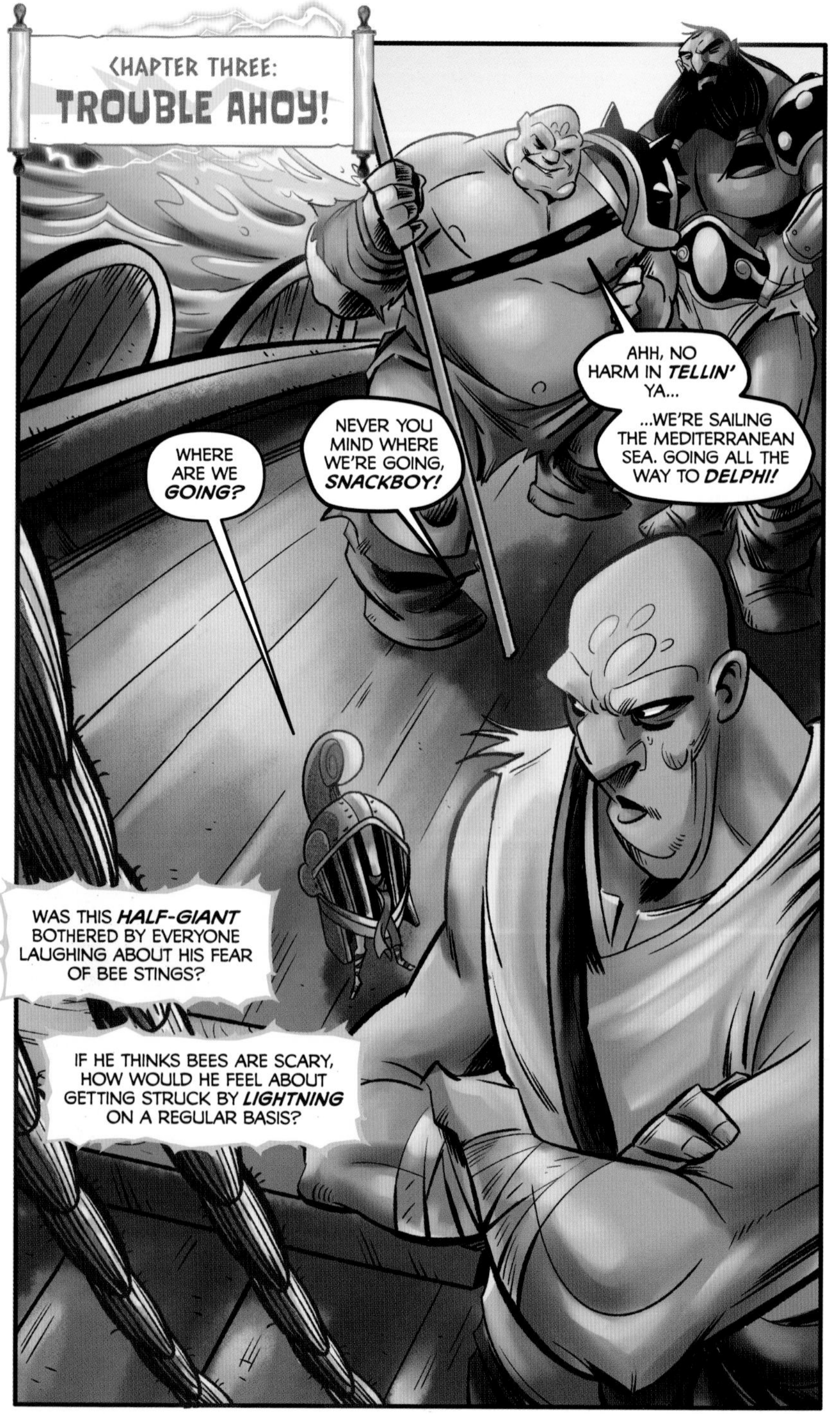
CHAPTER THREE:
TROUBLE AHOY!
WHERE ARE WE GOING?
NEVER YOU MIND WHERE WE'RE GOING, SNACKBOY!
AHH, NO HARM IN TELLIN' YA...
...WE'RE SAILING THE MEDITERRANEAN SEA. GOING ALL THE WAY TO DELPHI!
WAS THIS HALF-GIANT BOTHERED BY EVERYONE LAUGHING ABOUT HIS FEAR OF BEE STINGS?
IF HE THINKS BEES ARE SCARY, HOW WOULD HE FEEL ABOUT GETTING STRUCK BY LIGHTNING ON A REGULAR BASIS?

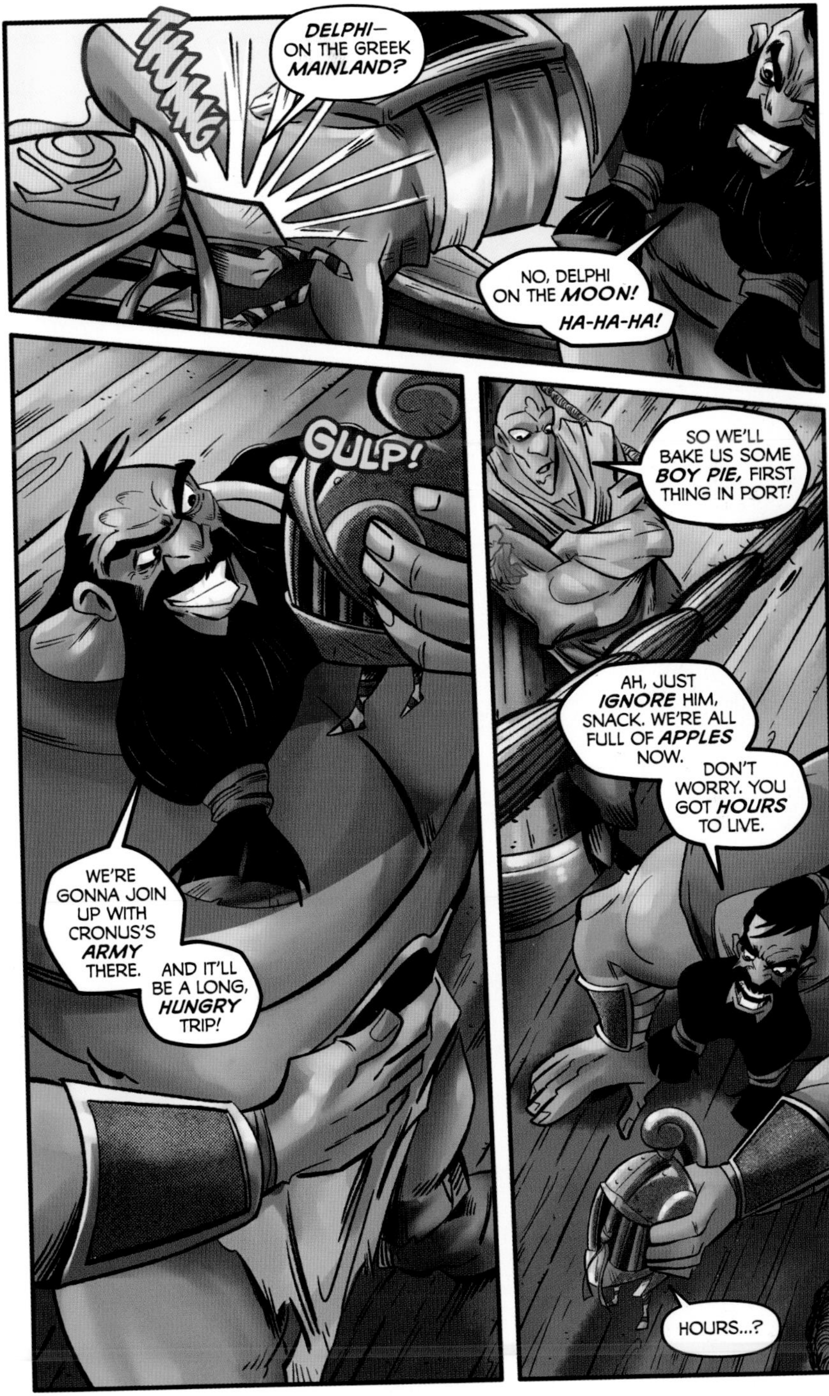
THUNG
DELPHI— ON THE GREEK MAINLAND?
NO, DELPHI ON THE MOON!
HA-HA-HA!
GULP!
WE'RE GONNA JOIN UP WITH CRONUS'S ARMY THERE.
AND IT'LL BE A LONG, HUNGRY TRIP!
SO WE'LL BAKE US SOME BOY PIE, FIRST THING IN PORT!
AH, JUST IGNORE HIM, SNACK. WE'RE ALL FULL OF APPLES NOW.
DON'T WORRY. YOU GOT HOURS TO LIVE.
HOURS...?

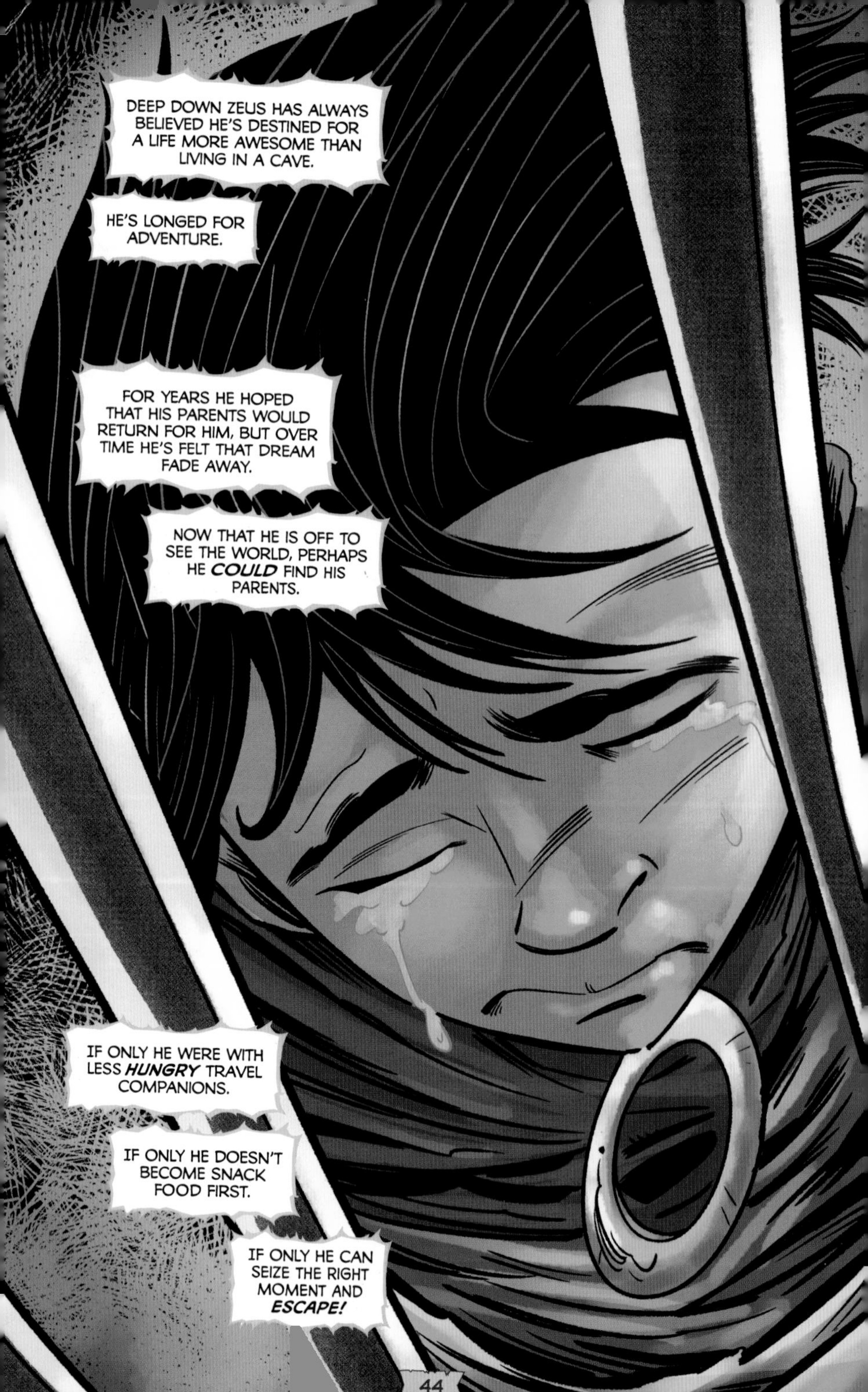
DEEP DOWN ZEUS HAS ALWAYS BELIEVED HE'S DESTINED FOR A LIFE MORE AWESOME THAN LIVING IN A CAVE.
HE'S LONGED FOR ADVENTURE.
FOR YEARS HE HOPED THAT HIS PARENTS WOULD RETURN FOR HIM, BUT OVER TIME HE'S FELT THAT DREAM FADE AWAY.
NOW THAT HE IS OFF TO SEE THE WORLD, PERHAPS HE *COULD* FIND HIS PARENTS.
IF ONLY HE WERE WITH LESS *HUNGRY* TRAVEL COMPANIONS.
IF ONLY HE DOESN'T BECOME SNACK FOOD FIRST.
IF ONLY HE CAN SEIZE THE RIGHT MOMENT AND *ESCAPE!*

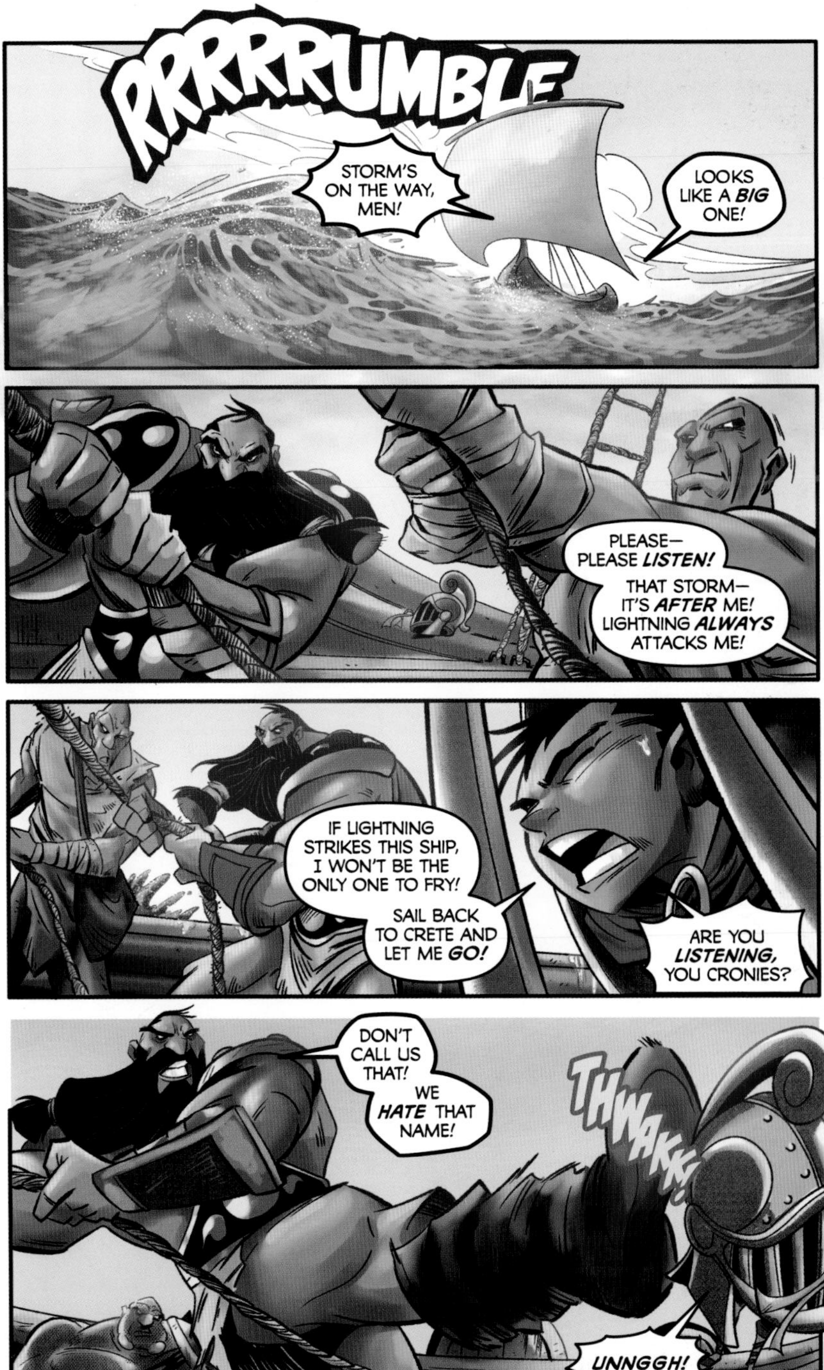
RRRRRUMBLE
STORM'S ON THE WAY, MEN!
LOOKS LIKE A BIG ONE!
PLEASE— PLEASE LISTEN!
THAT STORM— IT'S AFTER ME! LIGHTNING ALWAYS ATTACKS ME!
IF LIGHTNING STRIKES THIS SHIP, I WON'T BE THE ONLY ONE TO FRY!
SAIL BACK TO CRETE AND LET ME GO!
ARE YOU LISTENING, YOU CRONIES?
DON'T CALL US THAT!
WE HATE THAT NAME!
THWAKK
UNNGGH!

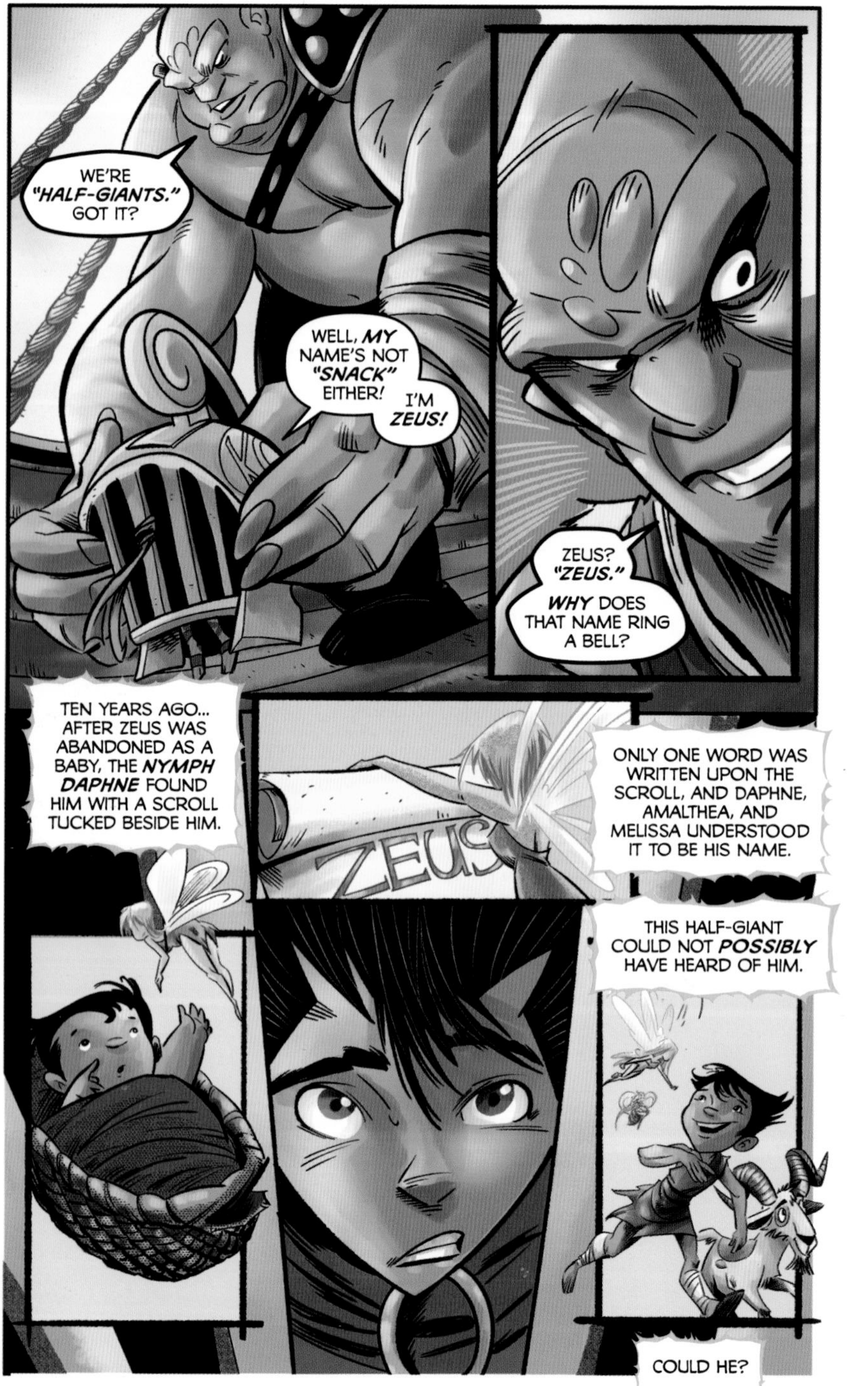
WE'RE "HALF-GIANTS." GOT IT?
WELL, MY NAME'S NOT "SNACK" EITHER!
I'M ZEUS!
ZEUS? "ZEUS."
WHY DOES THAT NAME RING A BELL?
TEN YEARS AGO... AFTER ZEUS WAS ABANDONED AS A BABY, THE NYMPH DAPHNE FOUND HIM WITH A SCROLL TUCKED BESIDE HIM.
ZEUS
ONLY ONE WORD WAS WRITTEN UPON THE SCROLL, AND DAPHNE, AMALTHEA, AND MELISSA UNDERSTOOD IT TO BE HIS NAME.
THIS HALF-GIANT COULD NOT POSSIBLY HAVE HEARD OF HIM.
COULD HE?

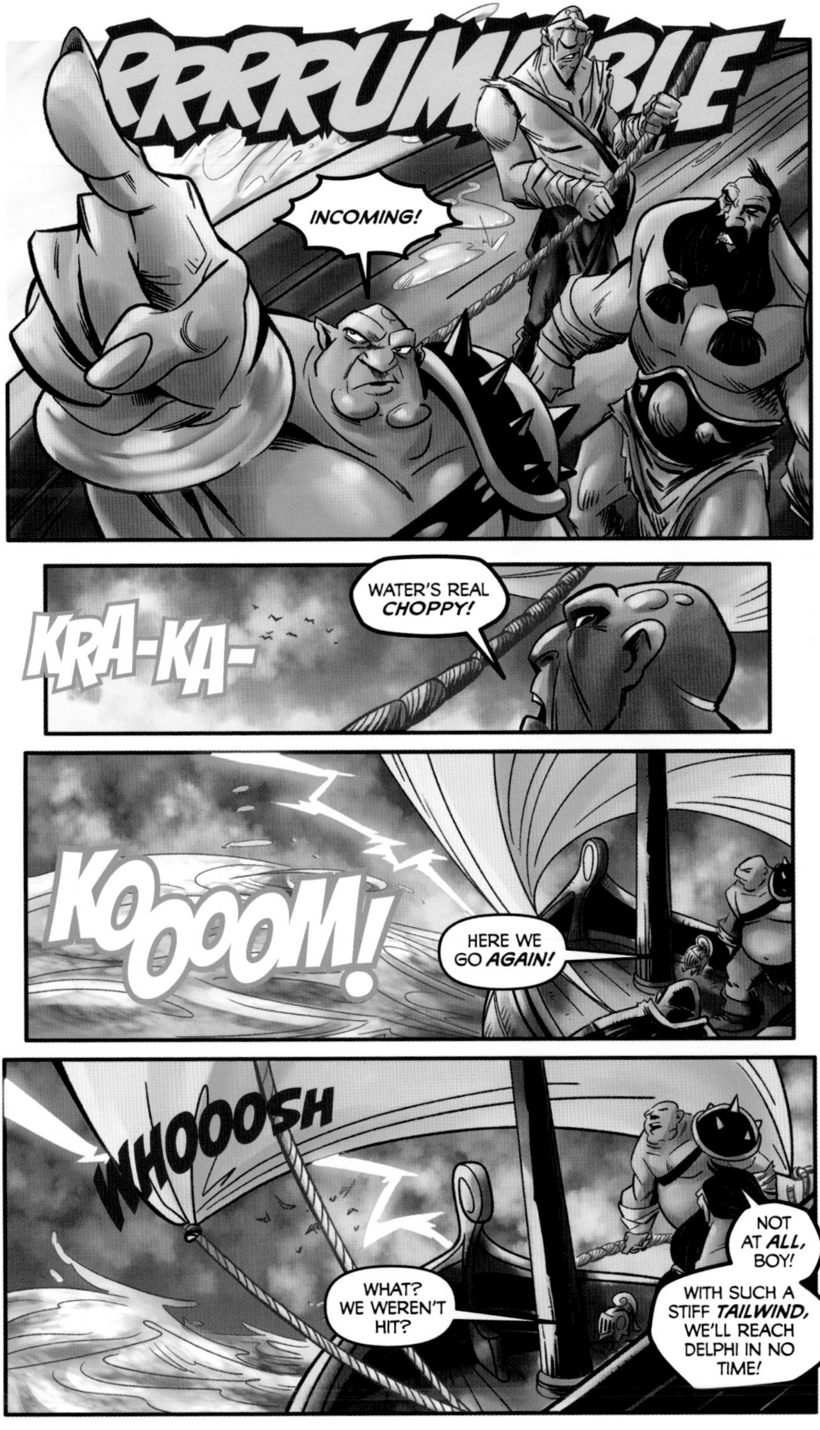
PRRRUMBLE
INCOMING!
KRA-KA-
WATER'S REAL CHOPPY!
KOOOOM!
HERE WE GO AGAIN!
WHOOOOSH
WHAT? WE WEREN'T HIT?
NOT AT ALL, BOY!
WITH SUCH A STIFF TAILWIND, WE'LL REACH DELPHI IN NO TIME!

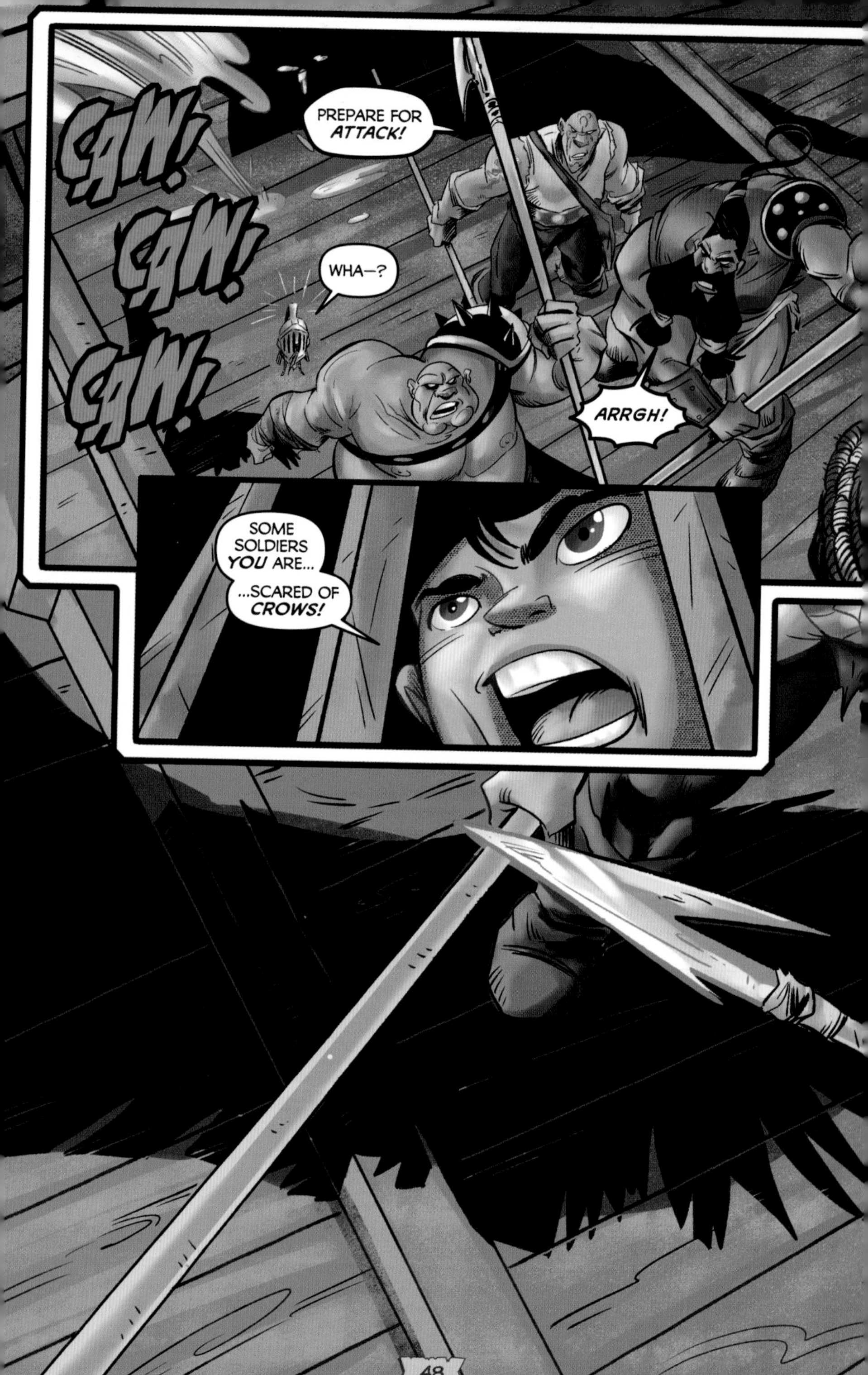
CAW!
CAW!
CAW!
PREPARE FOR ATTACK!
WHA—?
ARRGH!
SOME SOLDIERS YOU ARE...
...SCARED OF CROWS!

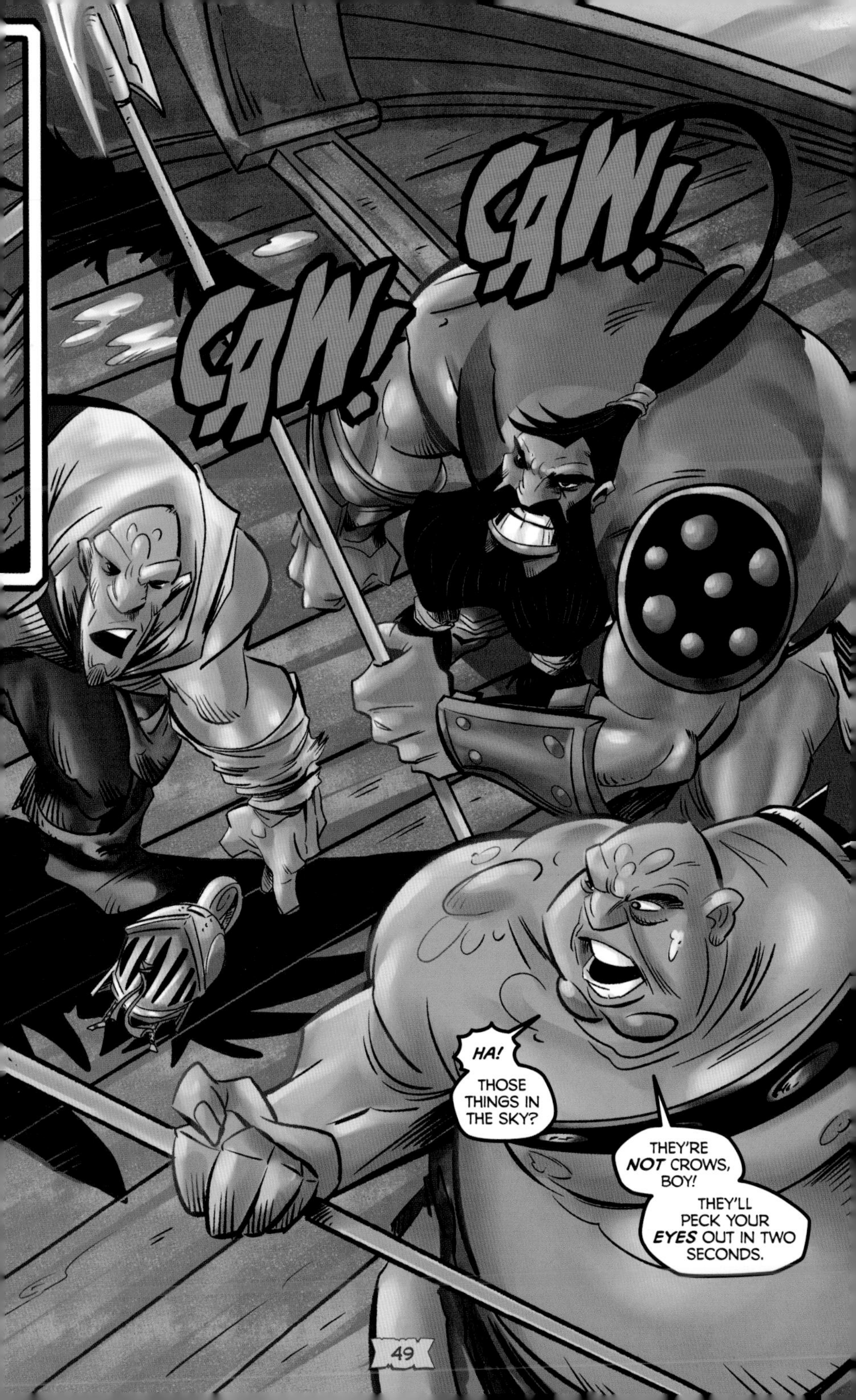
CAW!
CAW!
HA! THOSE THINGS IN THE SKY?
THEY'RE *NOT* CROWS, BOY!
THEY'LL PECK YOUR *EYES* OUT IN TWO SECONDS.

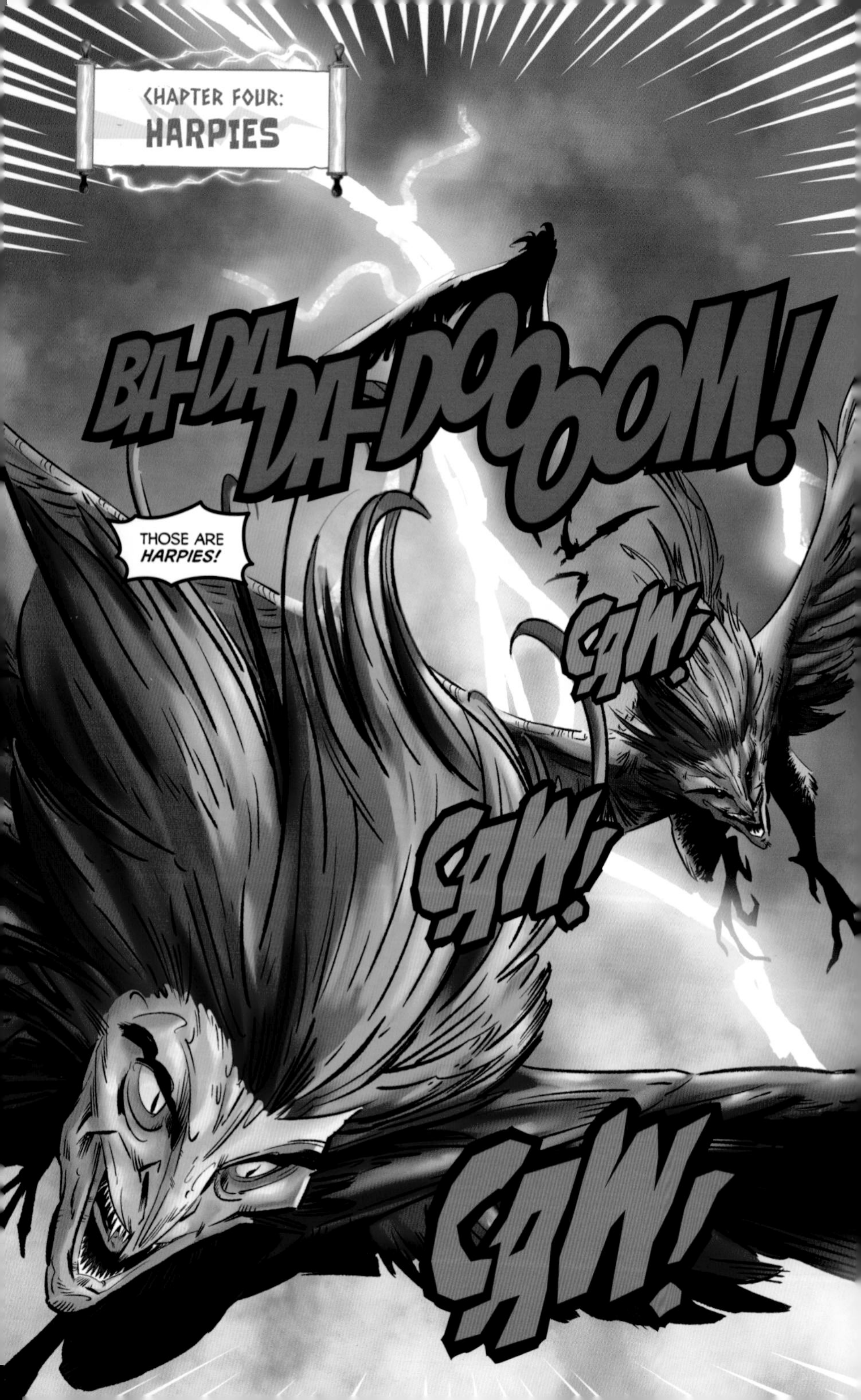
CHAPTER FOUR:
HARPIES
BA-DA DA-DOOOOOM!
THOSE ARE HARPIES!
CAW!
CAW!
CAW!

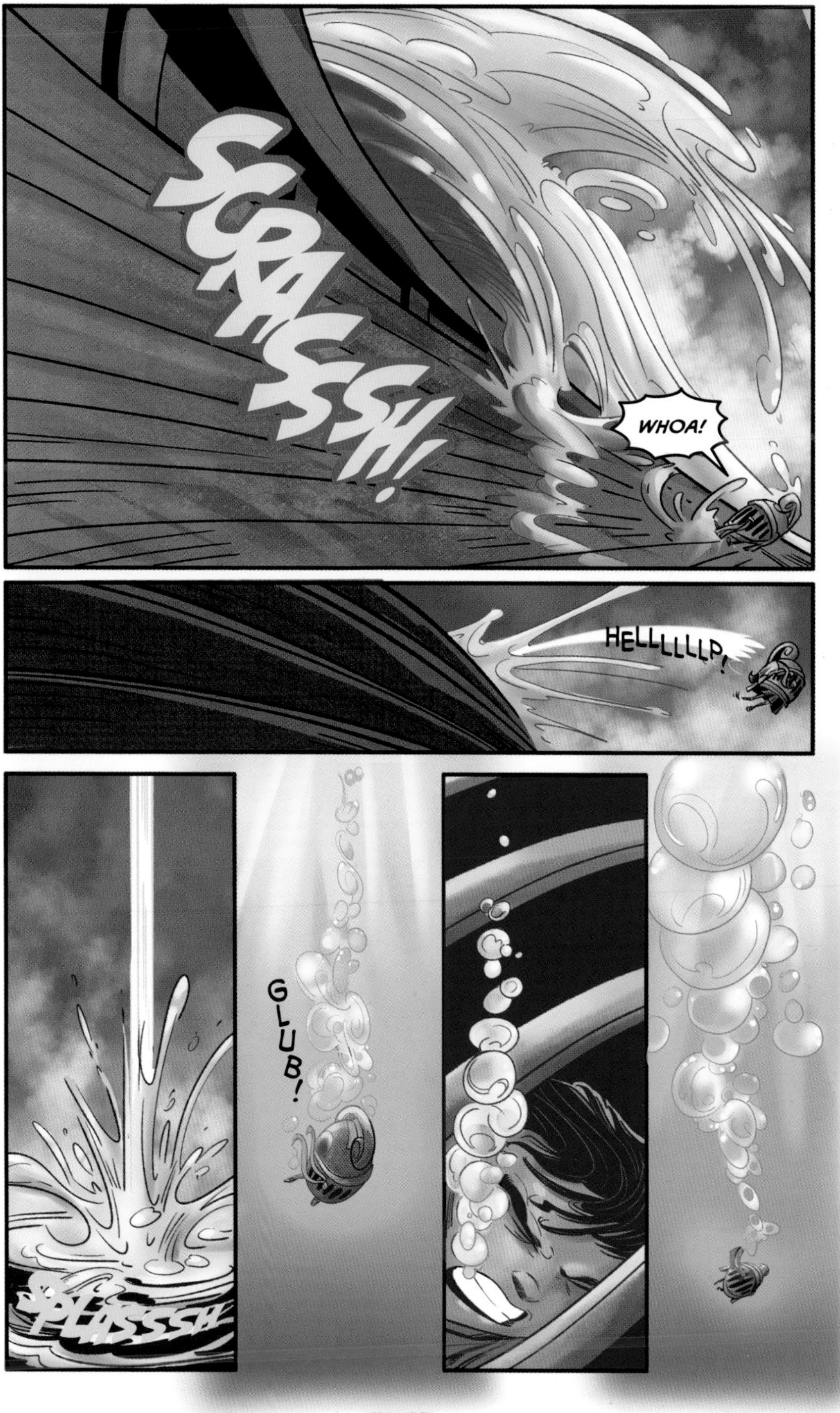
SCRASSSH!
WHOA!
HELLLLLLP!
SPLISSSH
GLUB!

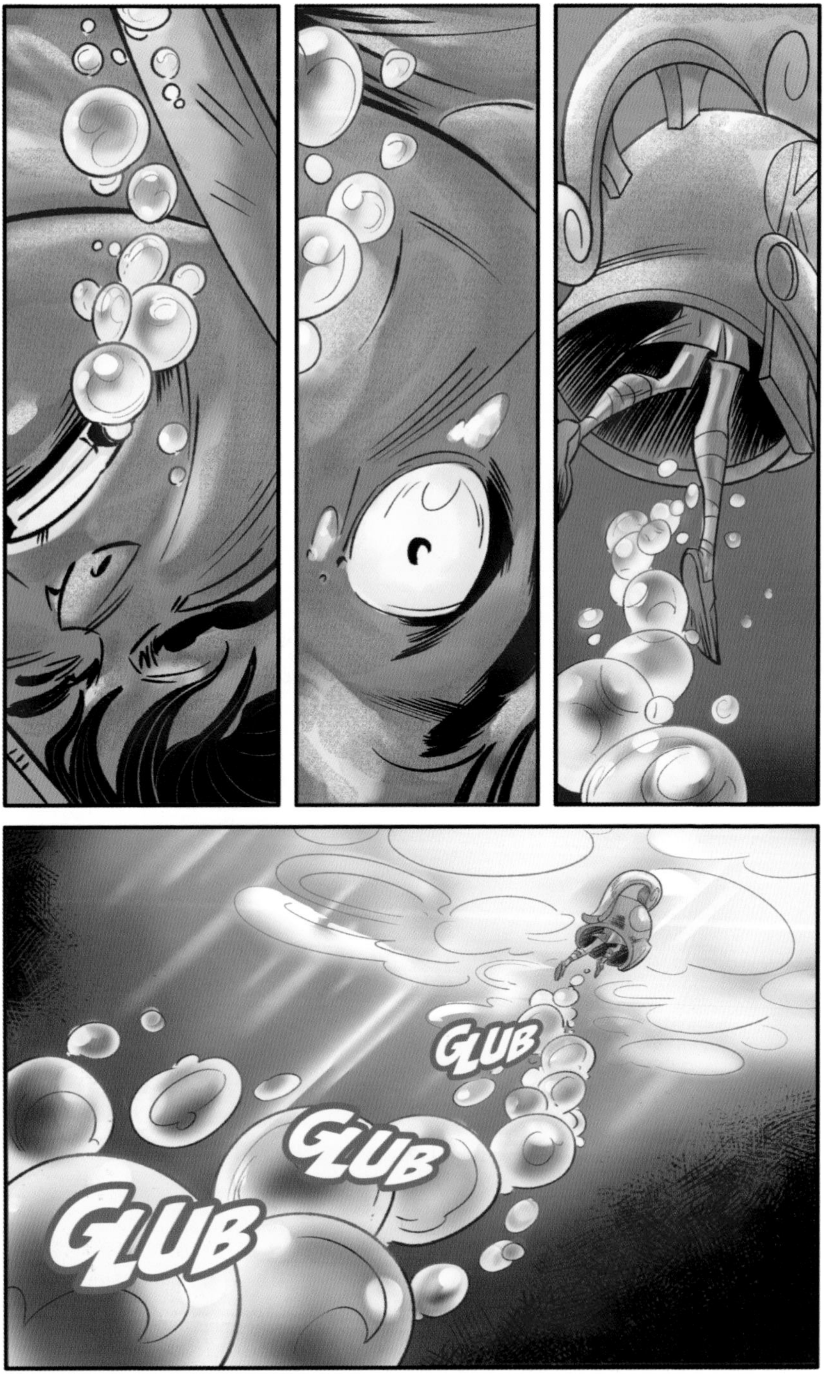
GLUB
GLUB
GLUB

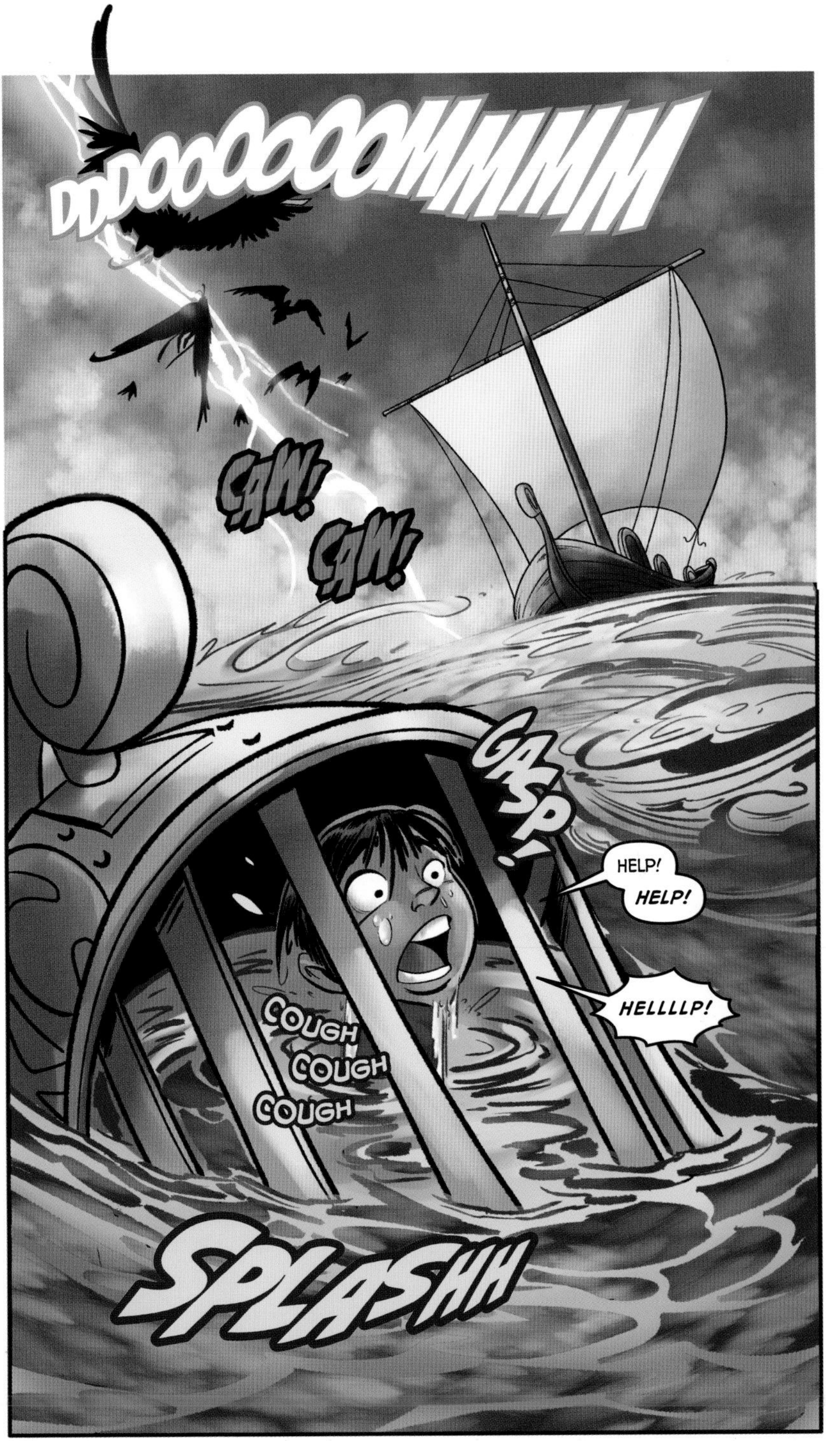
DDDOOOOOOMMMMM
CAW!
CAW!
GASP!
HELP!
HELP!
HELLLLP!
COUGH
COUGH
COUGH
SPLASHH

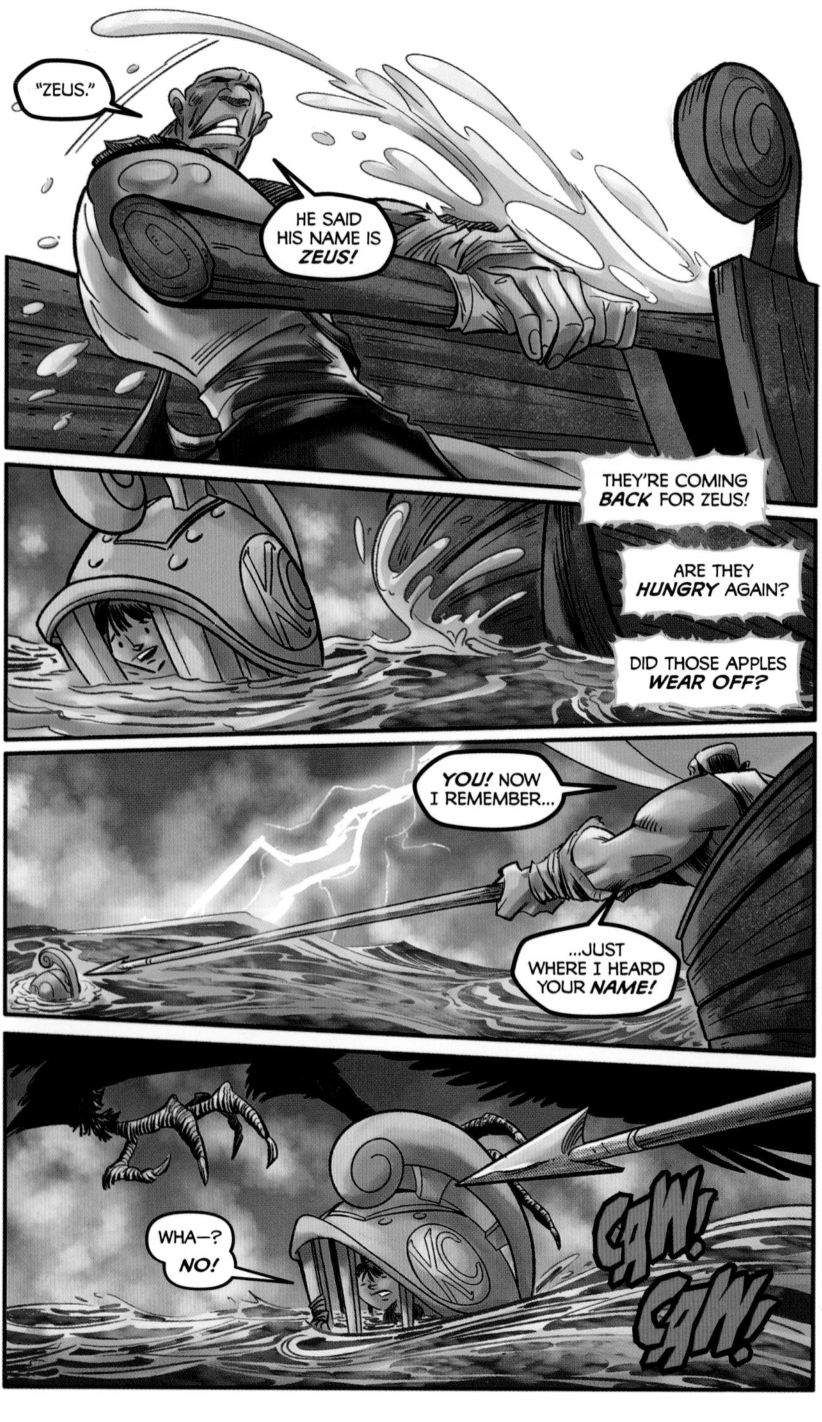
"ZEUS."
HE SAID HIS NAME IS *ZEUS!*
THEY'RE COMING *BACK* FOR ZEUS!
ARE THEY *HUNGRY* AGAIN?
DID THOSE APPLES *WEAR OFF?*
YOU! NOW I REMEMBER...
...JUST WHERE I HEARD YOUR *NAME!*
WHA—? *NO!*

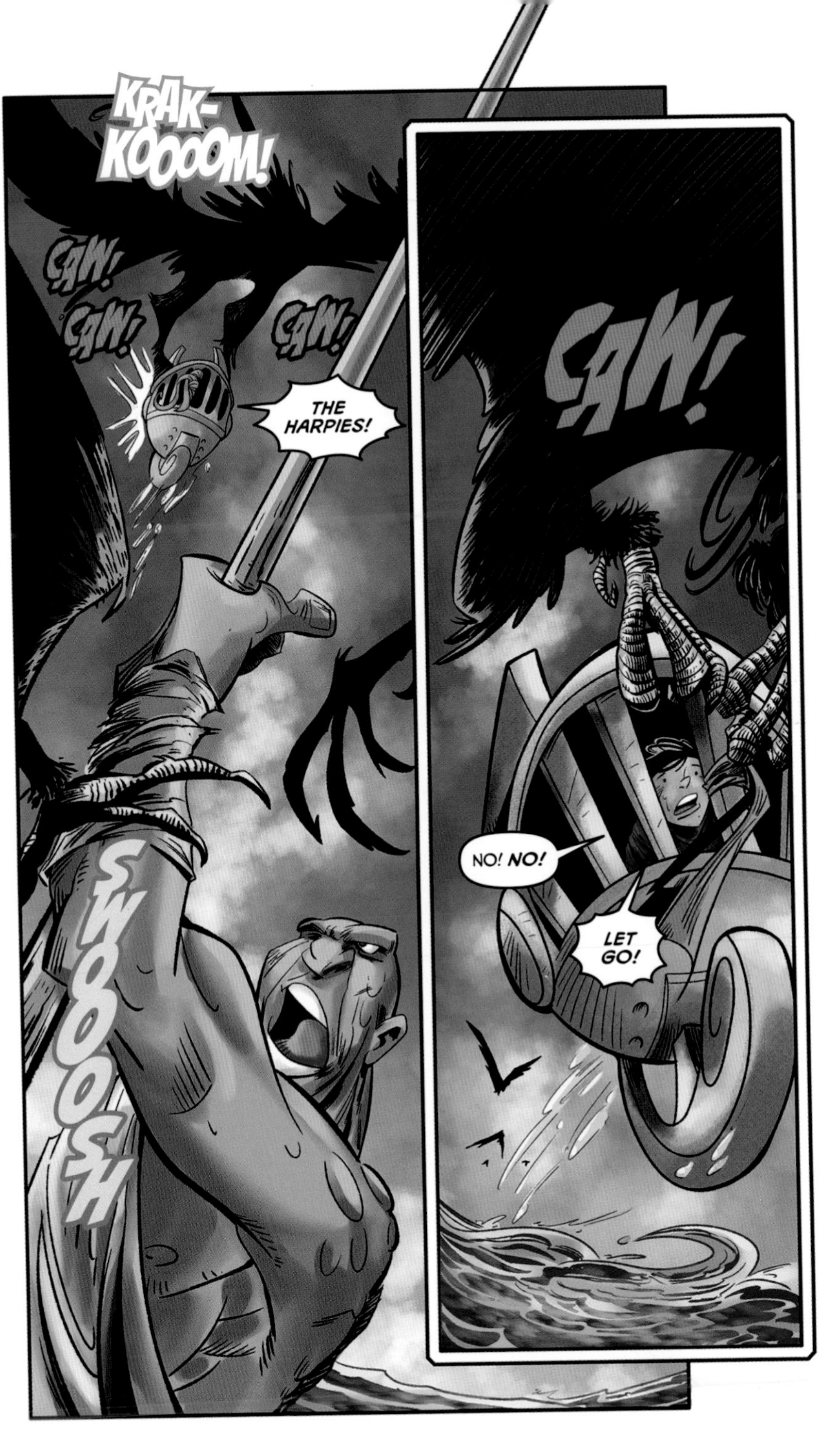
KRAK-KOOOOM!
CAW!
CAW!
CAW!
THE HARPIES!
SWOOOOSH
CAW!
NO! NO!
LET GO!

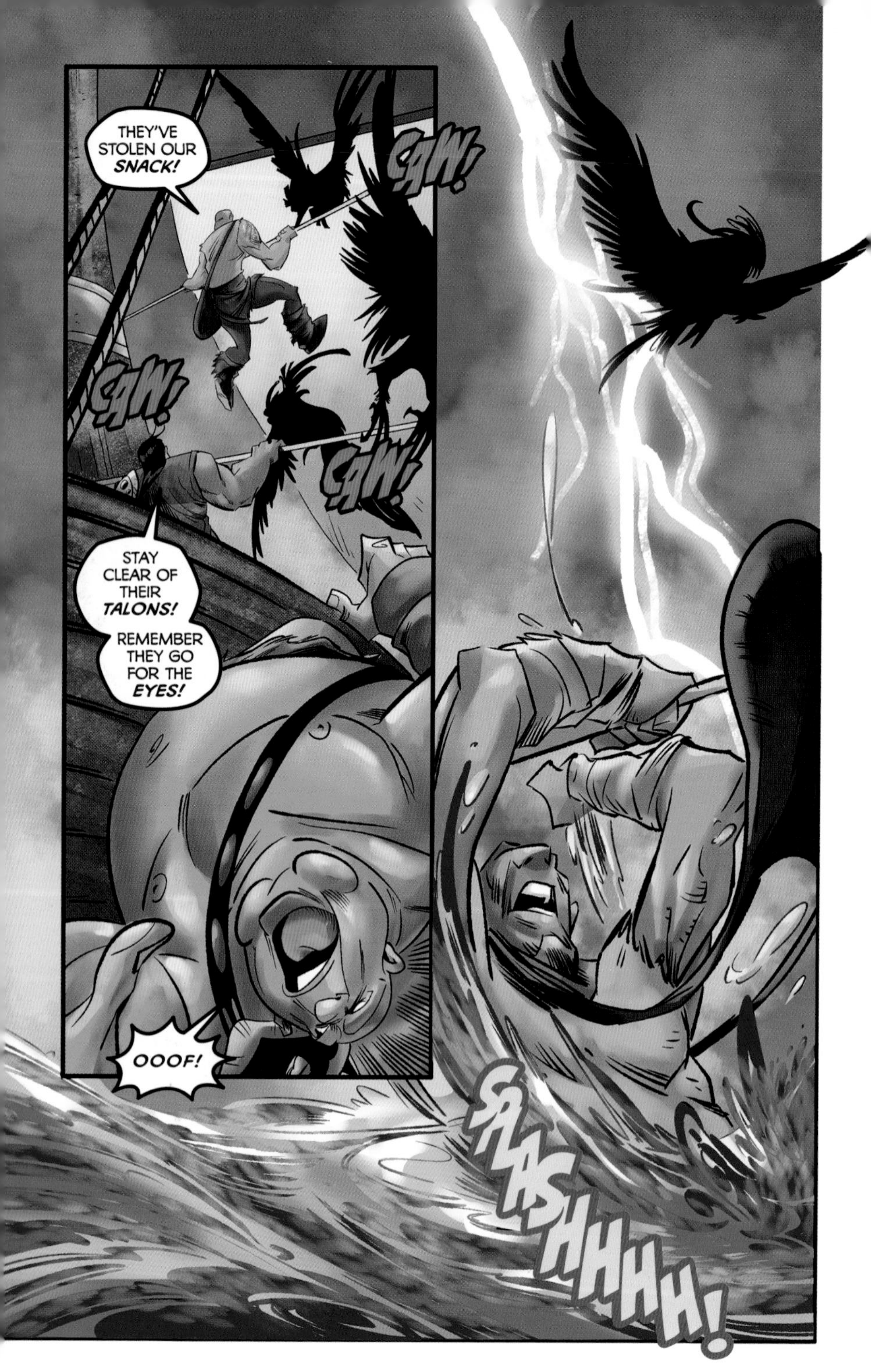
THEY'VE STOLEN OUR SNACK!
CAW!
CAW!
CAW!
STAY CLEAR OF THEIR TALONS!
REMEMBER THEY GO FOR THE EYES!
OOOF!
SPLASHHHHH!

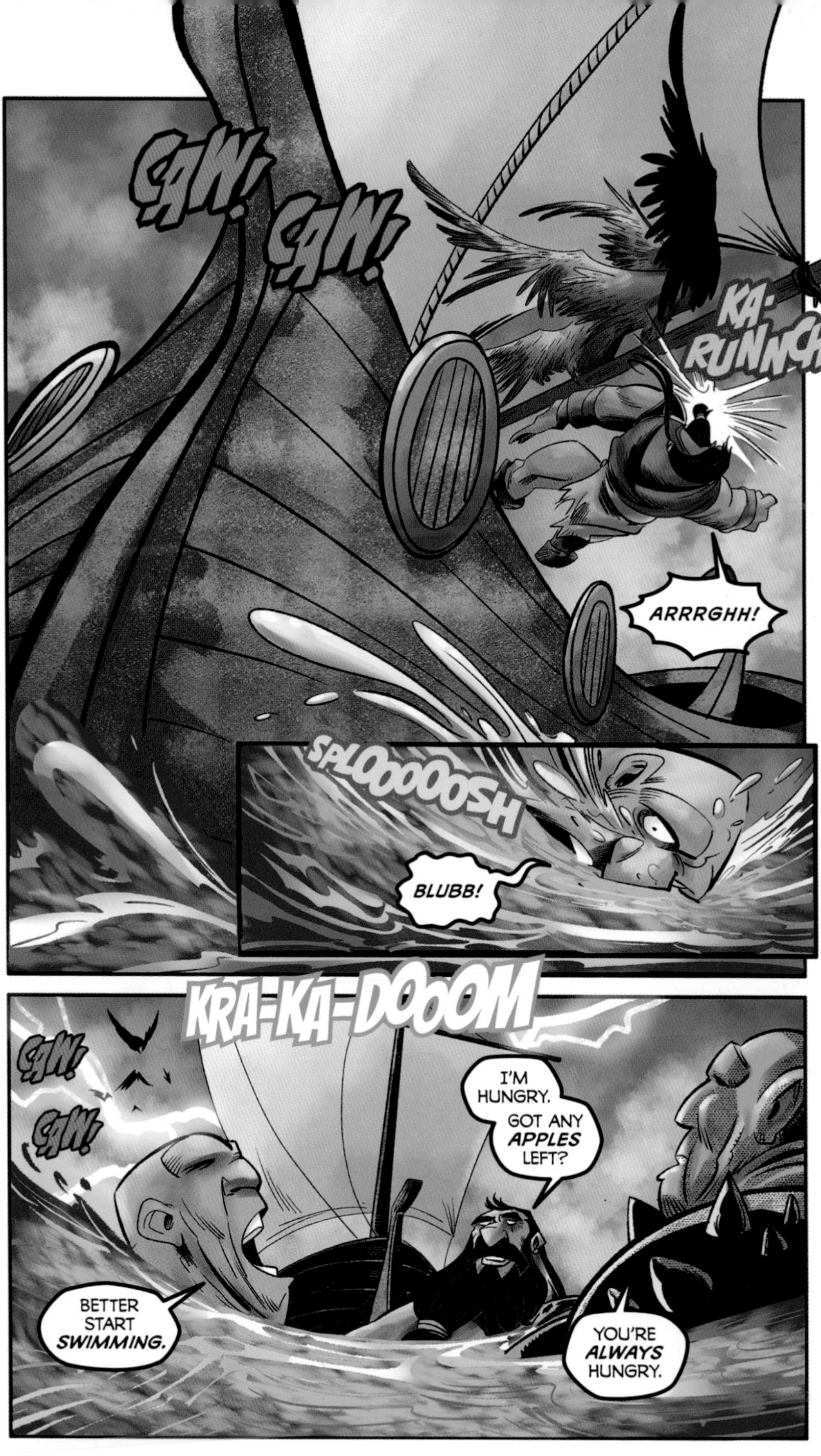
CAW!
CAW!
KA-
RUNNCH
ARRRGHH!
SPLOOOOOOSH
BLUBB!
KRA-KA-DOOOOM
CAW!
CAW!
I'M
HUNGRY.
GOT ANY
APPLES
LEFT?
BETTER
START
SWIMMING.
YOU'RE
ALWAYS
HUNGRY.

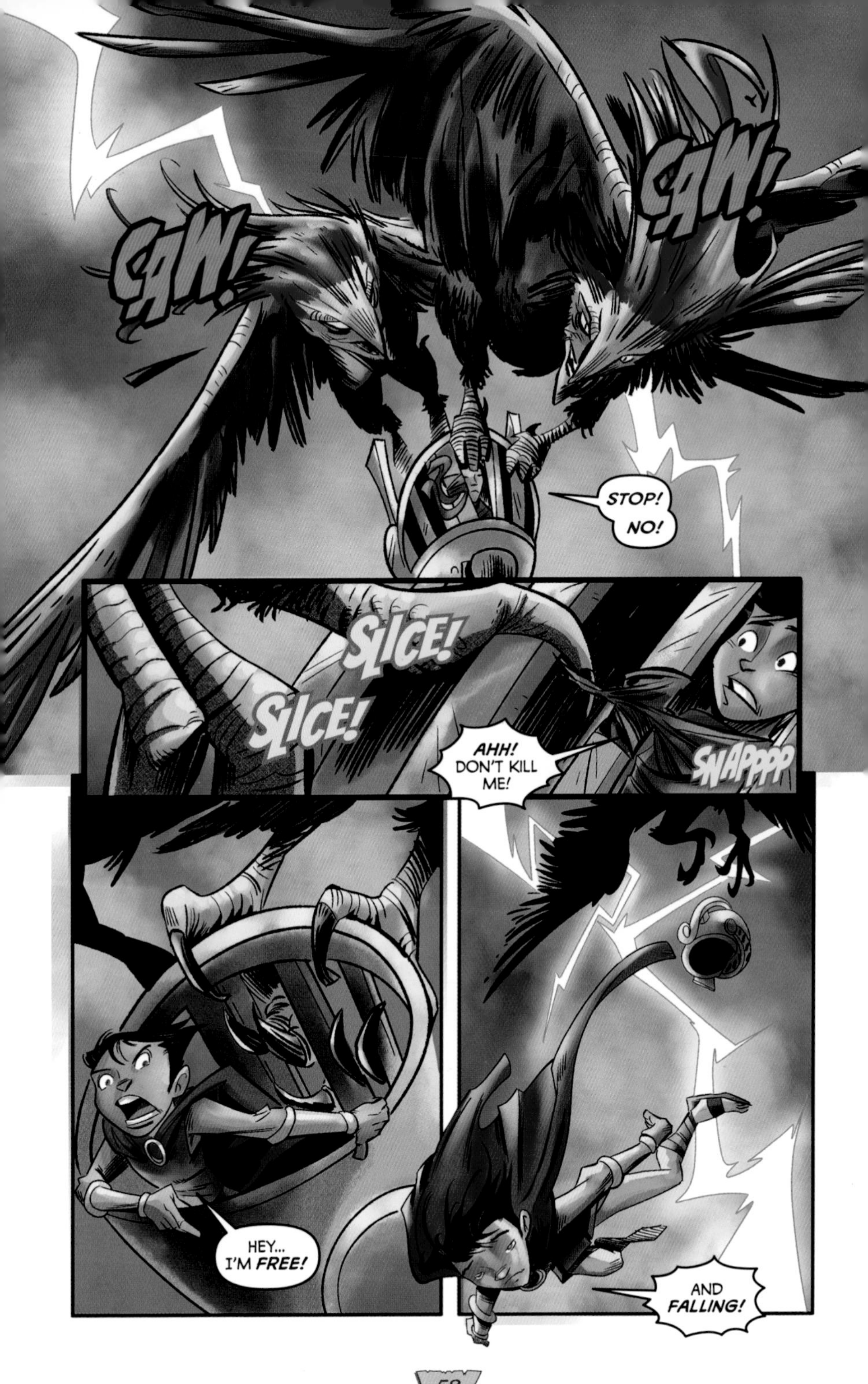
CAW!
CAW!
STOP! NO!
SLICE!
SLICE!
AHH! DON'T KILL ME!
SNAPPPP
HEY... I'M FREE!
AND FALLING!

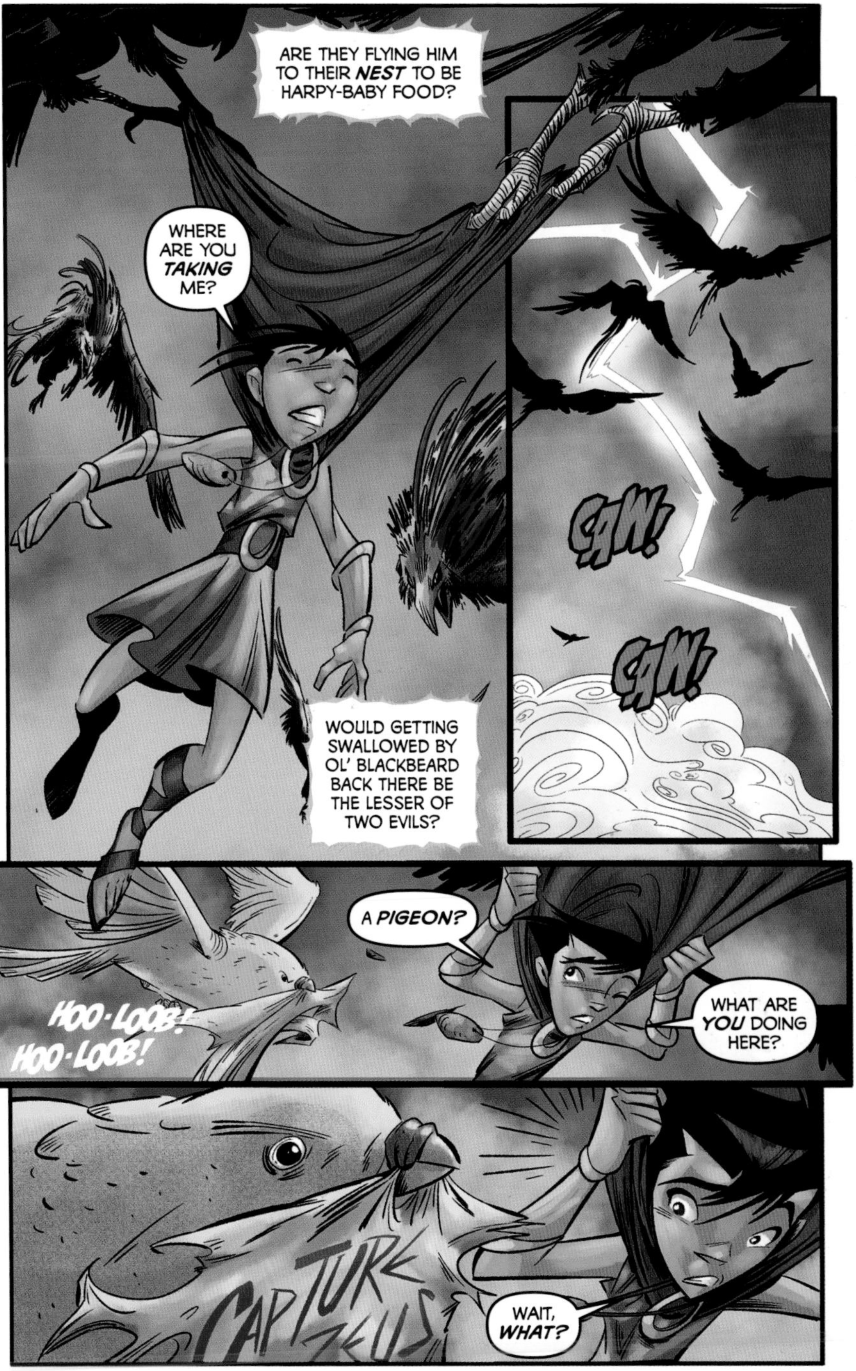
ARE THEY FLYING HIM TO THEIR *NEST* TO BE HARPY-BABY FOOD?
WHERE ARE YOU *TAKING* ME?
CAW!
CAW!
WOULD GETTING SWALLOWED BY OL' BLACKBEARD BACK THERE BE THE LESSER OF TWO EVILS?
A *PIGEON?*
WHAT ARE *YOU* DOING HERE?
HOO-LOOB!
HOO-LOOB!
CAPTURE ZEUS
WAIT, *WHAT?*

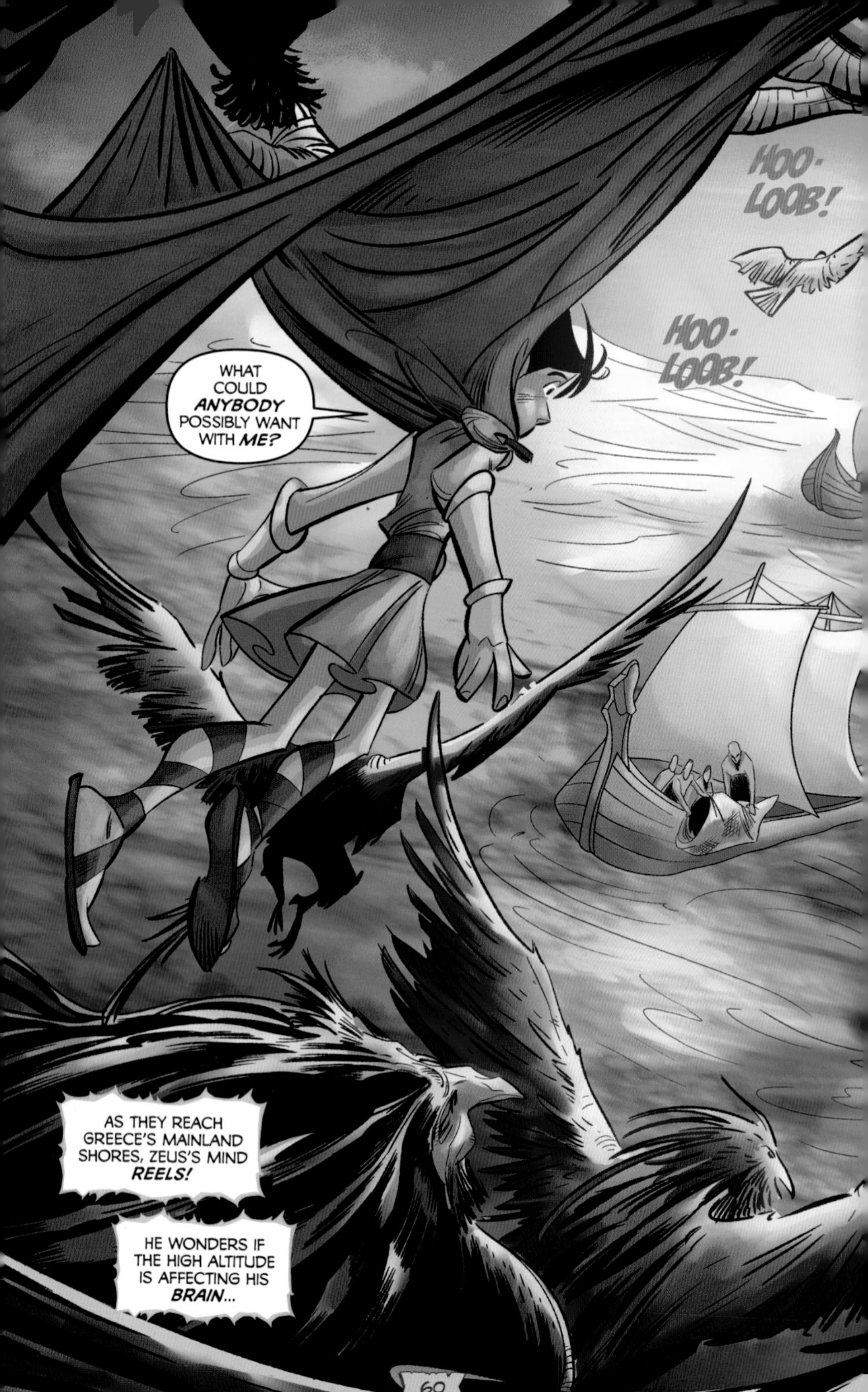
HOO-LOOB!
HOO-LOOB!
WHAT COULD ANYBODY POSSIBLY WANT WITH ME?
AS THEY REACH GREECE'S MAINLAND SHORES, ZEUS'S MIND REELS!
HE WONDERS IF THE HIGH ALTITUDE IS AFFECTING HIS BRAIN...

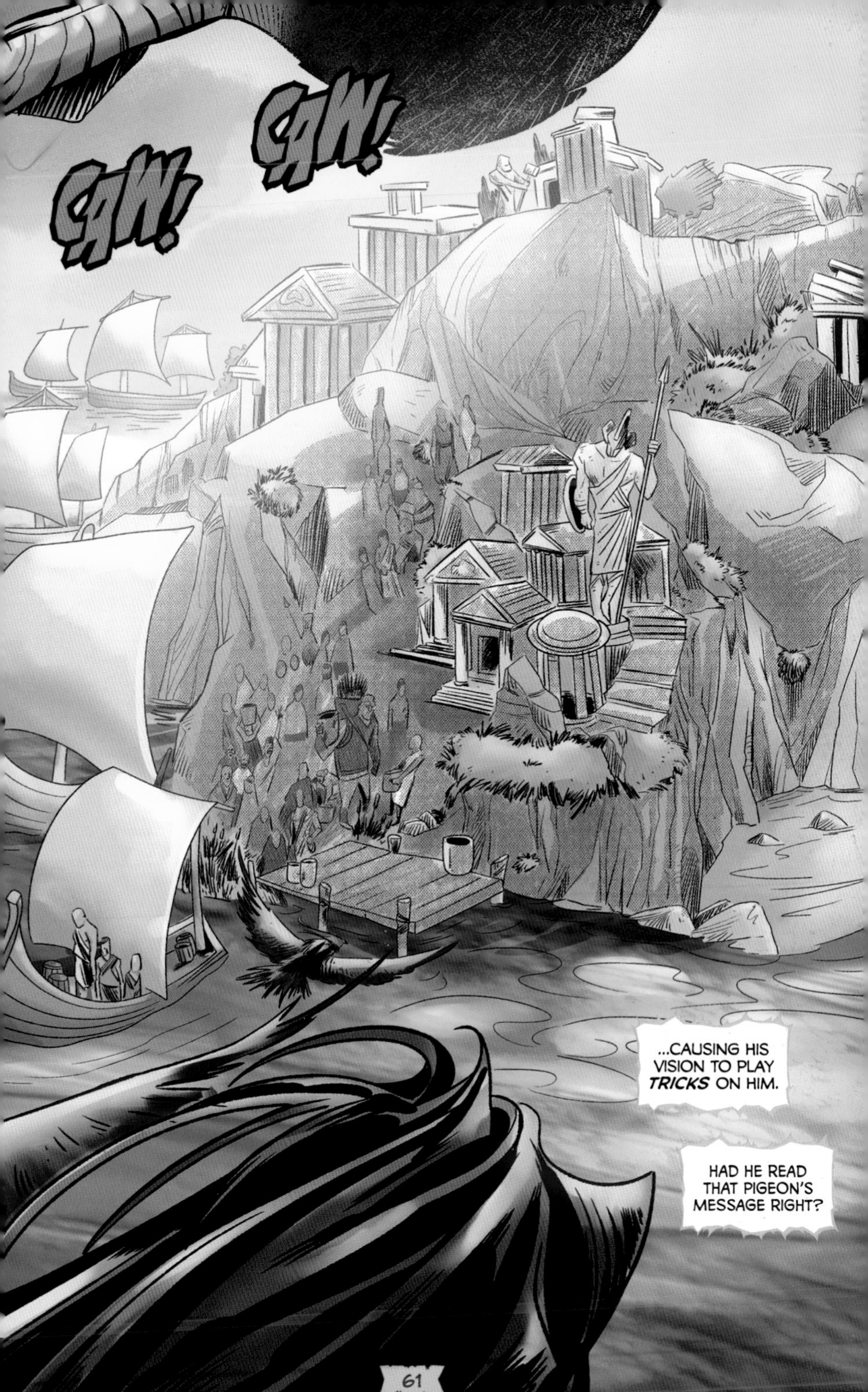
CAW!
CAW!
...CAUSING HIS VISION TO PLAY *TRICKS* ON HIM.
HAD HE READ THAT PIGEON'S MESSAGE RIGHT?

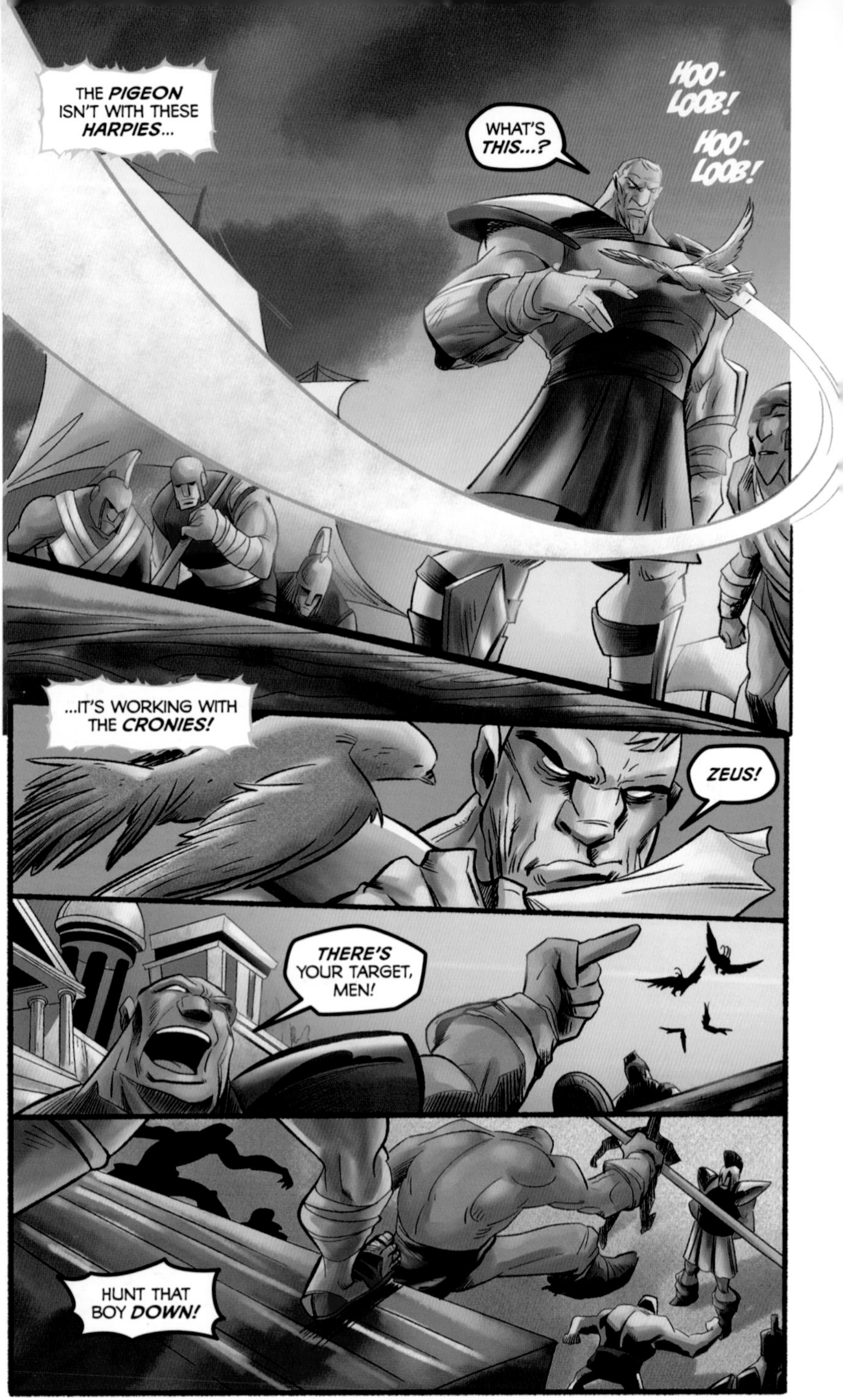
THE PIGEON ISN'T WITH THESE HARPIES...
WHAT'S THIS...?
HOO-LOOB!
HOO-LOOB!
...IT'S WORKING WITH THE CRONIES!
ZEUS!
THERE'S YOUR TARGET, MEN!
HUNT THAT BOY DOWN!

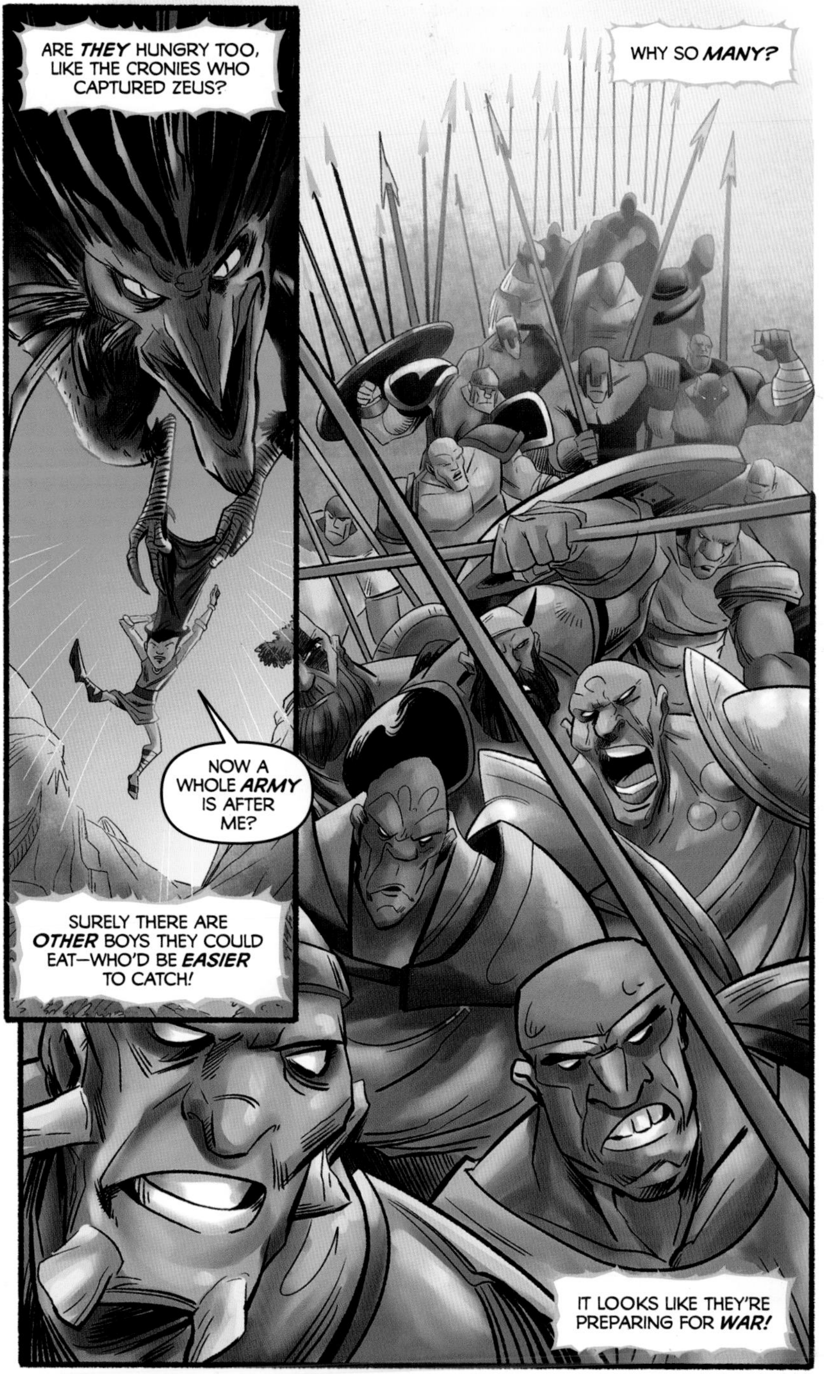
ARE THEY HUNGRY TOO, LIKE THE CRONIES WHO CAPTURED ZEUS?
WHY SO MANY?
NOW A WHOLE ARMY IS AFTER ME?
SURELY THERE ARE OTHER BOYS THEY COULD EAT—WHO'D BE EASIER TO CATCH!
IT LOOKS LIKE THEY'RE PREPARING FOR WAR!

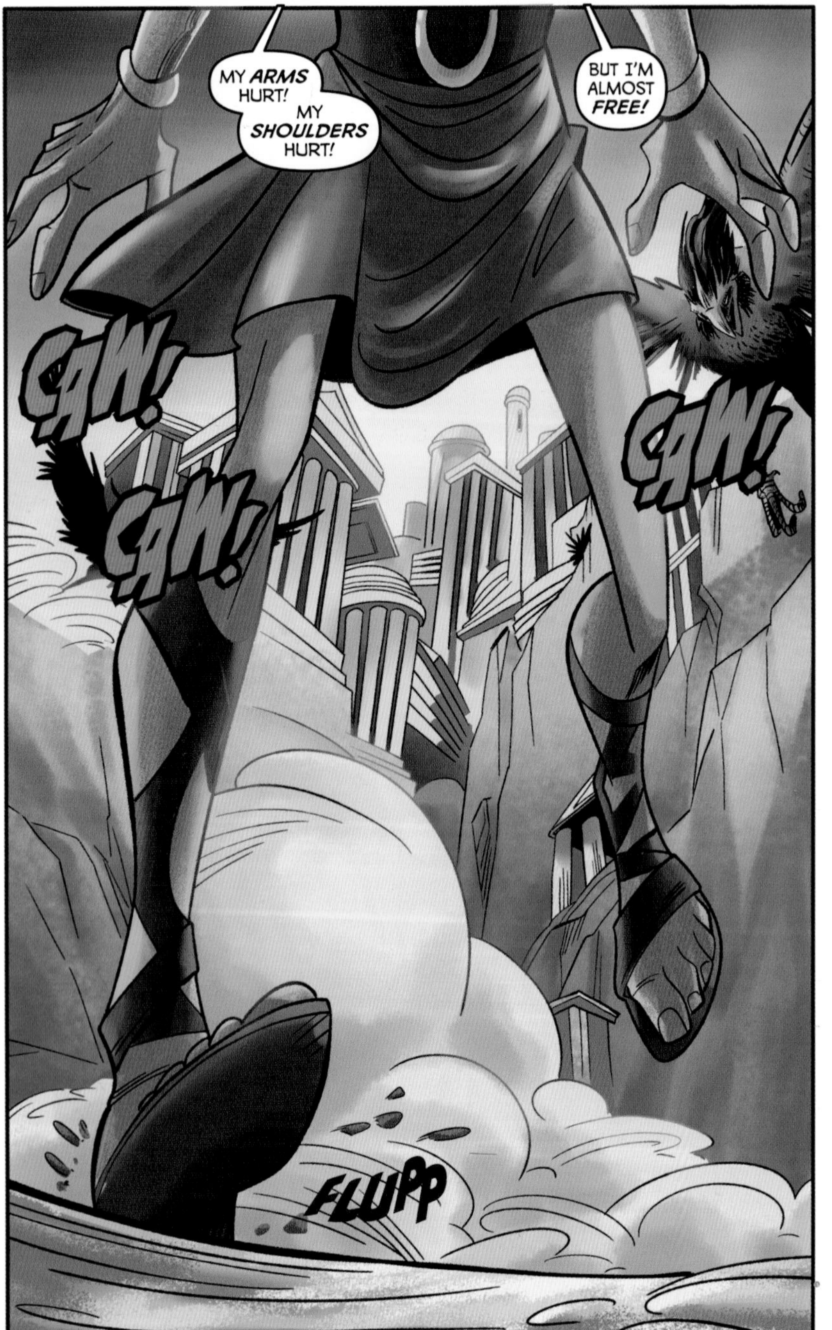
MY ARMS HURT! MY SHOULDERS HURT!
BUT I'M ALMOST FREE!
CAW!
CAW!
CAW!
FLUPP

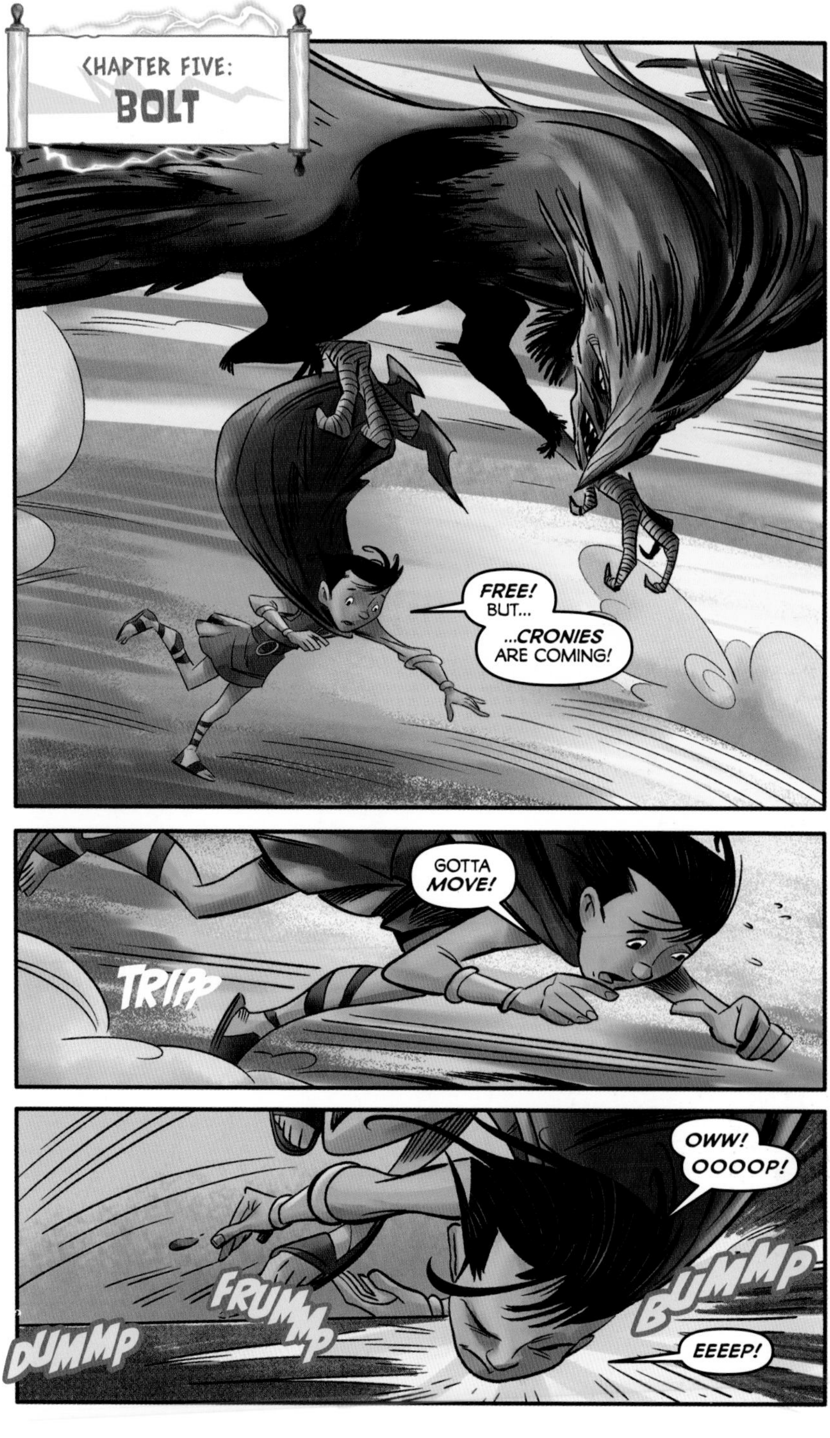
CHAPTER FIVE:
BOLT
FREE! BUT...
...CRONIES ARE COMING!
GOTTA MOVE!
TRIPP
OWW! OOOOP!
FRUMMP
DUMMP
BUMMP
EEEEP!

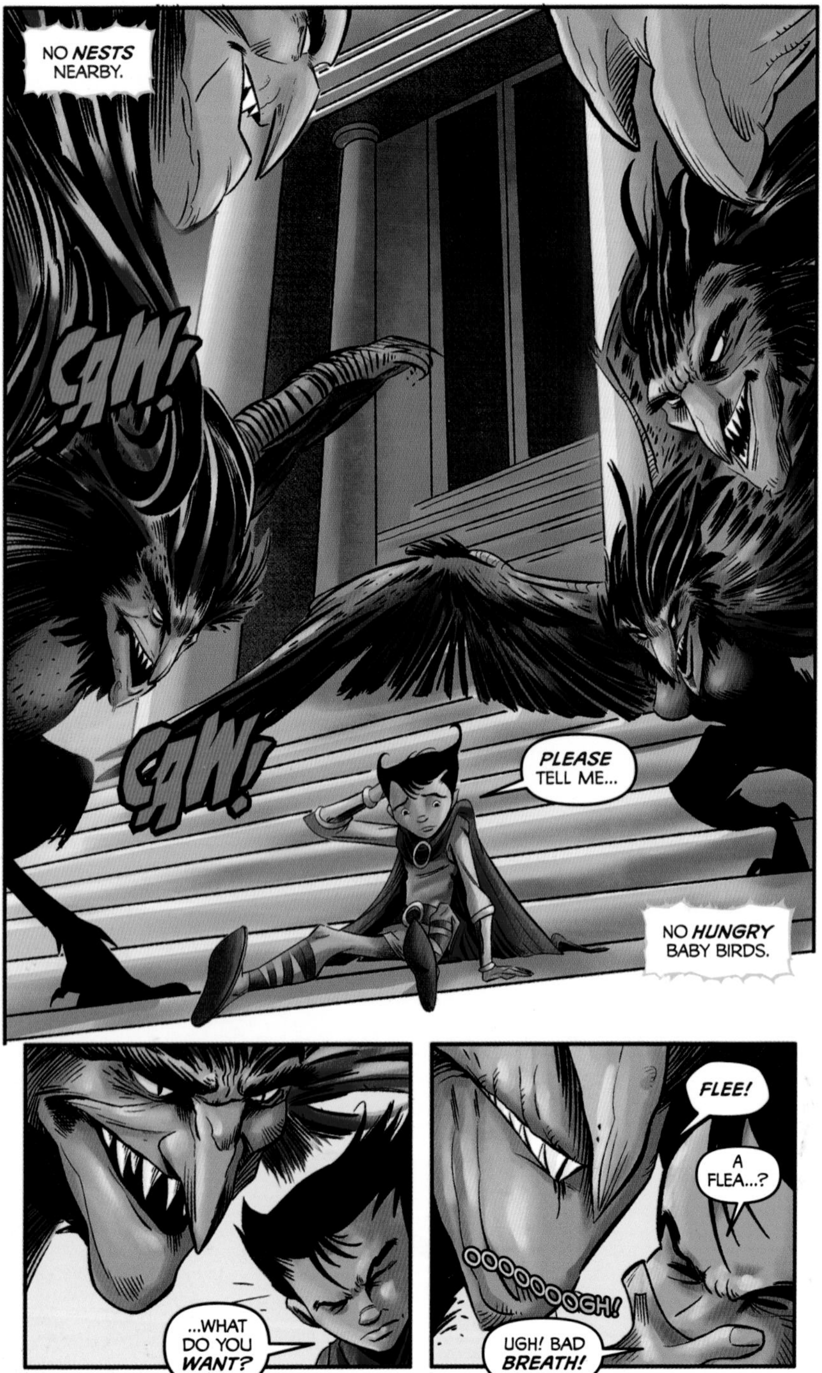

NO NESTS NEARBY.
CAW!
CAW!
PLEASE TELL ME...
NO HUNGRY BABY BIRDS.
...WHAT DO YOU WANT?
FLEE!
A FLEA...?
OOOOOOOGH!
UGH! BAD BREATH!

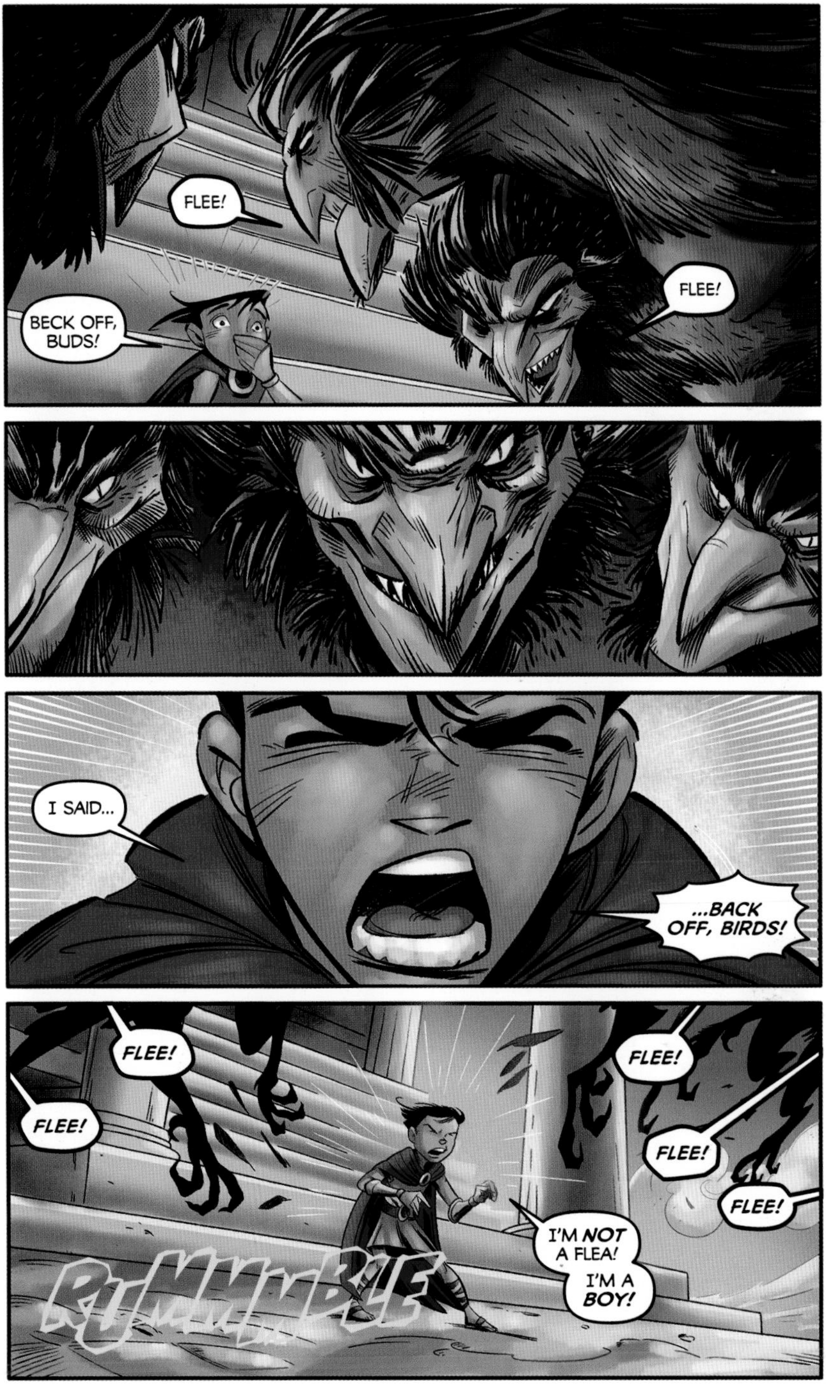
FLEE!
BECK OFF, BUDS!
FLEE!
I SAID...
...BACK OFF, BIRDS!
FLEE!
FLEE!
FLEE!
FLEE!
FLEE!
I'M NOT A FLEA!
I'M A BOY!
RUMMMBLE

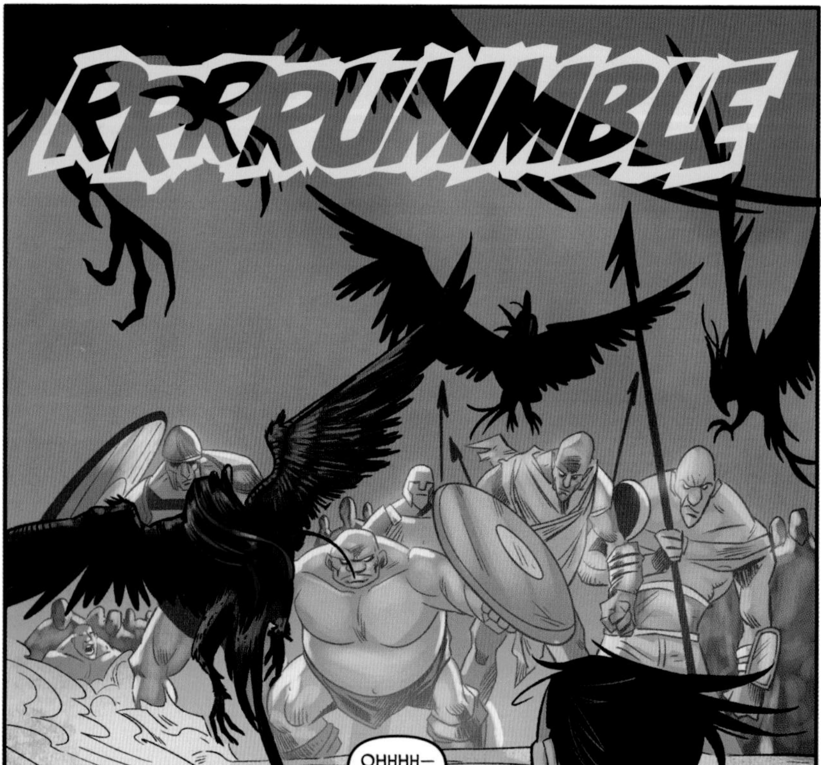
RRRRUMMBLE
OHHHH— "FLEE"!
AS IN "RUN"!

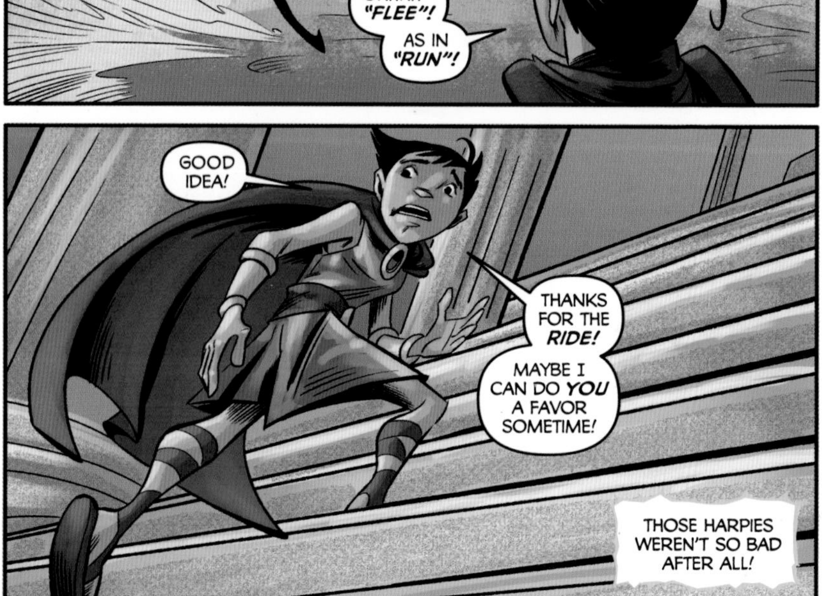
GOOD IDEA!
THANKS FOR THE RIDE!
MAYBE I CAN DO YOU A FAVOR SOMETIME!
THOSE HARPIES WEREN'T SO BAD AFTER ALL!

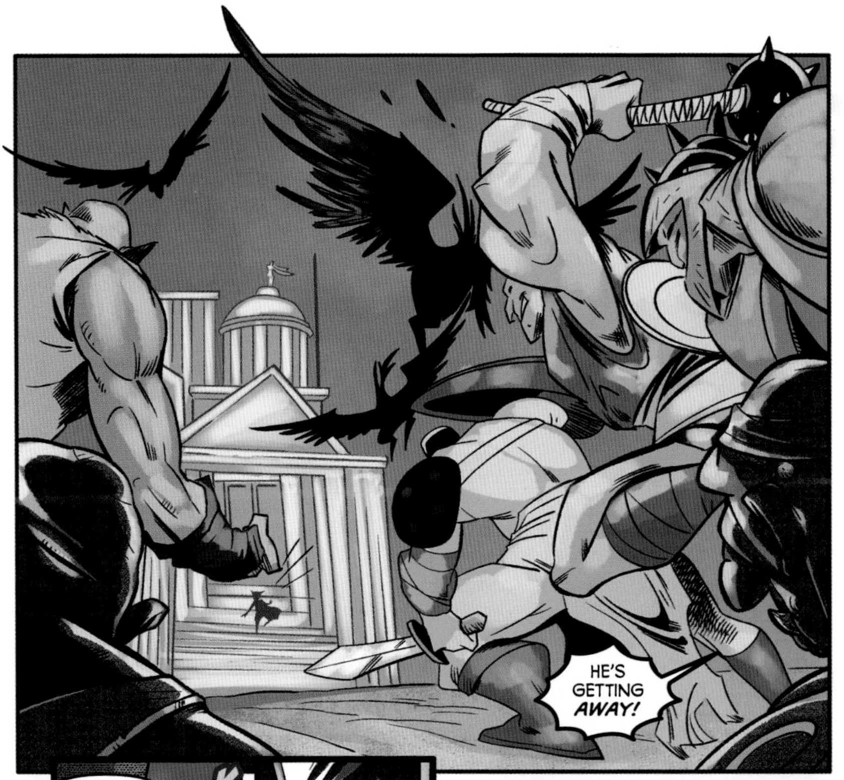
HE'S GETTING *AWAY!*

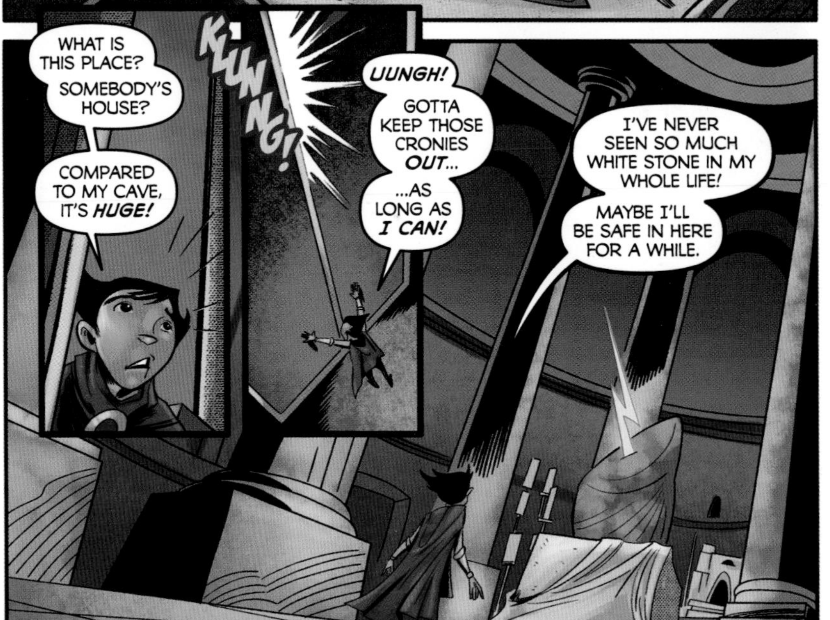
WHAT IS THIS PLACE?
SOMEBODY'S HOUSE?
COMPARED TO MY CAVE, IT'S *HUGE!*
KLUNNG!
UUNGH!
GOTTA KEEP THOSE CRONIES *OUT*...
...AS LONG AS *I CAN!*
I'VE NEVER SEEN SO MUCH WHITE STONE IN MY WHOLE LIFE!
MAYBE I'LL BE SAFE IN HERE FOR A WHILE.

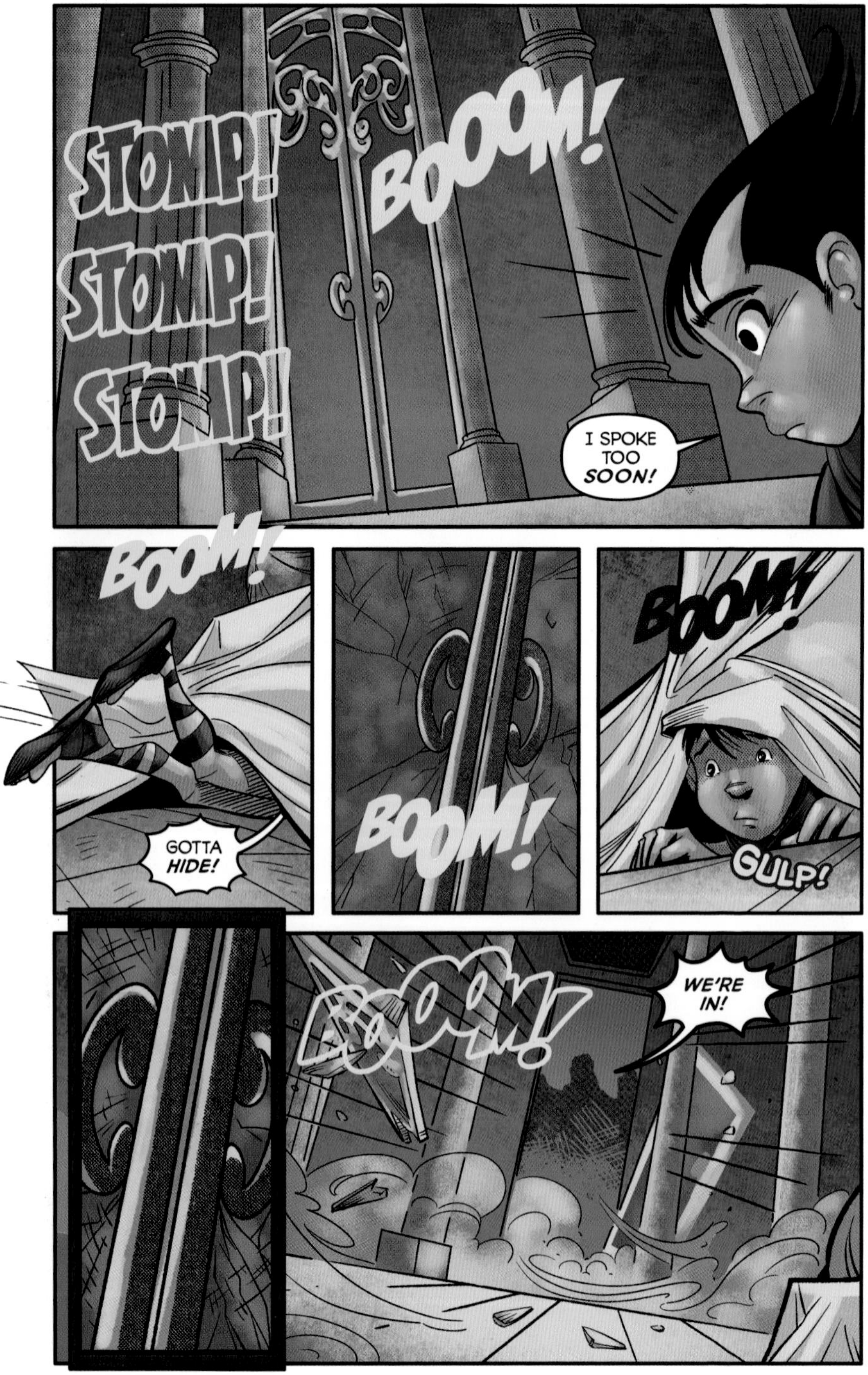
STOMP!
STOMP!
STOMP!
BOOOM!
I SPOKE TOO SOON!
BOOM!
GOTTA HIDE!
BOOM!
BOOM!
GULP!
BOOOM!
WE'RE IN!

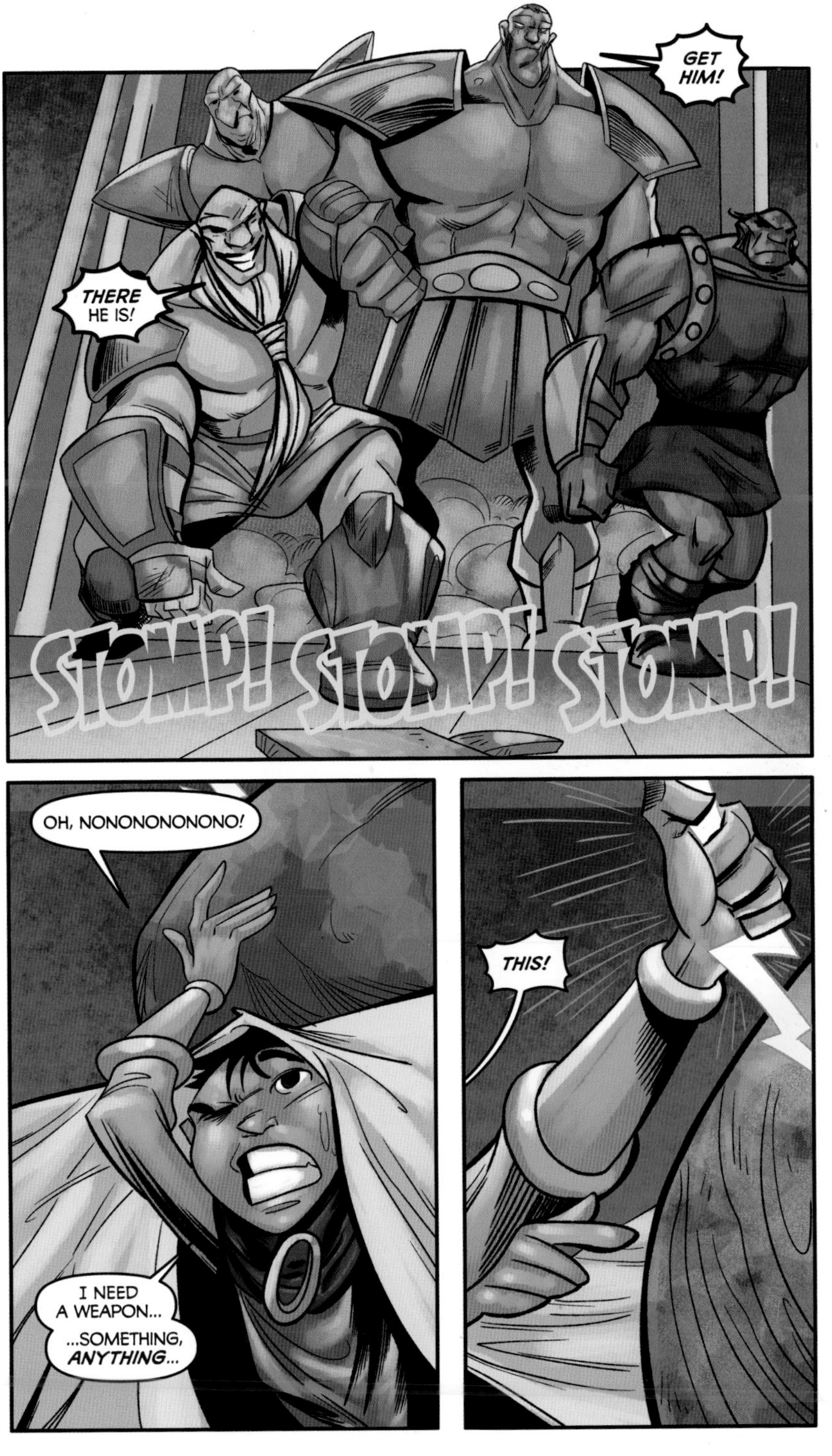

GET HIM!
THERE HE IS!
STOMP! STOMP! STOMP!
OH, NONONONONONO!
I NEED A WEAPON...
...SOMETHING, ANYTHING...
THIS!

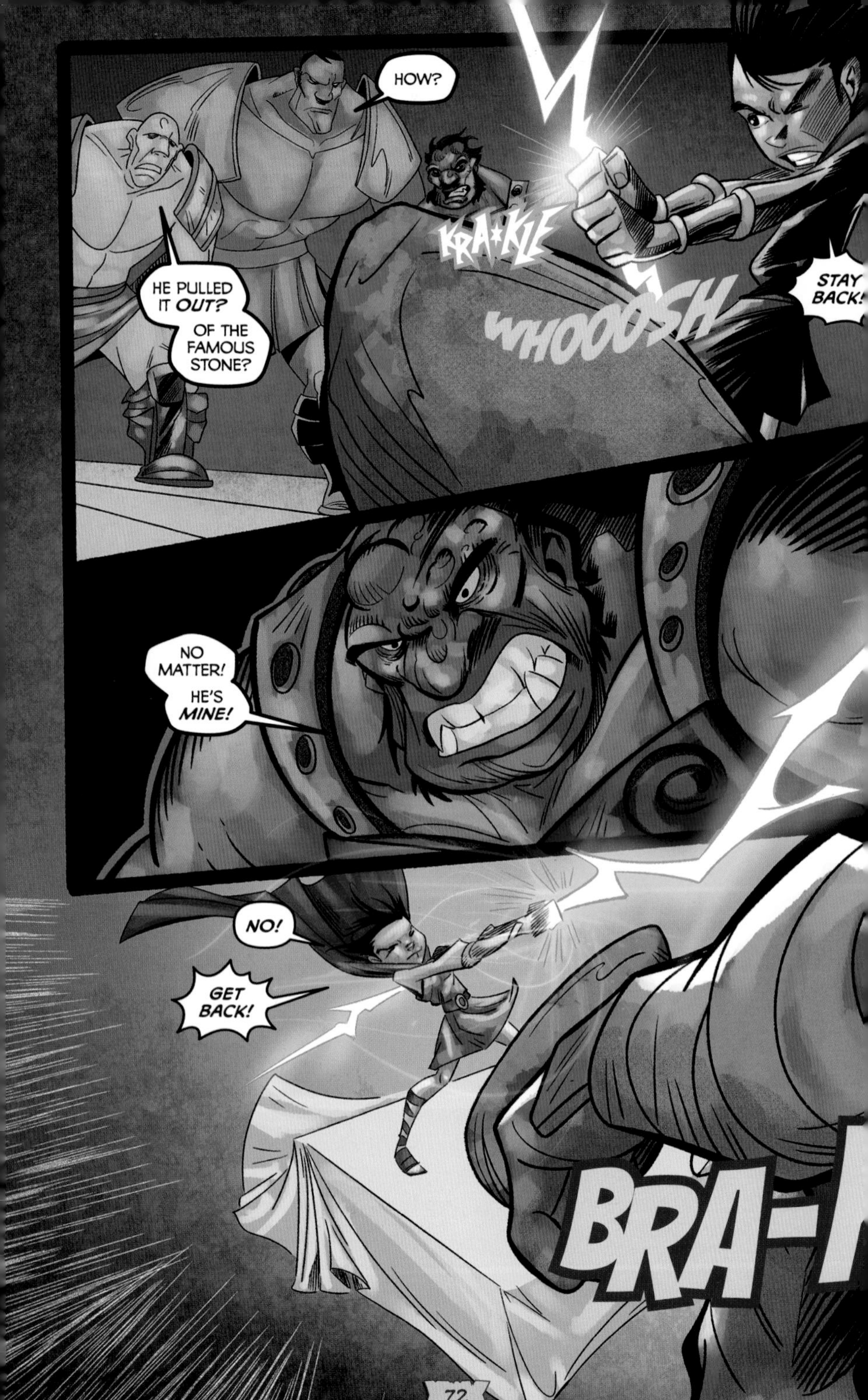
HOW?
HE PULLED IT OUT?
OF THE FAMOUS STONE?
KRA*KLE
WHOOOSH
STAY BACK!
NO MATTER!
HE'S MINE!
NO!
GET BACK!
BRA-

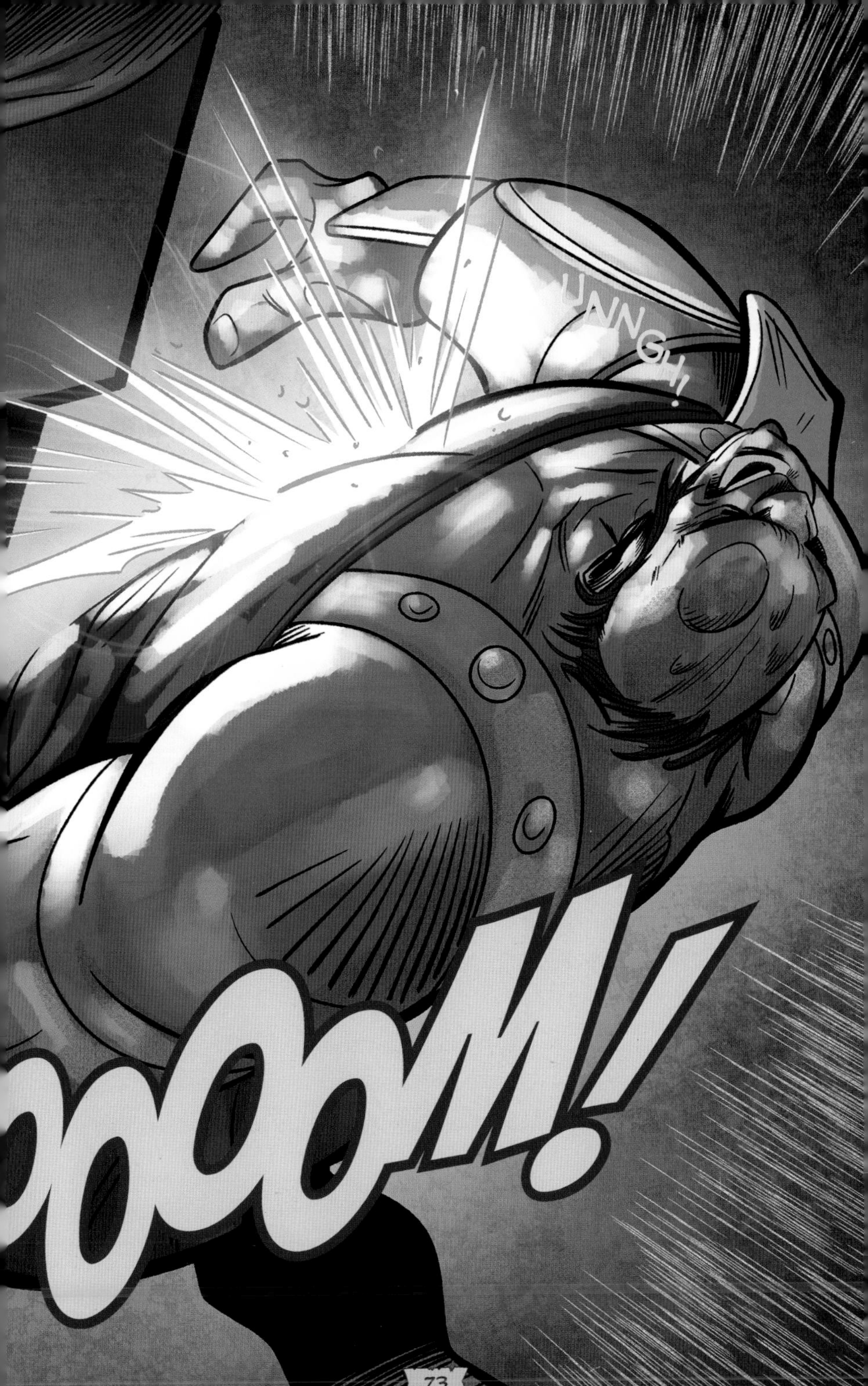
UNNGH!
OOOOM!

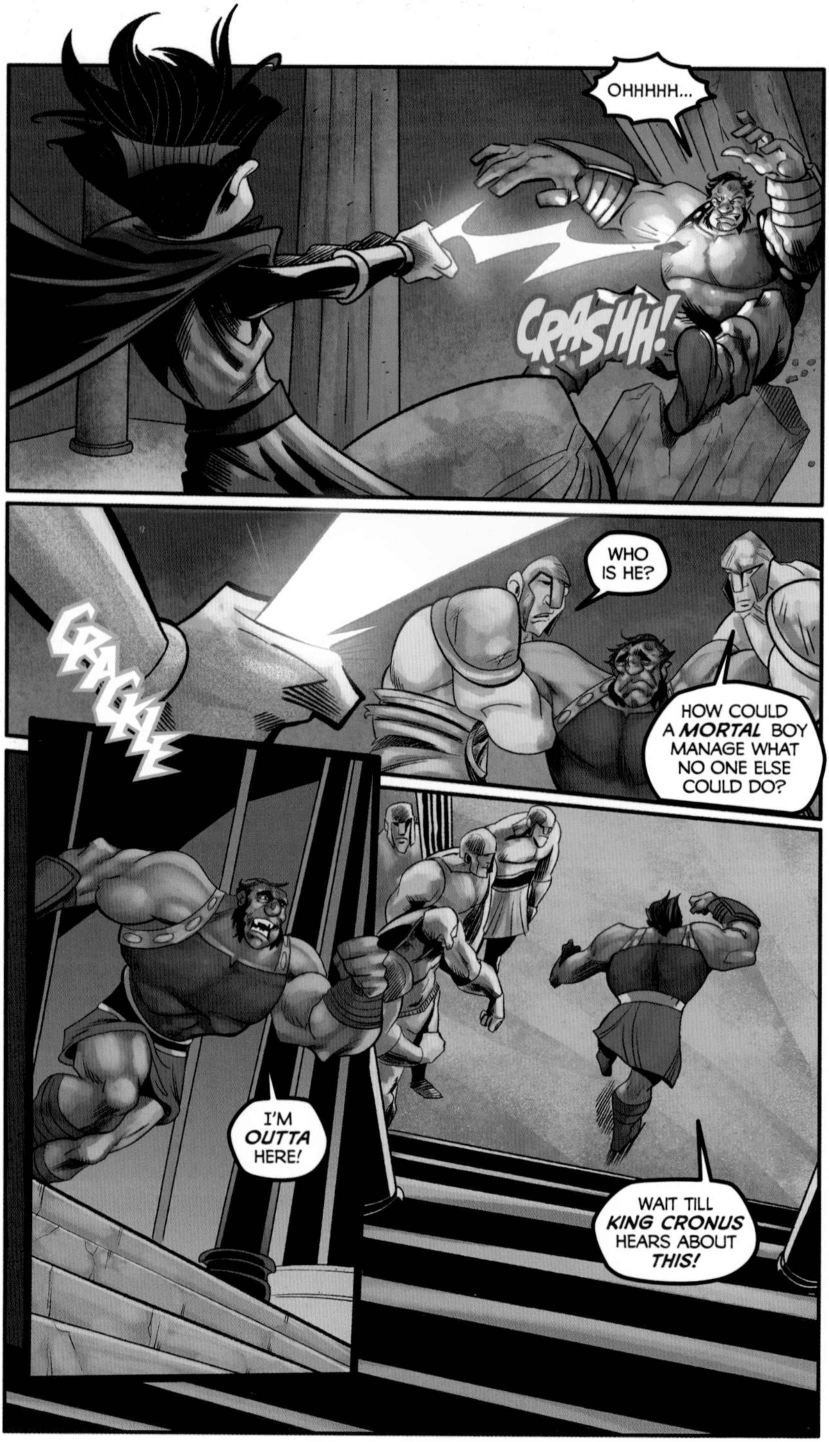
OHHHHH...
CRASHH!
CRACKLE
WHO IS HE?
HOW COULD A MORTAL BOY MANAGE WHAT NO ONE ELSE COULD DO?
I'M OUTTA HERE!
WAIT TILL KING CRONUS HEARS ABOUT THIS!

CHAPTER SIX:
THE WOMAN IN THE MIST

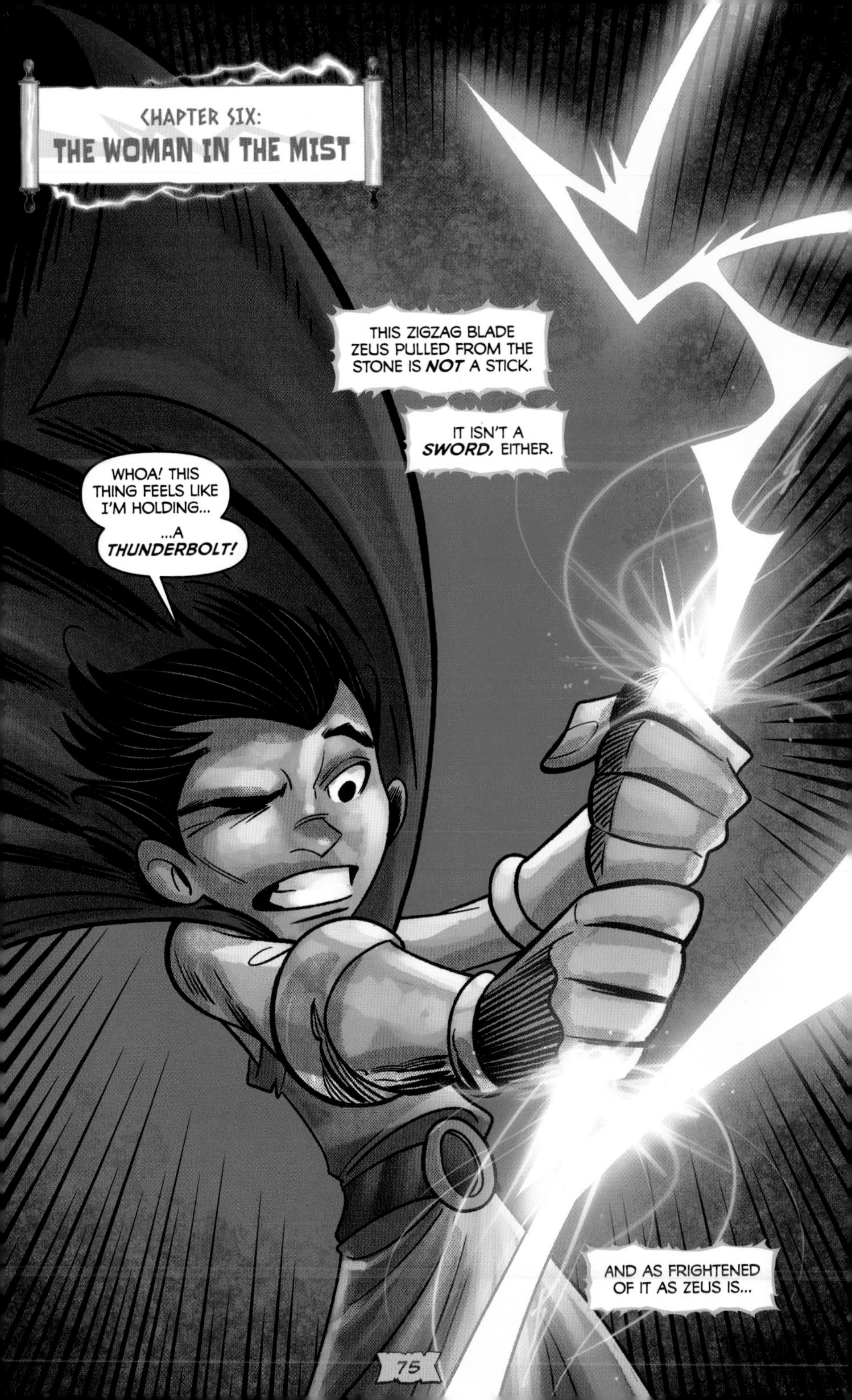
THIS ZIGZAG BLADE ZEUS PULLED FROM THE STONE IS NOT A STICK.
IT ISN'T A SWORD, EITHER.
WHOA! THIS THING FEELS LIKE I'M HOLDING... ...A THUNDERBOLT!
AND AS FRIGHTENED OF IT AS ZEUS IS...

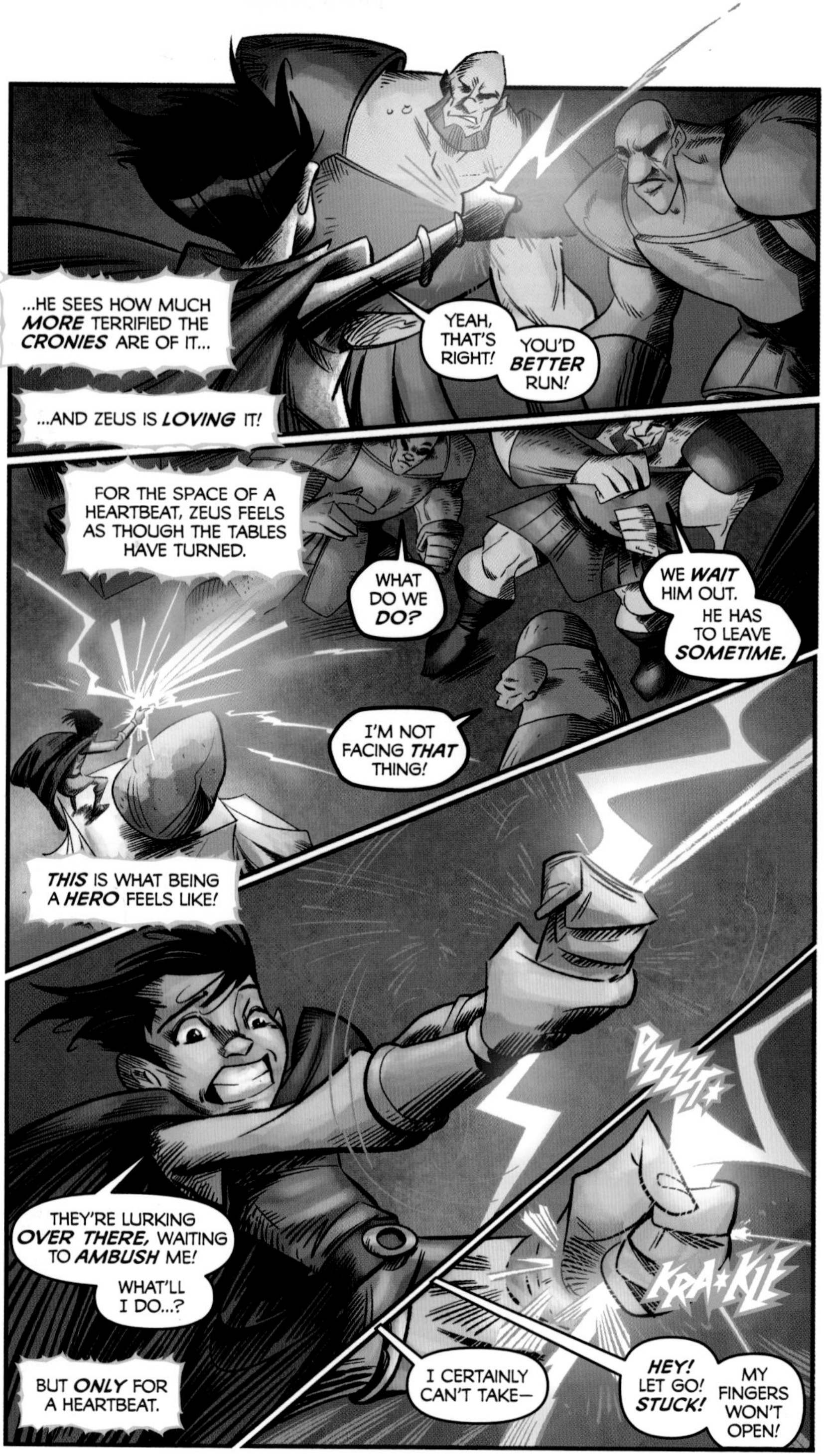

...HE SEES HOW MUCH MORE TERRIFIED THE CRONIES ARE OF IT...
YEAH, THAT'S RIGHT!
YOU'D BETTER RUN!
...AND ZEUS IS LOVING IT!
FOR THE SPACE OF A HEARTBEAT, ZEUS FEELS AS THOUGH THE TABLES HAVE TURNED.
WHAT DO WE DO?
WE WAIT HIM OUT.
HE HAS TO LEAVE SOMETIME.
I'M NOT FACING THAT THING!
THIS IS WHAT BEING A HERO FEELS LIKE!
THEY'RE LURKING OVER THERE, WAITING TO AMBUSH ME!
WHAT'LL I DO...?
BZZZT
KRA★KLE
BUT ONLY FOR A HEARTBEAT.
I CERTAINLY CAN'T TAKE—
HEY! LET GO! STUCK!
MY FINGERS WON'T OPEN!

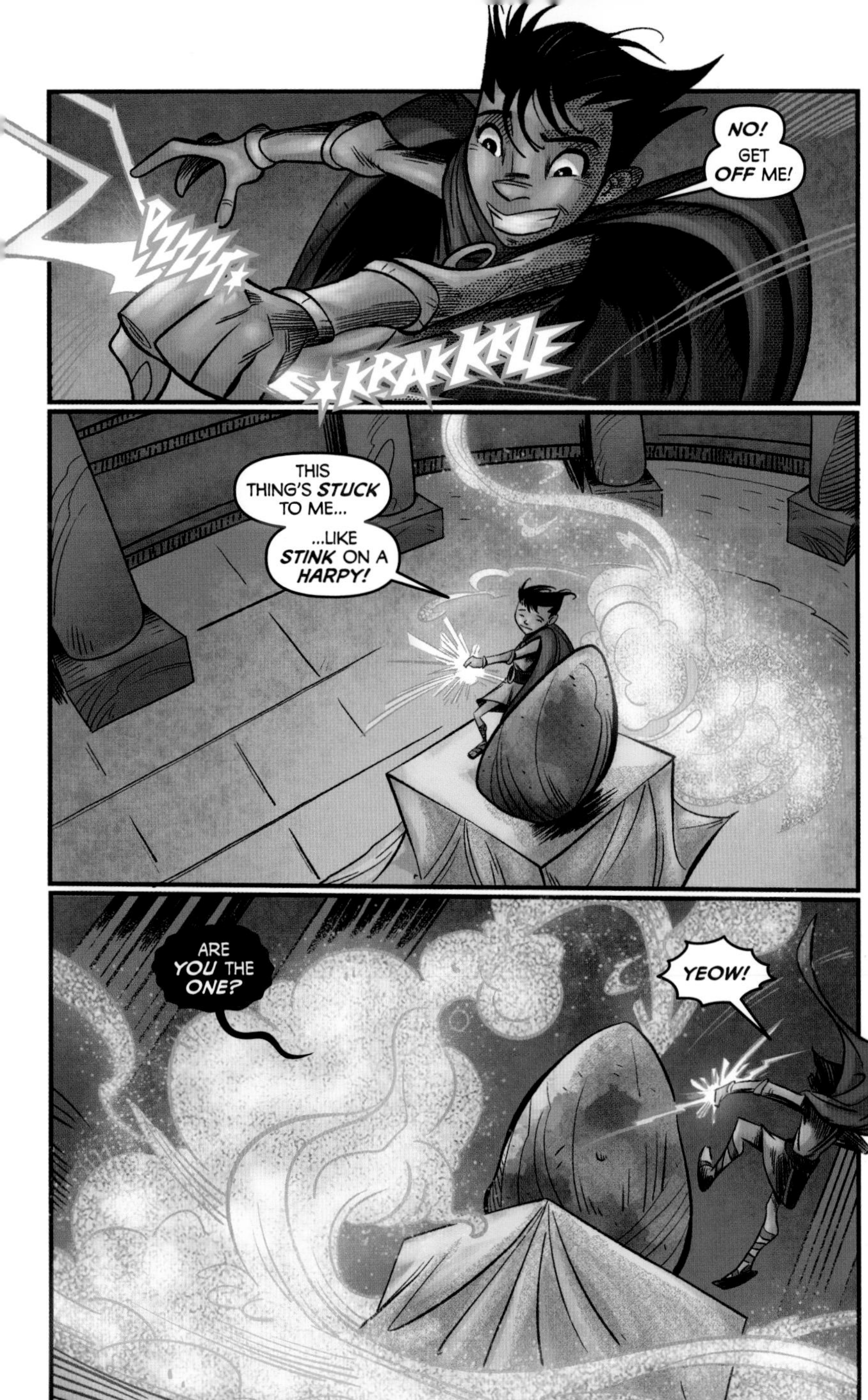
BZZZT
NO! GET OFF ME!
KRAKKKLE
THIS THING'S STUCK TO ME...
...LIKE STINK ON A HARPY!
ARE YOU THE ONE?
YEOW!

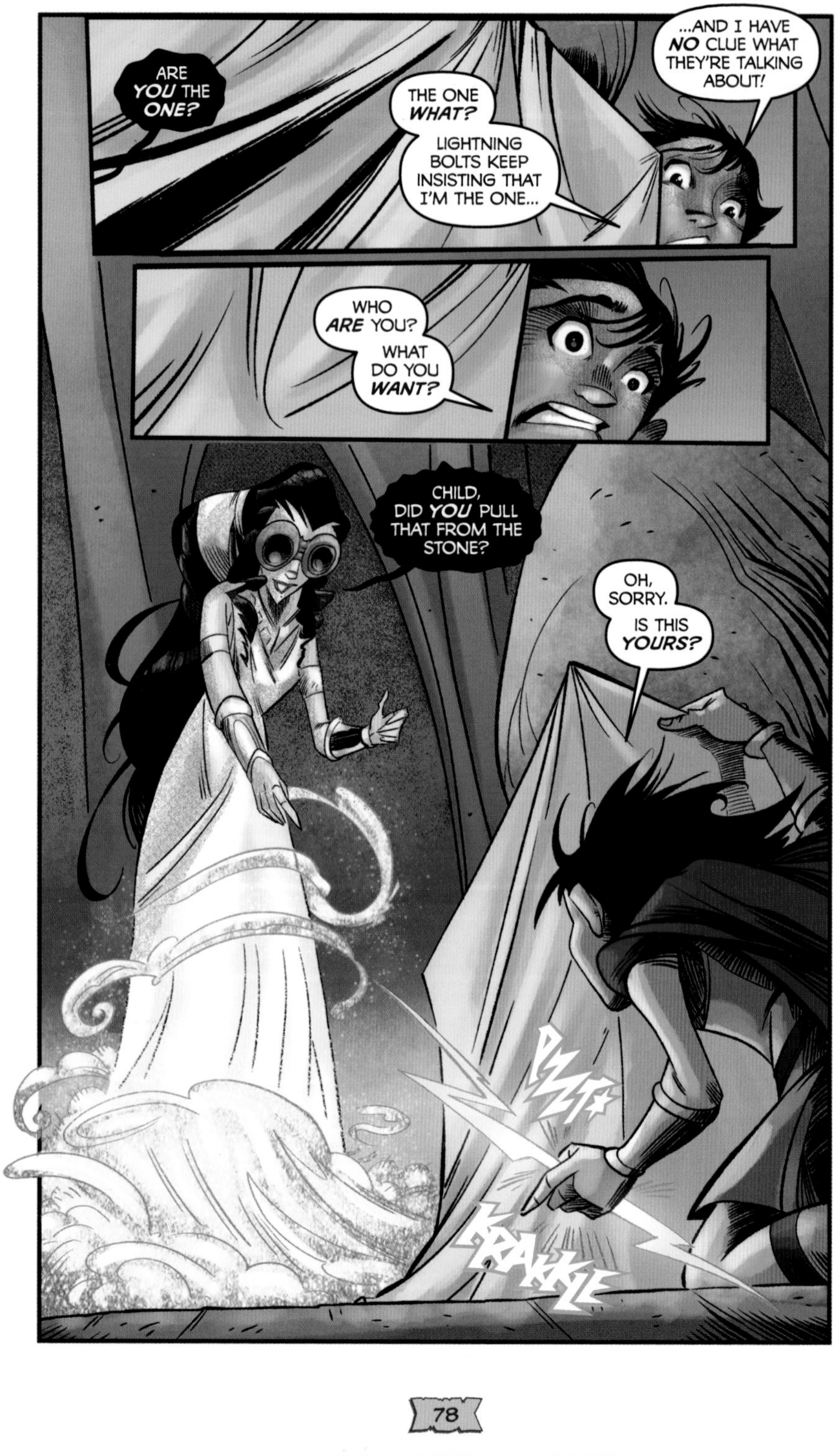
ARE YOU THE ONE?
THE ONE WHAT?
LIGHTNING BOLTS KEEP INSISTING THAT I'M THE ONE...
...AND I HAVE NO CLUE WHAT THEY'RE TALKING ABOUT!
WHO ARE YOU?
WHAT DO YOU WANT?
CHILD, DID YOU PULL THAT FROM THE STONE?
OH, SORRY.
IS THIS YOURS?
PZZT
KRAKKLE

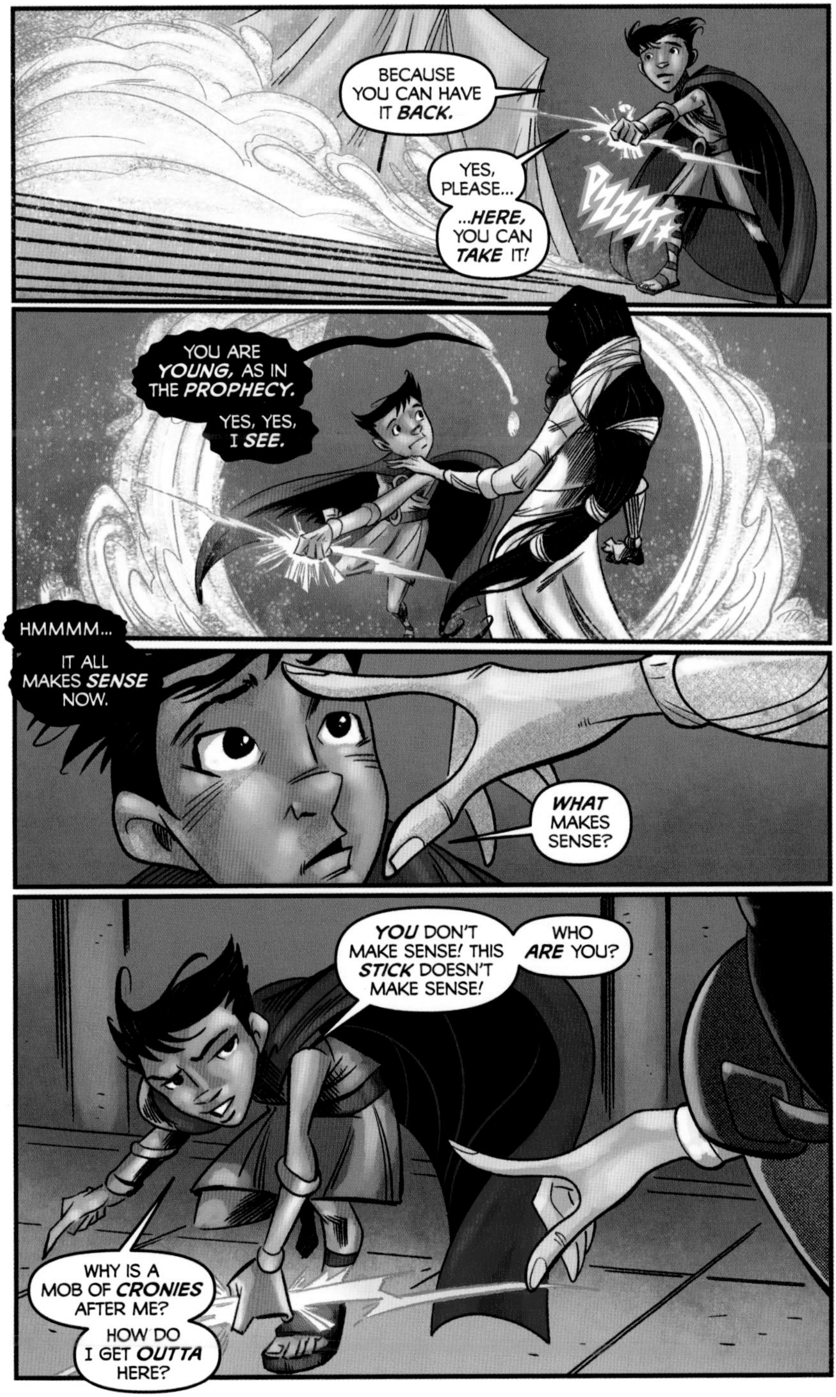
BECAUSE YOU CAN HAVE IT BACK.
YES, PLEASE...
...HERE, YOU CAN TAKE IT!
YOU ARE YOUNG, AS IN THE PROPHECY.
YES, YES, I SEE.
HMMMM...
IT ALL MAKES SENSE NOW.
WHAT MAKES SENSE?
YOU DON'T MAKE SENSE! THIS STICK DOESN'T MAKE SENSE!
WHO ARE YOU?
WHY IS A MOB OF CRONIES AFTER ME?
HOW DO I GET OUTTA HERE?

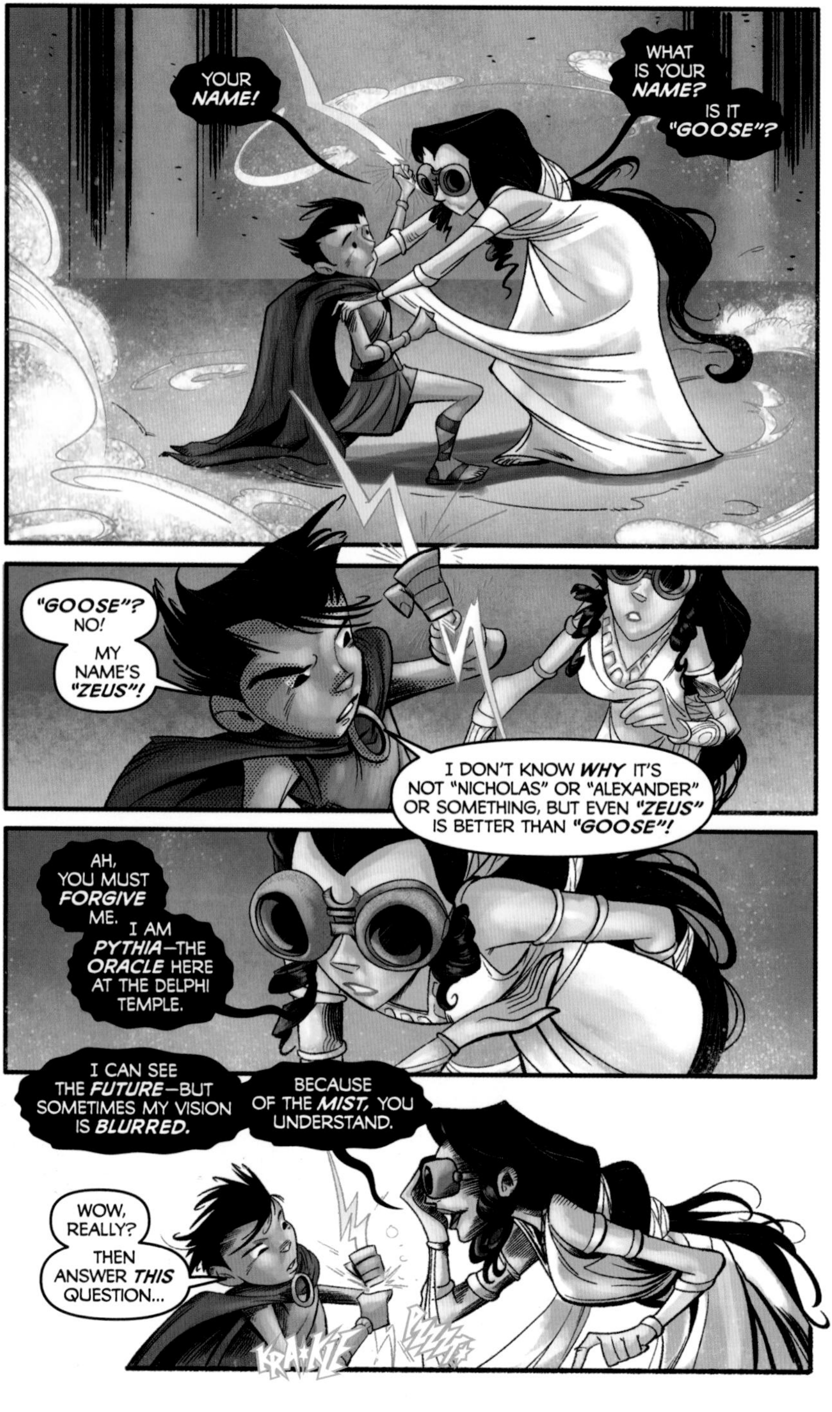
YOUR NAME!
WHAT IS YOUR NAME? IS IT "GOOSE"?
"GOOSE"? NO! MY NAME'S "ZEUS"!
I DON'T KNOW WHY IT'S NOT "NICHOLAS" OR "ALEXANDER" OR SOMETHING, BUT EVEN "ZEUS" IS BETTER THAN "GOOSE"!
AH, YOU MUST FORGIVE ME. I AM PYTHIA—THE ORACLE HERE AT THE DELPHI TEMPLE.
I CAN SEE THE FUTURE—BUT SOMETIMES MY VISION IS BLURRED.
BECAUSE OF THE MIST, YOU UNDERSTAND.
WOW, REALLY? THEN ANSWER THIS QUESTION...
KRA*KLE

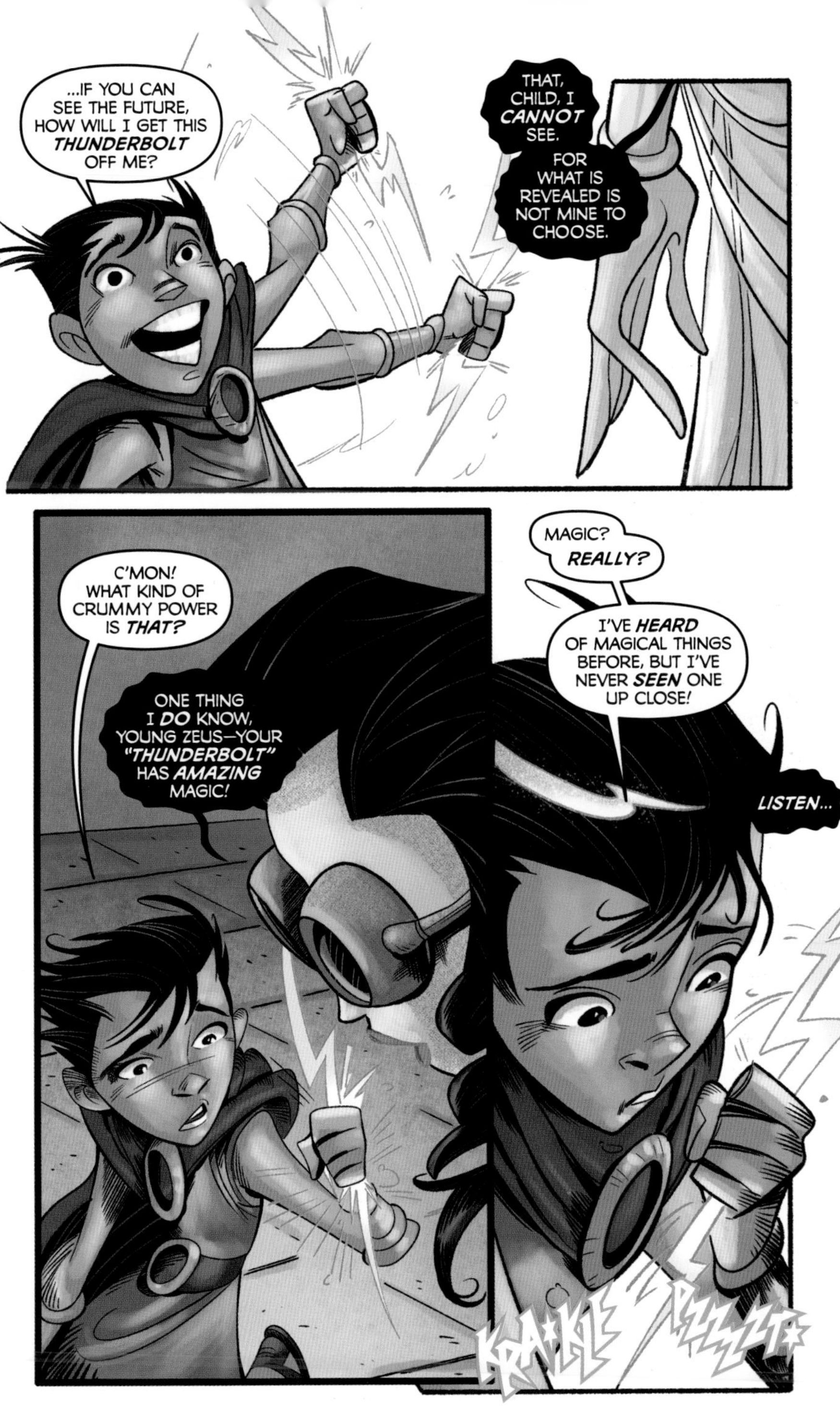
...IF YOU CAN SEE THE FUTURE, HOW WILL I GET THIS *THUNDERBOLT* OFF ME?
THAT, CHILD, I *CANNOT* SEE.
FOR WHAT IS REVEALED IS NOT MINE TO CHOOSE.
C'MON! WHAT KIND OF CRUMMY POWER IS *THAT?*
ONE THING I *DO* KNOW, YOUNG ZEUS—YOUR *"THUNDERBOLT"* HAS *AMAZING* MAGIC!
MAGIC? *REALLY?*
I'VE *HEARD* OF MAGICAL THINGS BEFORE, BUT I'VE NEVER *SEEN* ONE UP CLOSE!
LISTEN...
KRA*KLE PZZZT*

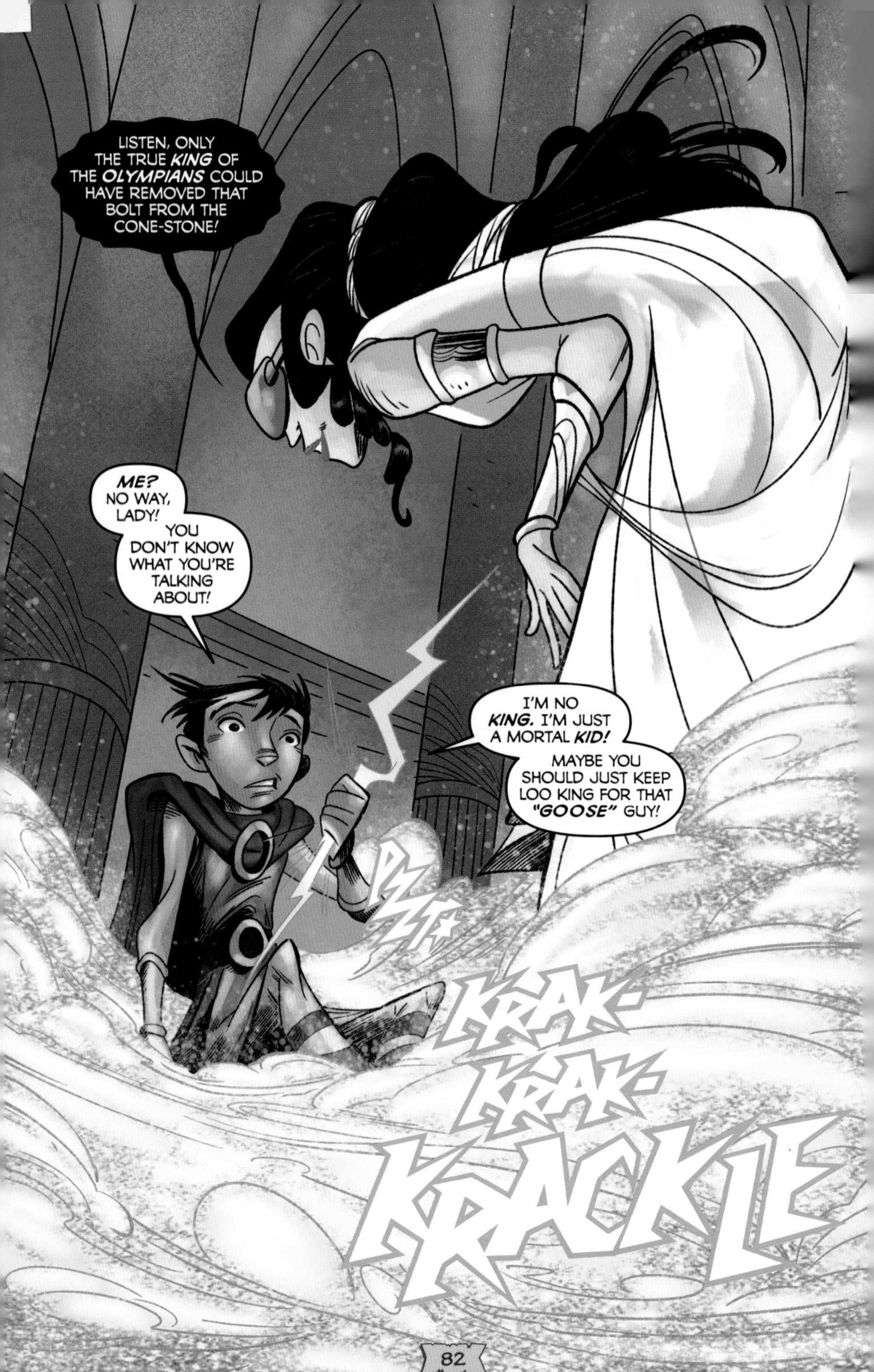
LISTEN, ONLY THE TRUE KING OF THE OLYMPIANS COULD HAVE REMOVED THAT BOLT FROM THE CONE-STONE!
ME? NO WAY, LADY!
YOU DON'T KNOW WHAT YOU'RE TALKING ABOUT!
I'M NO KING. I'M JUST A MORTAL KID!
MAYBE YOU SHOULD JUST KEEP LOO KING FOR THAT "GOOSE" GUY!
KRAK-
KRAK-
KRACKLE

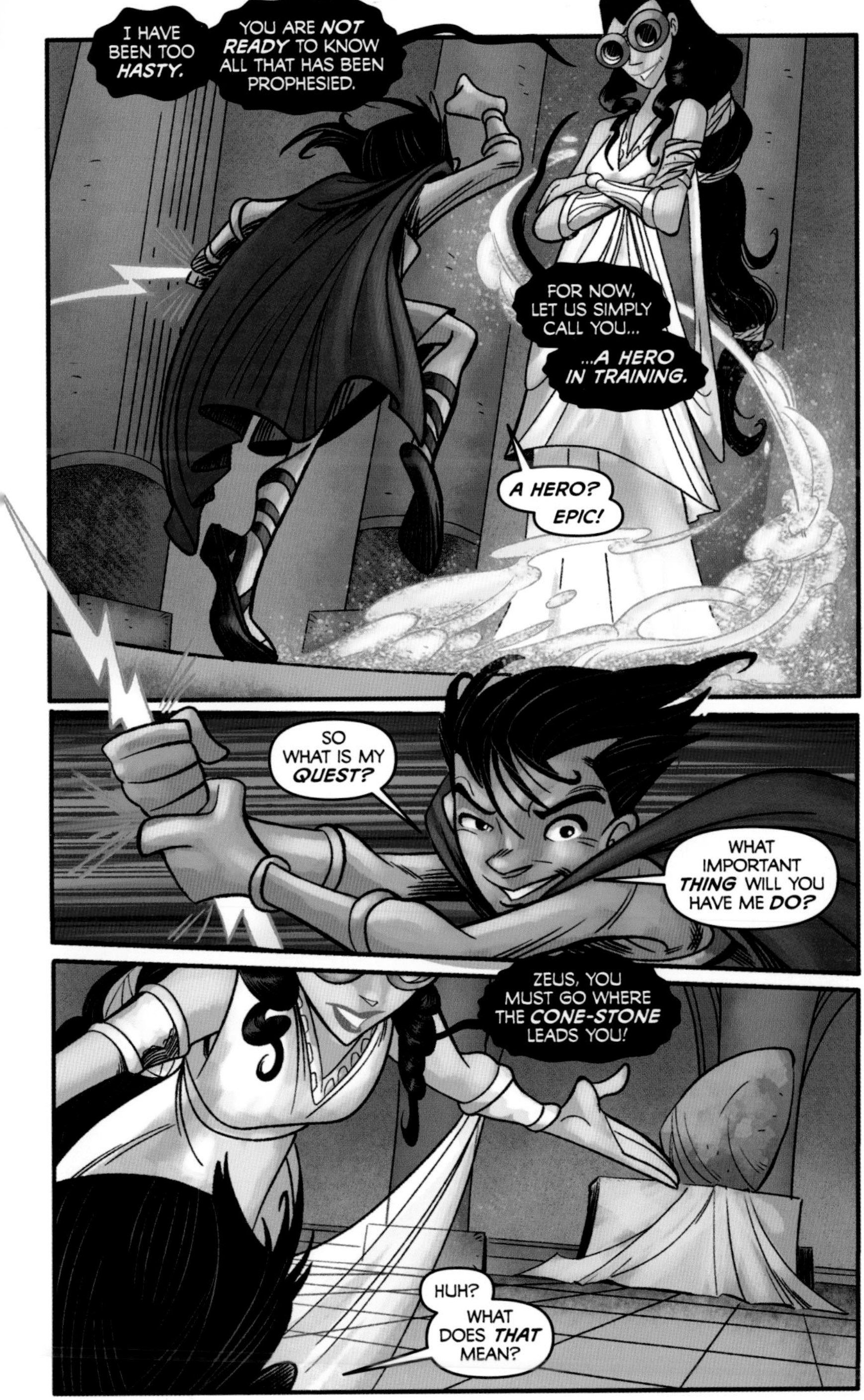
I HAVE BEEN TOO HASTY.
YOU ARE NOT READY TO KNOW ALL THAT HAS BEEN PROPHESIED.
FOR NOW, LET US SIMPLY CALL YOU...
...A HERO IN TRAINING.
A HERO? EPIC!
SO WHAT IS MY QUEST?
WHAT IMPORTANT THING WILL YOU HAVE ME DO?
ZEUS, YOU MUST GO WHERE THE CONE-STONE LEADS YOU!
HUH? WHAT DOES THAT MEAN?

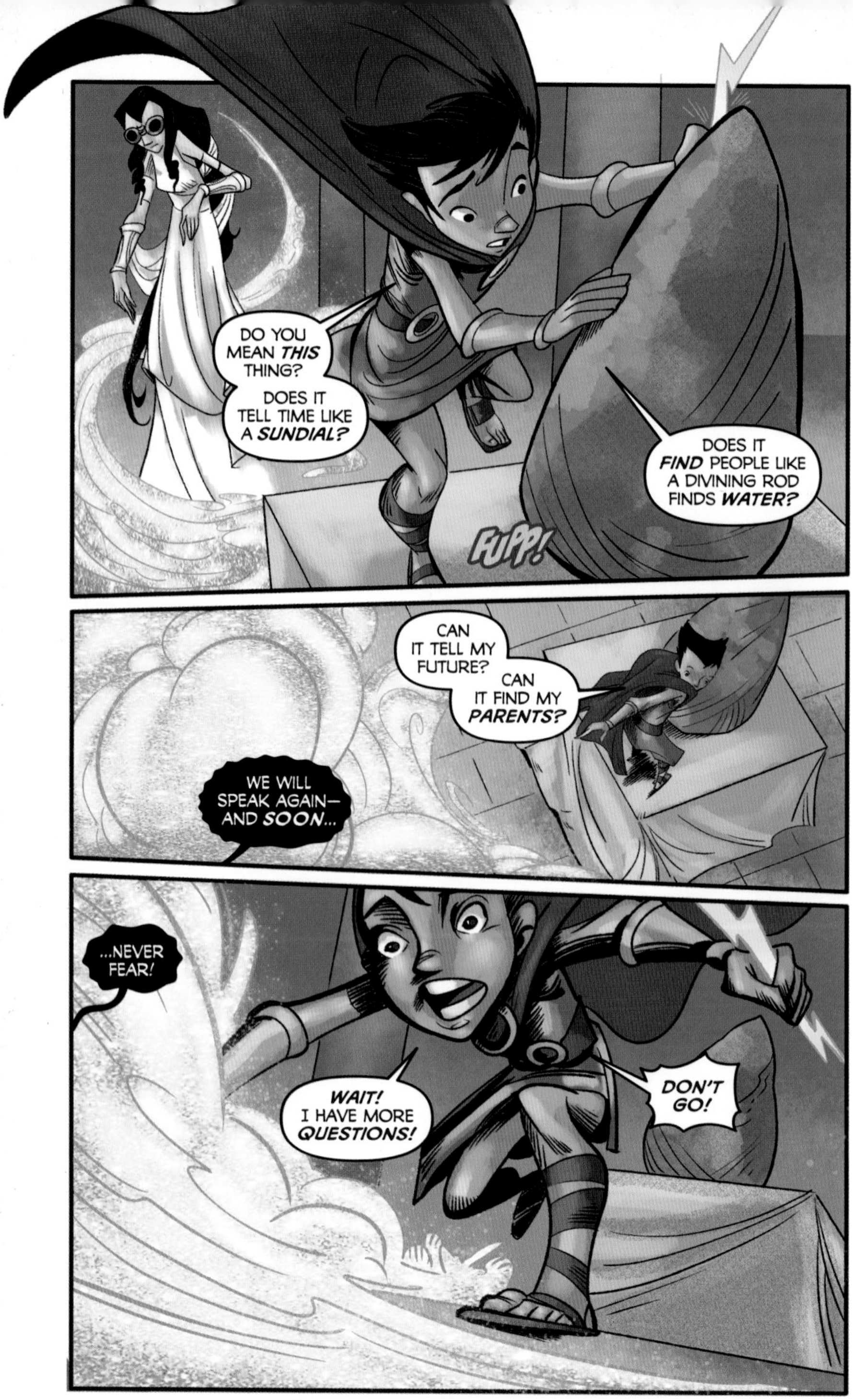
DO YOU MEAN *THIS* THING?
DOES IT TELL TIME LIKE A *SUNDIAL?*
DOES IT *FIND* PEOPLE LIKE A DIVINING ROD FINDS *WATER?*
FUPP!
CAN IT TELL MY FUTURE?
CAN IT FIND MY *PARENTS?*
WE WILL SPEAK AGAIN—AND *SOON*...
...NEVER FEAR!
WAIT! I HAVE MORE *QUESTIONS!*
DON'T GO!

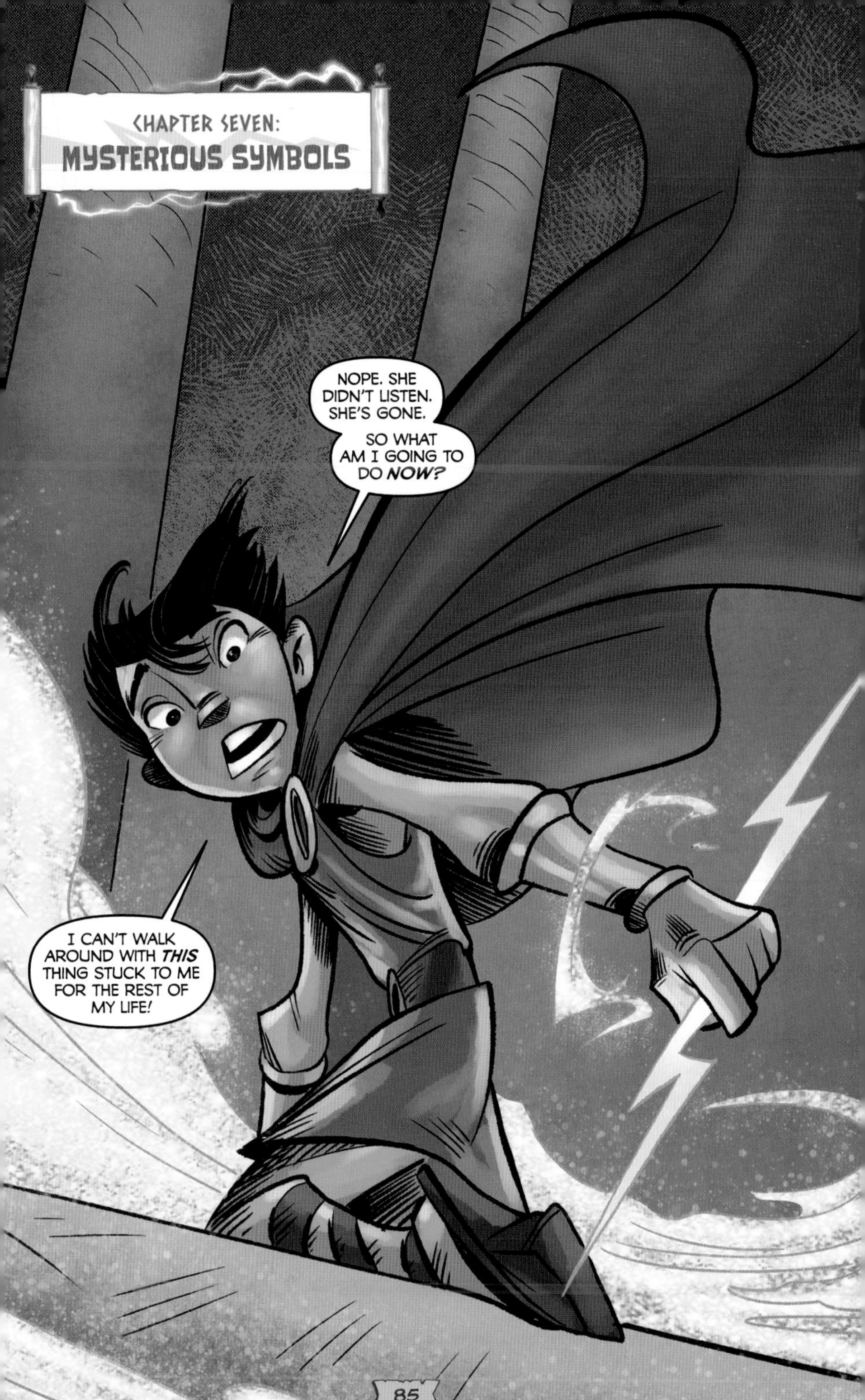
CHAPTER SEVEN:
MYSTERIOUS SYMBOLS
NOPE. SHE DIDN'T LISTEN. SHE'S GONE.
SO WHAT AM I GOING TO DO *NOW?*
I CAN'T WALK AROUND WITH *THIS* THING STUCK TO ME FOR THE REST OF MY LIFE!

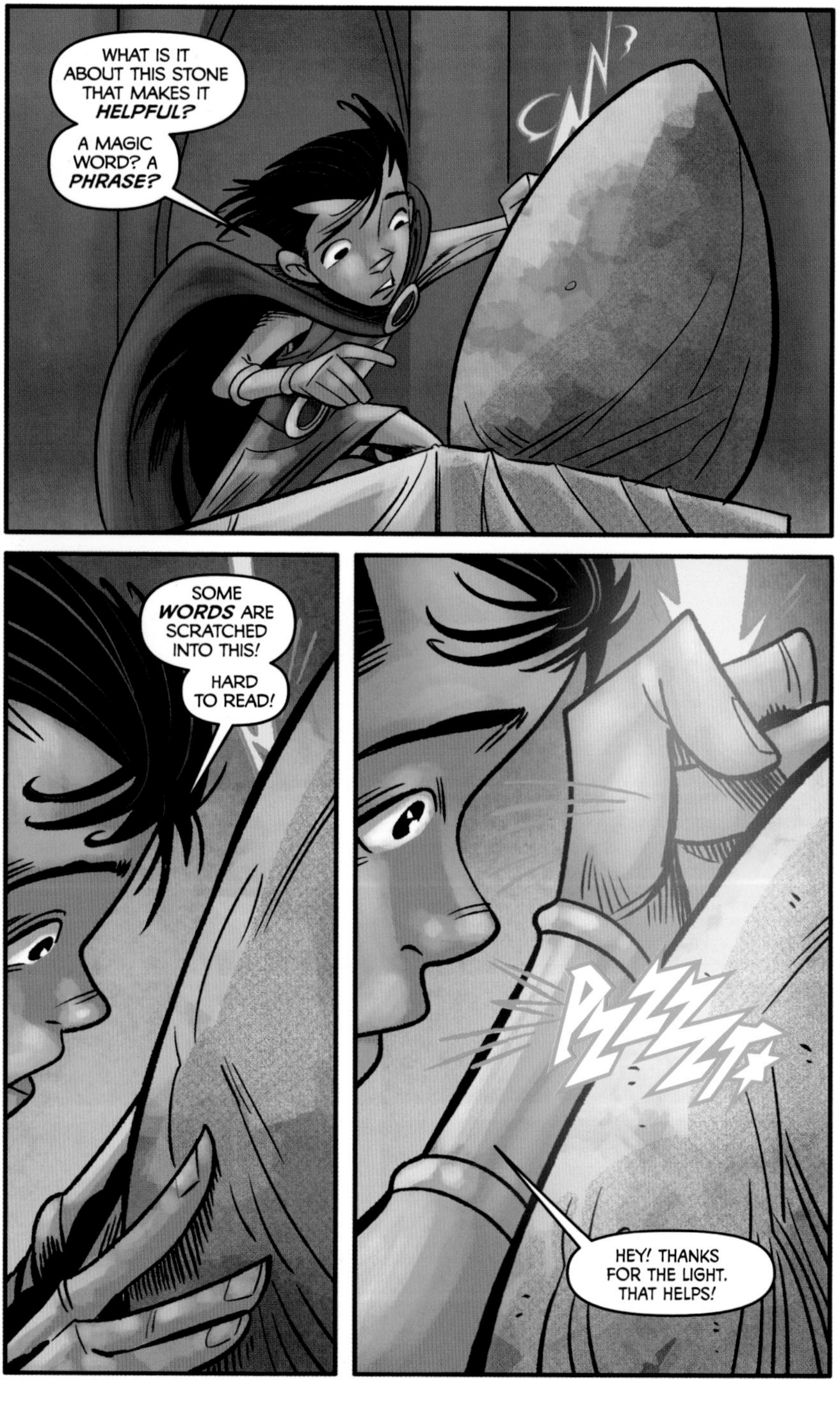
WHAT IS IT ABOUT THIS STONE THAT MAKES IT ***HELPFUL?***
A MAGIC WORD? A ***PHRASE?***
SOME ***WORDS*** ARE SCRATCHED INTO THIS!
HARD TO READ!
HEY! THANKS FOR THE LIGHT. THAT HELPS!

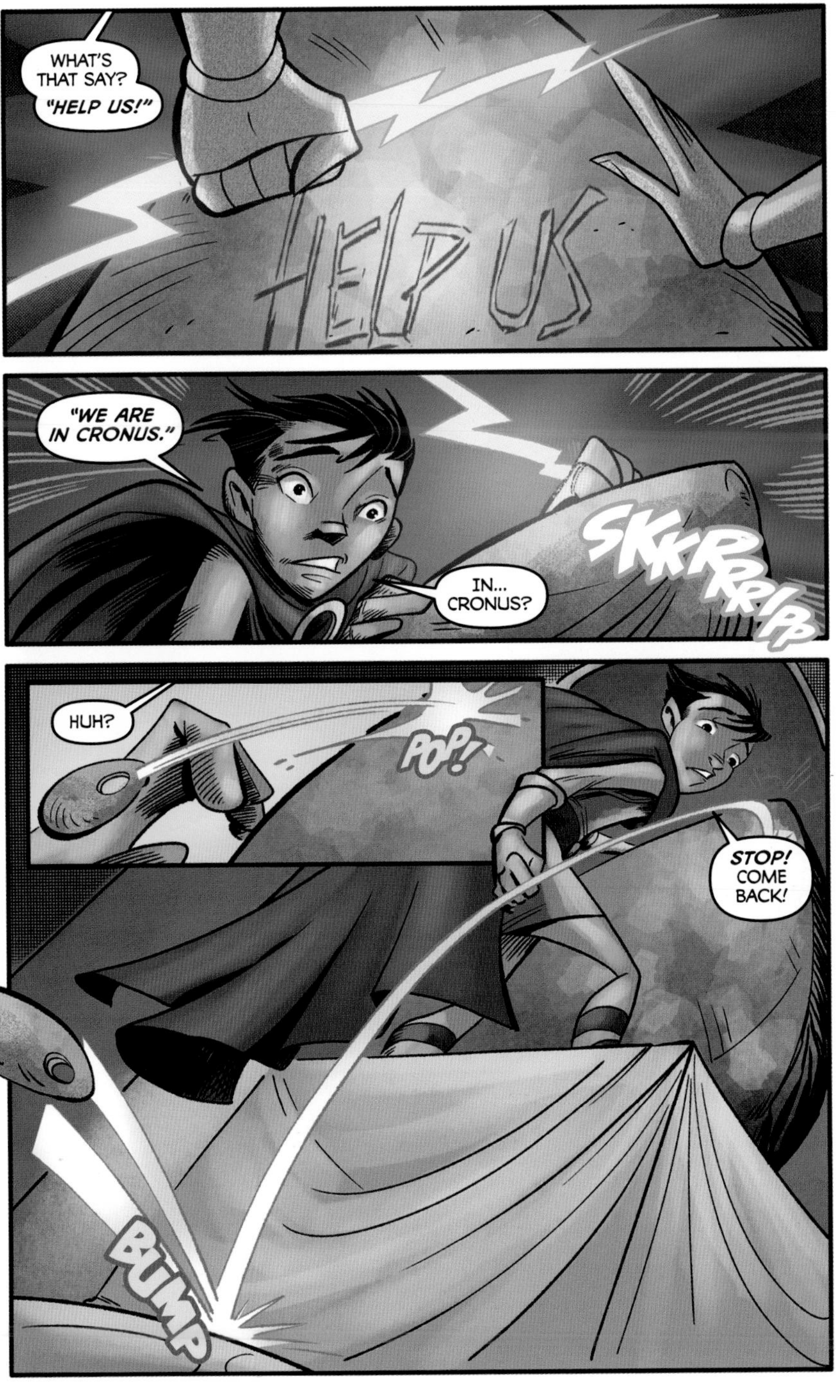
WHAT'S THAT SAY? "HELP US!"
HELP US
"WE ARE IN CRONUS."
SKKRRRIPP
IN... CRONUS?
HUH?
POP!
STOP! COME BACK!
BUMP

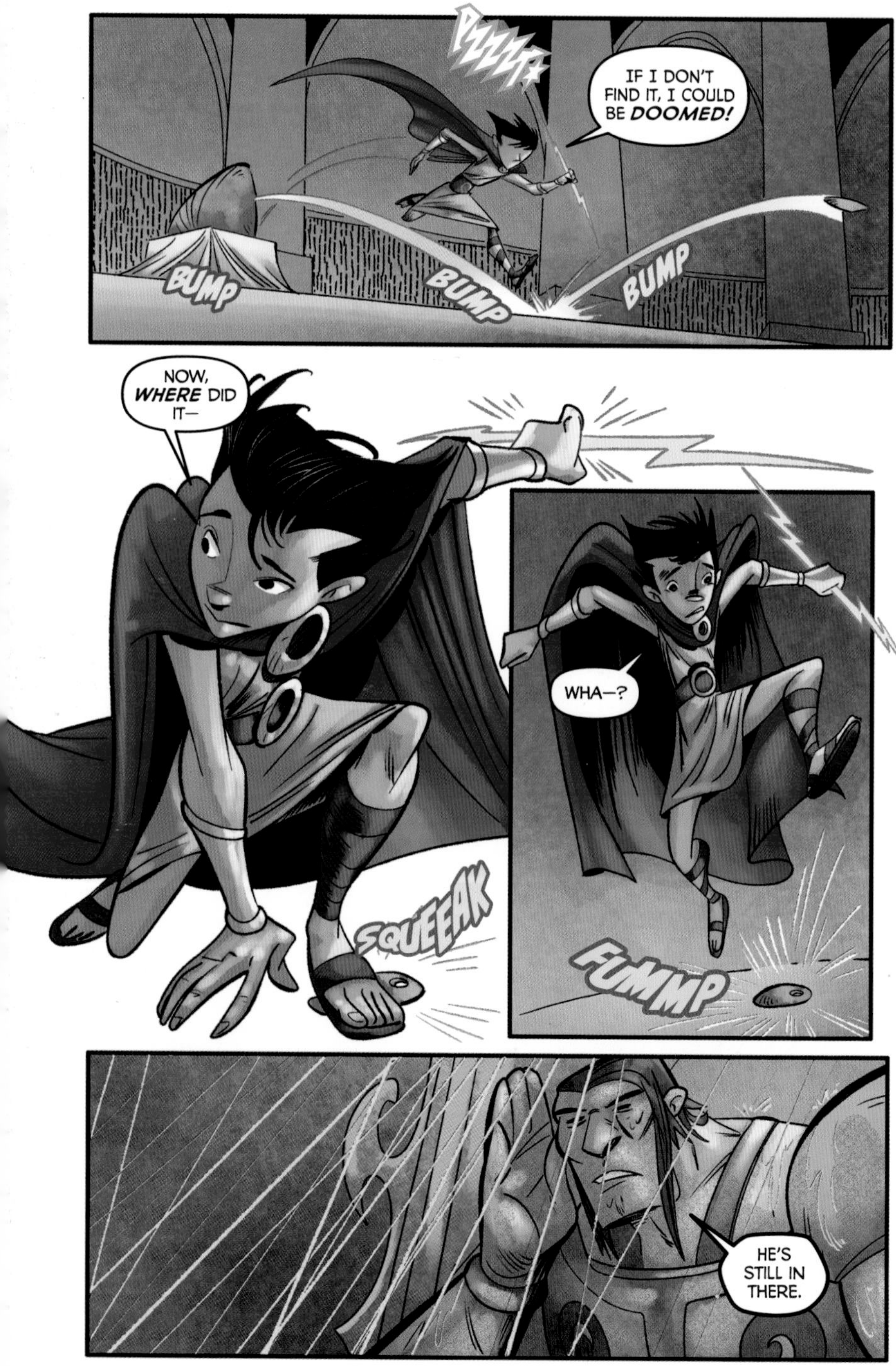

IF I DON'T FIND IT, I COULD BE ***DOOMED!***
BUMP
BUMP
BUMP
NOW, ***WHERE*** DID IT—
SQUEEAK
WHA—?
FUMMP
HE'S STILL IN THERE.

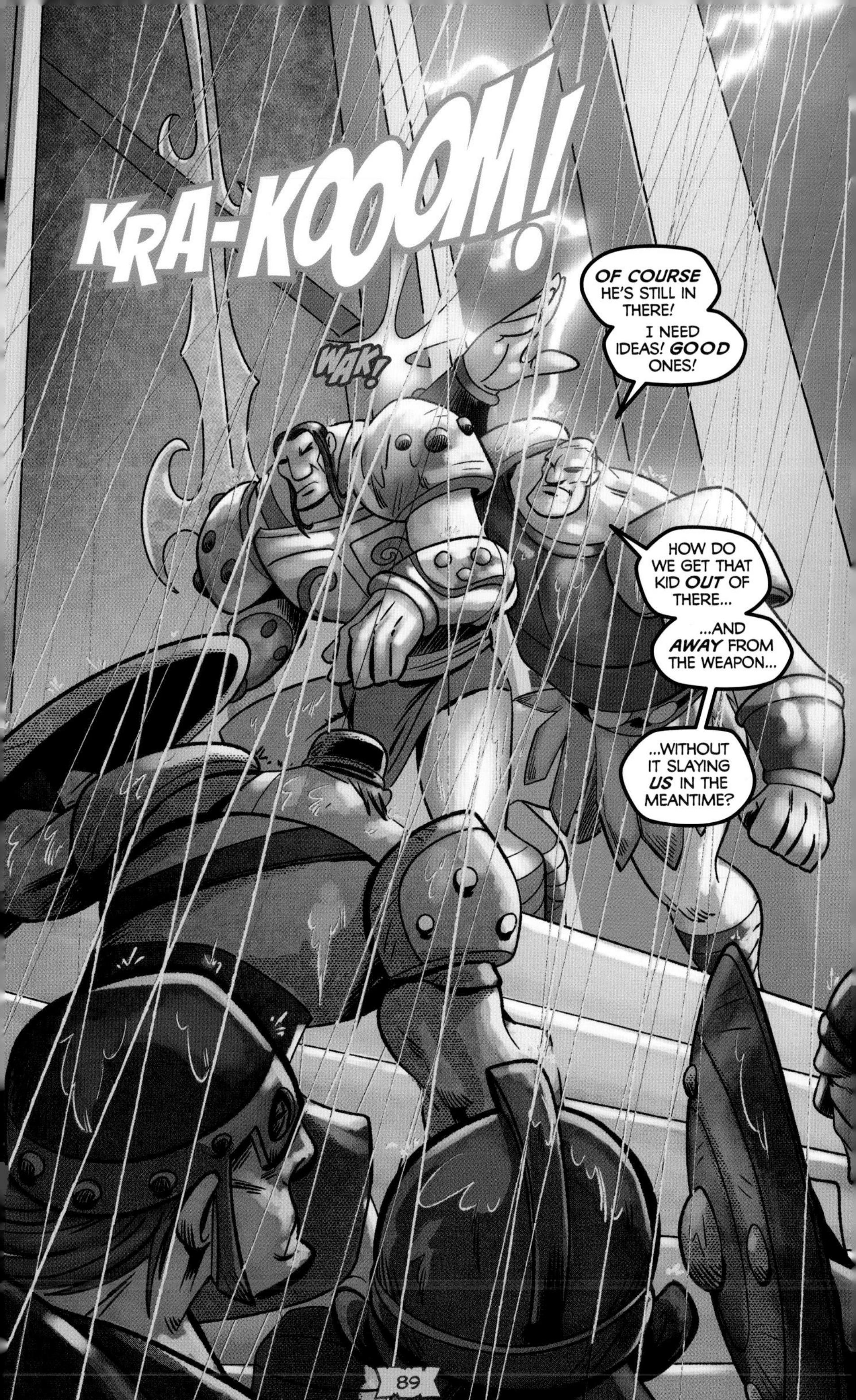
KRA-KOOOM!
WAK!
OF COURSE HE'S STILL IN THERE!
I NEED IDEAS! GOOD ONES!
HOW DO WE GET THAT KID OUT OF THERE...
...AND AWAY FROM THE WEAPON...
...WITHOUT IT SLAYING US IN THE MEANTIME?

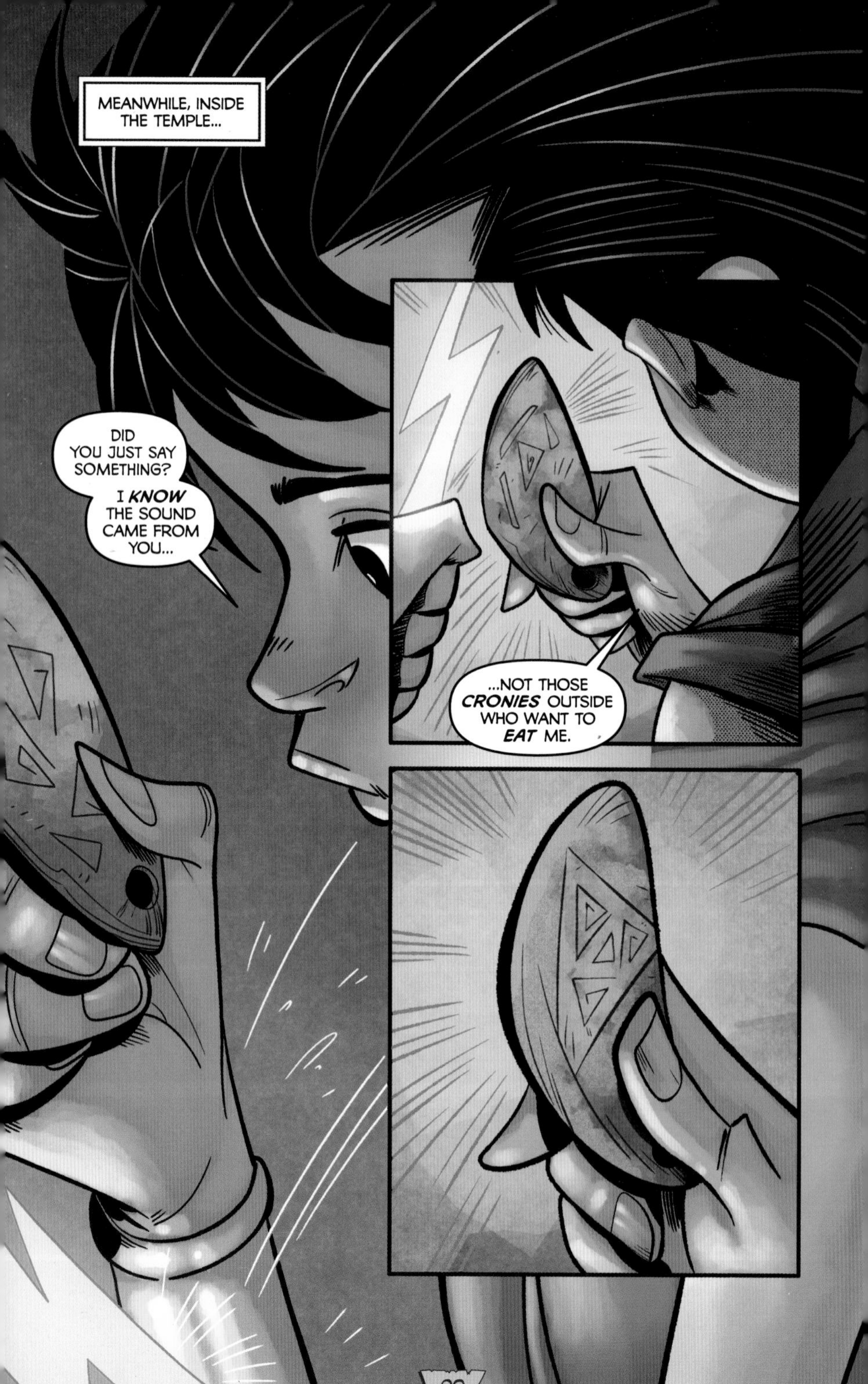
MEANWHILE, INSIDE THE TEMPLE...
DID YOU JUST SAY SOMETHING? I KNOW THE SOUND CAME FROM YOU...
...NOT THOSE CRONIES OUTSIDE WHO WANT TO EAT ME.

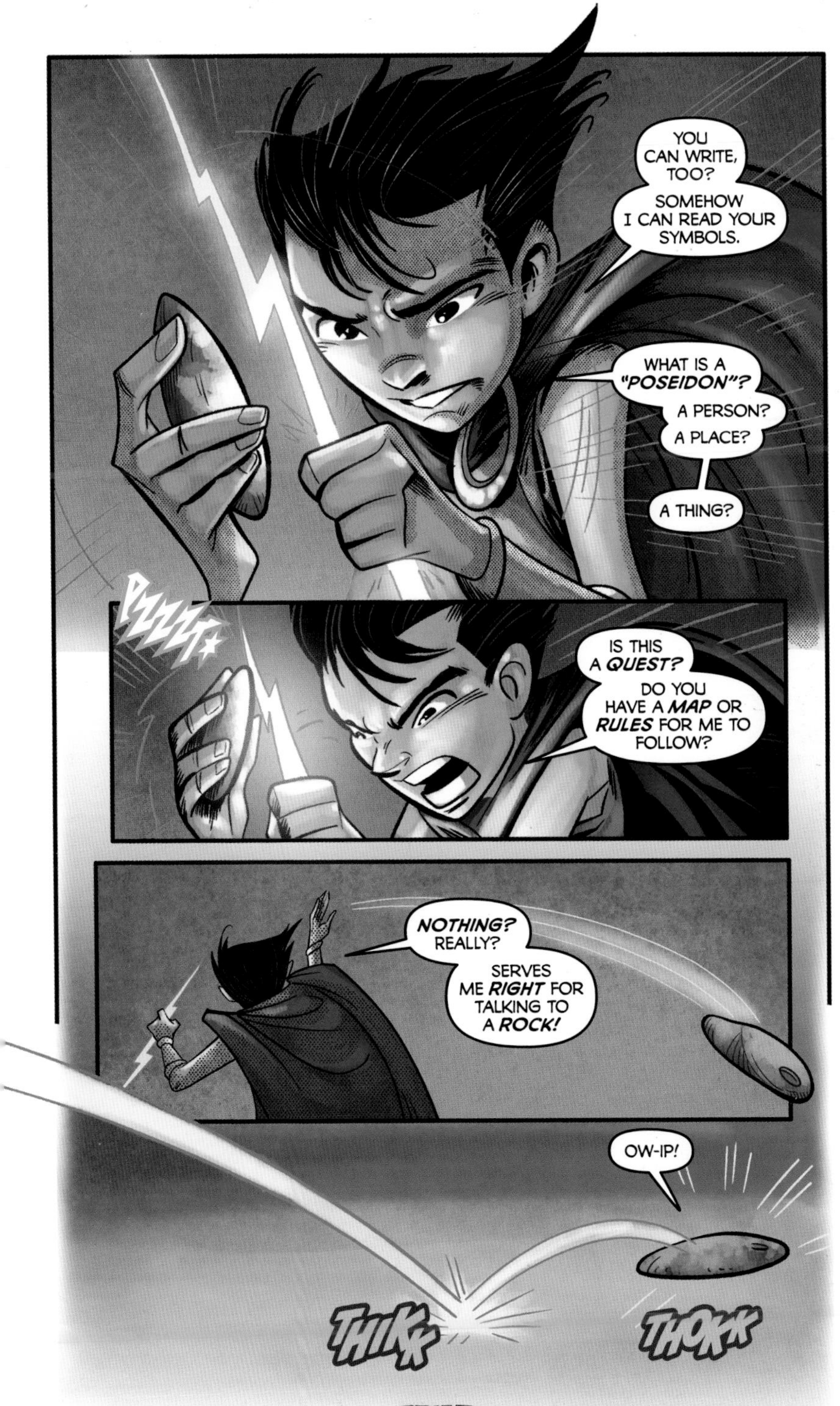
YOU CAN WRITE, TOO?
SOMEHOW I CAN READ YOUR SYMBOLS.
WHAT IS A "POSEIDON"?
A PERSON?
A PLACE?
A THING?
PZZZZT
IS THIS A QUEST?
DO YOU HAVE A MAP OR RULES FOR ME TO FOLLOW?
NOTHING? REALLY?
SERVES ME RIGHT FOR TALKING TO A ROCK!
OW-IP!
THIKK
THOKK

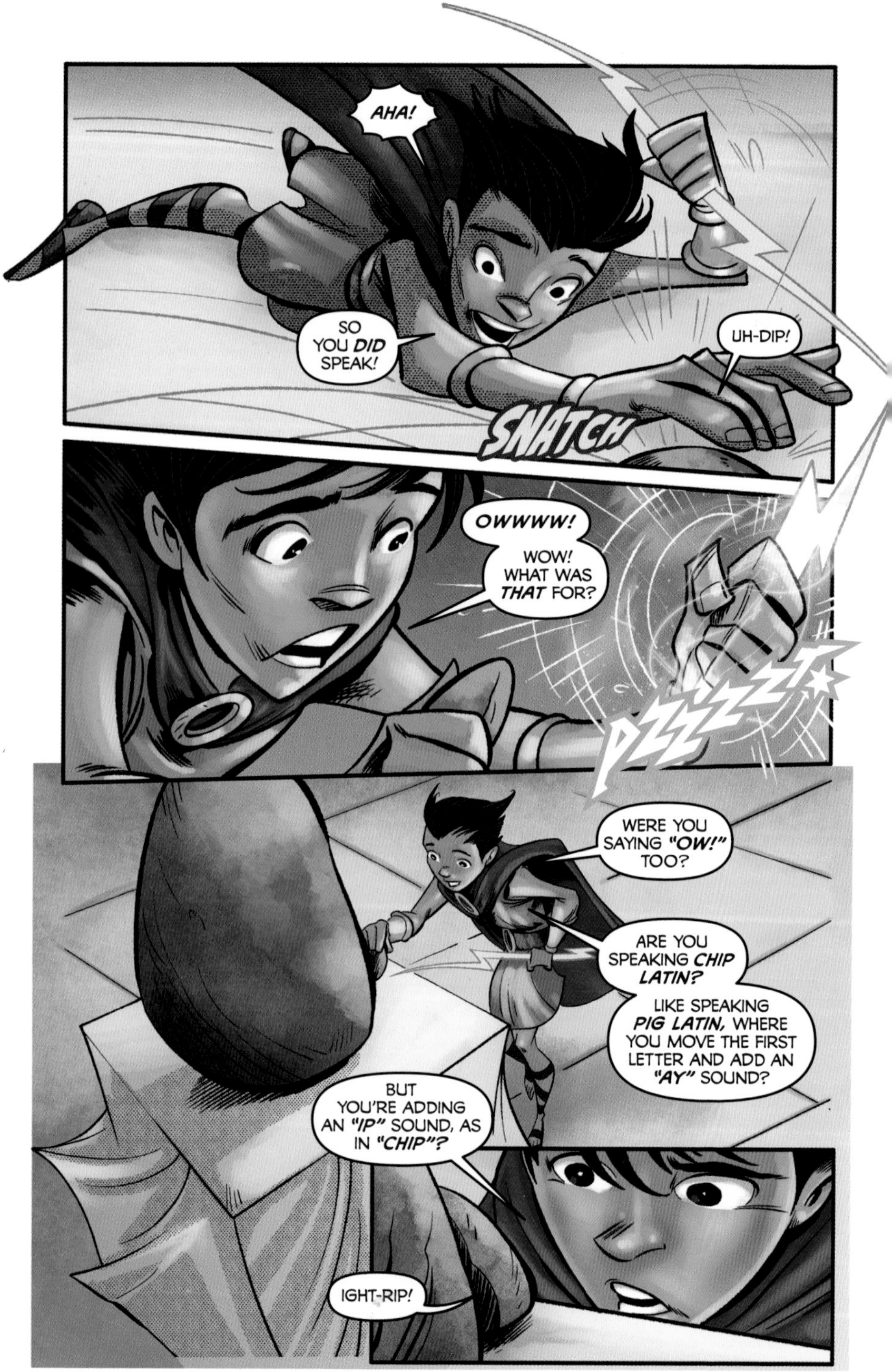
AHA!
SO YOU DID SPEAK!
UH-DIP!
SNATCH
OWWWW!
WOW! WHAT WAS THAT FOR?
PZZZZT
WERE YOU SAYING "OW!" TOO?
ARE YOU SPEAKING CHIP LATIN?
LIKE SPEAKING PIG LATIN, WHERE YOU MOVE THE FIRST LETTER AND ADD AN "AY" SOUND?
BUT YOU'RE ADDING AN "IP" SOUND, AS IN "CHIP"?
IGHT-RIP!

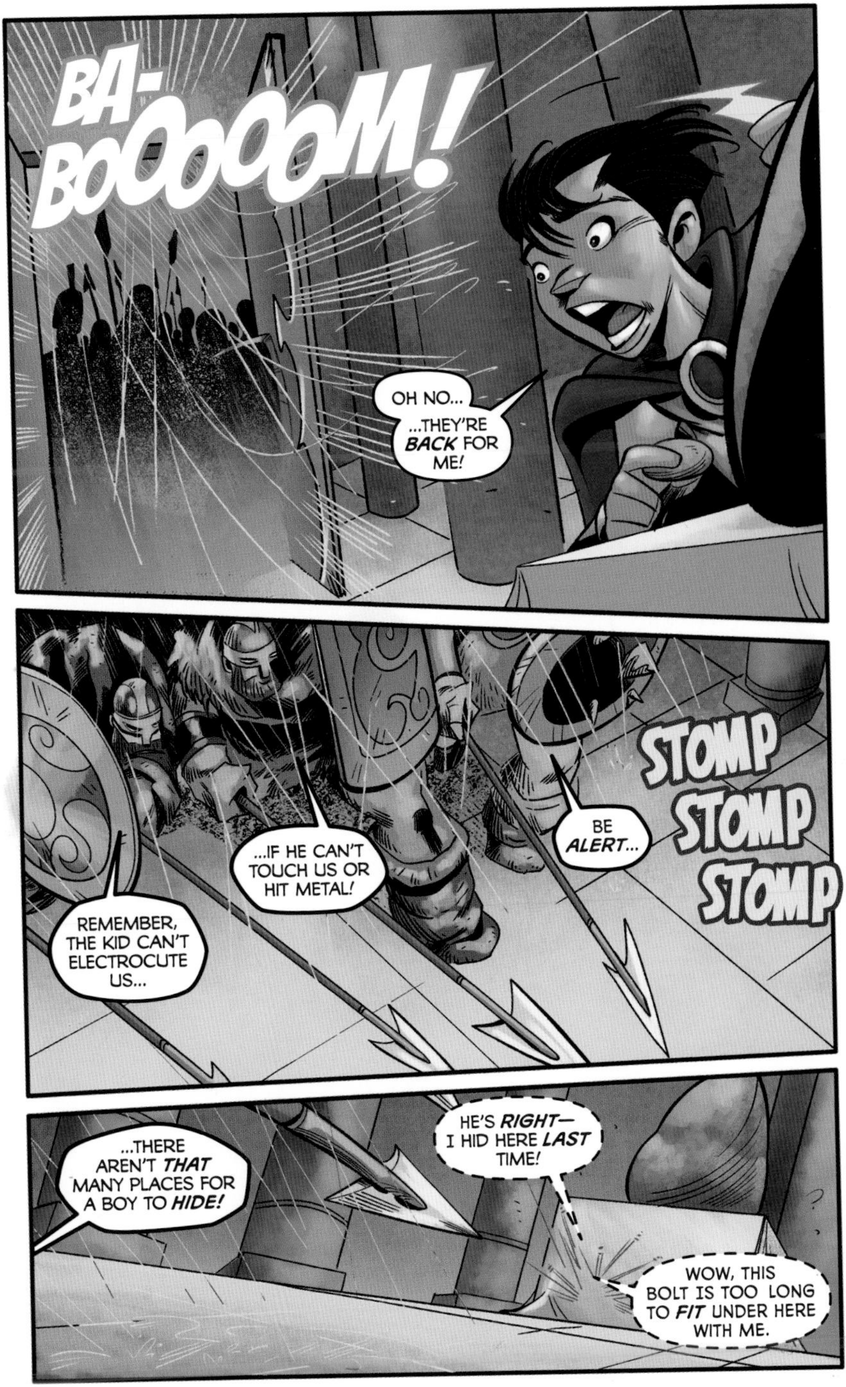
BA-BOOOOOM!
OH NO...
...THEY'RE BACK FOR ME!
STOMP STOMP STOMP
BE ALERT...
...IF HE CAN'T TOUCH US OR HIT METAL!
REMEMBER, THE KID CAN'T ELECTROCUTE US...
...THERE AREN'T THAT MANY PLACES FOR A BOY TO HIDE!
HE'S RIGHT— I HID HERE LAST TIME!
WOW, THIS BOLT IS TOO LONG TO FIT UNDER HERE WITH ME.

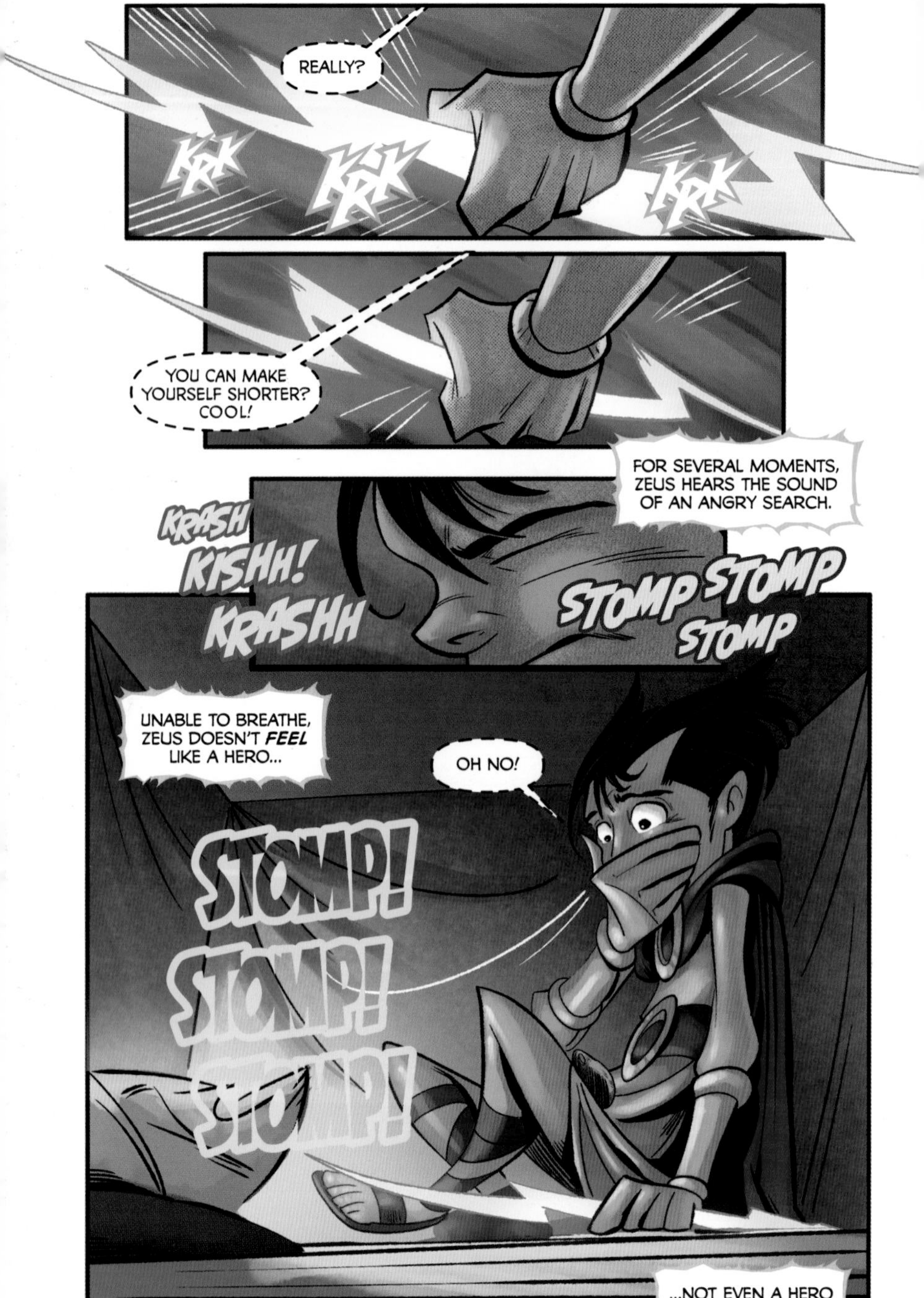
REALLY?
KRK
KRK
KRK
YOU CAN MAKE YOURSELF SHORTER? COOL!
FOR SEVERAL MOMENTS, ZEUS HEARS THE SOUND OF AN ANGRY SEARCH.
KRASH
KISHH!
KRASHH
STOMP STOMP
STOMP
UNABLE TO BREATHE, ZEUS DOESN'T *FEEL* LIKE A HERO...
OH NO!
STOMP!
STOMP!
STOMP!
...NOT EVEN A HERO IN ***TRAINING!***

CHAPTER EIGHT:
THE BIG, BAD BULLY KING

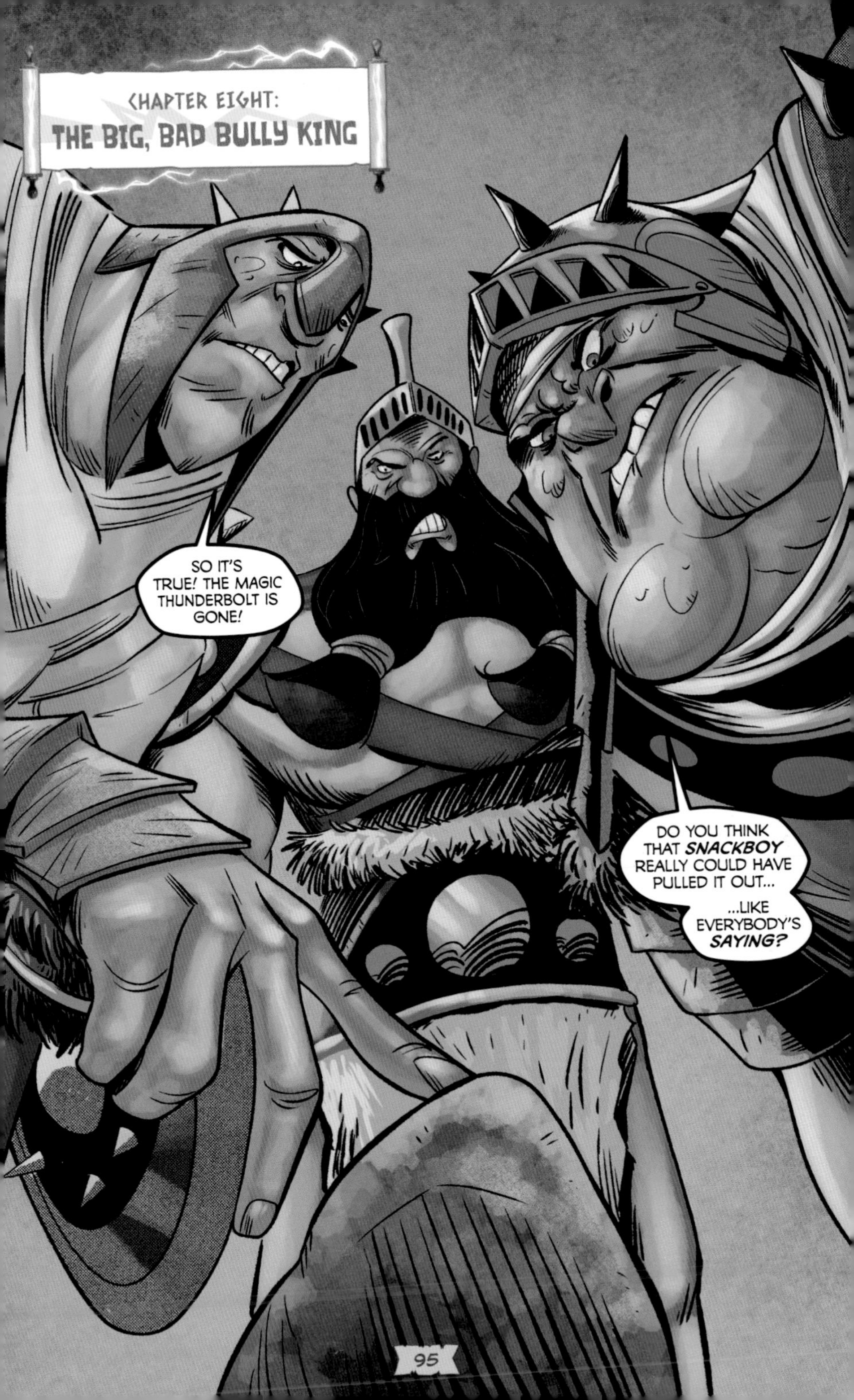
SO IT'S TRUE! THE MAGIC THUNDERBOLT IS GONE!
DO YOU THINK THAT ***SNACKBOY*** REALLY COULD HAVE PULLED IT OUT...
...LIKE EVERYBODY'S ***SAYING?***

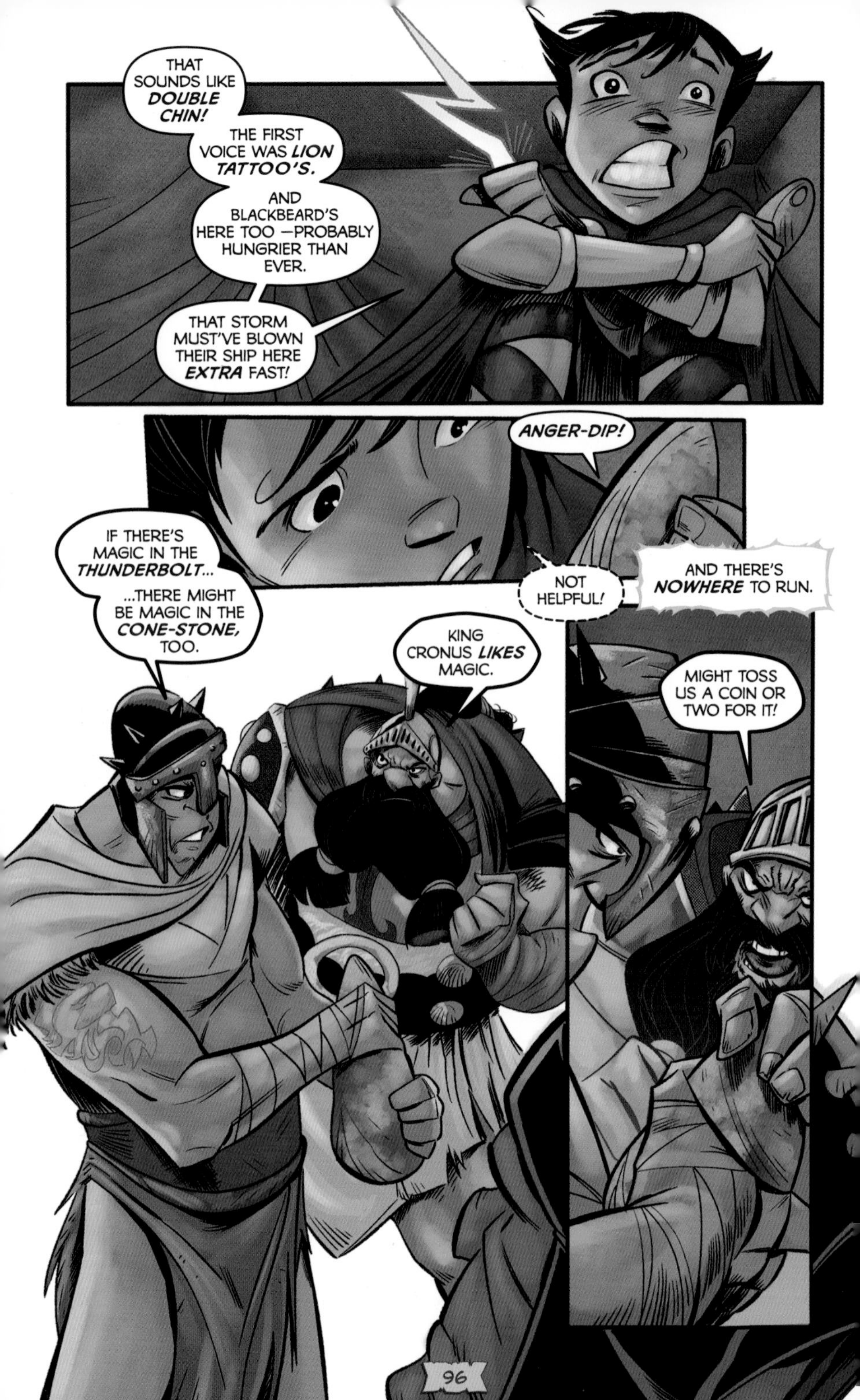

THAT SOUNDS LIKE ***DOUBLE CHIN!***
THE FIRST VOICE WAS ***LION TATTOO'S.***
AND BLACKBEARD'S HERE TOO —PROBABLY HUNGRIER THAN EVER.
THAT STORM MUST'VE BLOWN THEIR SHIP HERE ***EXTRA*** FAST!
ANGER-DIP!
IF THERE'S MAGIC IN THE ***THUNDERBOLT...***
...THERE MIGHT BE MAGIC IN THE ***CONE-STONE,*** TOO.
KING CRONUS ***LIKES*** MAGIC.
NOT HELPFUL!
AND THERE'S ***NOWHERE*** TO RUN.
MIGHT TOSS US A COIN OR TWO FOR IT!

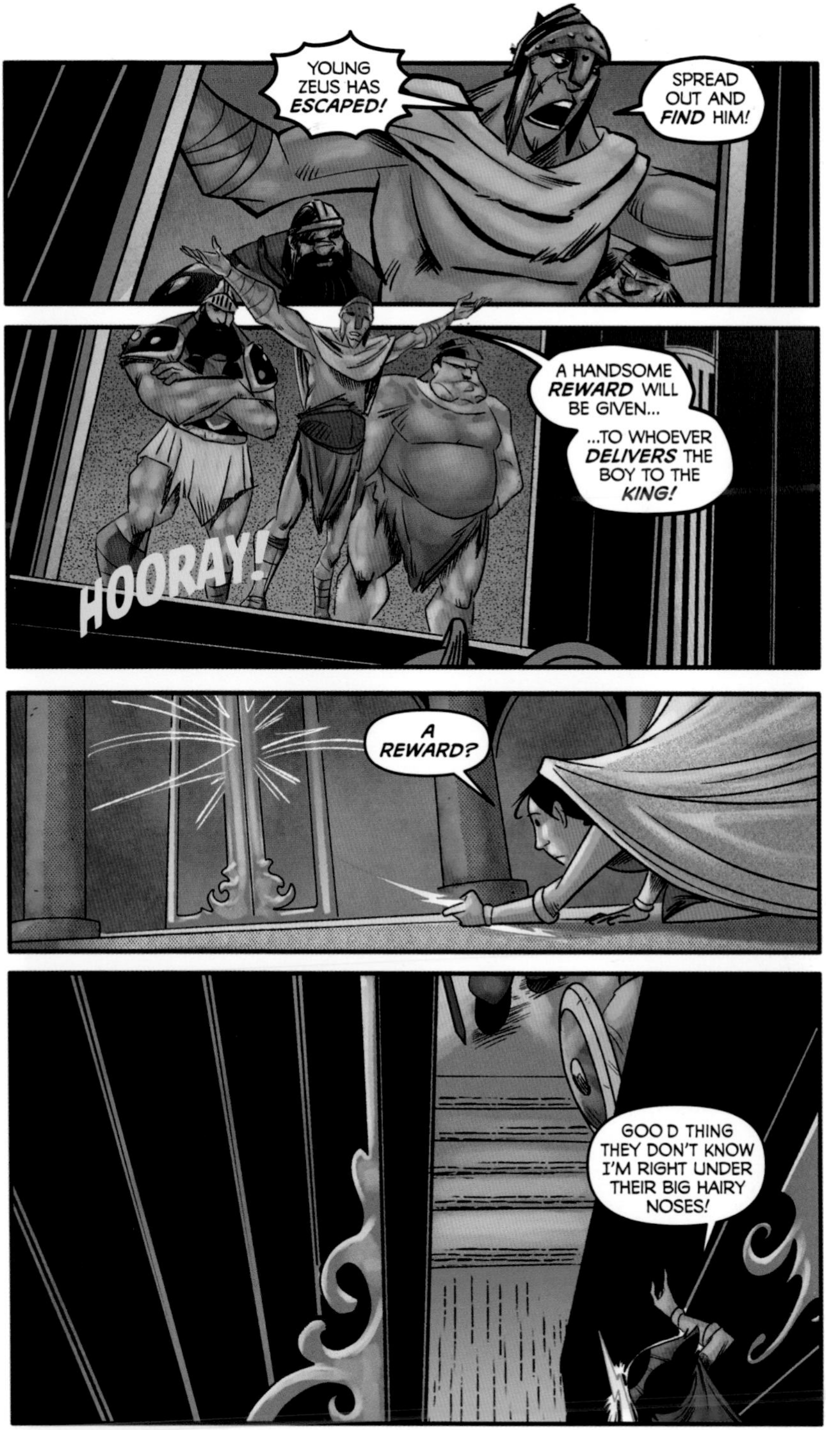
YOUNG ZEUS HAS *ESCAPED!*
SPREAD OUT AND *FIND* HIM!
A HANDSOME *REWARD* WILL BE GIVEN...
...TO WHOEVER *DELIVERS* THE BOY TO THE *KING!*
HOORAY!
A REWARD?
GOO D THING THEY DON'T KNOW I'M RIGHT UNDER THEIR BIG HAIRY NOSES!

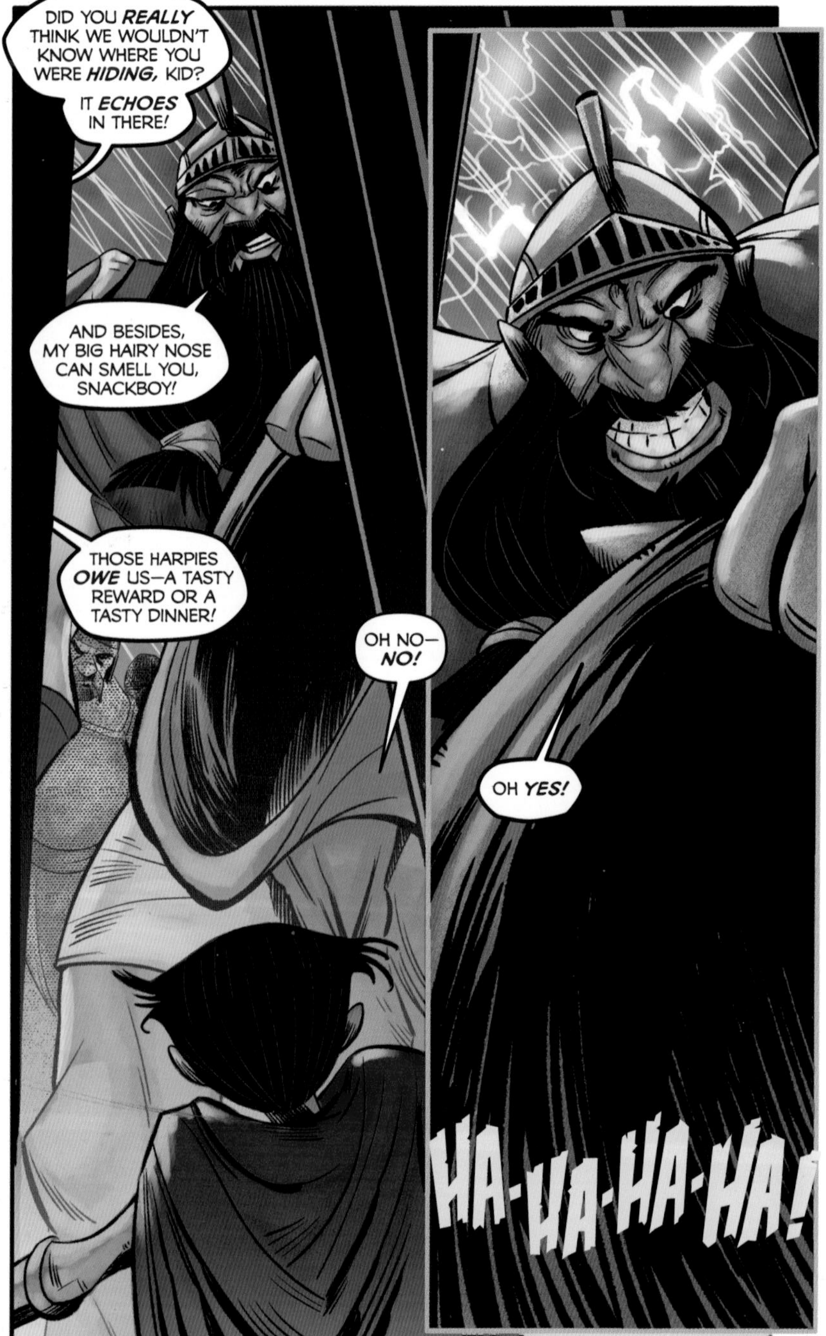
DID YOU *REALLY* THINK WE WOULDN'T KNOW WHERE YOU WERE *HIDING,* KID?
IT *ECHOES* IN THERE!
AND BESIDES, MY BIG HAIRY NOSE CAN SMELL YOU, SNACKBOY!
THOSE HARPIES *OWE* US—A TASTY REWARD OR A TASTY DINNER!
OH NO— *NO!*
OH *YES!*
HA-HA-HA-HA!

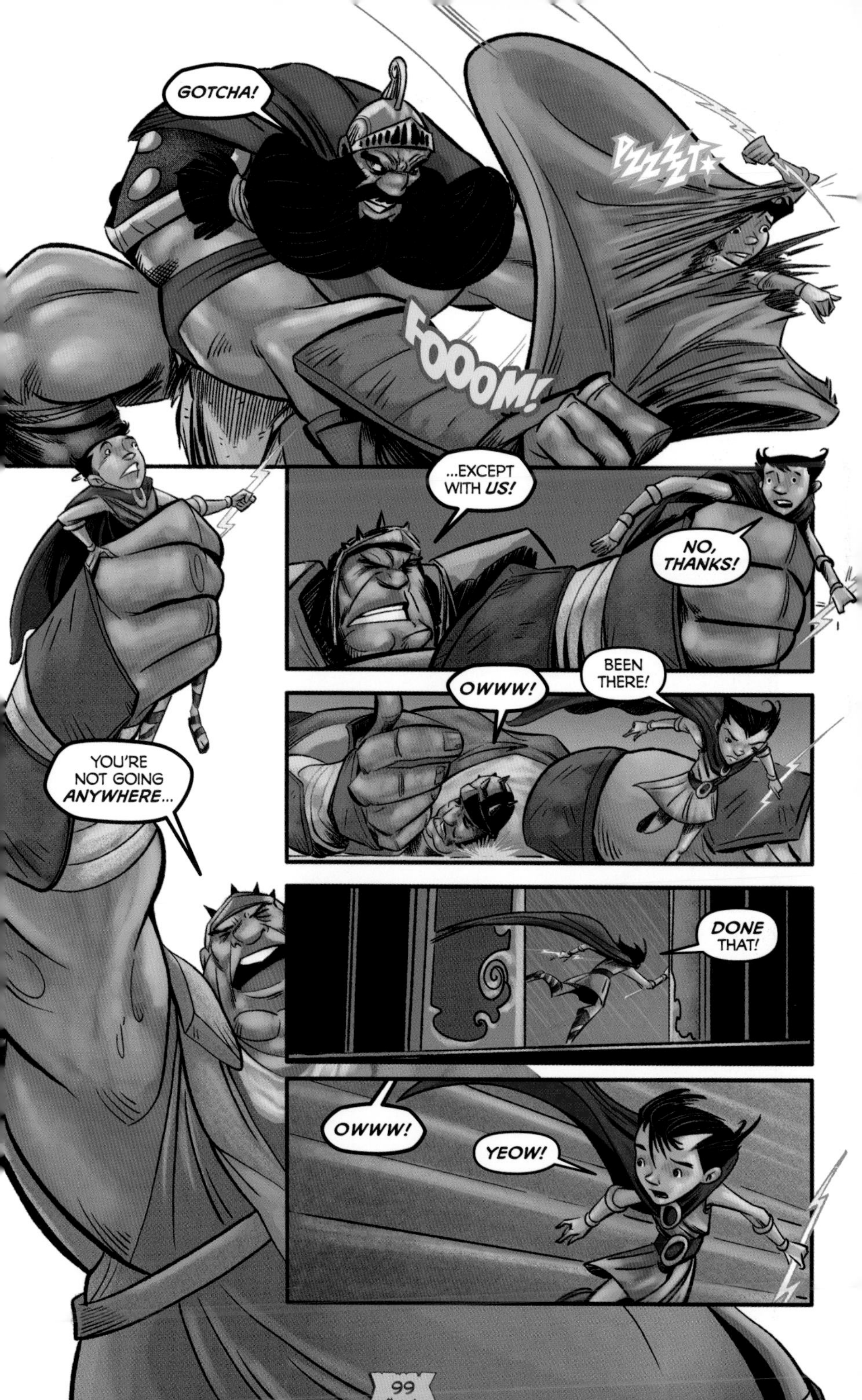
GOTCHA!
PZZZZT
FOOOM!
YOU'RE NOT GOING ANYWHERE...
...EXCEPT WITH US!
NO, THANKS!
OWWW!
BEEN THERE!
DONE THAT!
OWWW!
YEOW!

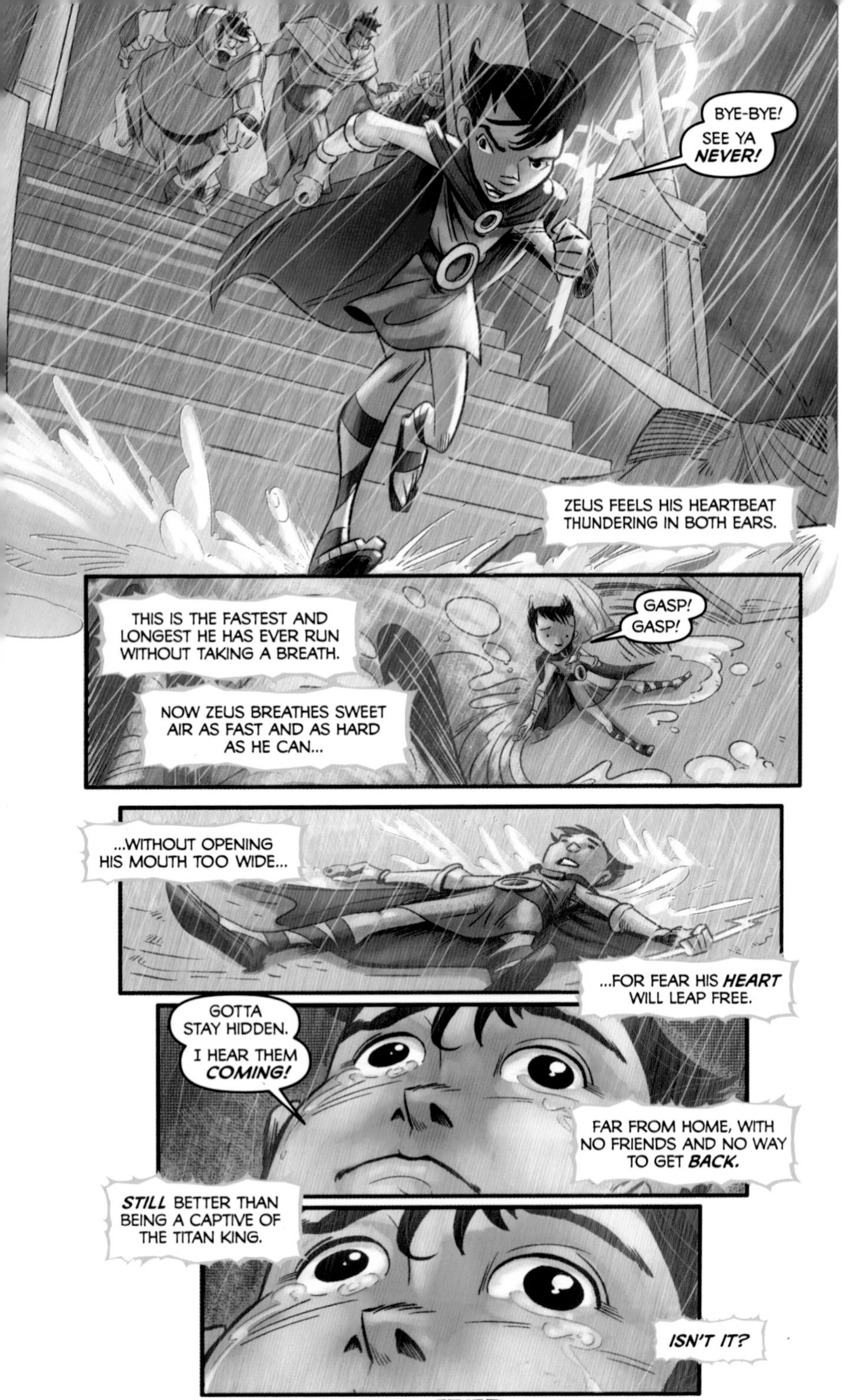
BYE-BYE! SEE YA NEVER!
ZEUS FEELS HIS HEARTBEAT THUNDERING IN BOTH EARS.
THIS IS THE FASTEST AND LONGEST HE HAS EVER RUN WITHOUT TAKING A BREATH.
GASP! GASP!
NOW ZEUS BREATHES SWEET AIR AS FAST AND AS HARD AS HE CAN...
...WITHOUT OPENING HIS MOUTH TOO WIDE...
...FOR FEAR HIS HEART WILL LEAP FREE.
GOTTA STAY HIDDEN.
I HEAR THEM COMING!
FAR FROM HOME, WITH NO FRIENDS AND NO WAY TO GET BACK.
STILL BETTER THAN BEING A CAPTIVE OF THE TITAN KING.
ISN'T IT?

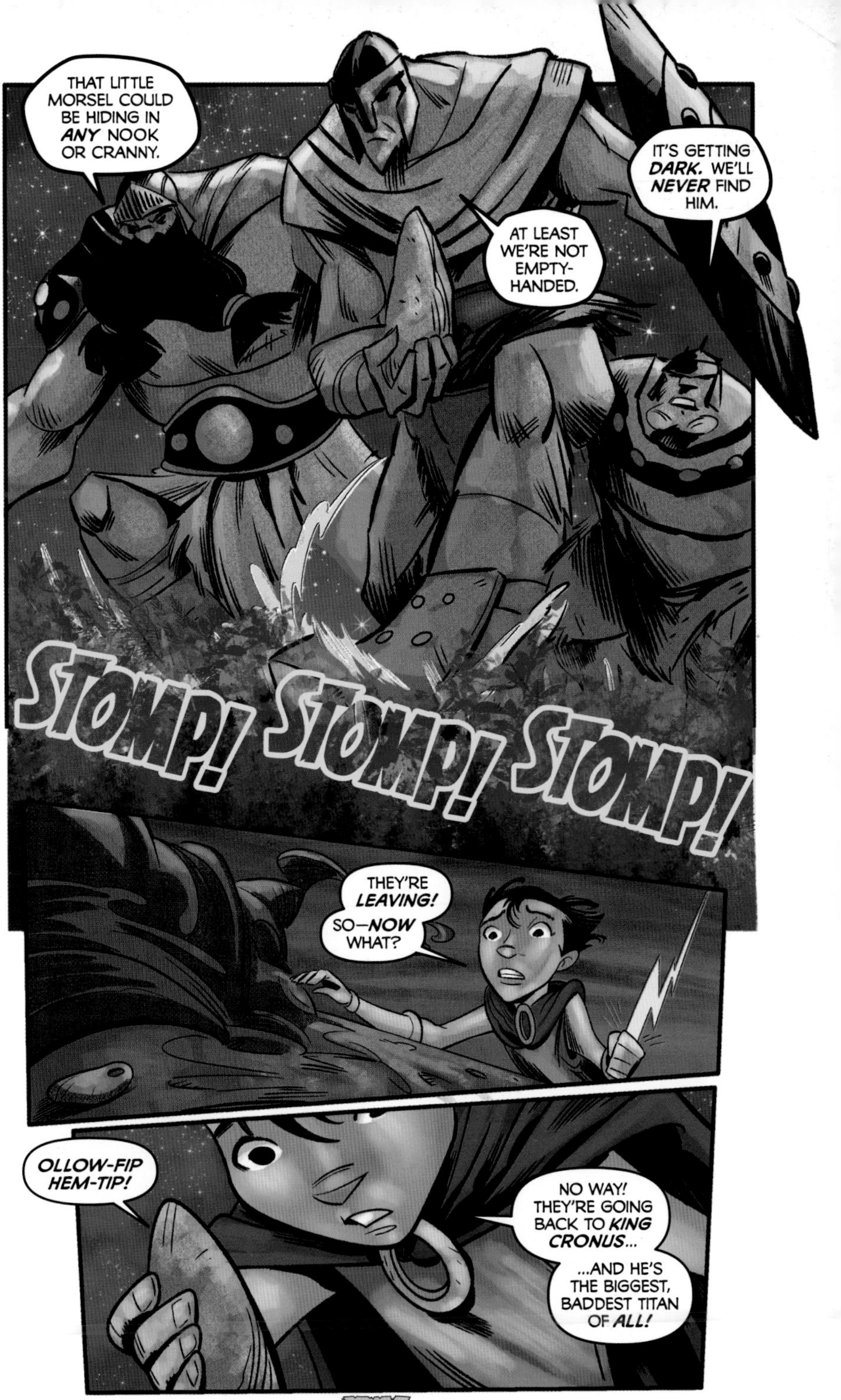
THAT LITTLE MORSEL COULD BE HIDING IN ANY NOOK OR CRANNY.
AT LEAST WE'RE NOT EMPTY-HANDED.
IT'S GETTING DARK. WE'LL NEVER FIND HIM.
STOMP! STOMP! STOMP!
THEY'RE LEAVING! SO—NOW WHAT?
OLLOW-FIP HEM-TIP!
NO WAY! THEY'RE GOING BACK TO KING CRONUS...
...AND HE'S THE BIGGEST, BADDEST TITAN OF ALL!

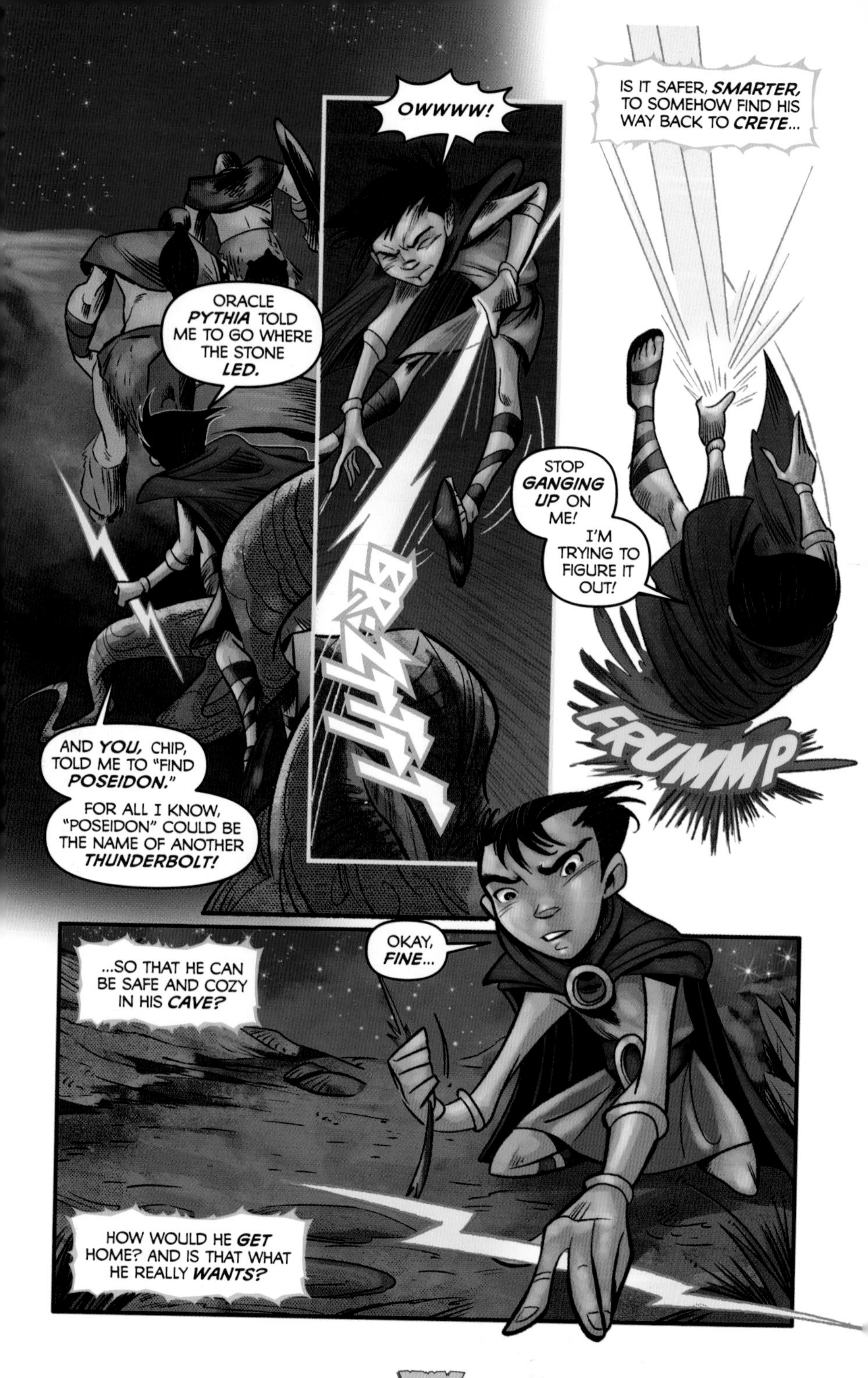
ORACLE PYTHIA TOLD ME TO GO WHERE THE STONE LED.
AND YOU, CHIP, TOLD ME TO "FIND POSEIDON."
FOR ALL I KNOW, "POSEIDON" COULD BE THE NAME OF ANOTHER THUNDERBOLT!
OWWWW!
IS IT SAFER, SMARTER, TO SOMEHOW FIND HIS WAY BACK TO CRETE...
STOP GANGING UP ON ME!
I'M TRYING TO FIGURE IT OUT!
FRUMMP
...SO THAT HE CAN BE SAFE AND COZY IN HIS CAVE?
OKAY, FINE...
HOW WOULD HE GET HOME? AND IS THAT WHAT HE REALLY WANTS?

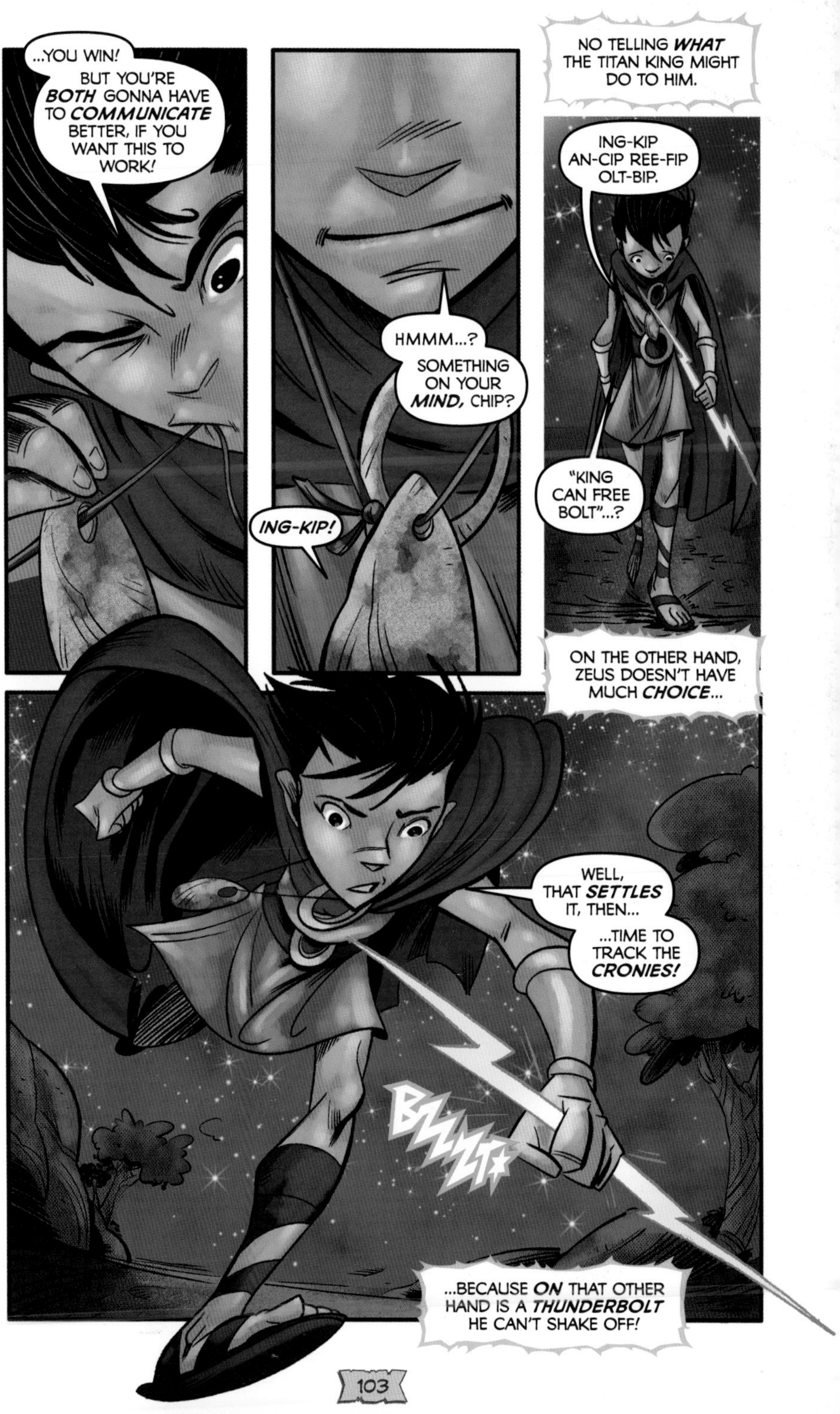

...YOU WIN! BUT YOU'RE BOTH GONNA HAVE TO COMMUNICATE BETTER, IF YOU WANT THIS TO WORK!
HMMM...? SOMETHING ON YOUR MIND, CHIP?
ING-KIP!
NO TELLING WHAT THE TITAN KING MIGHT DO TO HIM.
ING-KIP AN-CIP REE-FIP OLT-BIP.
"KING CAN FREE BOLT"...?
ON THE OTHER HAND, ZEUS DOESN'T HAVE MUCH CHOICE...
WELL, THAT SETTLES IT, THEN...
...TIME TO TRACK THE CRONIES!
BZZZT
...BECAUSE ON THAT OTHER HAND IS A THUNDERBOLT HE CAN'T SHAKE OFF!

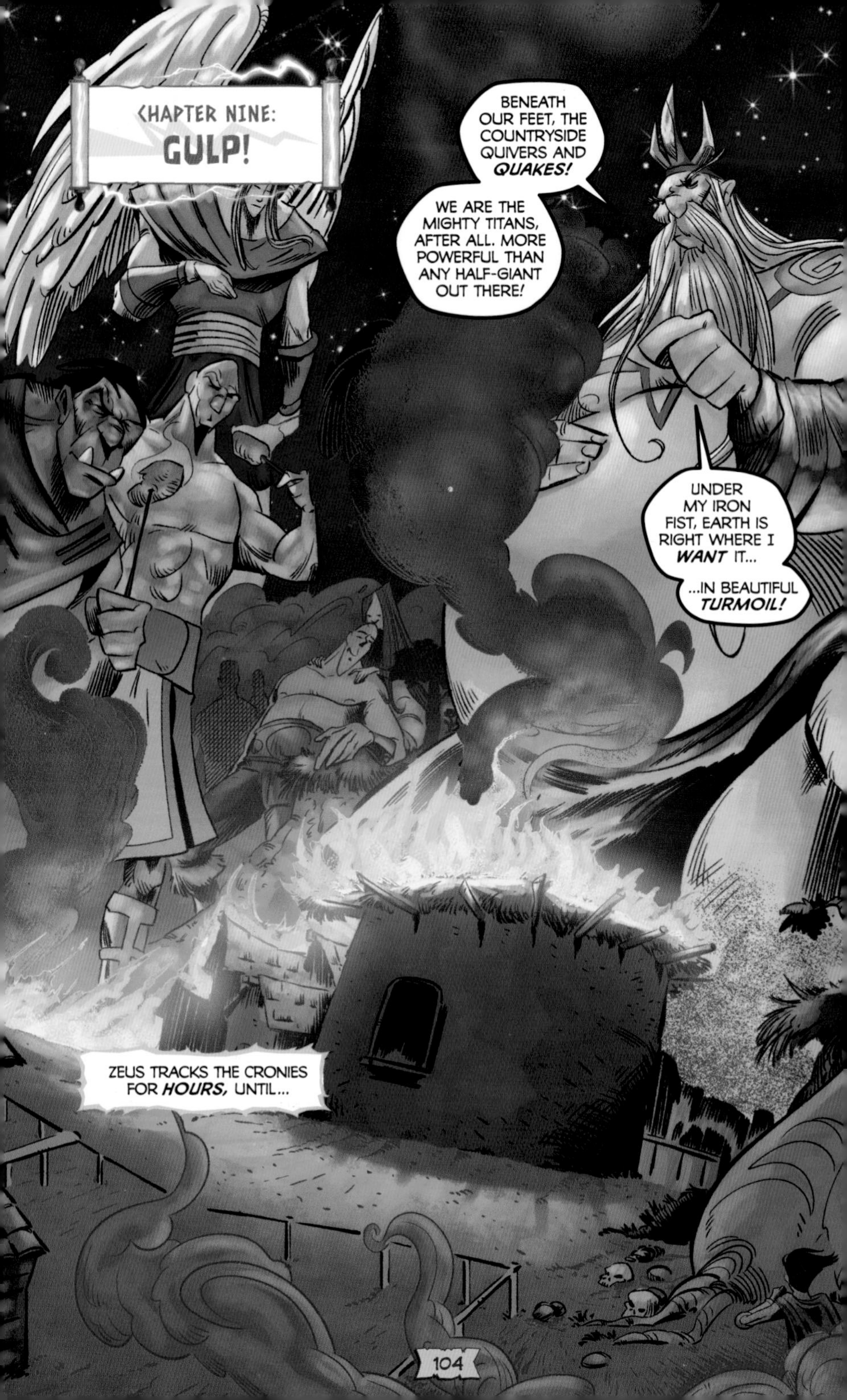
CHAPTER NINE:
GULP!
BENEATH OUR FEET, THE COUNTRYSIDE QUIVERS AND QUAKES!
WE ARE THE MIGHTY TITANS, AFTER ALL. MORE POWERFUL THAN ANY HALF-GIANT OUT THERE!
UNDER MY IRON FIST, EARTH IS RIGHT WHERE I WANT IT...
...IN BEAUTIFUL TURMOIL!
ZEUS TRACKS THE CRONIES FOR HOURS, UNTIL...

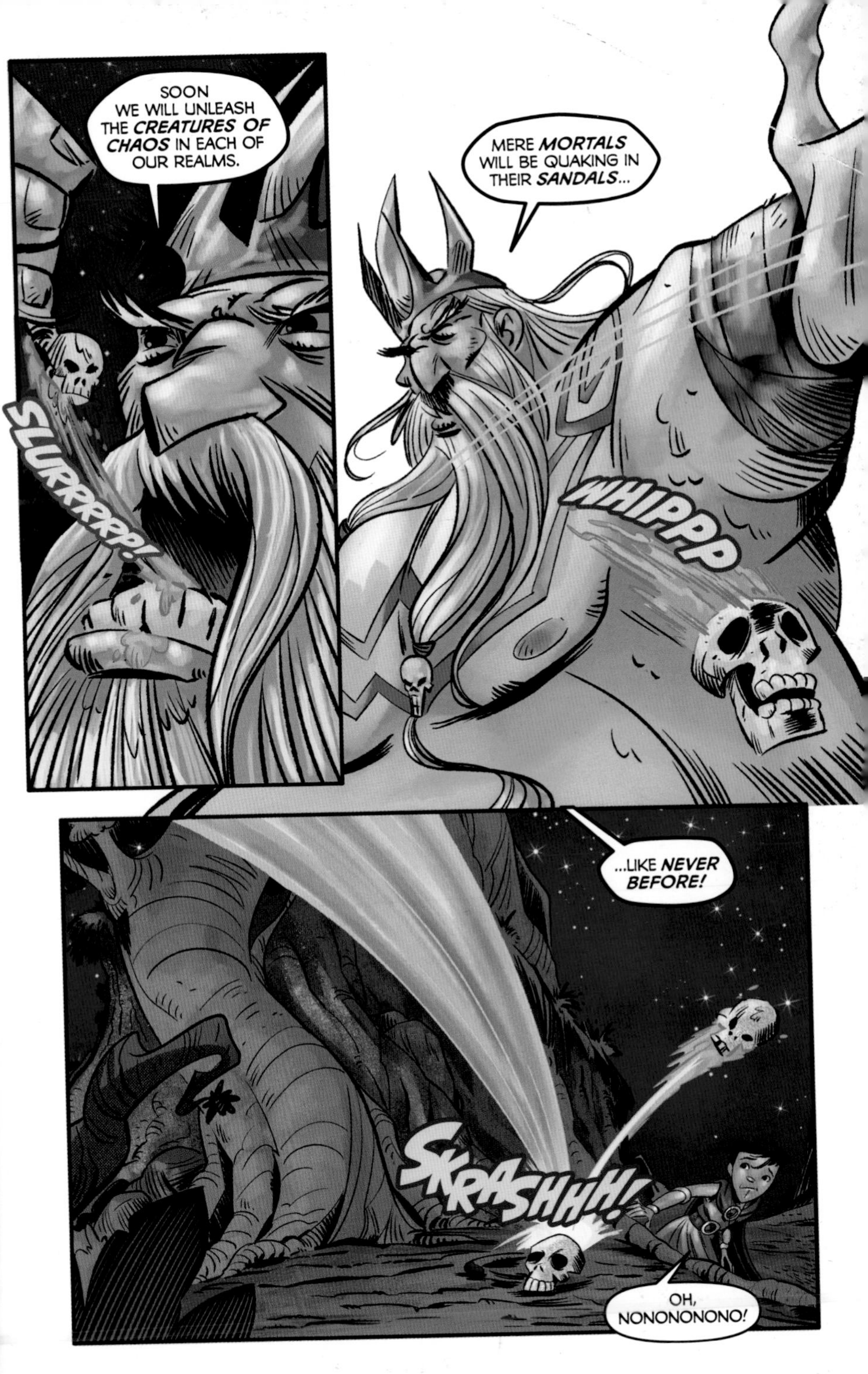
SOON WE WILL UNLEASH THE CREATURES OF CHAOS IN EACH OF OUR REALMS.
SLURRRRP!
MERE MORTALS WILL BE QUAKING IN THEIR SANDALS...
WHIPPP
...LIKE NEVER BEFORE!
SKRASHHH!
OH, NONONONONO!

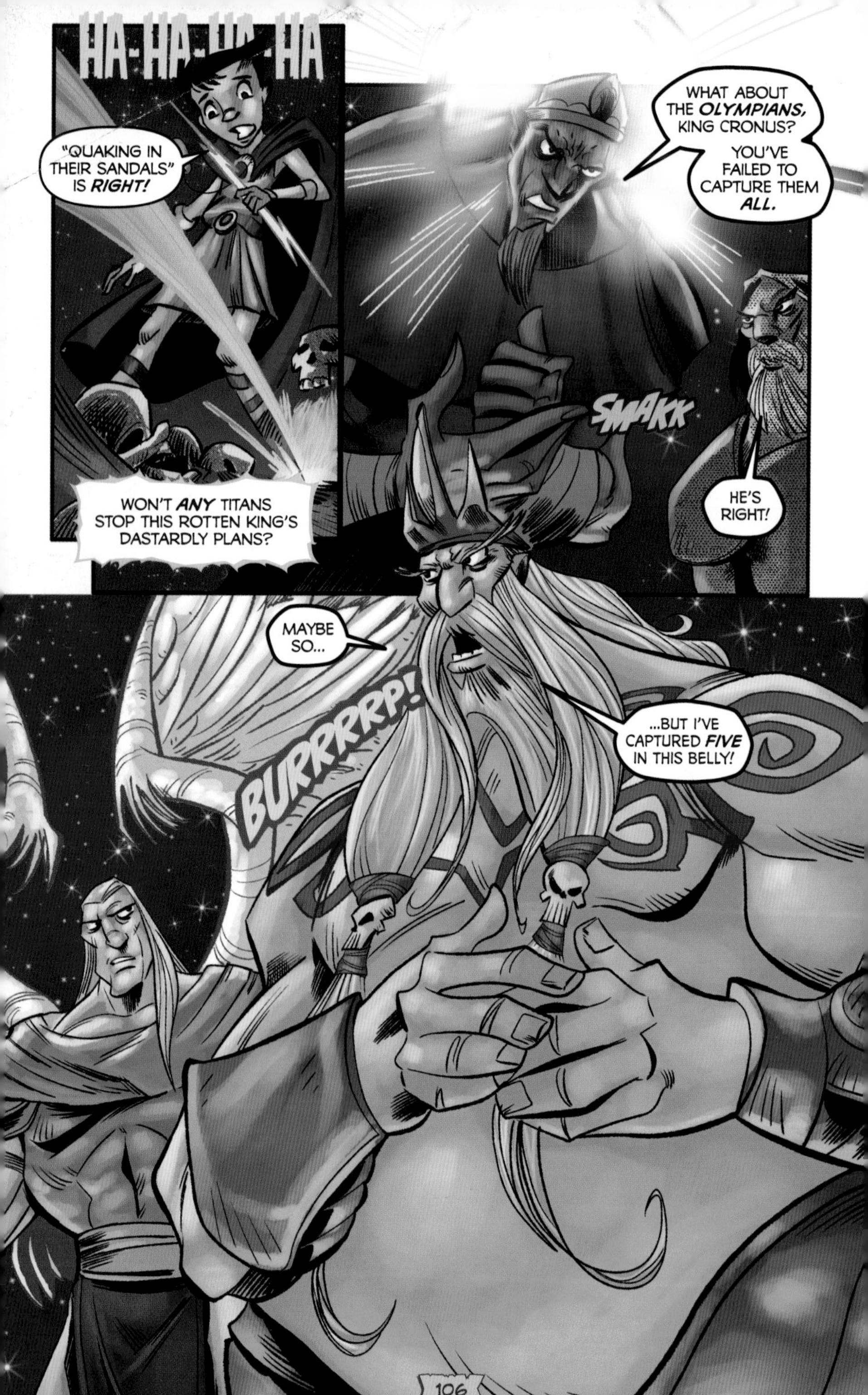
HA-HA-HA-HA
"QUAKING IN THEIR SANDALS" IS RIGHT!
WON'T ANY TITANS STOP THIS ROTTEN KING'S DASTARDLY PLANS?
WHAT ABOUT THE OLYMPIANS, KING CRONUS?
YOU'VE FAILED TO CAPTURE THEM ALL.
SMAKK
HE'S RIGHT!
MAYBE SO...
BURRRRP!
...BUT I'VE CAPTURED FIVE IN THIS BELLY!

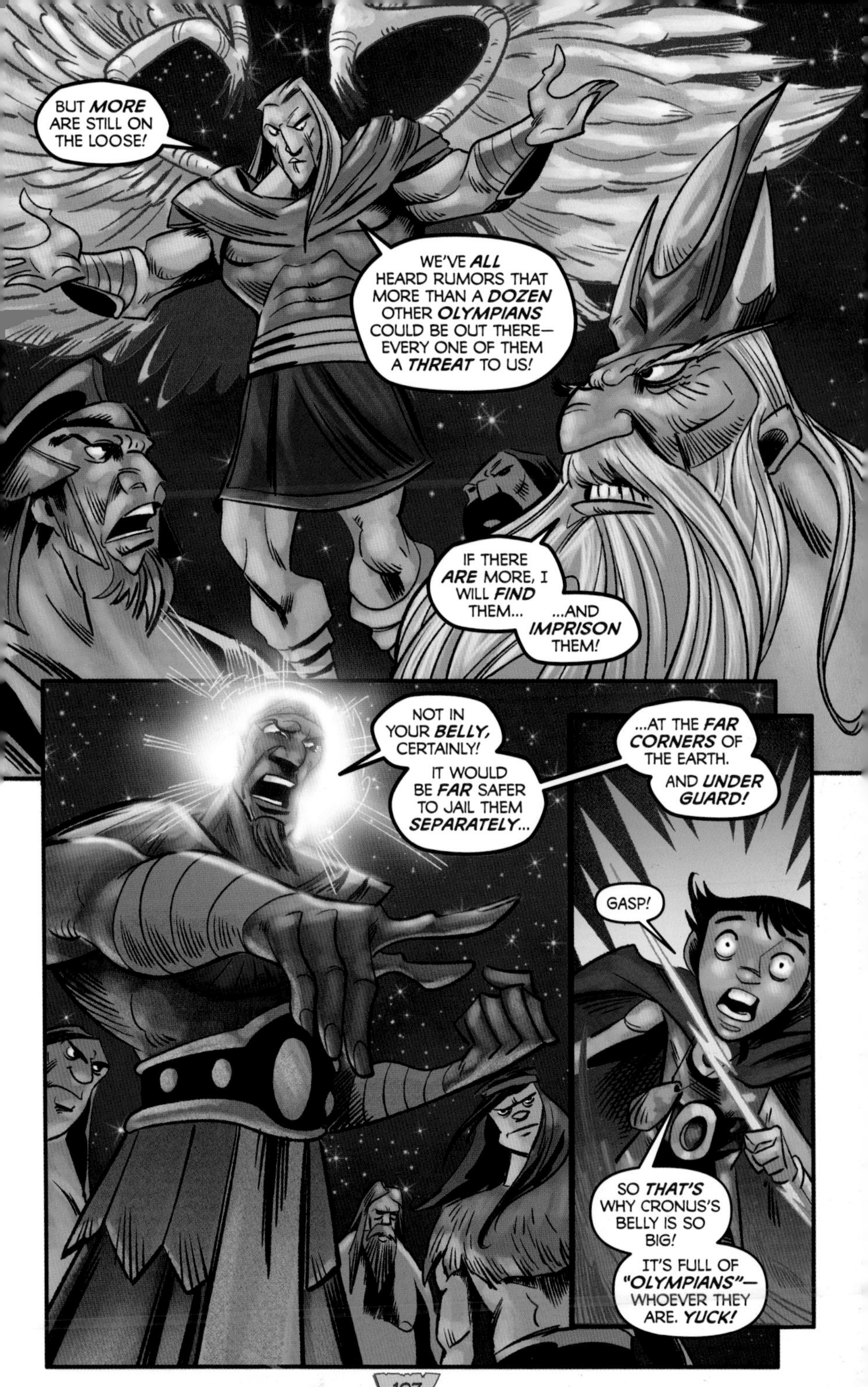
BUT MORE ARE STILL ON THE LOOSE!
WE'VE ALL HEARD RUMORS THAT MORE THAN A DOZEN OTHER OLYMPIANS COULD BE OUT THERE— EVERY ONE OF THEM A THREAT TO US!
IF THERE ARE MORE, I WILL FIND THEM...
...AND IMPRISON THEM!
NOT IN YOUR BELLY, CERTAINLY!
IT WOULD BE FAR SAFER TO JAIL THEM SEPARATELY...
...AT THE FAR CORNERS OF THE EARTH.
AND UNDER GUARD!
GASP!
SO THAT'S WHY CRONUS'S BELLY IS SO BIG!
IT'S FULL OF "OLYMPIANS"— WHOEVER THEY ARE. YUCK!

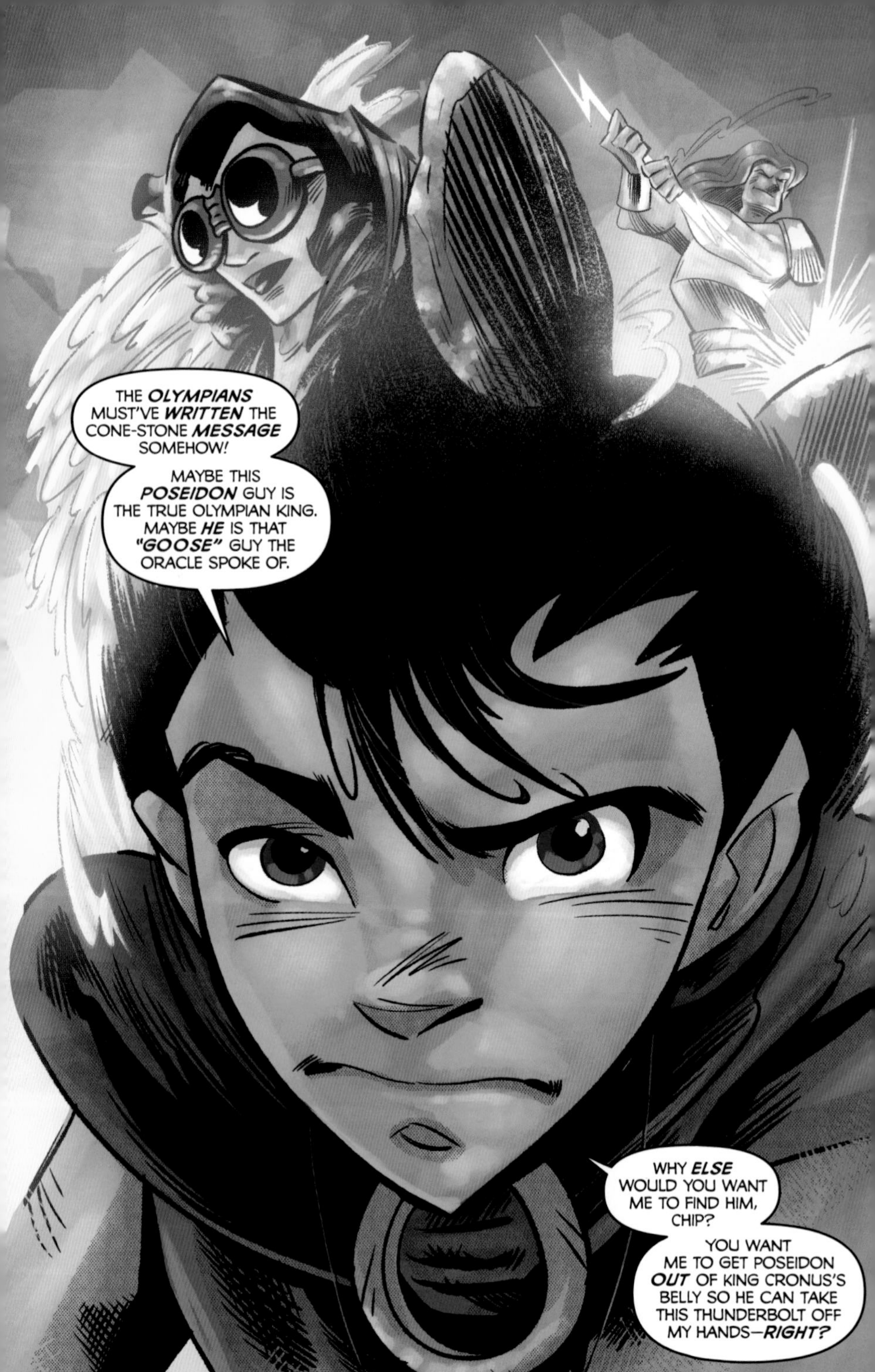
THE *OLYMPIANS* MUST'VE *WRITTEN* THE CONE-STONE *MESSAGE* SOMEHOW!
MAYBE THIS *POSEIDON* GUY IS THE TRUE OLYMPIAN KING. MAYBE *HE* IS THAT *"GOOSE"* GUY THE ORACLE SPOKE OF.
WHY *ELSE* WOULD YOU WANT ME TO FIND HIM, CHIP?
YOU WANT ME TO GET POSEIDON *OUT* OF KING CRONUS'S BELLY SO HE CAN TAKE THIS THUNDERBOLT OFF MY HANDS—*RIGHT?*

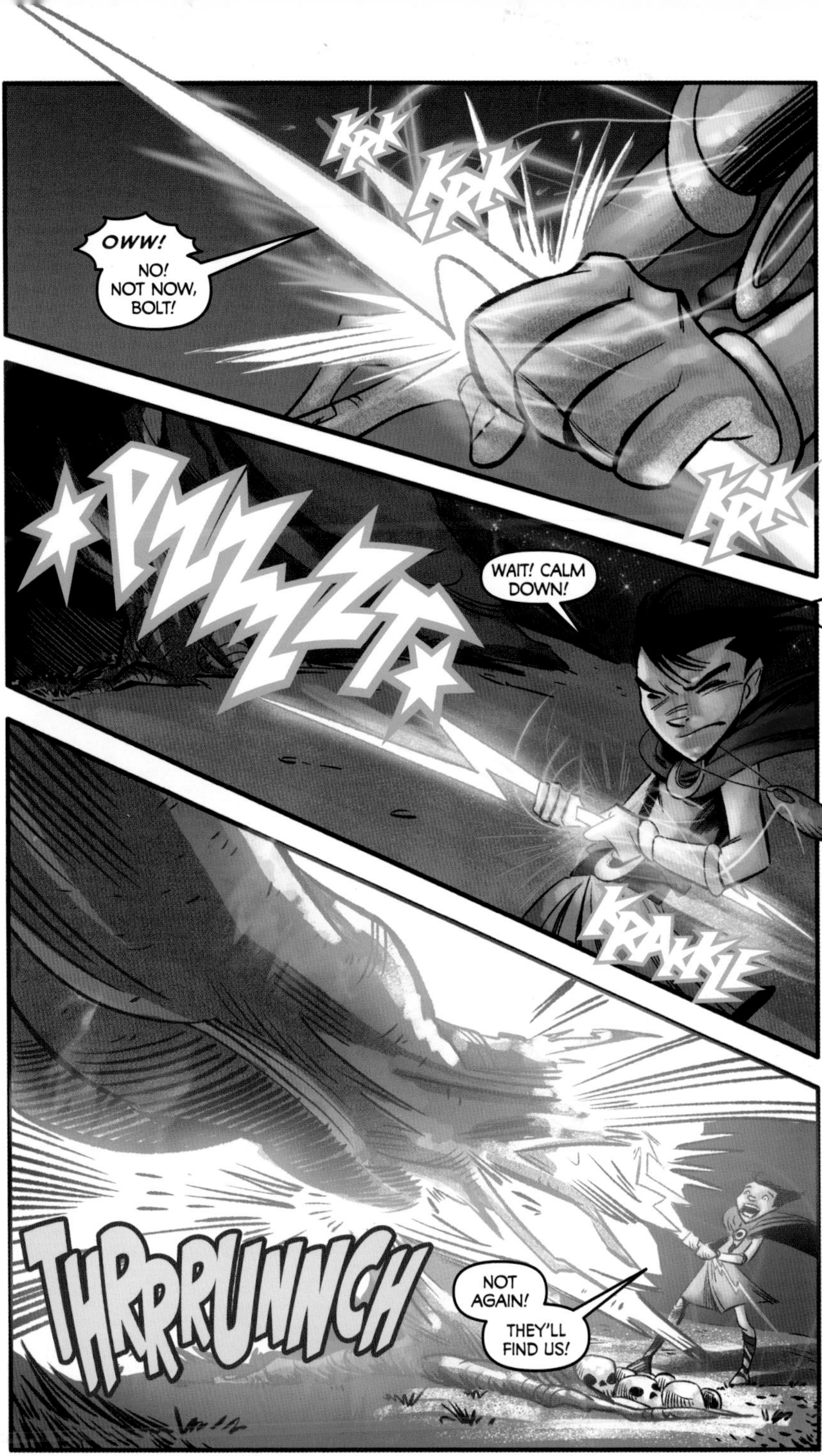
KRK
KRK
OWW!
NO! NOT NOW, BOLT!
KRK
PZZZZT
WAIT! CALM DOWN!
KRAKKLE
THRRUNNCH
NOT AGAIN!
THEY'LL FIND US!

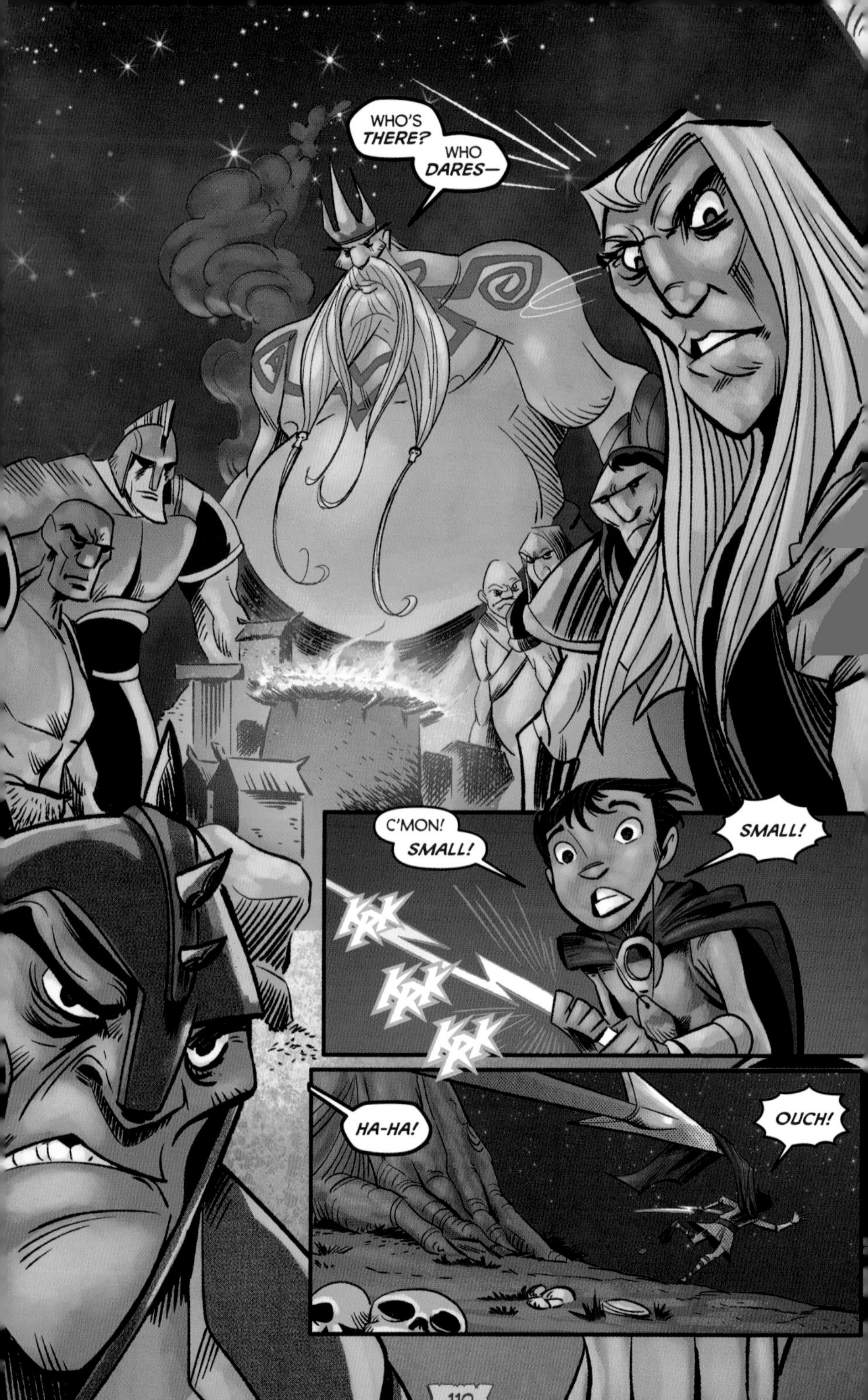
WHO'S THERE?
WHO DARES—
C'MON! SMALL!
SMALL!
KRK
KRK
KRK
HA-HA!
OUCH!

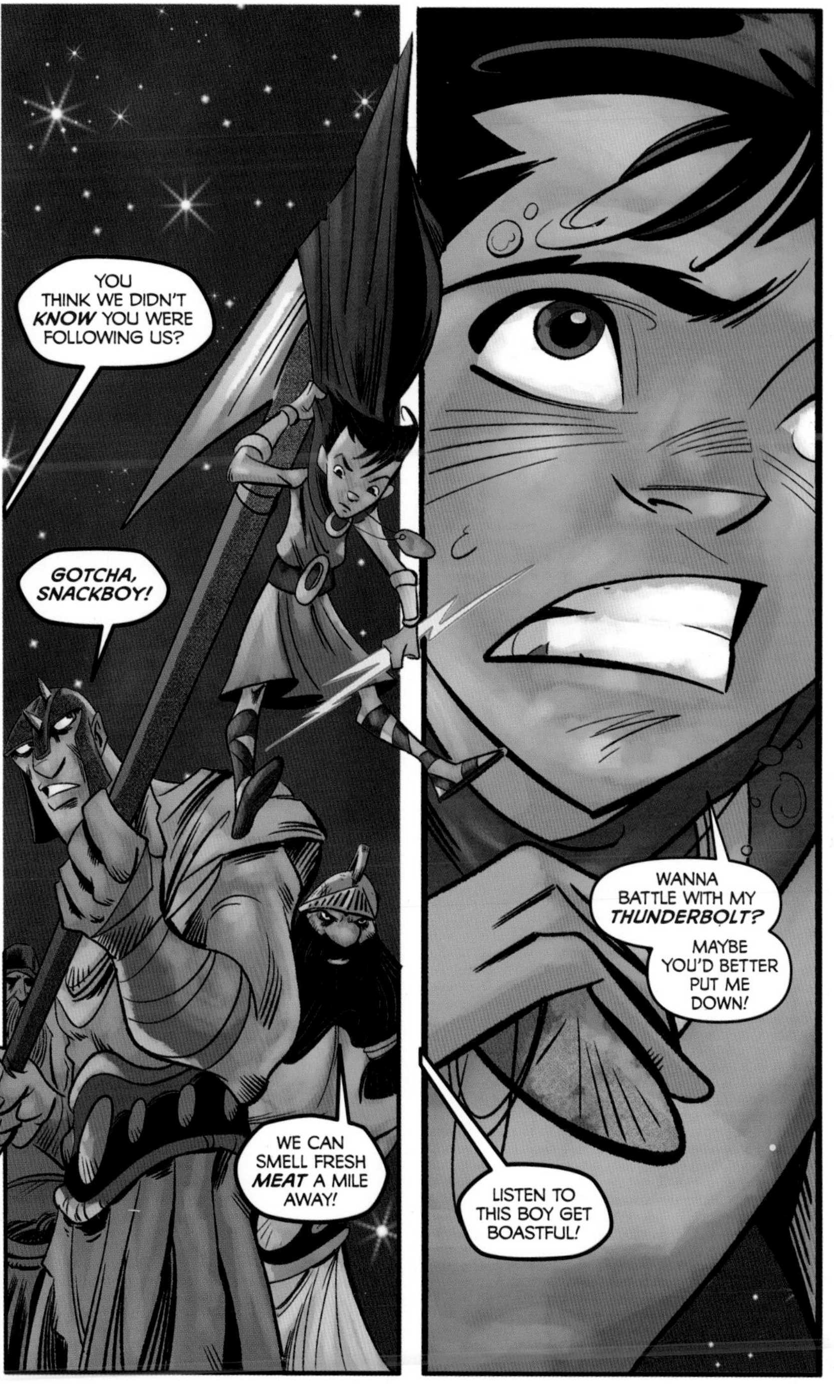
YOU THINK WE DIDN'T KNOW YOU WERE FOLLOWING US?
GOTCHA, SNACKBOY!
WE CAN SMELL FRESH MEAT A MILE AWAY!
WANNA BATTLE WITH MY THUNDERBOLT?
MAYBE YOU'D BETTER PUT ME DOWN!
LISTEN TO THIS BOY GET BOASTFUL!

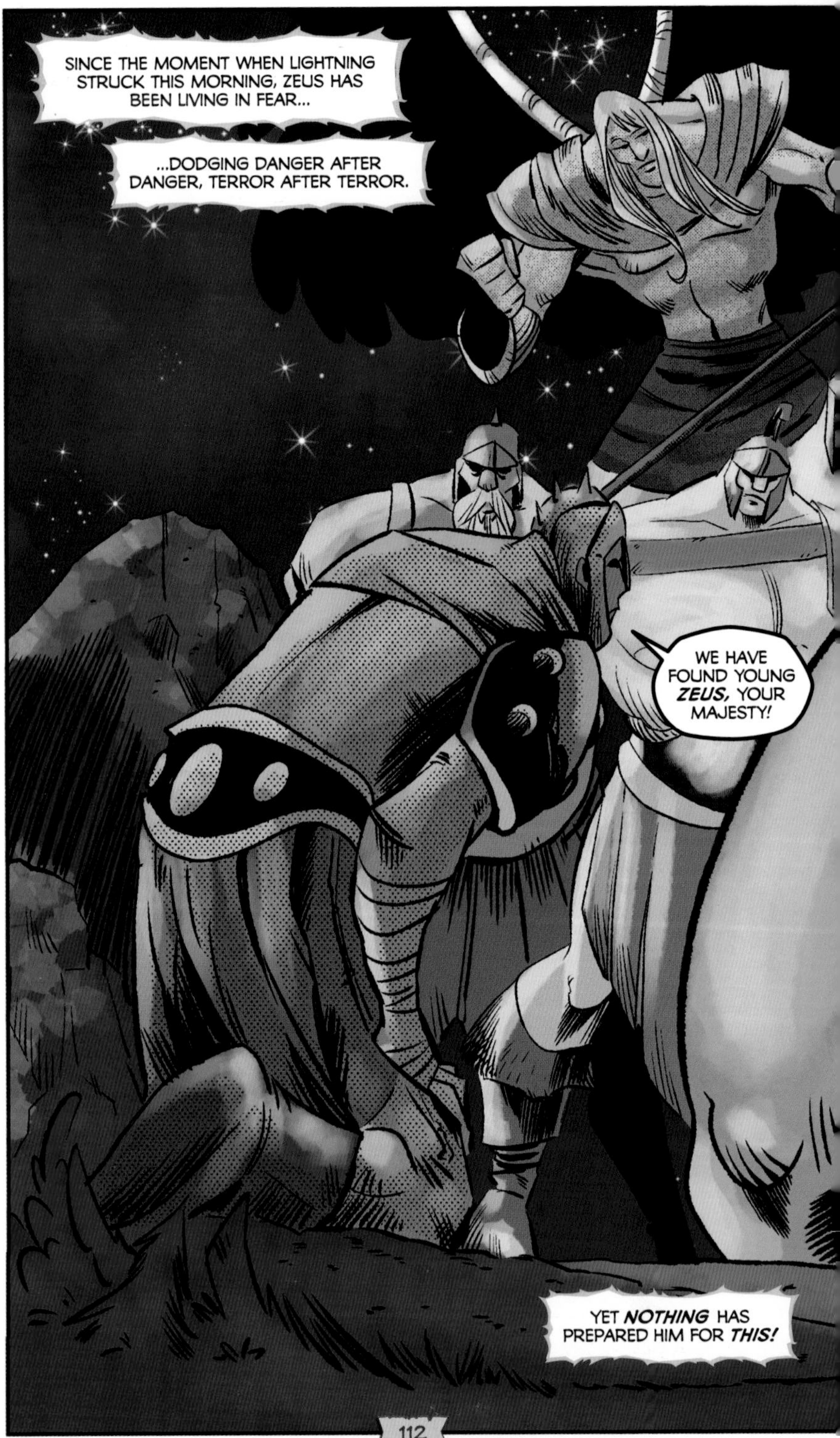
SINCE THE MOMENT WHEN LIGHTNING STRUCK THIS MORNING, ZEUS HAS BEEN LIVING IN FEAR...
...DODGING DANGER AFTER DANGER, TERROR AFTER TERROR.
WE HAVE FOUND YOUNG *ZEUS,* YOUR MAJESTY!
YET ***NOTHING*** HAS PREPARED HIM FOR ***THIS!***

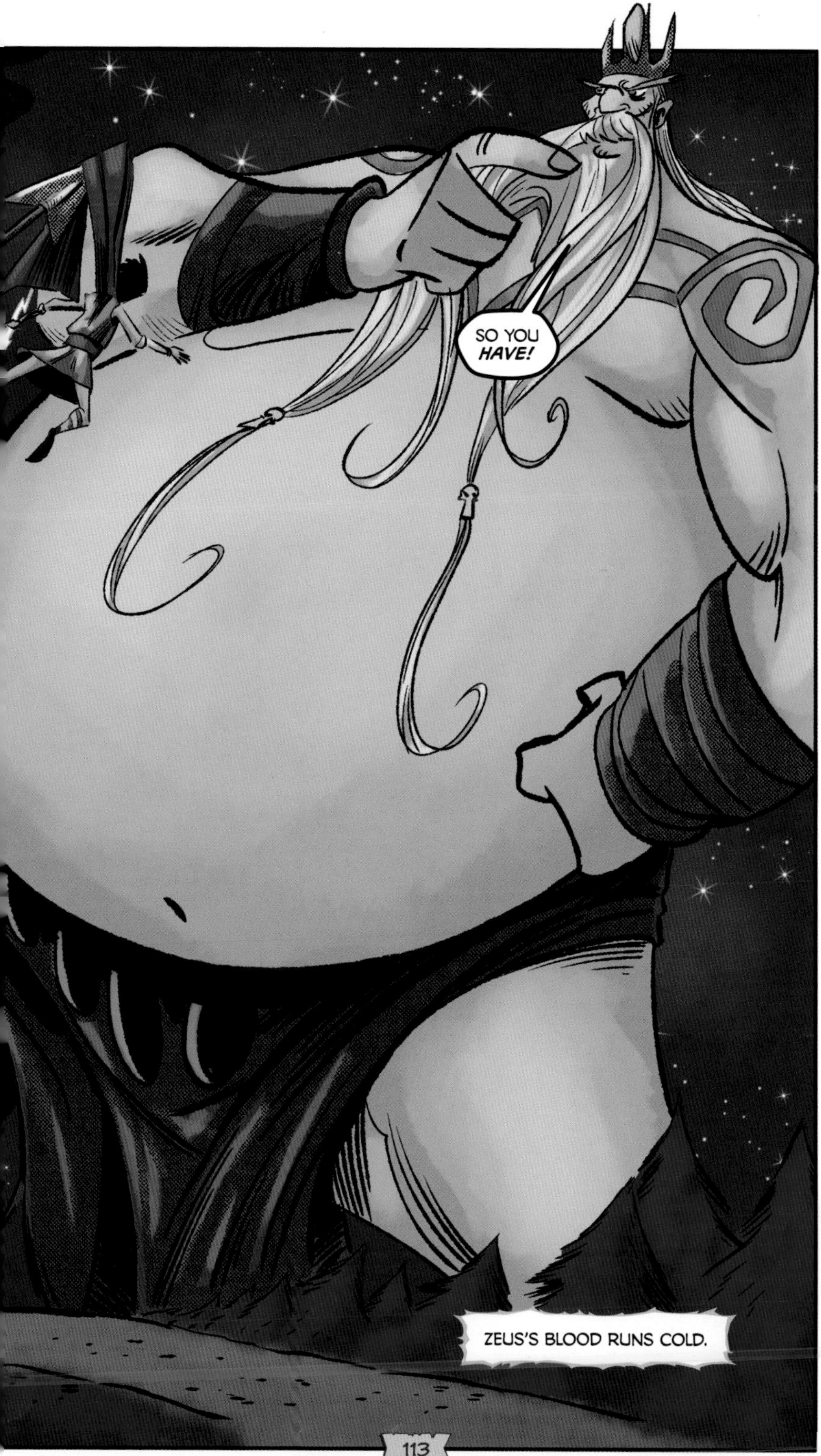
SO YOU HAVE!
ZEUS'S BLOOD RUNS COLD.

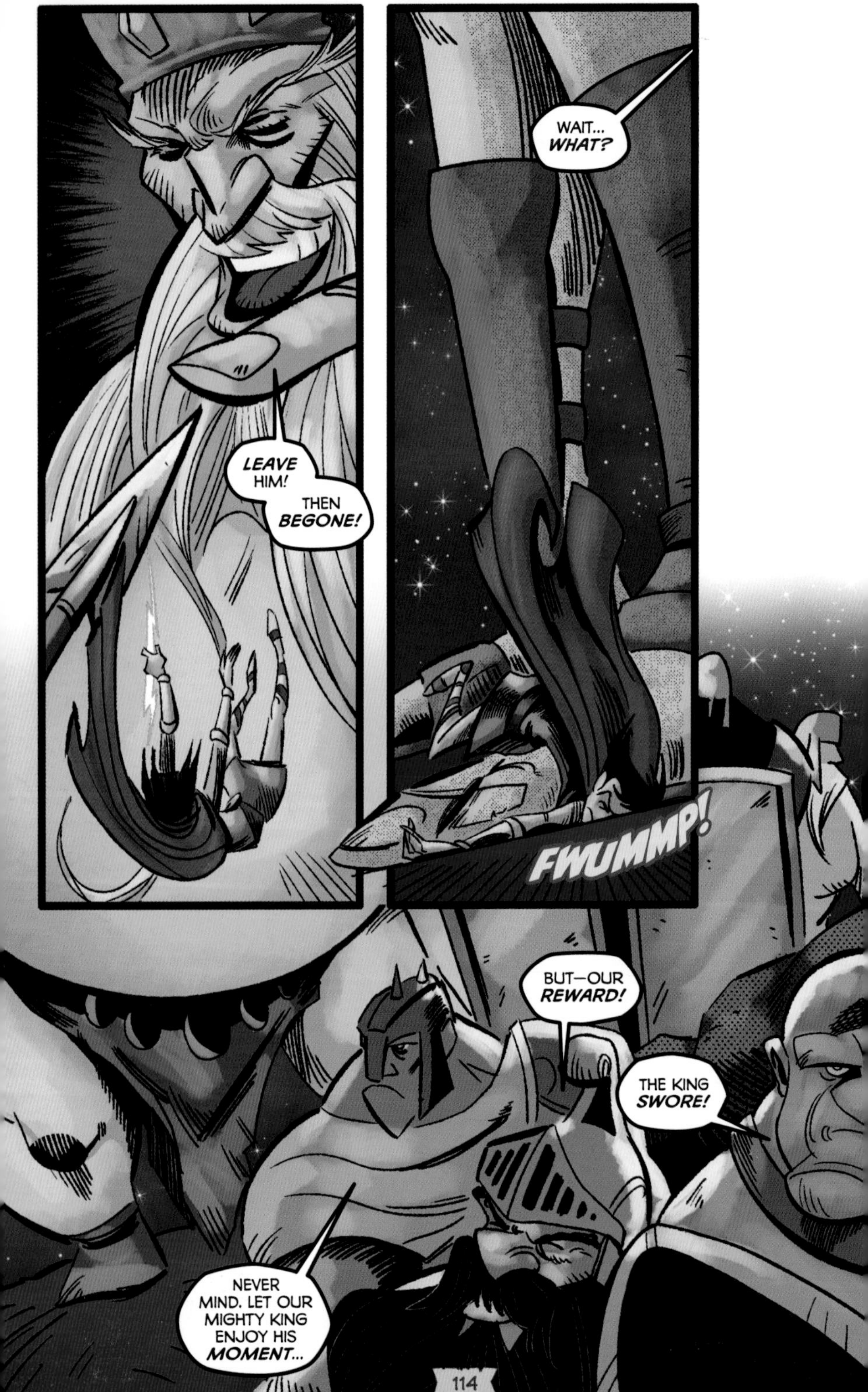
LEAVE HIM! THEN BEGONE!
WAIT... WHAT?
FWUMMP!
BUT—OUR REWARD!
THE KING SWORE!
NEVER MIND. LET OUR MIGHTY KING ENJOY HIS MOMENT...

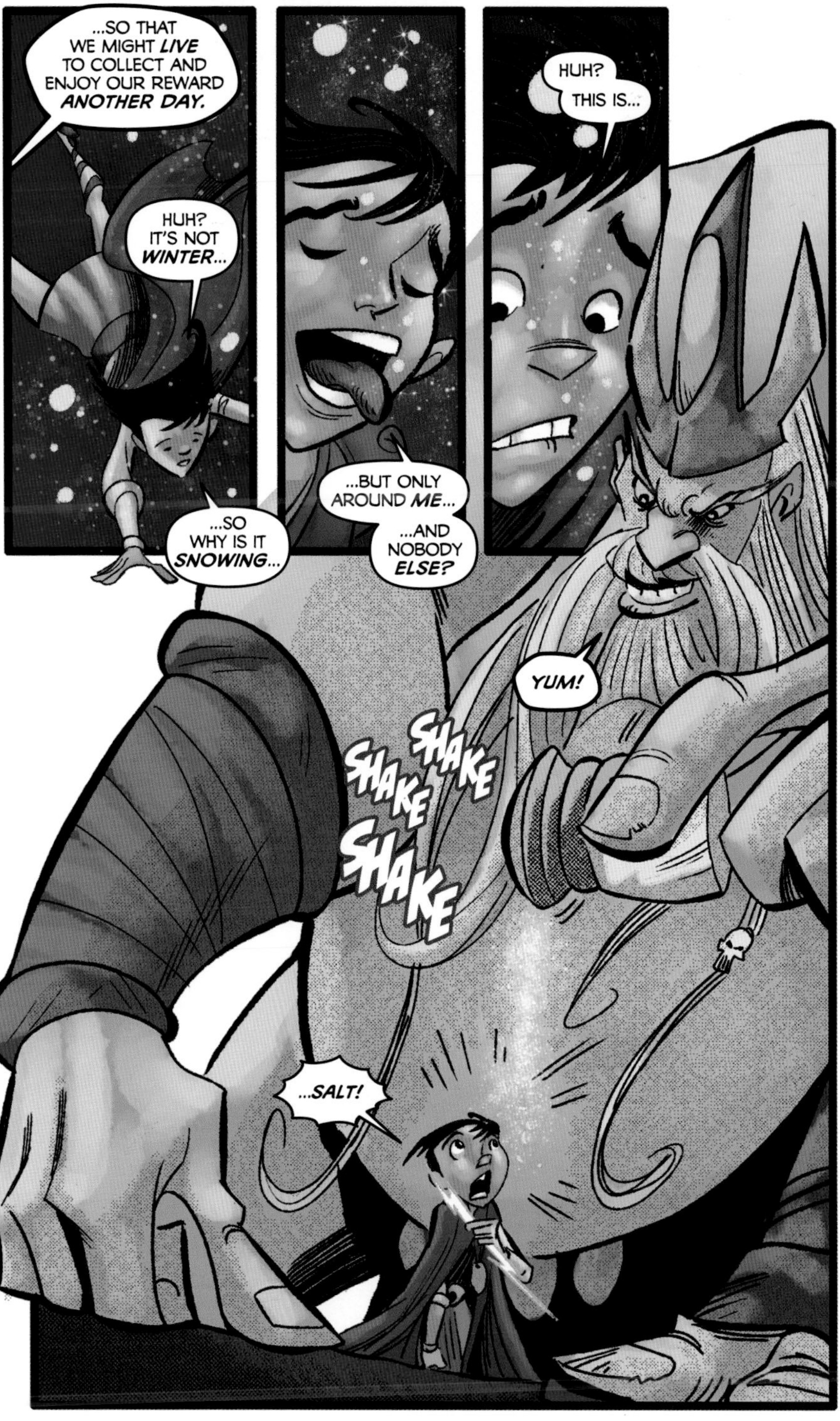
...SO THAT WE MIGHT LIVE TO COLLECT AND ENJOY OUR REWARD ANOTHER DAY.
HUH? IT'S NOT WINTER...
...SO WHY IS IT SNOWING...
...BUT ONLY AROUND ME...
...AND NOBODY ELSE?
HUH?
THIS IS...
YUM!
SHAKE
SHAKE
SHAKE
...SALT!

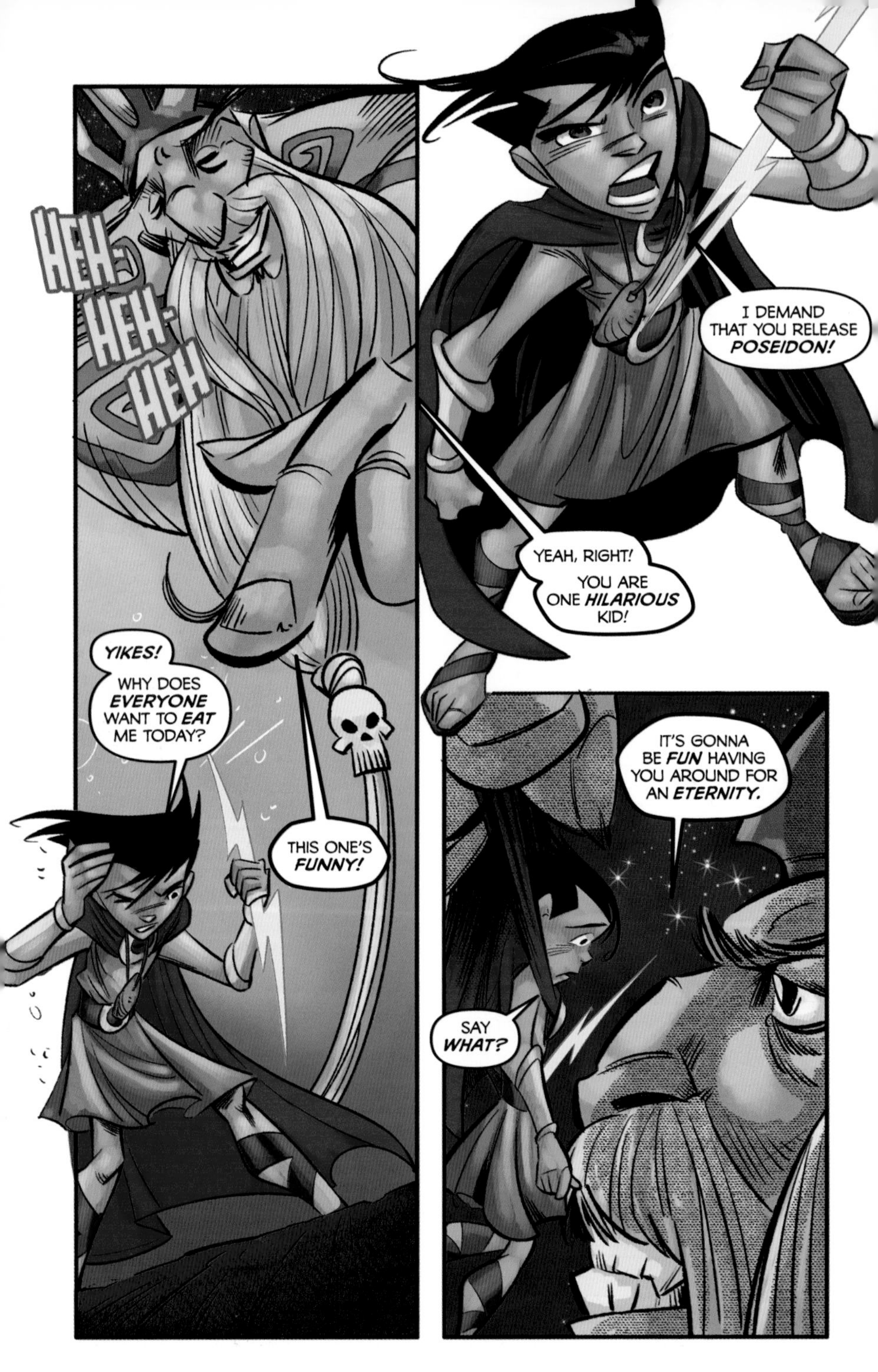
HEH-HEH-HEH
I DEMAND THAT YOU RELEASE POSEIDON!
YEAH, RIGHT!
YOU ARE ONE HILARIOUS KID!
YIKES!
WHY DOES EVERYONE WANT TO EAT ME TODAY?
THIS ONE'S FUNNY!
IT'S GONNA BE FUN HAVING YOU AROUND FOR AN ETERNITY.
SAY WHAT?

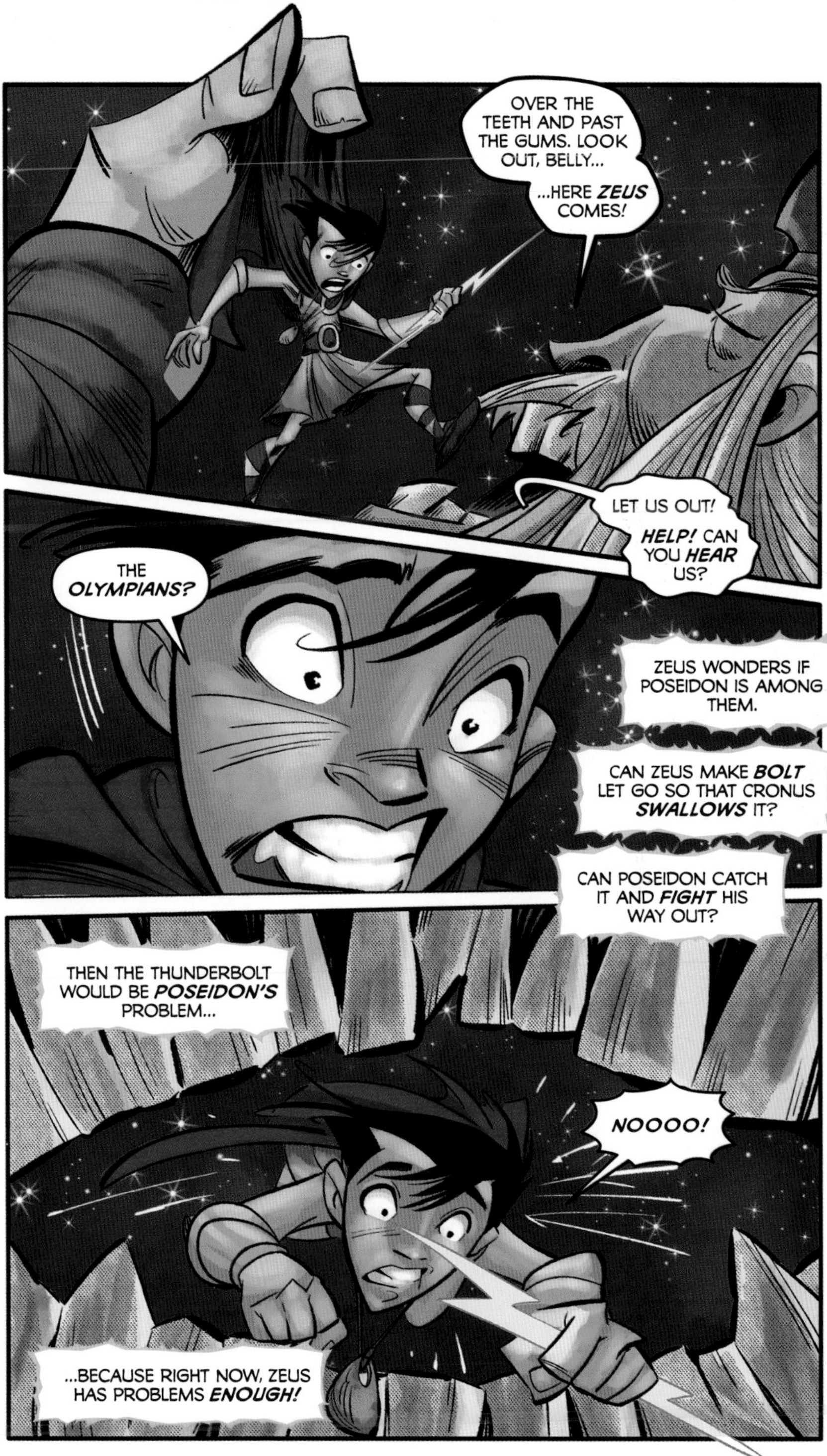
OVER THE TEETH AND PAST THE GUMS. LOOK OUT, BELLY...
...HERE *ZEUS* COMES!
LET US OUT!
HELP! CAN YOU *HEAR* US?
THE *OLYMPIANS?*
ZEUS WONDERS IF POSEIDON IS AMONG THEM.
CAN ZEUS MAKE *BOLT* LET GO SO THAT CRONUS *SWALLOWS* IT?
CAN POSEIDON CATCH IT AND *FIGHT* HIS WAY OUT?
THEN THE THUNDERBOLT WOULD BE *POSEIDON'S* PROBLEM...
NOOOO!
...BECAUSE RIGHT NOW, ZEUS HAS PROBLEMS *ENOUGH!*

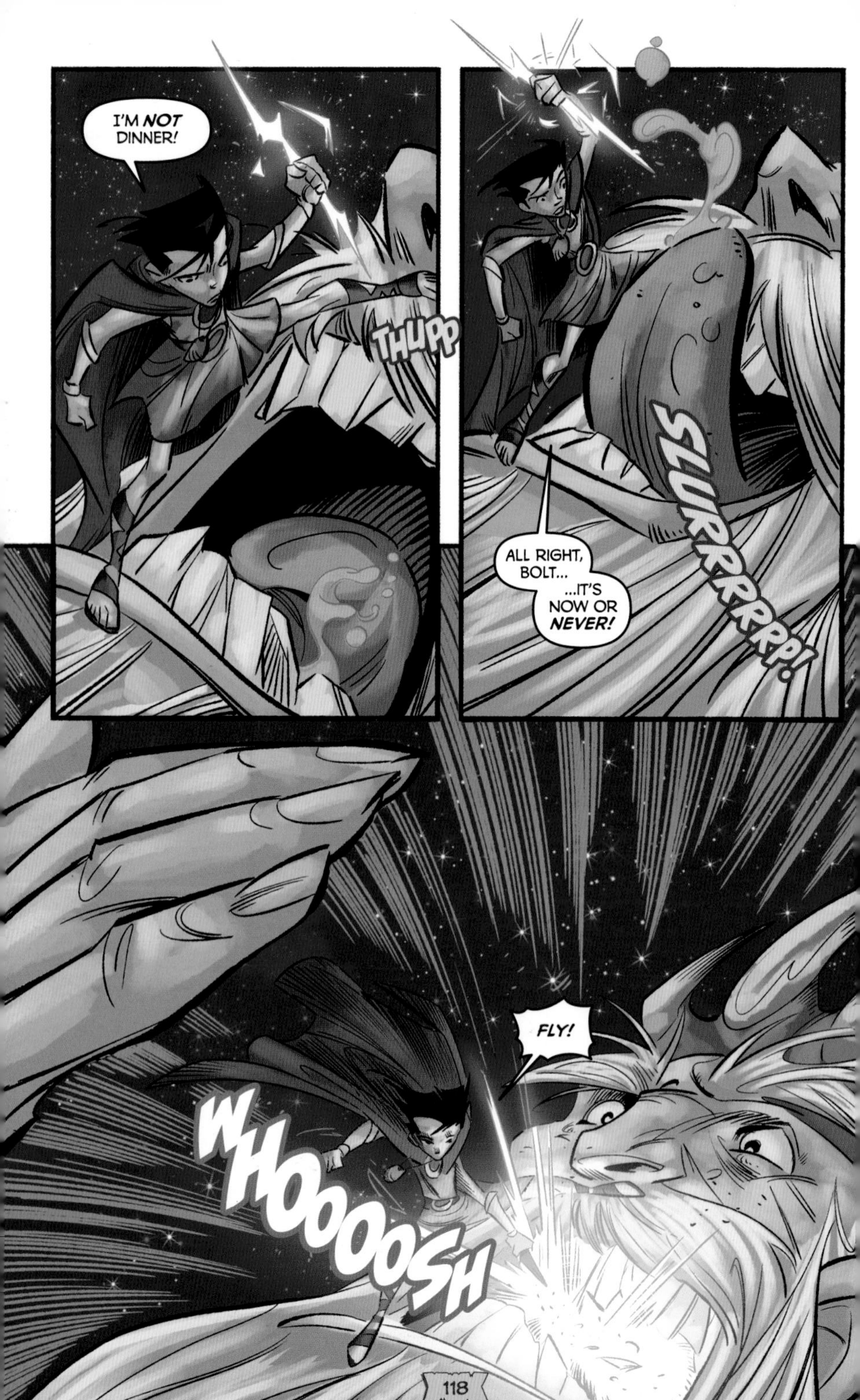
I'M NOT DINNER!
THUPP
SLURRRRRP!
ALL RIGHT, BOLT...
...IT'S NOW OR NEVER!
FLY!
WHOOOOSH

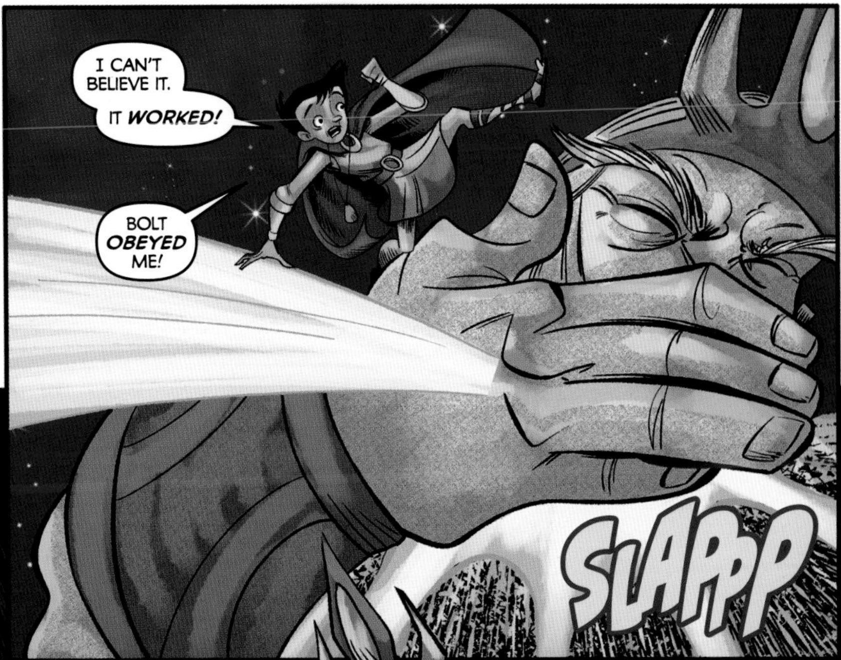
I CAN'T BELIEVE IT.
IT WORKED!
BOLT OBEYED ME!
SLAPP

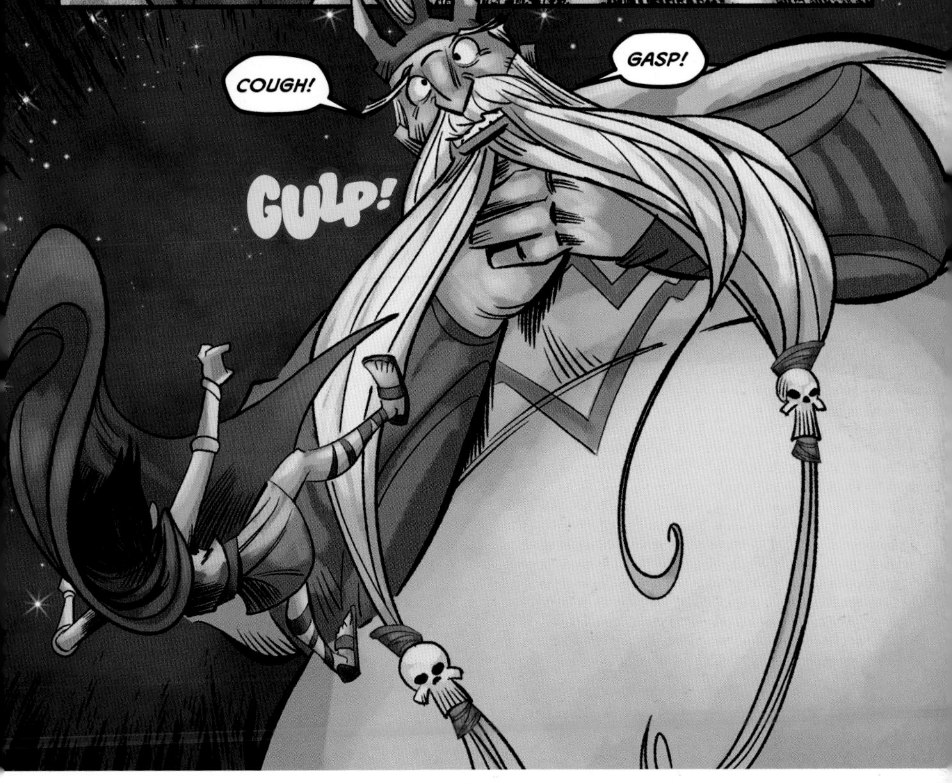
COUGH!
GASP!
GULP!

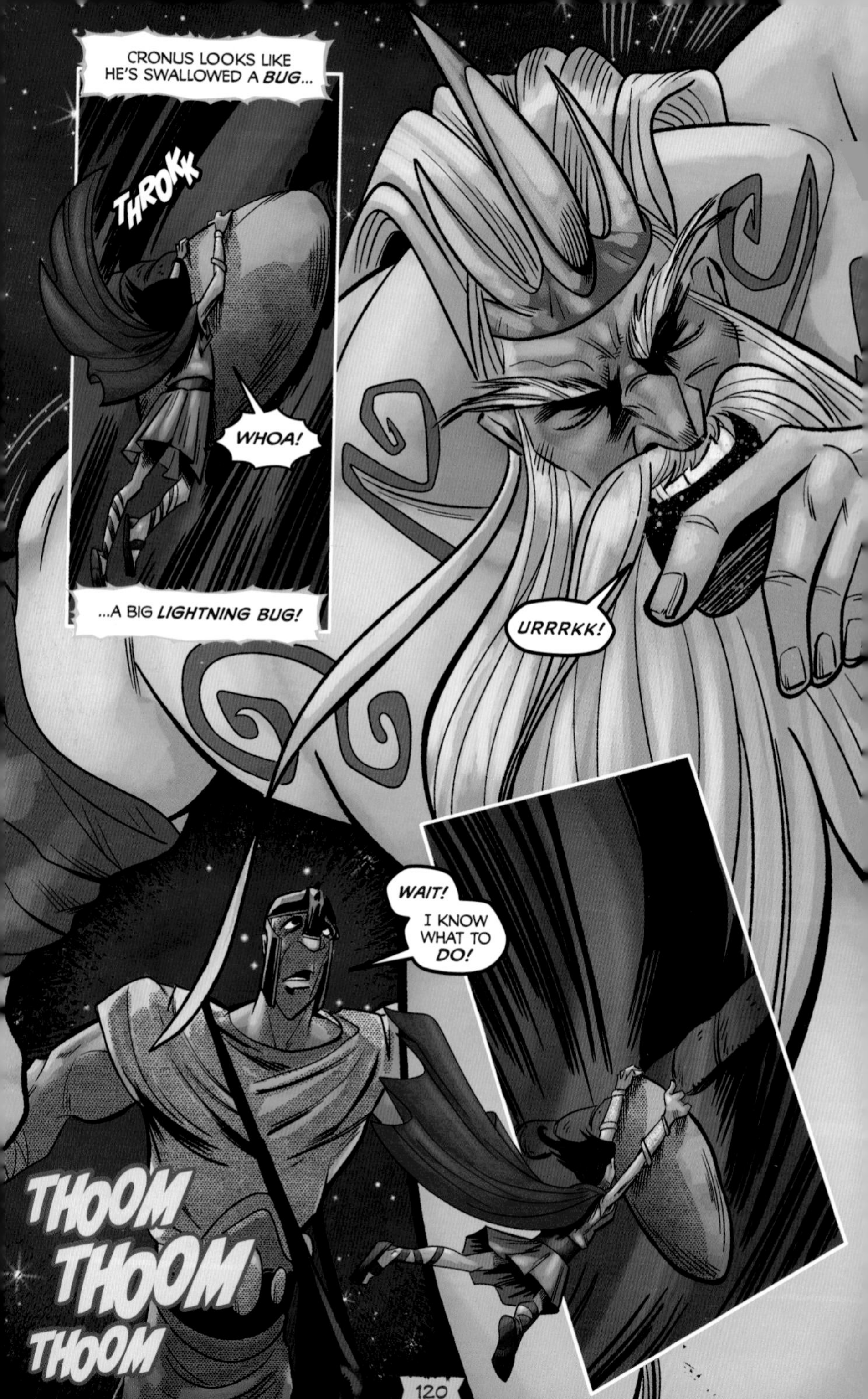
CRONUS LOOKS LIKE HE'S SWALLOWED A *BUG*...
THROKK
WHOA!
...A BIG *LIGHTNING BUG!*
URRRKK!
WAIT!
I KNOW WHAT TO *DO!*
THOOM THOOM THOOM

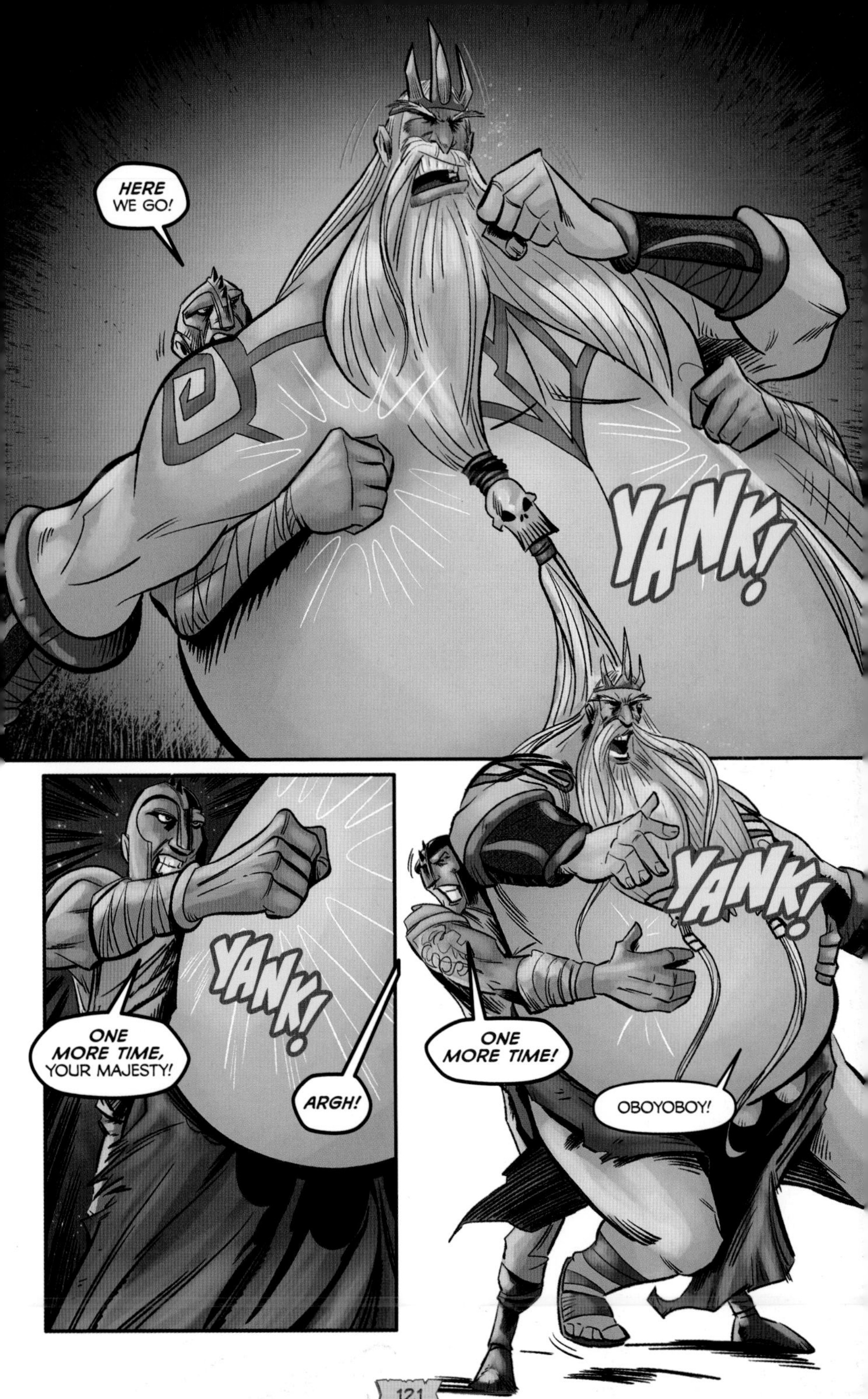
HERE WE GO!
YANK!
ONE MORE TIME, YOUR MAJESTY!
YANK!
ARGH!
YANK!
ONE MORE TIME!
OBOYOBOY!

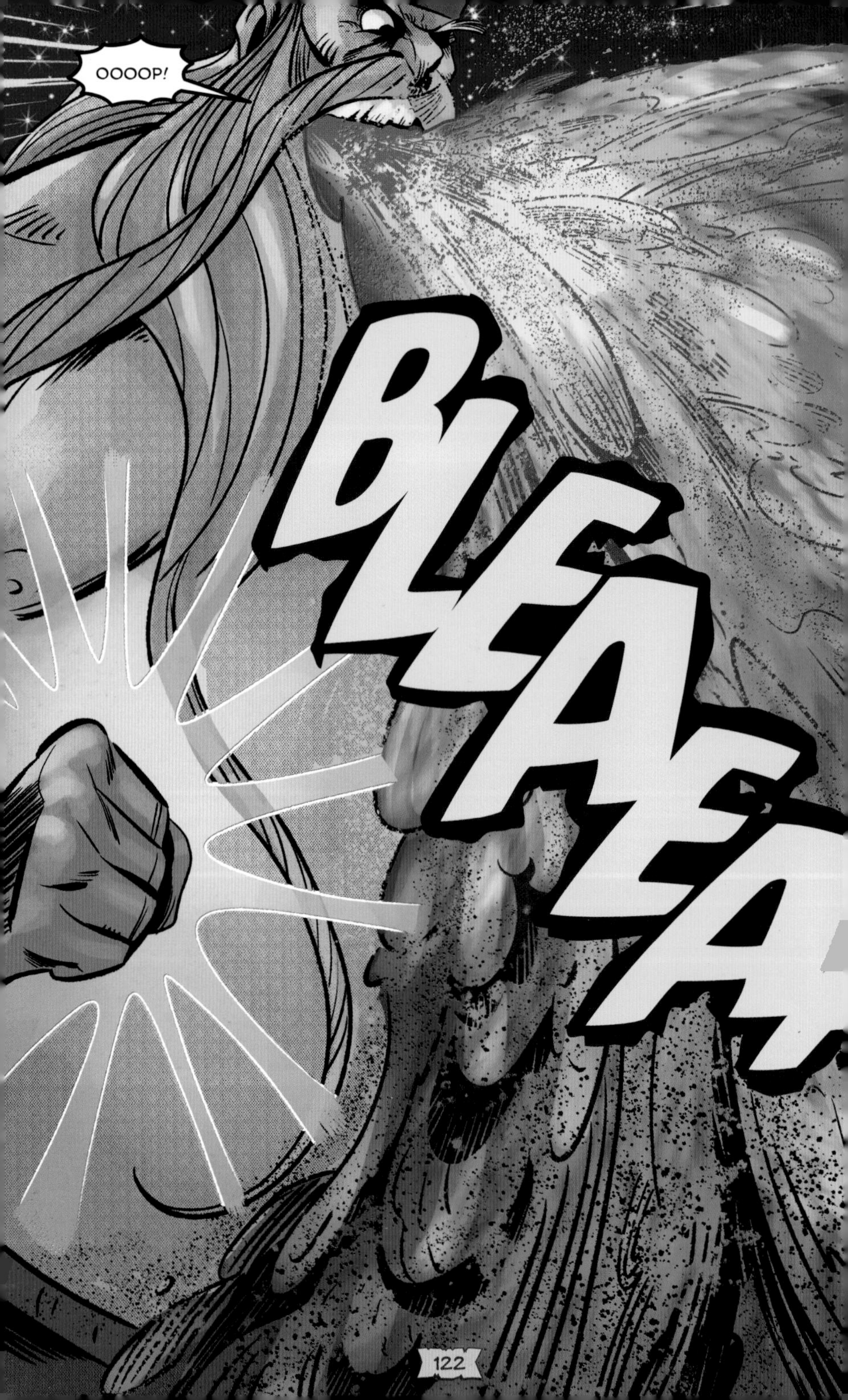
OOOOP!
BLAAAA

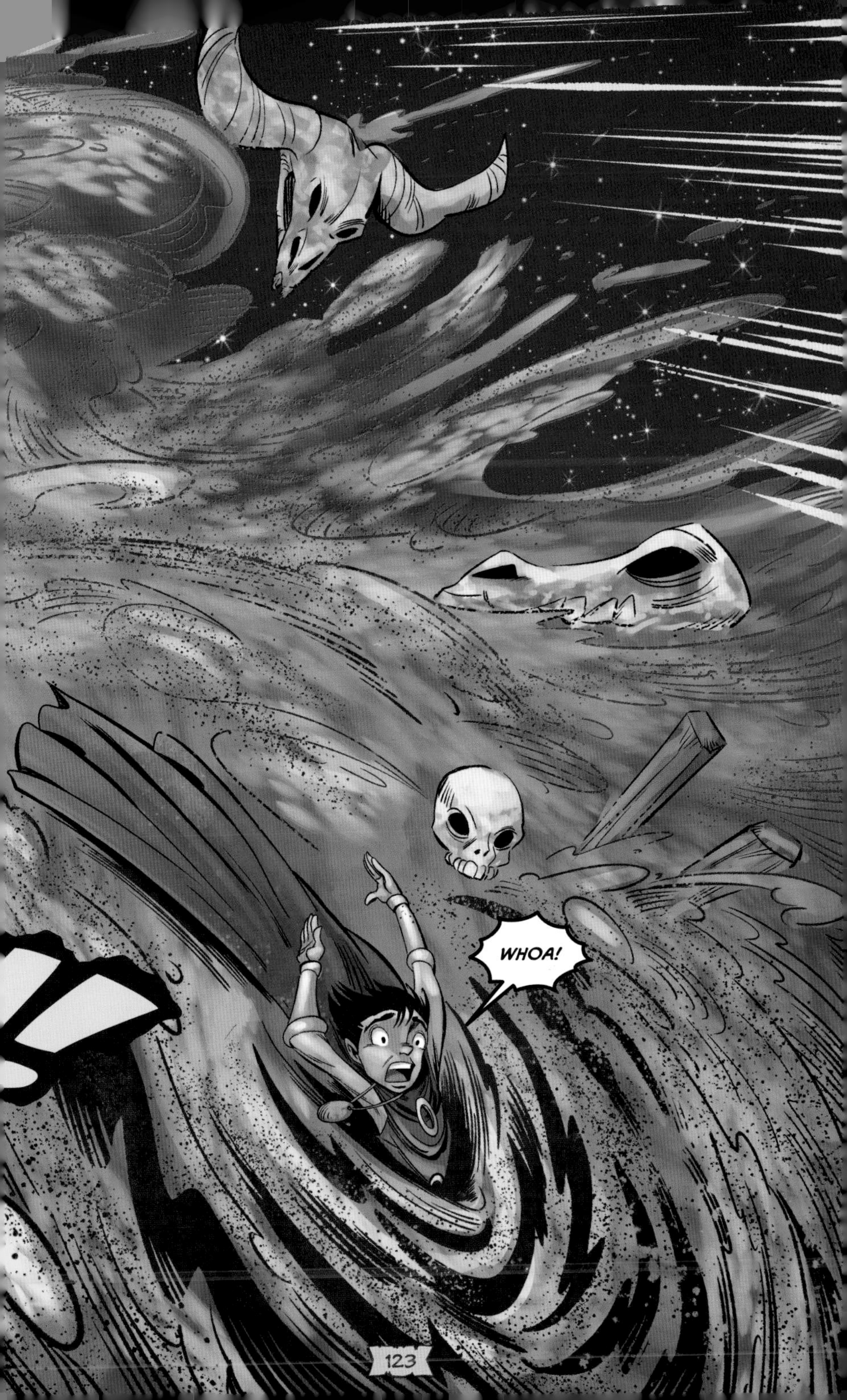
WHOA!

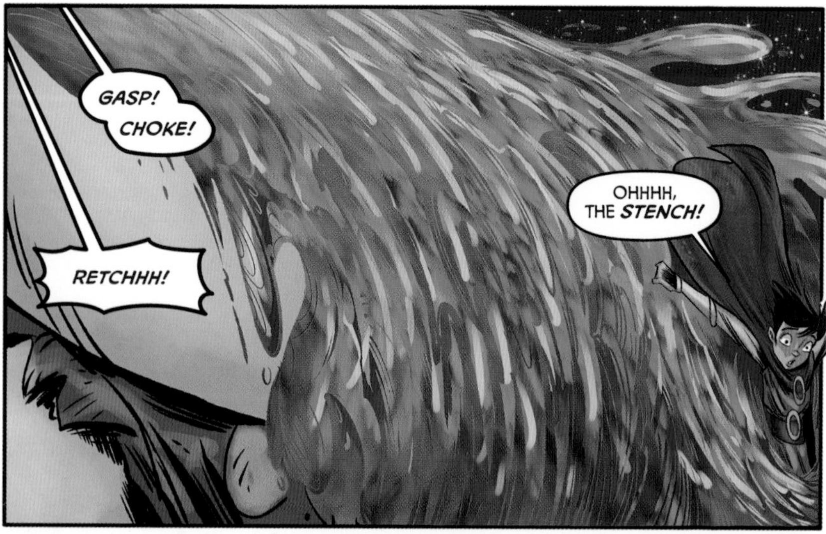
GASP!
CHOKE!
RETCHHH!
OHHHH, THE STENCH!

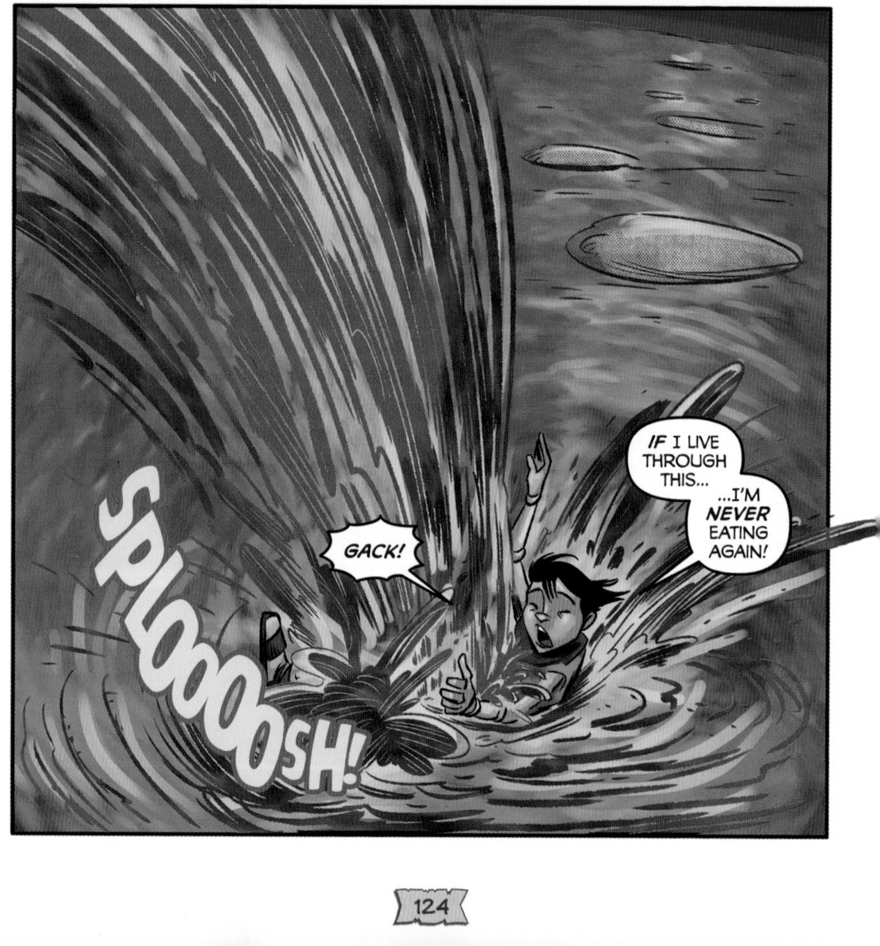
IF I LIVE THROUGH THIS...
...I'M NEVER EATING AGAIN!
GACK!
SPLOOOOOSH!

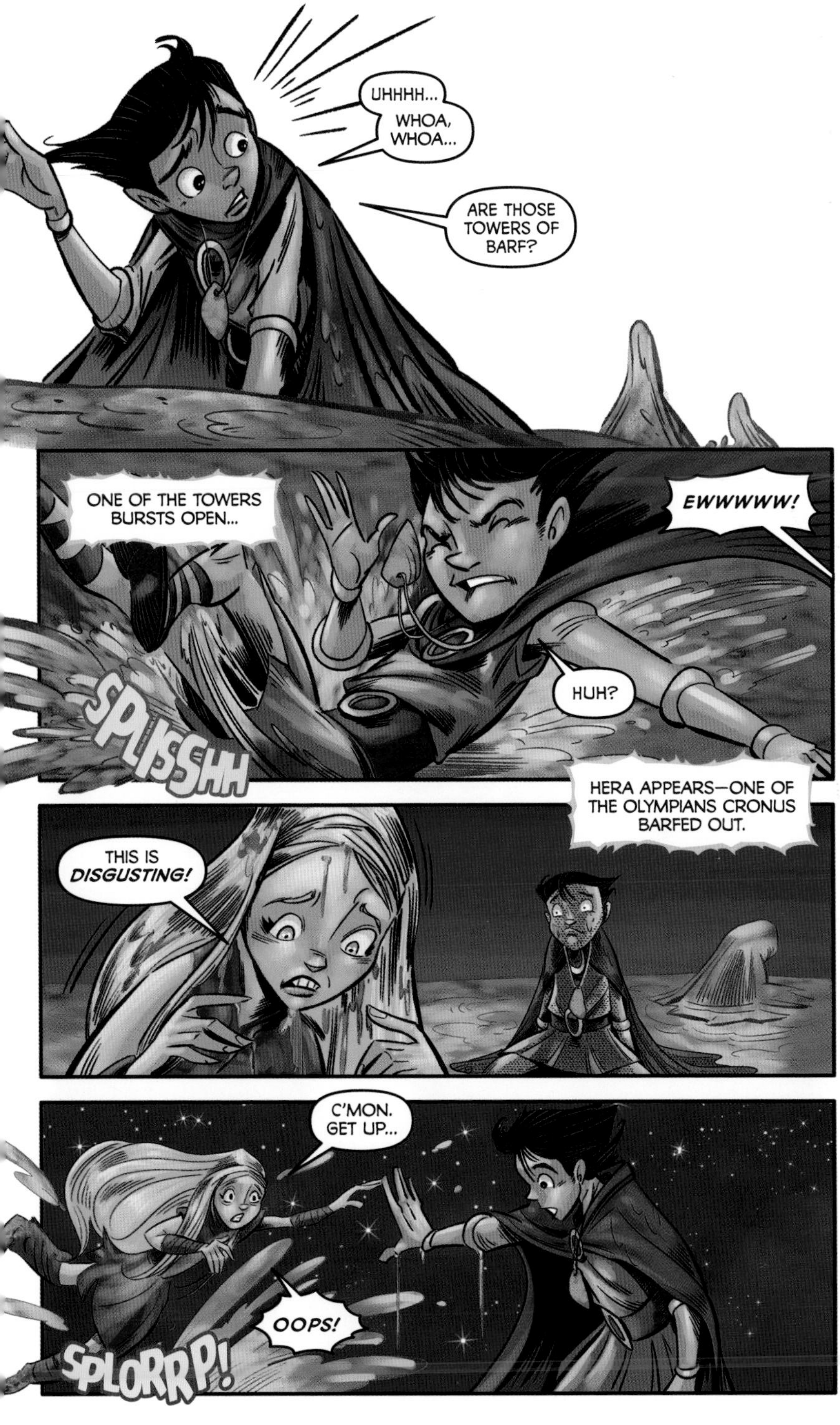
UHHHH...
WHOA, WHOA...
ARE THOSE TOWERS OF BARF?
ONE OF THE TOWERS BURSTS OPEN...
EWWWWW!
SPLISSHH
HUH?
HERA APPEARS—ONE OF THE OLYMPIANS CRONUS BARFED OUT.
THIS IS *DISGUSTING!*
C'MON. GET UP...
OOPS!
SPLORRP!

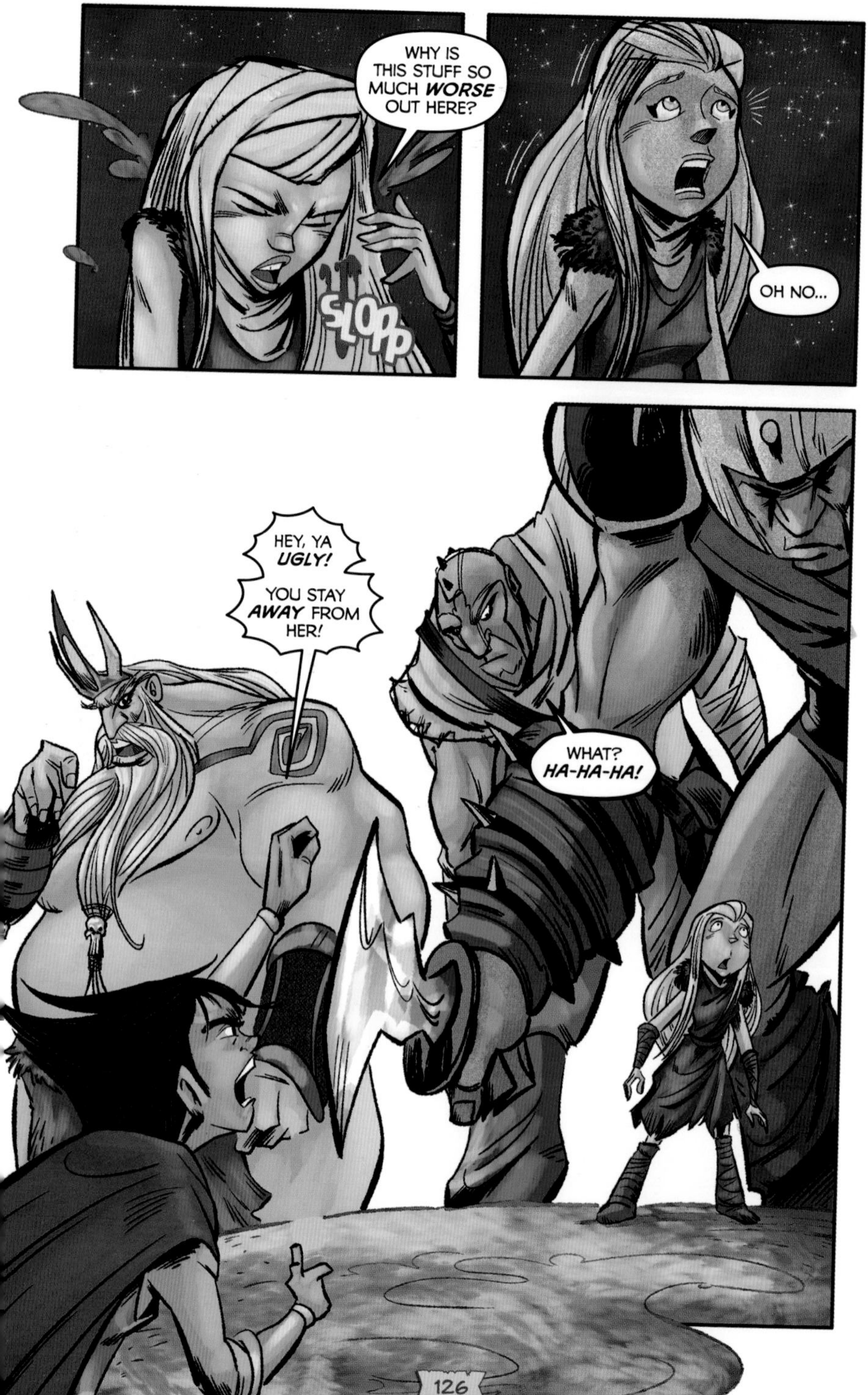

WHY IS THIS STUFF SO MUCH ***WORSE*** OUT HERE?
SLOPP
OH NO...
HEY, YA ***UGLY!***
YOU STAY ***AWAY*** FROM HER!
WHAT? ***HA-HA-HA!***

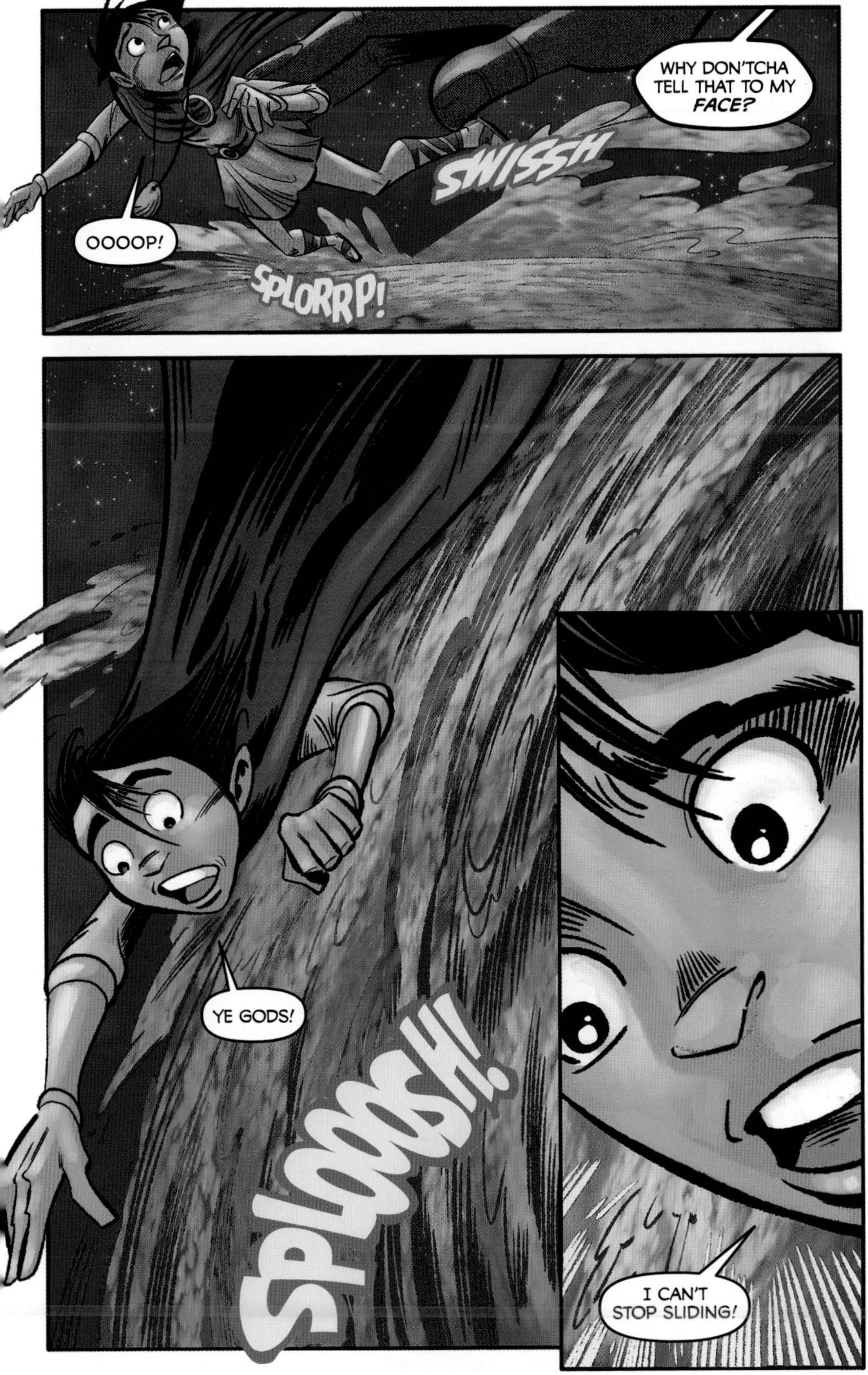
WHY DON'TCHA TELL THAT TO MY *FACE?*
SWISSH
OOOOP!
SPLORRP!
YE GODS!
SPLOOOSH!!
I CAN'T STOP SLIDING!

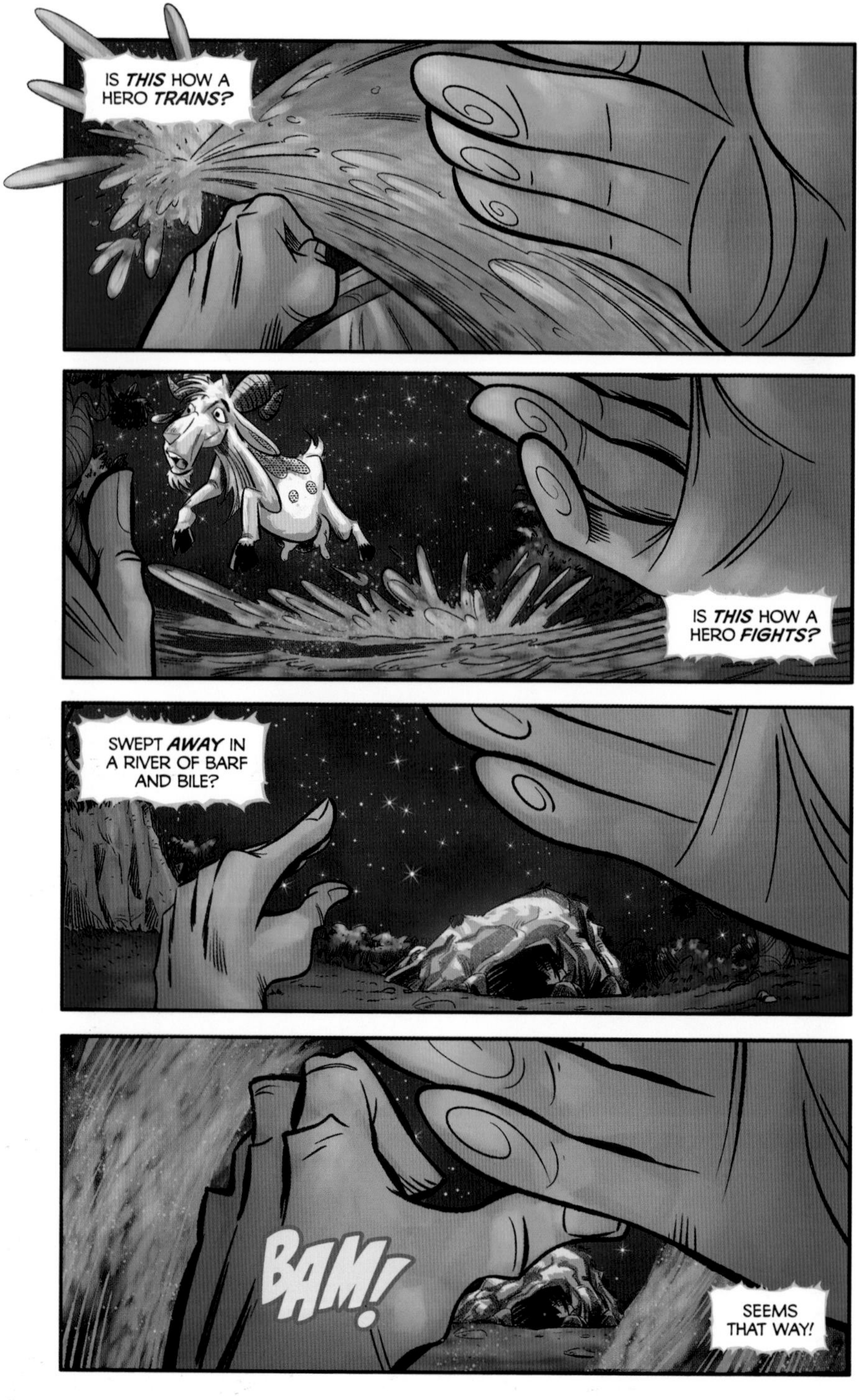
IS THIS HOW A HERO TRAINS?
IS THIS HOW A HERO FIGHTS?
SWEPT AWAY IN A RIVER OF BARF AND BILE?
BAM!
SEEMS THAT WAY!

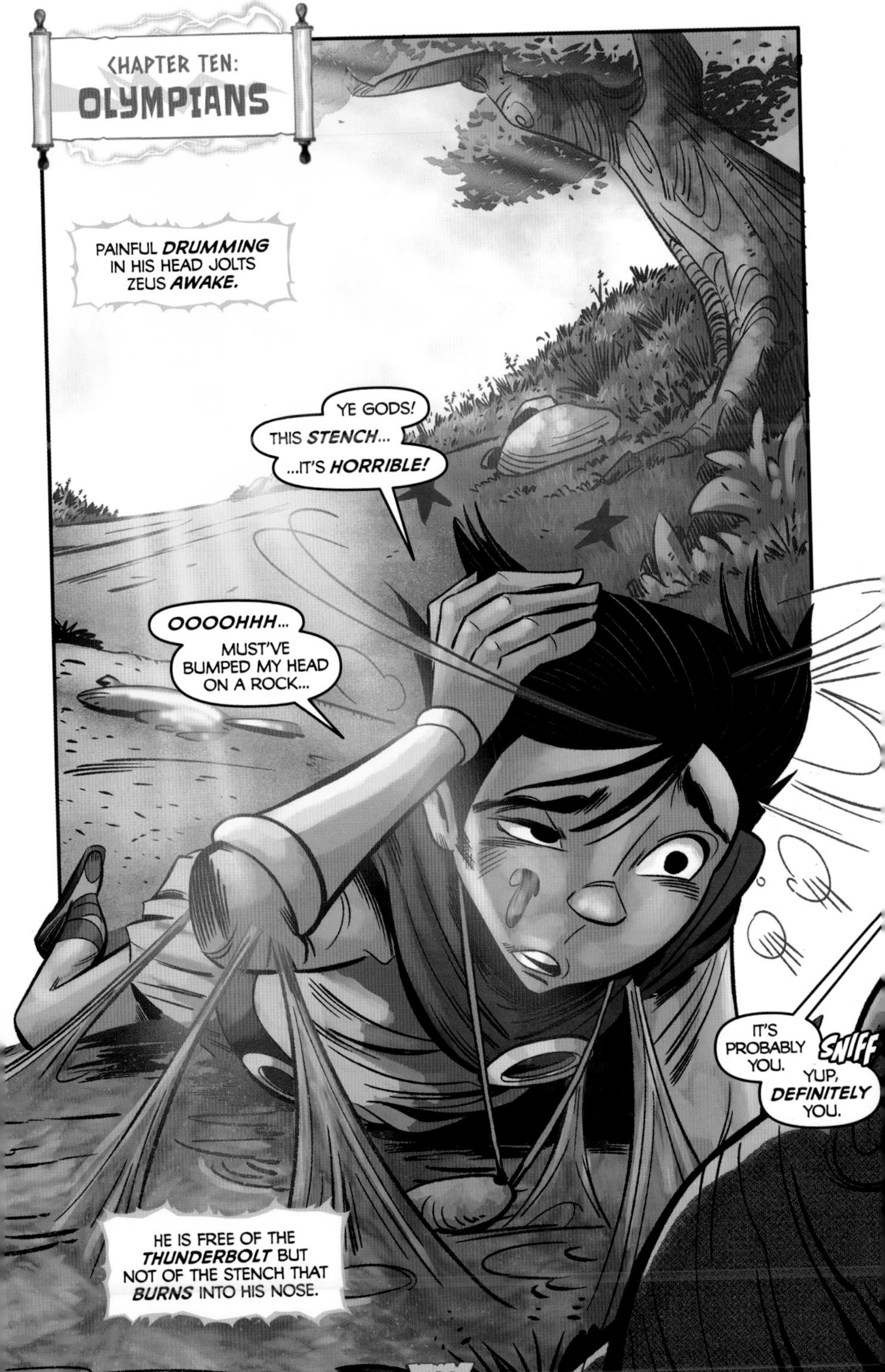
CHAPTER TEN:
OLYMPIANS
PAINFUL DRUMMING IN HIS HEAD JOLTS ZEUS AWAKE.
YE GODS!
THIS STENCH...
...IT'S HORRIBLE!
OOOOHHH... MUST'VE BUMPED MY HEAD ON A ROCK...
IT'S PROBABLY YOU.
SNIFF
YUP, DEFINITELY YOU.
HE IS FREE OF THE THUNDERBOLT BUT NOT OF THE STENCH THAT BURNS INTO HIS NOSE.

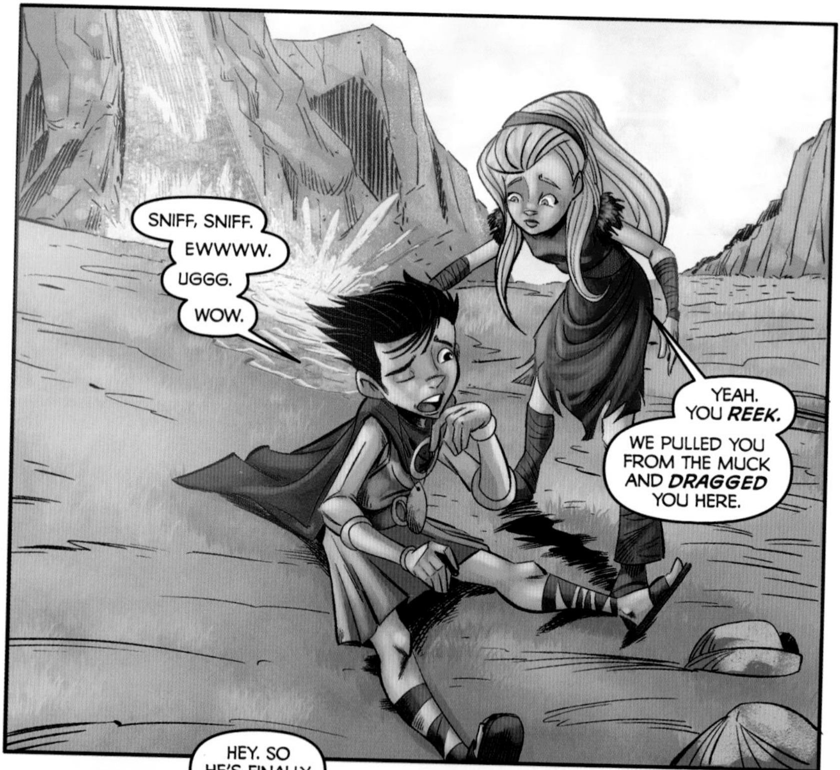
SNIFF, SNIFF.
EWWWW.
UGGG.
WOW.
YEAH. YOU **REEK.**
WE PULLED YOU FROM THE MUCK AND **DRAGGED** YOU HERE.

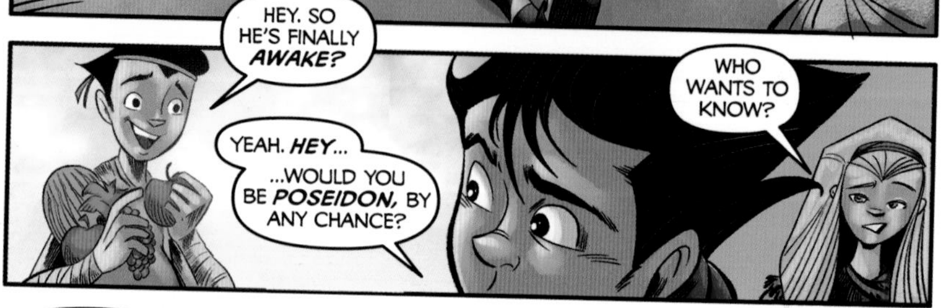
HEY. SO HE'S FINALLY ***AWAKE?***
YEAH. ***HEY...***
...WOULD YOU BE ***POSEIDON,*** BY ANY CHANCE?
WHO WANTS TO KNOW?

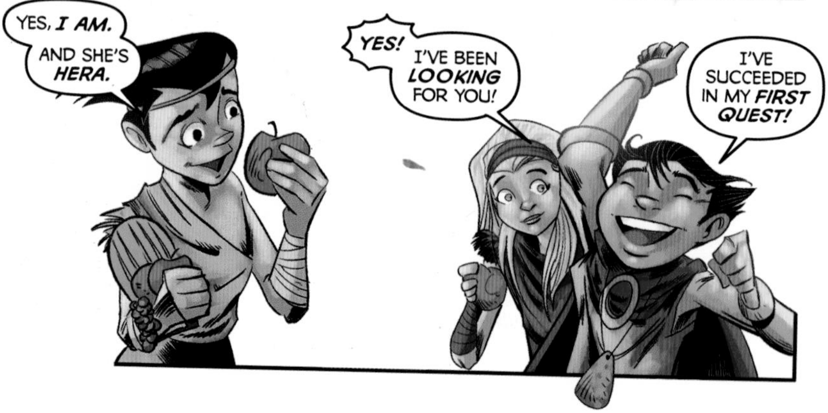
YES, ***I AM.***
AND SHE'S ***HERA.***
YES!
I'VE BEEN ***LOOKING*** FOR YOU!
I'VE SUCCEEDED IN MY ***FIRST QUEST!***

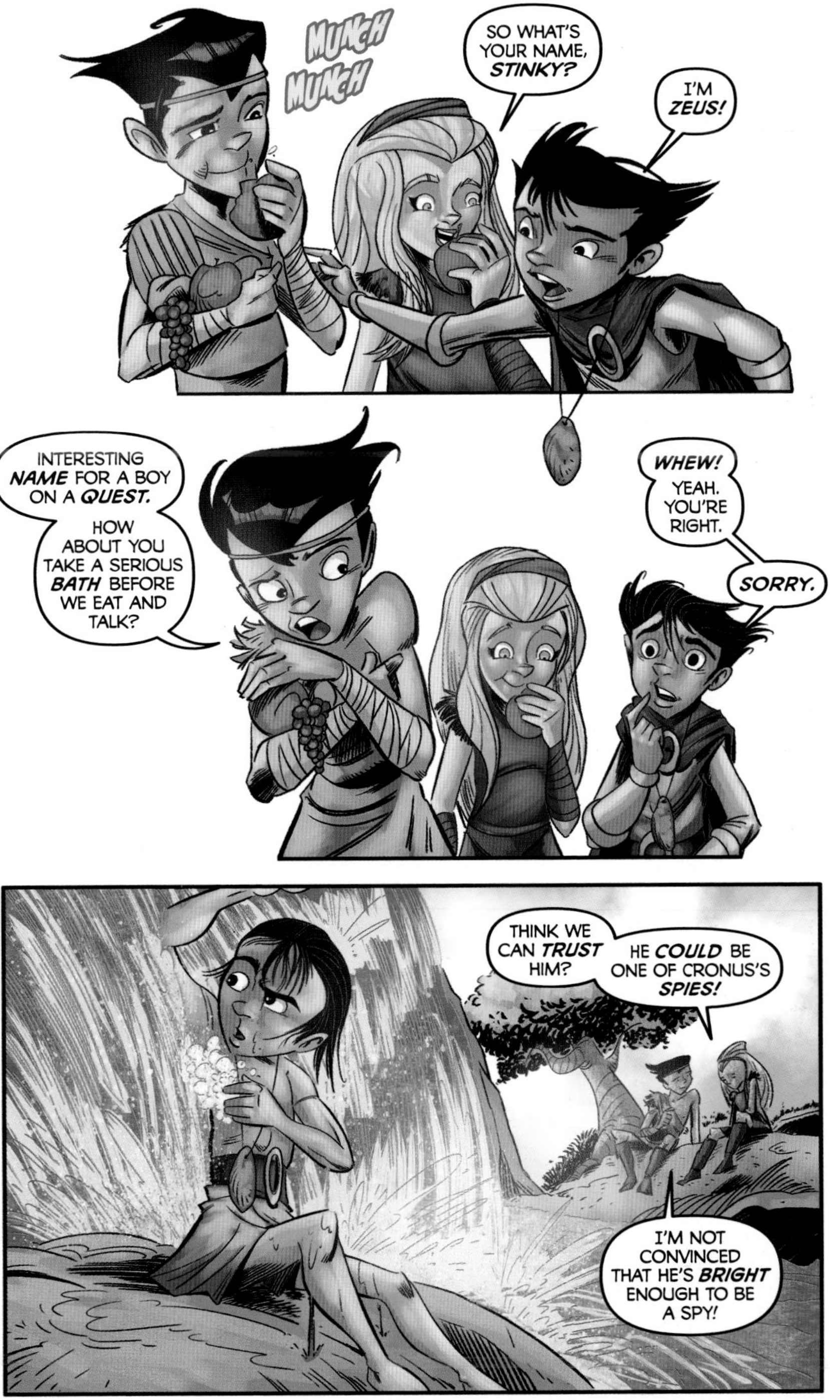
MUNCH MUNCH
SO WHAT'S YOUR NAME, STINKY?
I'M ZEUS!
INTERESTING NAME FOR A BOY ON A QUEST.
HOW ABOUT YOU TAKE A SERIOUS BATH BEFORE WE EAT AND TALK?
WHEW! YEAH. YOU'RE RIGHT.
SORRY.
THINK WE CAN TRUST HIM?
HE COULD BE ONE OF CRONUS'S SPIES!
I'M NOT CONVINCED THAT HE'S BRIGHT ENOUGH TO BE A SPY!

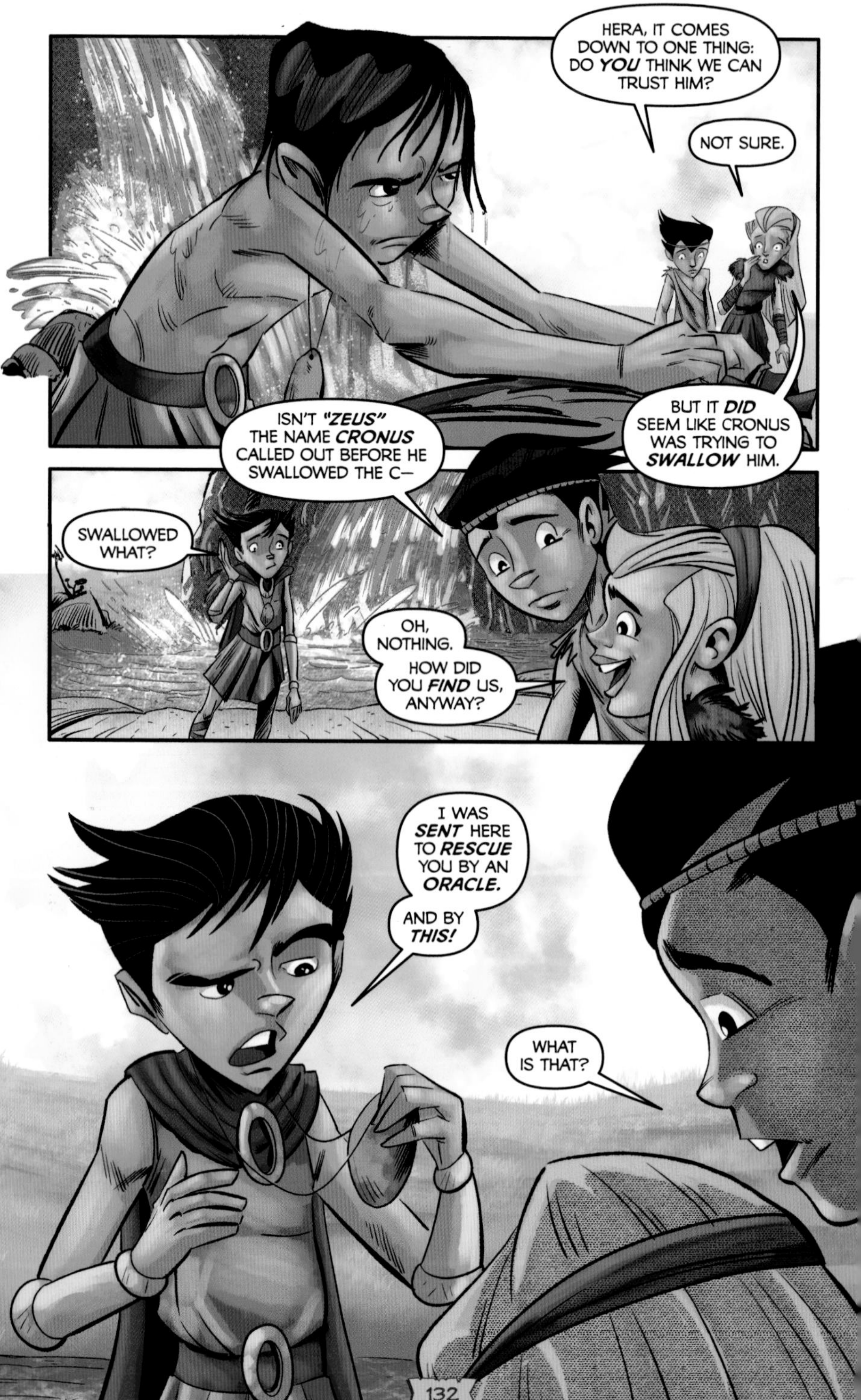
HERA, IT COMES DOWN TO ONE THING: DO YOU THINK WE CAN TRUST HIM?
NOT SURE.
BUT IT DID SEEM LIKE CRONUS WAS TRYING TO SWALLOW HIM.
ISN'T "ZEUS" THE NAME CRONUS CALLED OUT BEFORE HE SWALLOWED THE C—
SWALLOWED WHAT?
OH, NOTHING.
HOW DID YOU FIND US, ANYWAY?
I WAS SENT HERE TO RESCUE YOU BY AN ORACLE.
AND BY THIS!
WHAT IS THAT?

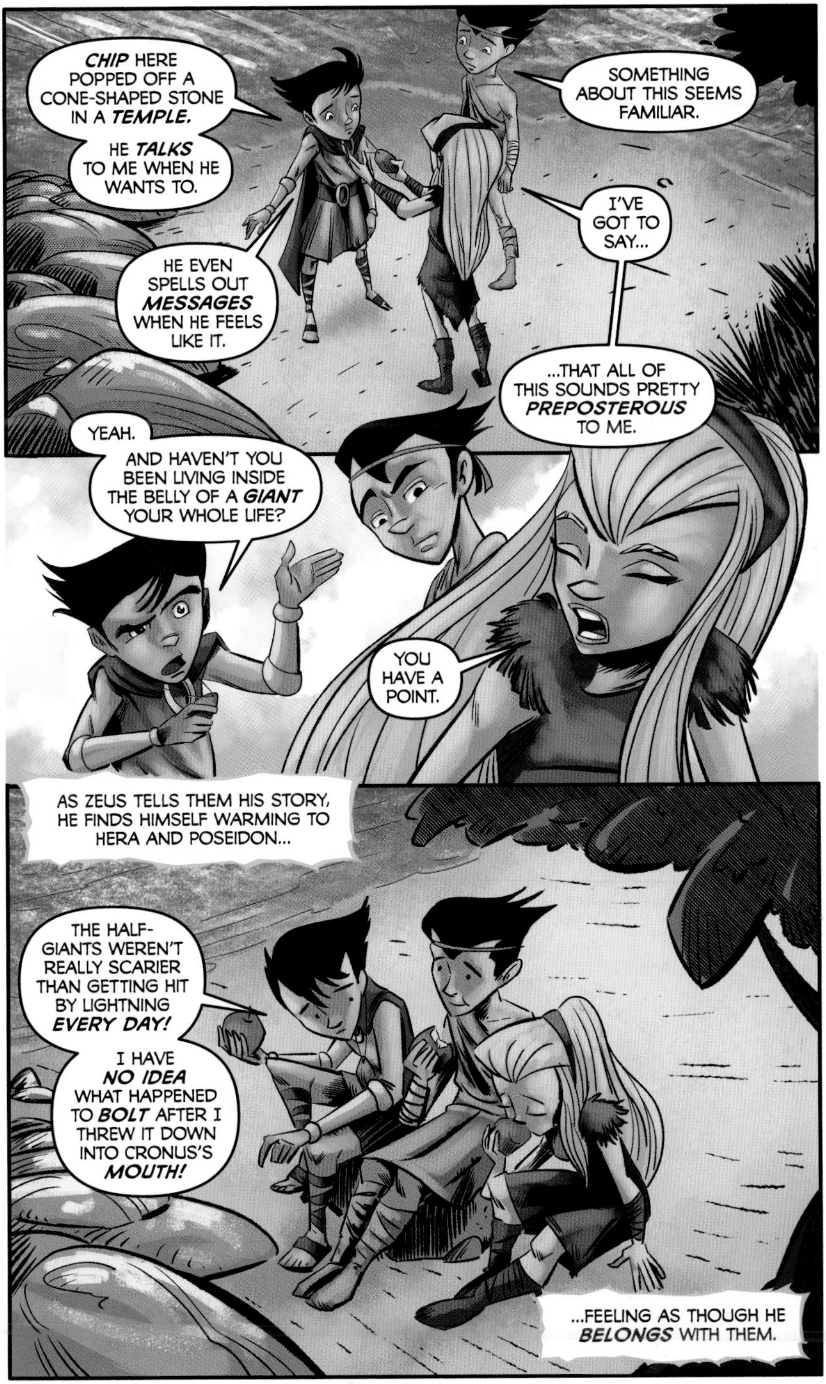
CHIP HERE POPPED OFF A CONE-SHAPED STONE IN A TEMPLE.
HE TALKS TO ME WHEN HE WANTS TO.
SOMETHING ABOUT THIS SEEMS FAMILIAR.
HE EVEN SPELLS OUT MESSAGES WHEN HE FEELS LIKE IT.
I'VE GOT TO SAY...
...THAT ALL OF THIS SOUNDS PRETTY PREPOSTEROUS TO ME.
YEAH.
AND HAVEN'T YOU BEEN LIVING INSIDE THE BELLY OF A GIANT YOUR WHOLE LIFE?
YOU HAVE A POINT.
AS ZEUS TELLS THEM HIS STORY, HE FINDS HIMSELF WARMING TO HERA AND POSEIDON...
THE HALF-GIANTS WEREN'T REALLY SCARIER THAN GETTING HIT BY LIGHTNING EVERY DAY!
I HAVE NO IDEA WHAT HAPPENED TO BOLT AFTER I THREW IT DOWN INTO CRONUS'S MOUTH!
...FEELING AS THOUGH HE BELONGS WITH THEM.

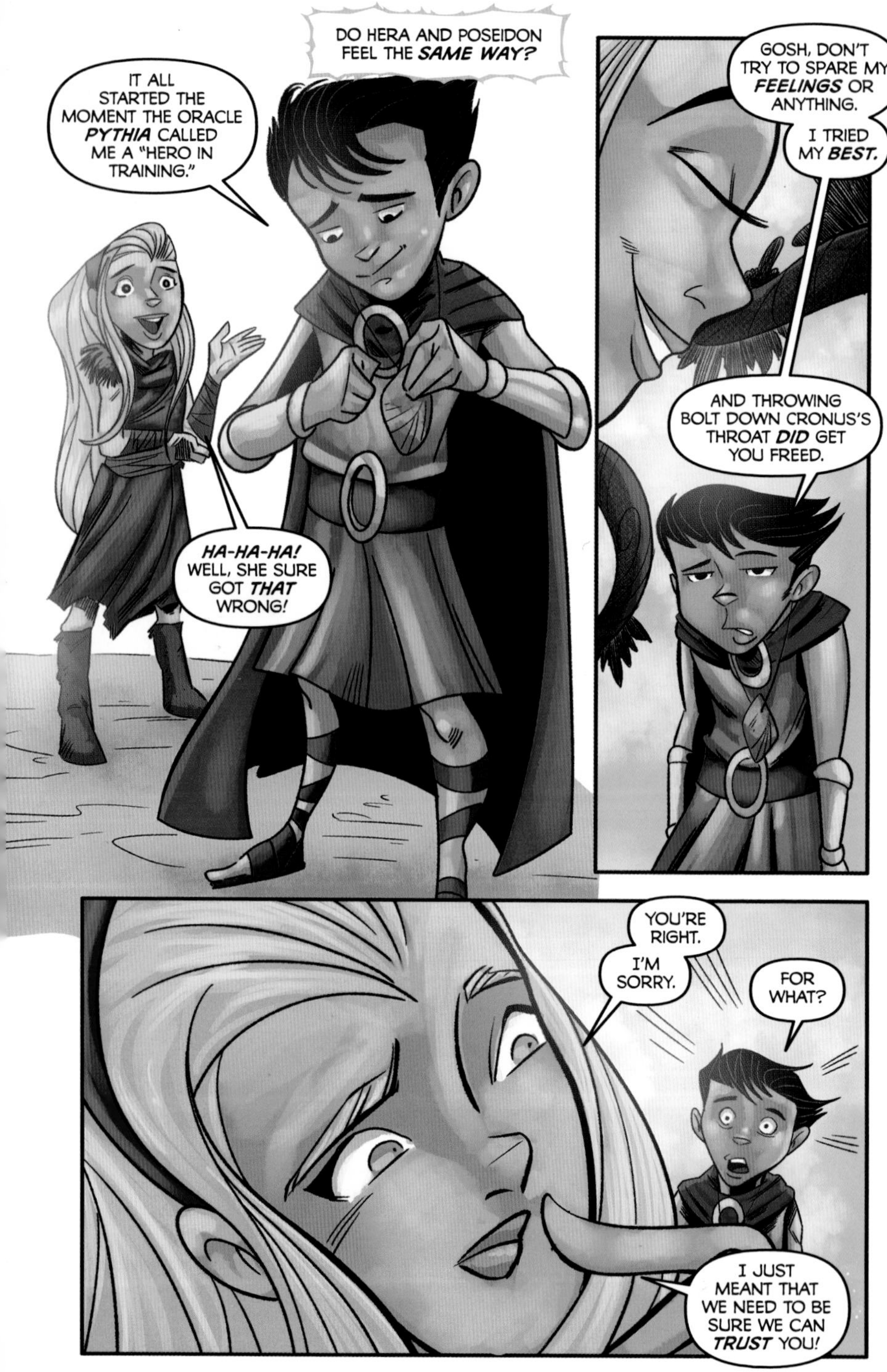
DO HERA AND POSEIDON FEEL THE *SAME WAY?*
IT ALL STARTED THE MOMENT THE ORACLE *PYTHIA* CALLED ME A "HERO IN TRAINING."
HA-HA-HA! WELL, SHE SURE GOT *THAT* WRONG!
GOSH, DON'T TRY TO SPARE MY *FEELINGS* OR ANYTHING.
I TRIED MY *BEST.*
AND THROWING BOLT DOWN CRONUS'S THROAT *DID* GET YOU FREED.
YOU'RE RIGHT.
I'M SORRY.
FOR WHAT?
I JUST MEANT THAT WE NEED TO BE SURE WE CAN *TRUST* YOU!

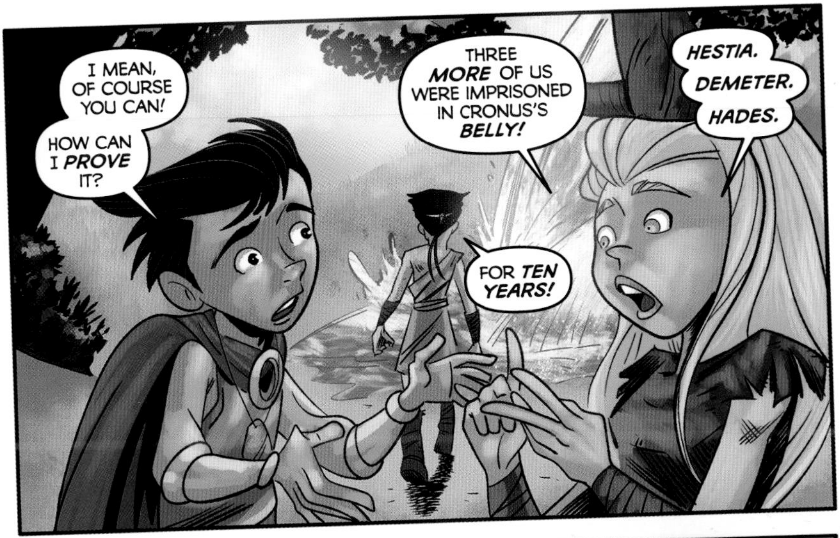
I MEAN, OF COURSE YOU CAN!
HOW CAN I PROVE IT?
THREE MORE OF US WERE IMPRISONED IN CRONUS'S BELLY!
FOR TEN YEARS!
HESTIA.
DEMETER.
HADES.

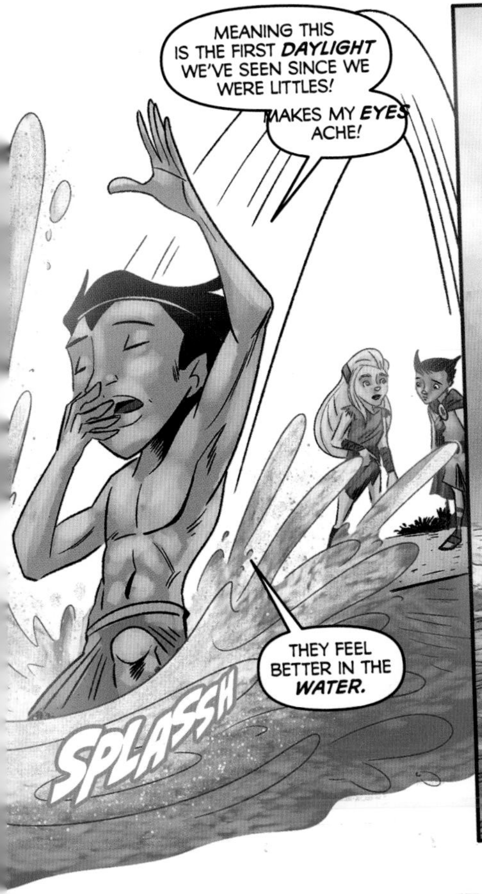
MEANING THIS IS THE FIRST DAYLIGHT WE'VE SEEN SINCE WE WERE LITTLES!
MAKES MY EYES ACHE!
THEY FEEL BETTER IN THE WATER.
SPLASSH

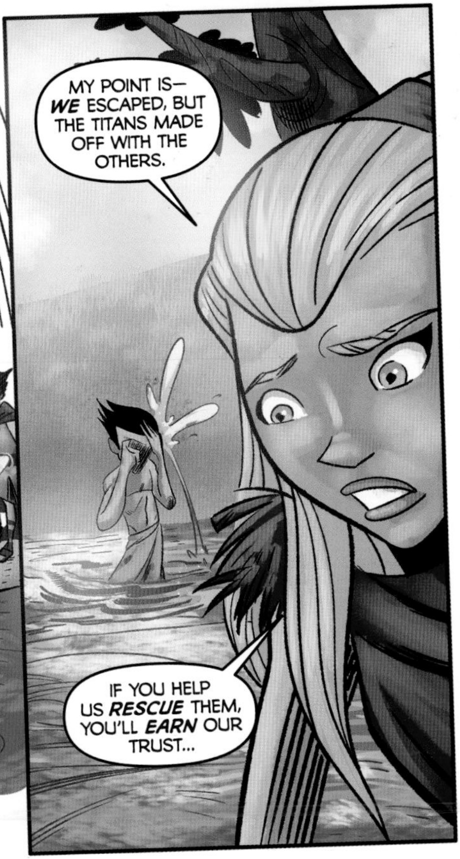
MY POINT IS— WE ESCAPED, BUT THE TITANS MADE OFF WITH THE OTHERS.
IF YOU HELP US RESCUE THEM, YOU'LL EARN OUR TRUST...

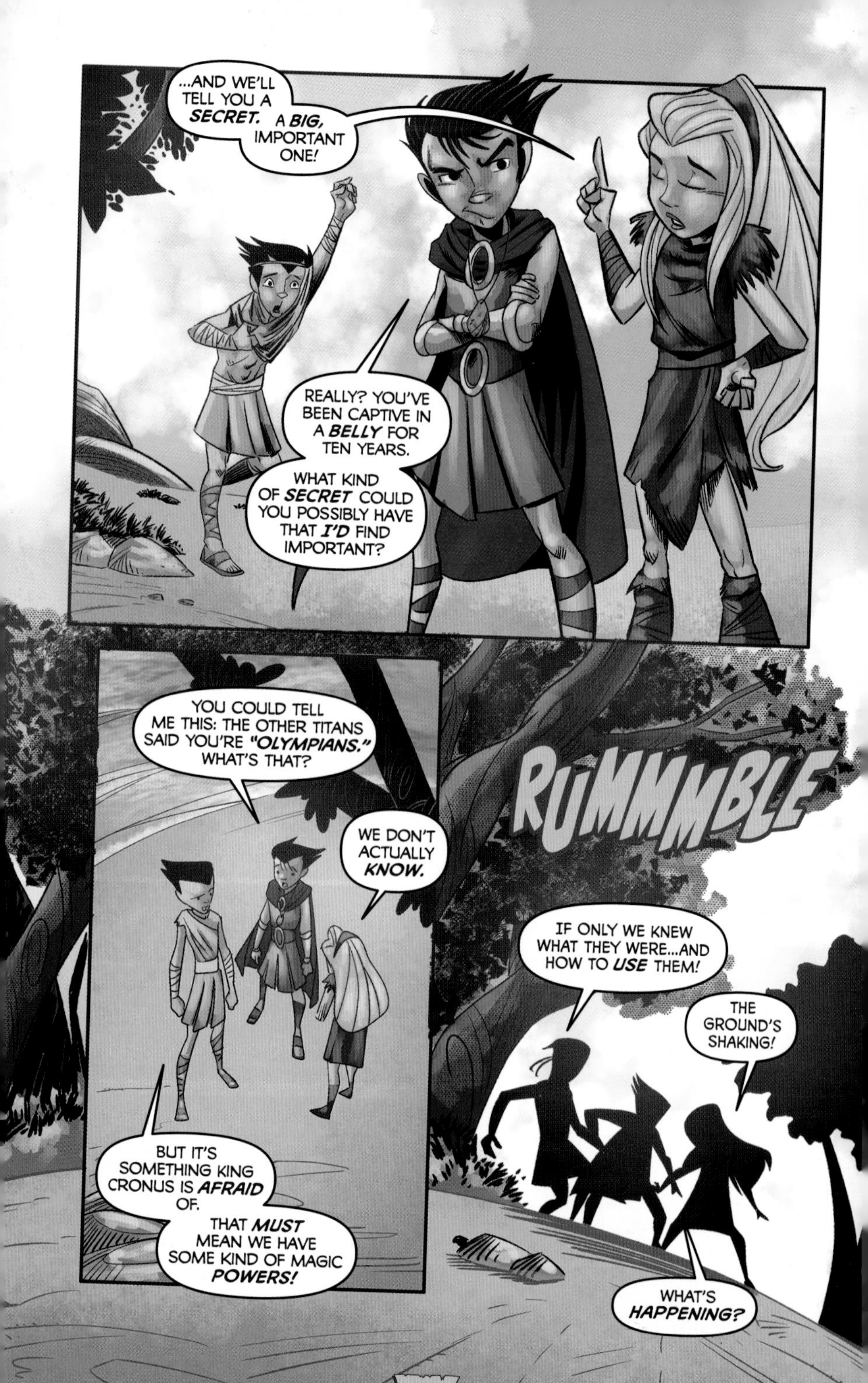
...AND WE'LL TELL YOU A SECRET. A BIG, IMPORTANT ONE!
REALLY? YOU'VE BEEN CAPTIVE IN A BELLY FOR TEN YEARS.
WHAT KIND OF SECRET COULD YOU POSSIBLY HAVE THAT I'D FIND IMPORTANT?
YOU COULD TELL ME THIS: THE OTHER TITANS SAID YOU'RE "OLYMPIANS." WHAT'S THAT?
WE DON'T ACTUALLY KNOW.
BUT IT'S SOMETHING KING CRONUS IS AFRAID OF.
THAT MUST MEAN WE HAVE SOME KIND OF MAGIC POWERS!
RUMMMBLE
IF ONLY WE KNEW WHAT THEY WERE...AND HOW TO USE THEM!
THE GROUND'S SHAKING!
WHAT'S HAPPENING?

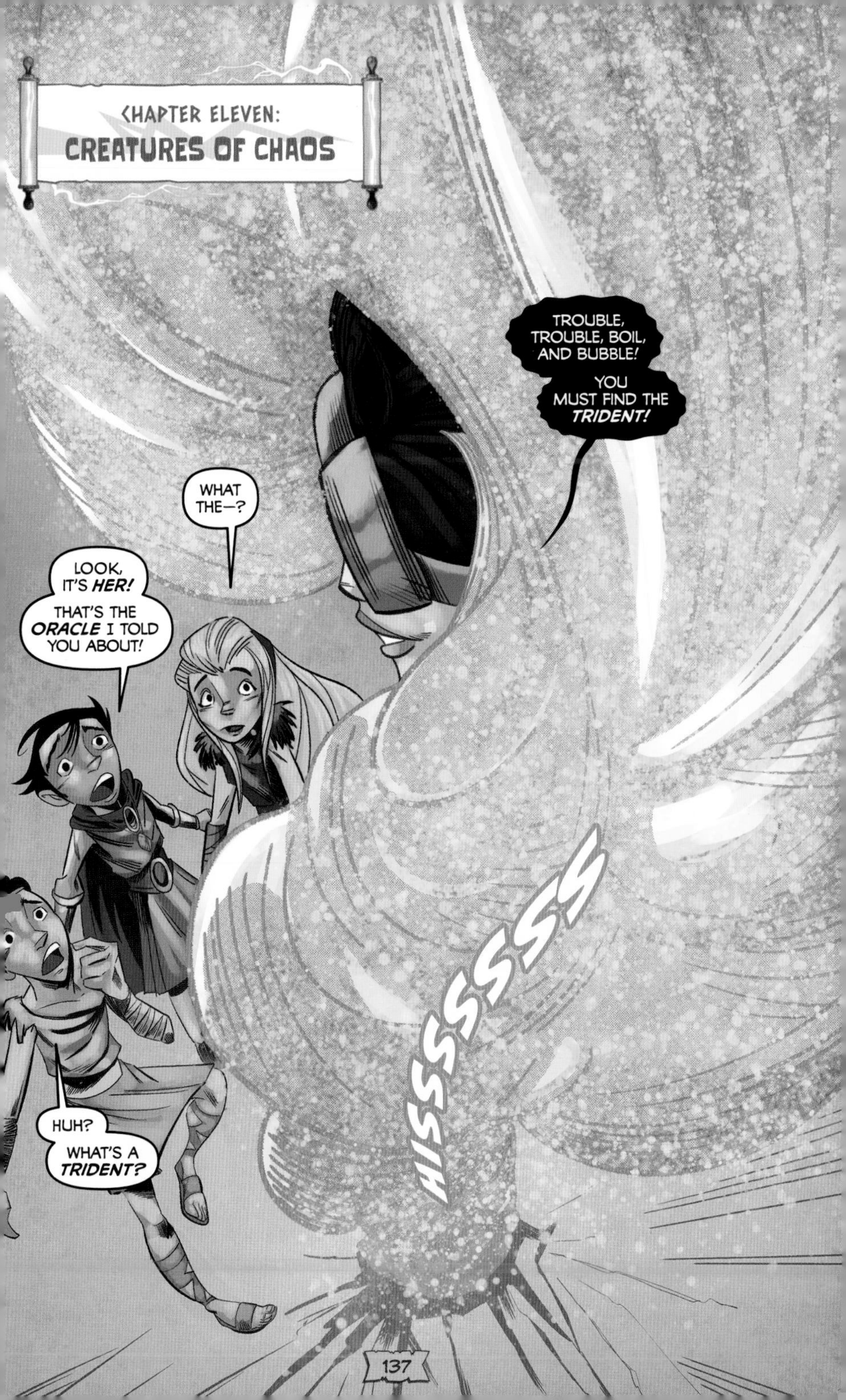

CHAPTER ELEVEN:
CREATURES OF CHAOS
TROUBLE, TROUBLE, BOIL, AND BUBBLE!
YOU MUST FIND THE TRIDENT!
WHAT THE—?
LOOK, IT'S HER!
THAT'S THE ORACLE I TOLD YOU ABOUT!
HUH? WHAT'S A TRIDENT?
HISSSSSSSS

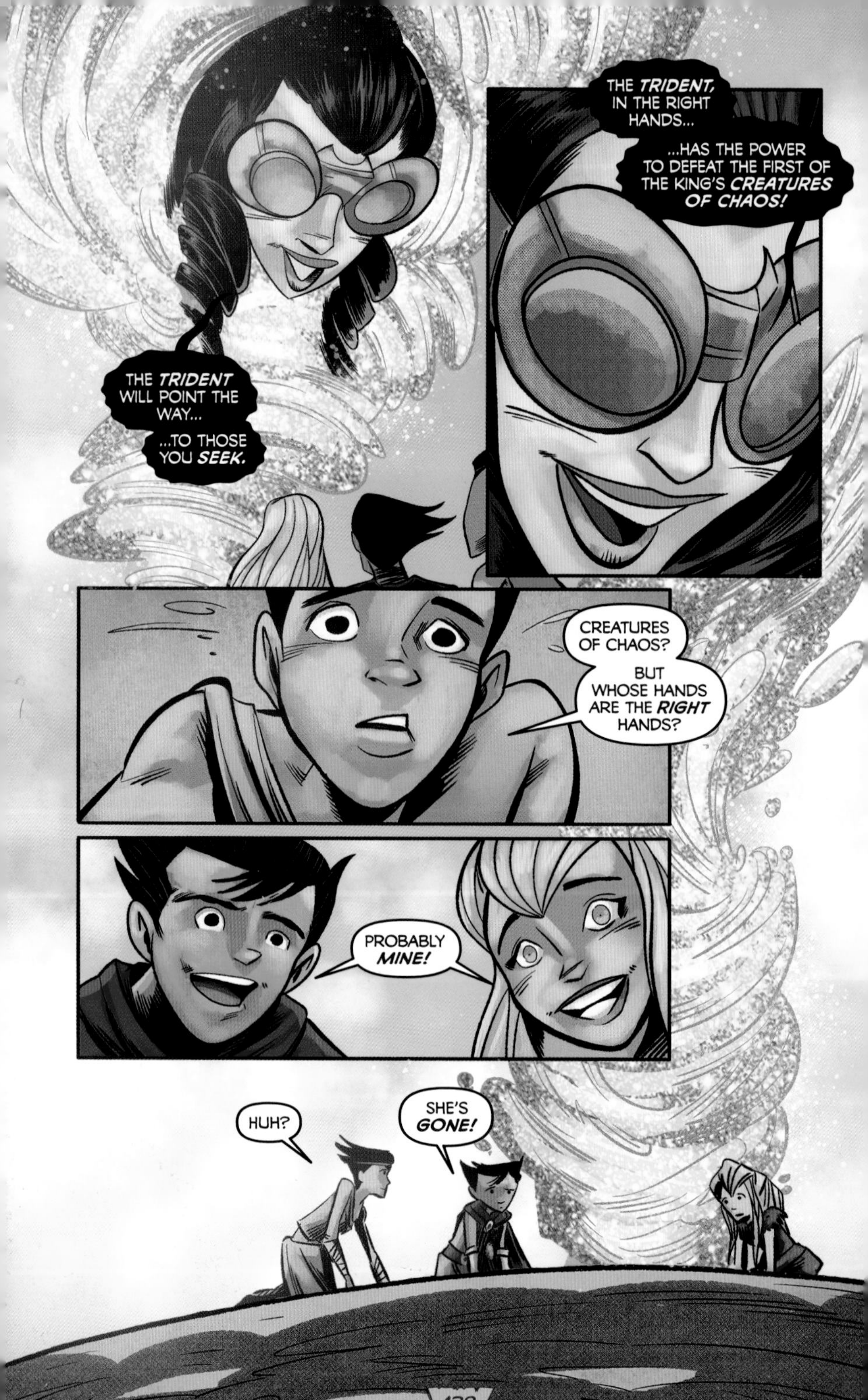
THE TRIDENT WILL POINT THE WAY...
...TO THOSE YOU SEEK.
THE TRIDENT, IN THE RIGHT HANDS...
...HAS THE POWER TO DEFEAT THE FIRST OF THE KING'S CREATURES OF CHAOS!
CREATURES OF CHAOS?
BUT WHOSE HANDS ARE THE RIGHT HANDS?
PROBABLY MINE!
HUH?
SHE'S GONE!

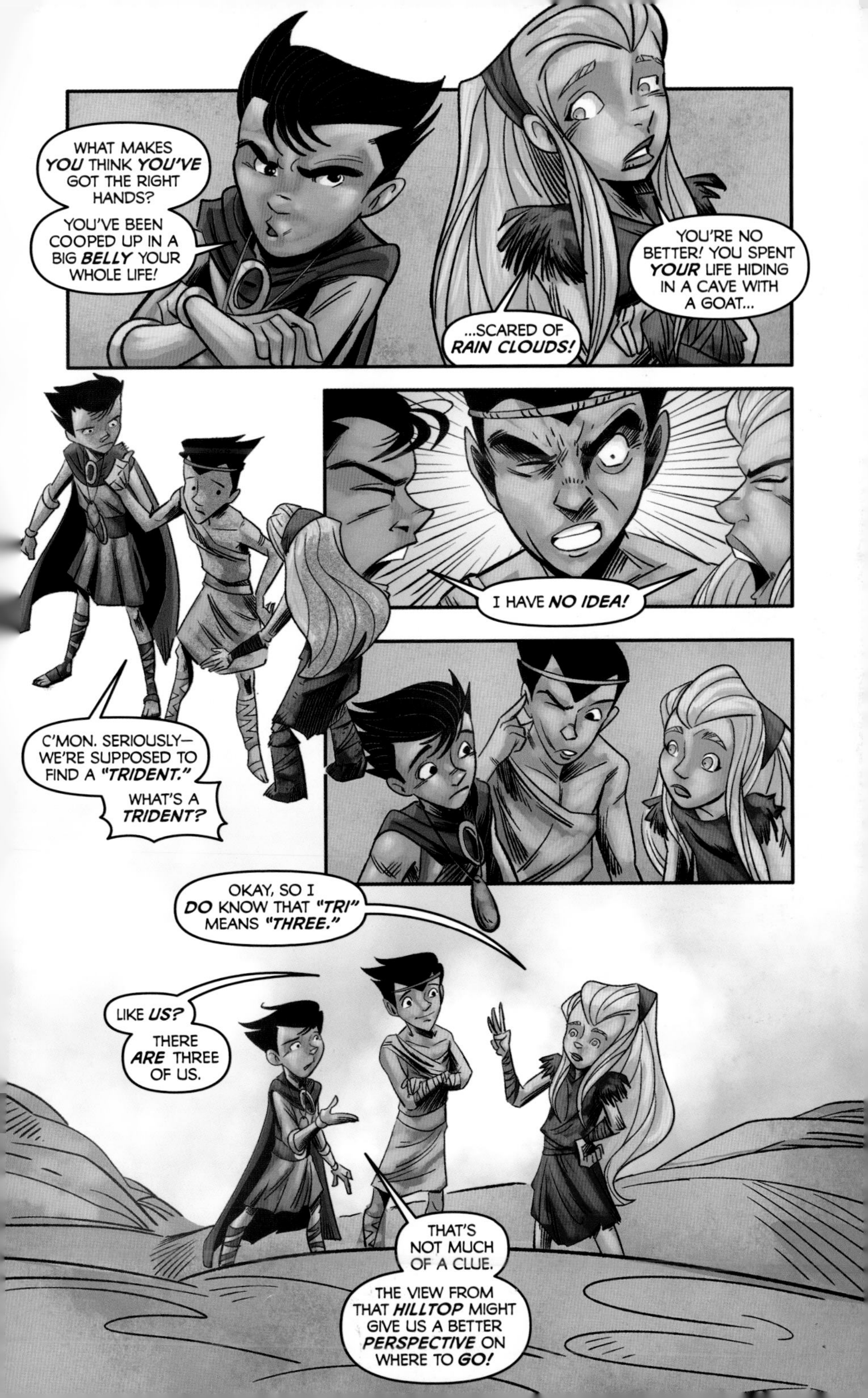
WHAT MAKES YOU THINK YOU'VE GOT THE RIGHT HANDS?
YOU'VE BEEN COOPED UP IN A BIG BELLY YOUR WHOLE LIFE!
YOU'RE NO BETTER! YOU SPENT YOUR LIFE HIDING IN A CAVE WITH A GOAT...
...SCARED OF RAIN CLOUDS!
I HAVE NO IDEA!
C'MON. SERIOUSLY— WE'RE SUPPOSED TO FIND A "TRIDENT."
WHAT'S A TRIDENT?
OKAY, SO I DO KNOW THAT "TRI" MEANS "THREE."
LIKE US?
THERE ARE THREE OF US.
THAT'S NOT MUCH OF A CLUE.
THE VIEW FROM THAT HILLTOP MIGHT GIVE US A BETTER PERSPECTIVE ON WHERE TO GO!

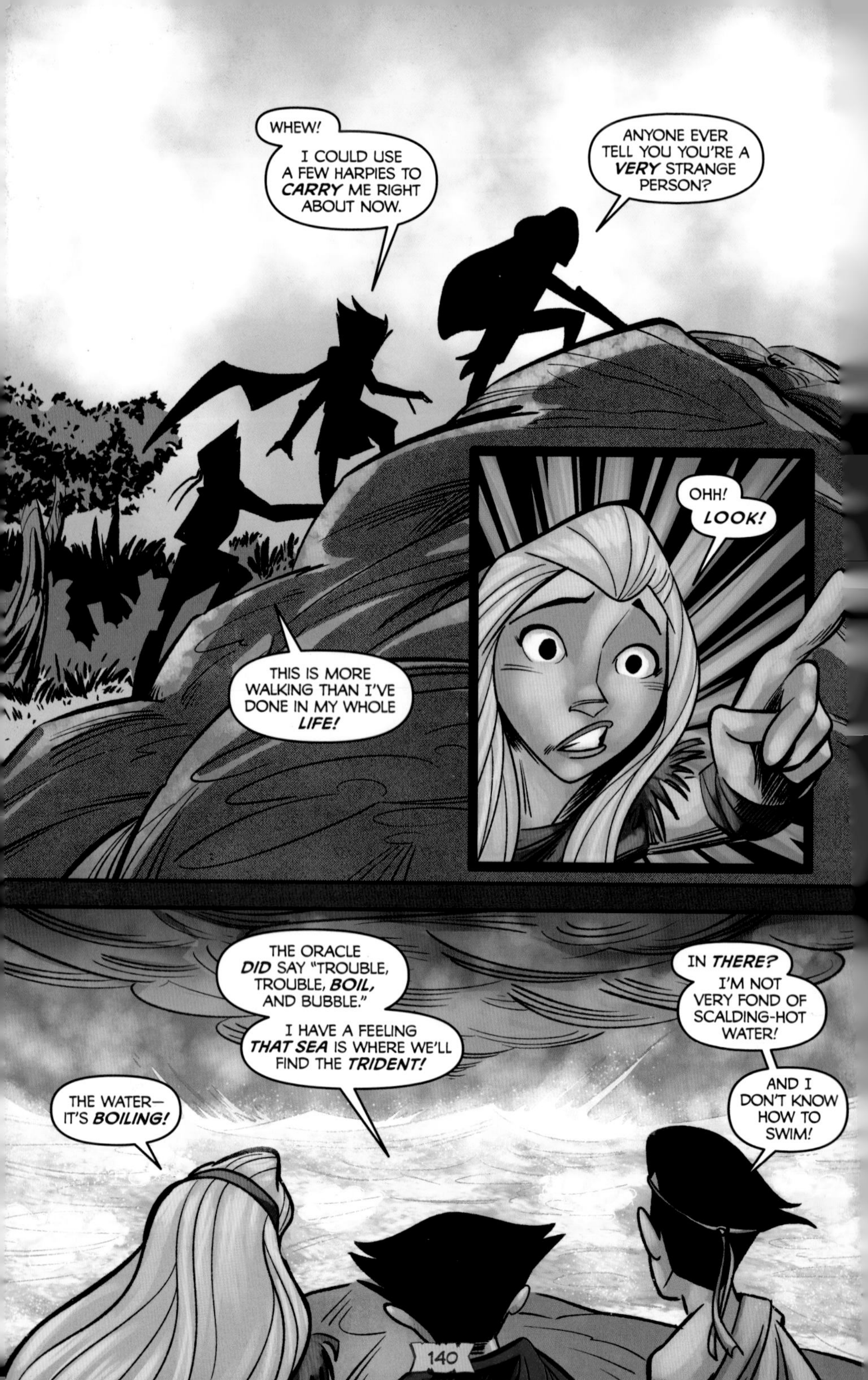
WHEW!
I COULD USE A FEW HARPIES TO CARRY ME RIGHT ABOUT NOW.
ANYONE EVER TELL YOU YOU'RE A VERY STRANGE PERSON?
THIS IS MORE WALKING THAN I'VE DONE IN MY WHOLE LIFE!
OHH! LOOK!
THE WATER— IT'S BOILING!
THE ORACLE DID SAY "TROUBLE, TROUBLE, BOIL, AND BUBBLE."
I HAVE A FEELING THAT SEA IS WHERE WE'LL FIND THE TRIDENT!
IN THERE?
I'M NOT VERY FOND OF SCALDING-HOT WATER!
AND I DON'T KNOW HOW TO SWIM!

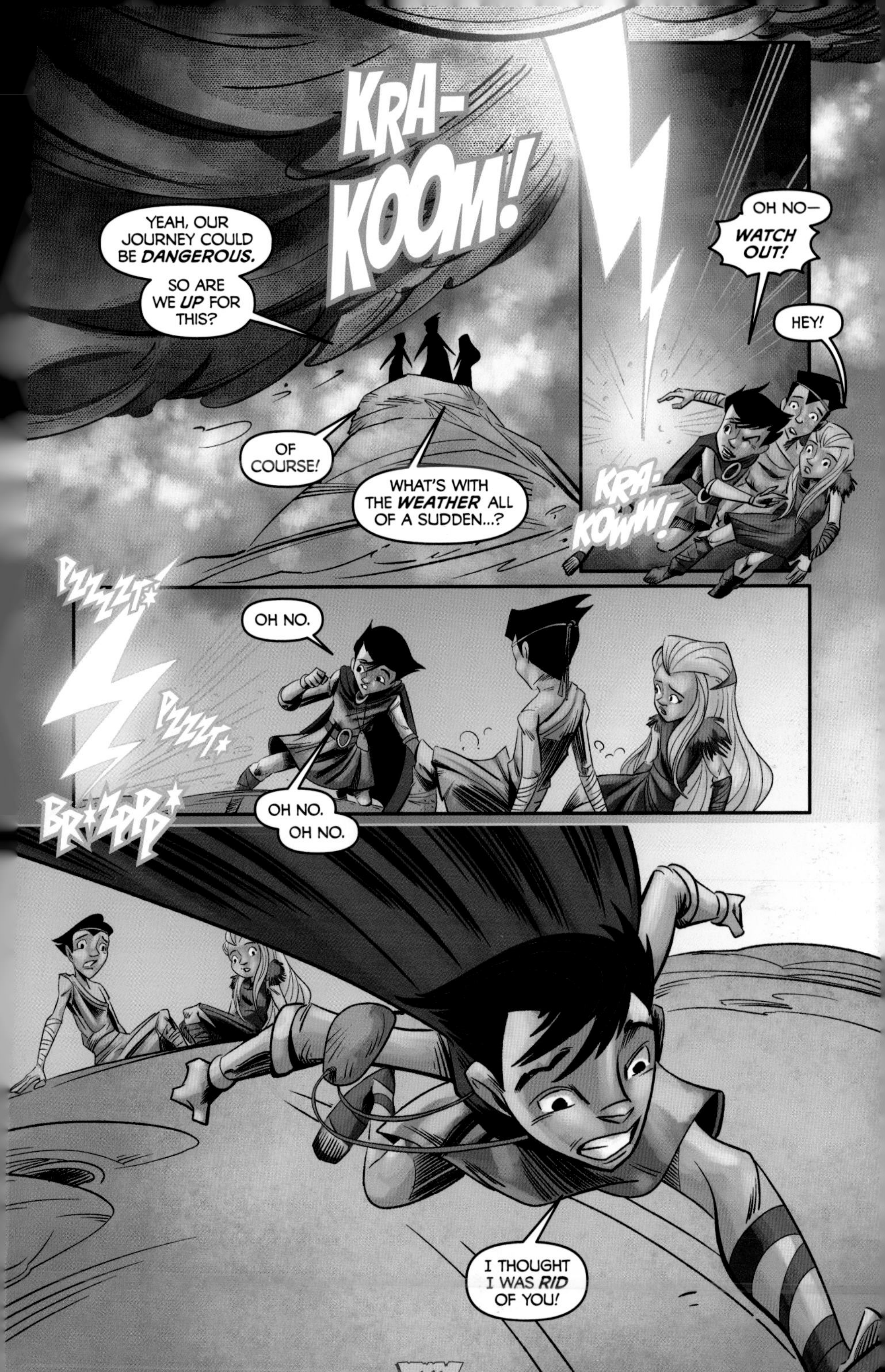
KRA-KOOM!
YEAH, OUR JOURNEY COULD BE DANGEROUS.
SO ARE WE UP FOR THIS?
OF COURSE!
WHAT'S WITH THE WEATHER ALL OF A SUDDEN...?
OH NO— WATCH OUT!
HEY!
KRA-KOWW!
PZZZZT!
PZZZT!
BR-ZAPP!
OH NO.
OH NO. OH NO.
I THOUGHT I WAS RID OF YOU!

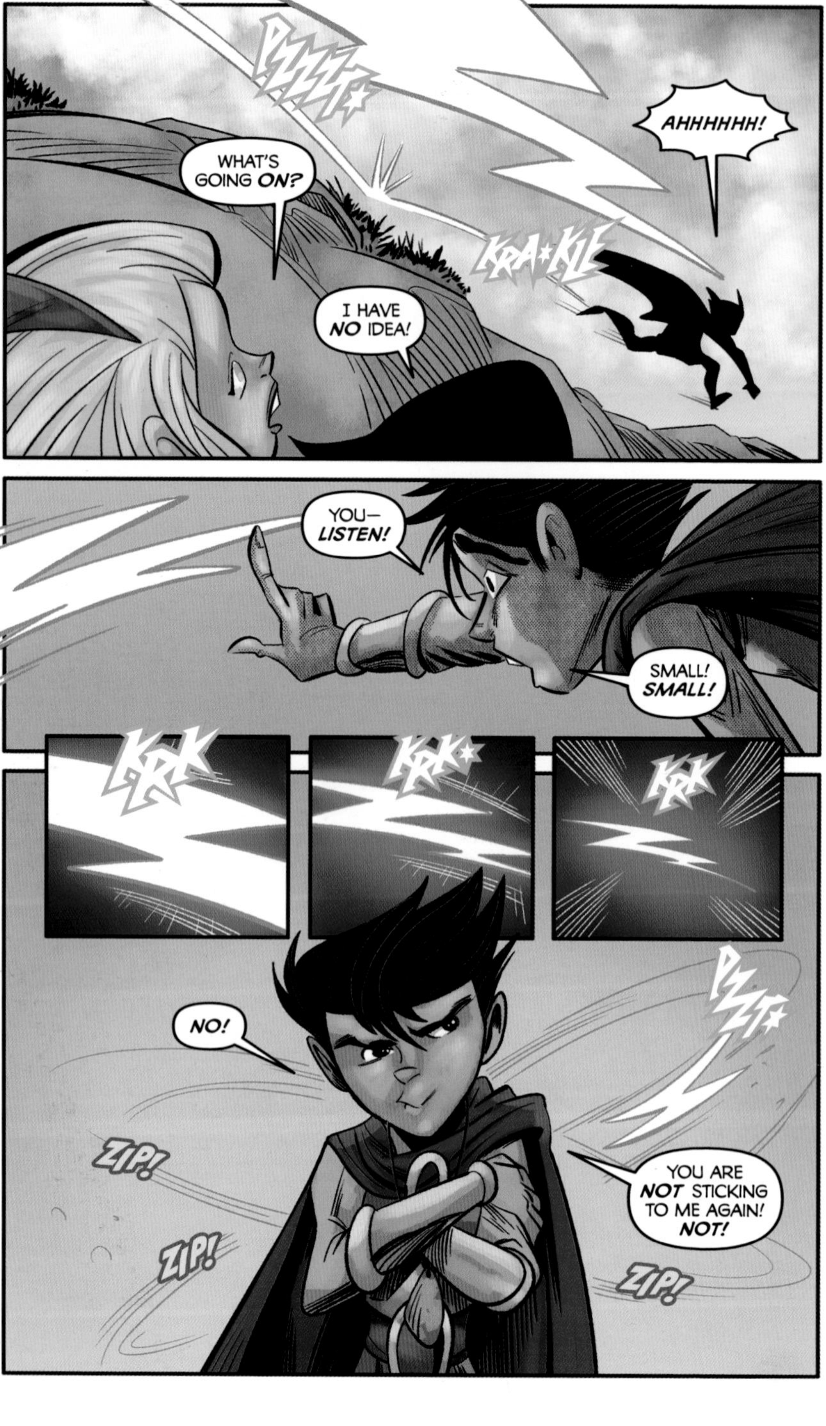
WHAT'S GOING ON?
AHHHHHH!
I HAVE NO IDEA!
YOU— LISTEN!
SMALL! SMALL!
KRK
KRK
KRK
NO!
YOU ARE NOT STICKING TO ME AGAIN! NOT!
ZIP!
ZIP!
ZIP!

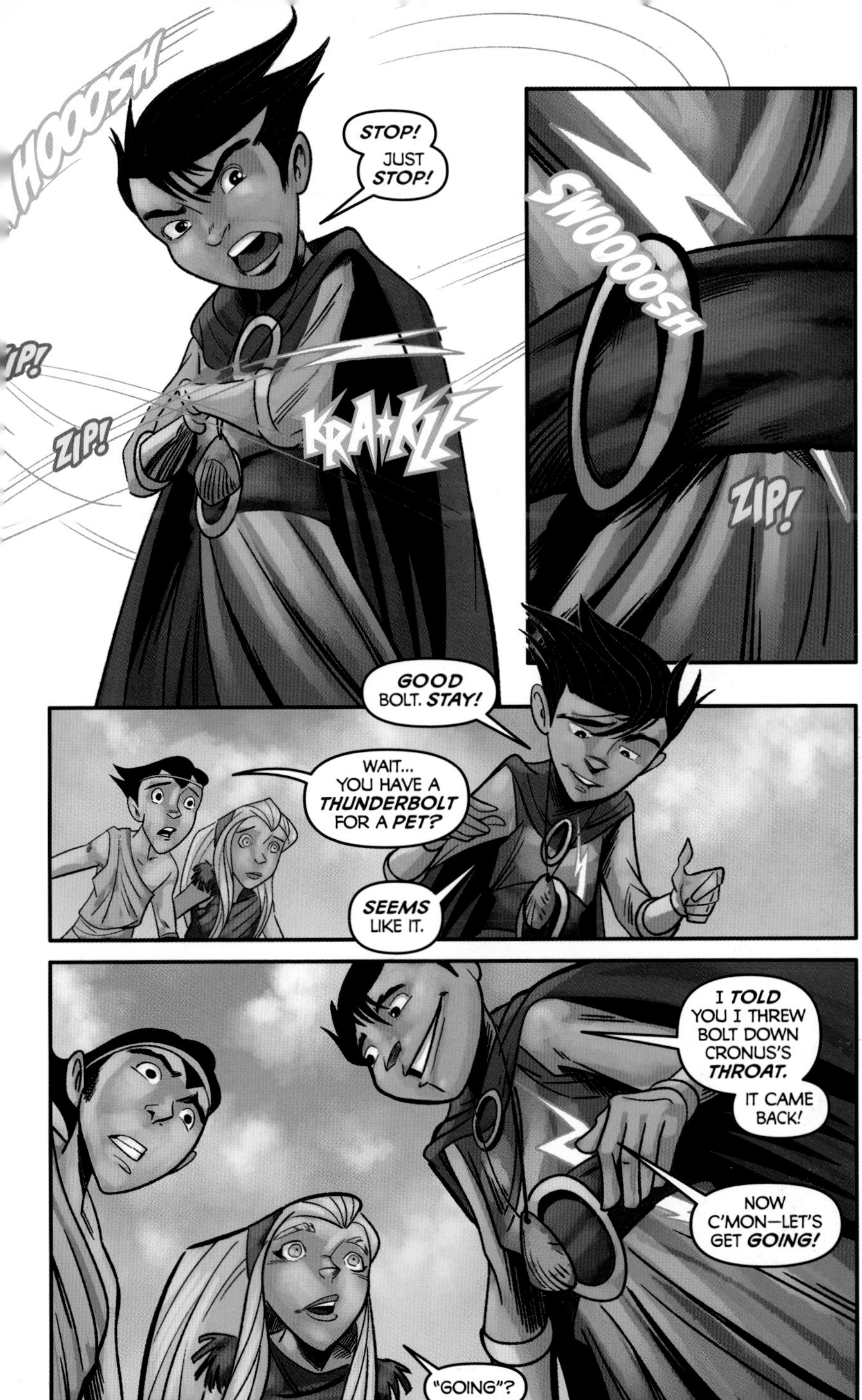
HOOOSH
STOP! JUST STOP!
IP!
ZIP!
KRA*KLE
SWOOOOSH
ZIP!
GOOD BOLT. STAY!
WAIT... YOU HAVE A THUNDERBOLT FOR A PET?
SEEMS LIKE IT.
I TOLD YOU I THREW BOLT DOWN CRONUS'S THROAT.
IT CAME BACK!
NOW C'MON—LET'S GET GOING!
"GOING"?

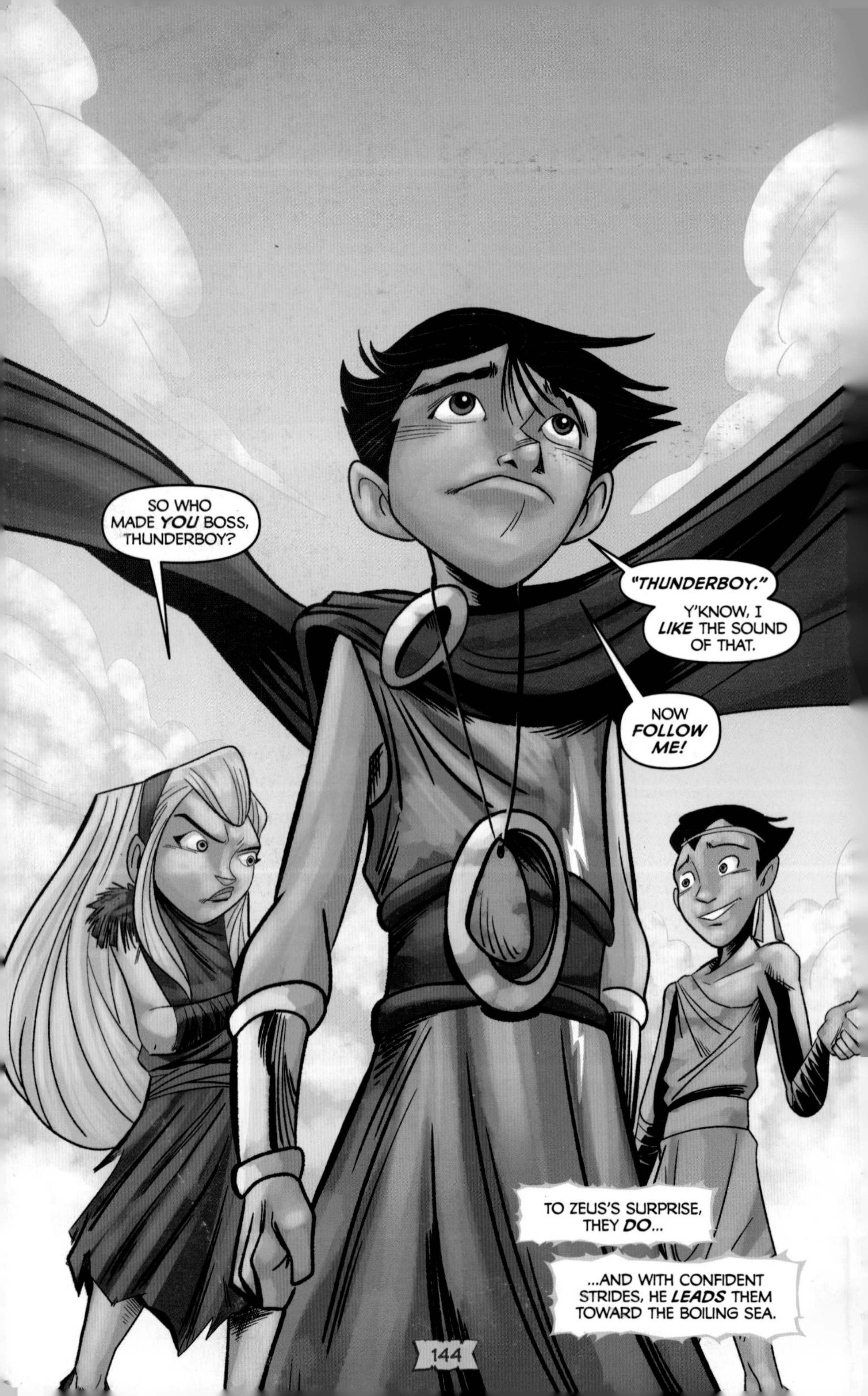
SO WHO MADE *YOU* BOSS, THUNDERBOY?
"THUNDERBOY."
Y'KNOW, I *LIKE* THE SOUND OF THAT.
NOW *FOLLOW ME!*
TO ZEUS'S SURPRISE, THEY *DO*...
...AND WITH CONFIDENT STRIDES, HE *LEADS* THEM TOWARD THE BOILING SEA.